To my husband, always. And to my readers, especially
those who gave me a chance with my first Avon series and
have followed me into this second one. I hope you find the
Ruthvens' stories as fun to read as they were to write.

A Study in Scoundrels

Also by Christy Carlyle

Romancing the Rules series
Rules for a Rogue

The Accidental Heirs series
One Dangerous Desire
One Tempting Proposal
One Scandalous Kiss

Coming Soon
How to Woo a Wallflower

A STUDY IN SCOUNDRELS

A Romancing the Rules Novel

CHRISTY CARLYLE

AVONIMPULSE
An Imprint of HarperCollinsPublishers

Excerpt from *Rules for a Rogue* copyright © 2017 by Christy Carlyle.

Digital Edition APRIL 2017 ISBN: 978-0-06-257237-0
Print Edition ISBN: 978-0-06-257238-7

Avon Impulse and the Avon Impulse logo are registered trademarks of HarperCollins Publishers in the United States of America.

Avon and HarperCollins are registered trademarks of HarperCollins Publishers in the United States of America and other countries.

FIRST EDITION

17 18 19 20 21   HDC   10 9 8 7 6 5 4 3 2 1

ACKNOWLEDGMENTS

Thanks to my fabulous editor, Elle. Your wisdom and encouragement make every book better. Jan and Karen, you're both amazing. Every time I read your work, I'm inspired. How did I ever get by without your thoughtful critiques, help with plotting, and fabulous feedback? And a huge thanks to you, Charis, for letting me talk through my "road trip" tale with you.

A Study in Scoundrels

PROLOGUE

June 20, 1877

Four and one would become his new lucky numbers because his fourteenth was proving to be the best birthday yet.

Jasper Grey, second son of the Earl of Stanhope, considered mischief an art, and he worked very hard at becoming a master artist.

With a bit of bravado and a flawless poker face, he'd won every last note and coin off a cluster of fools at the White Horse pub. Almost more than he could cram into his fist. Enough to buy him dozens of dreadfuls. He'd get *Crimes of London* and *The Black Band* and every other penny-blood that his mother insisted he never ever read.

They weren't local men. He'd never seen them at the village public house before, but they let him into their card game just the same. No doubt they'd taken in his tailored clothes and youthful face and considered him an easy mark.

The only easy bit had been playing cards well enough to unburden the dunces of all of their blunt.

Bending at the waist, he braced a hand on his thigh and worked to catch his breath. In case the fools thought to follow him, he'd cut across the meadow and run all the way to the lake on his family's estate. Nothing felt better on a hot summer day than a dip in the lake. Hidden by a copse of ancient oaks, the water kept cool even when the sun beat down from morning to night.

"What have you got up to now, Jas?" Richard stepped from behind a tree near the path that led to Longcross, the family estate. His brother cuffed him around the back of the neck before laying a broad arm across his shoulders. "The White Horse publican says some visitors from London are complaining about a young scalawag cheating them at cards."

Eight years older and several heads taller, Rich had the nose of a bloodhound when it came to sniffing out Jasper's mischievous deeds.

"I never cheated. A bit of fakery perhaps. I'm better at hiding my hand than they are." Jasper shrugged. "Father always says one shouldn't suffer fools." He didn't need to remind his brother that their father usually repeated the phrase when referring to his second and continuously disappointing son.

"At some point, you'll have to stop seeking mischief." Rich ran a hand through his blond hair before tugging the bottom edge of the fancy waistcoat he'd taken to wearing. Since turning two and twenty a few months past, his brother had become a good deal more interested in fashion than fun.

"Why?"

Rich chuckled. "You're growing up, Jas. Time to start planning for the future."

"Like you?" Jasper teased. "Planning to ask Miss Rebecca Hartley to marry you?"

"She'll say yes," Rich boasted.

Jasper had no doubt she would. Becca was two years older than Rich and far from the prettiest girl in the county, but they'd long fancied each other. And she was clever. She'd even beaten Jasper at cribbage. Once.

"Maybe I shouldn't have joined the men's card game." They were tough and burly, and none was thrilled to have his pockets emptied of coin. After losing several rounds, they'd continued to play, convinced their luck would turn. "But trust me, Rich. These men were imbeciles."

"Imp seals, are we?" The tallest of the four men emerged from the tree line. His cronies joined him one by one, building a wall of brawny bodies and scowling faces.

"See what I mean?" Jasper teased as he tipped his brother a smirk.

"We don't want any trouble, gentlemen." Rich stepped forward, shoving Jasper behind him.

"Too late," the shortest thug sneered. "Your wee friend already found it."

Richard squared his shoulders, and Jasper watched as his brother curled his massive hands into fists.

"Come, gents." Jasper sidestepped around Richard. "Let's return to the White Horse, and I'll give you a chance to win back your losses." His brother was a fine fighter, but Jasper wasn't naïve enough to think they could take on four grown men.

Unfortunately, his words only seemed to stoke their ire. The shortest slipped an object from his coat and slapped the roughhewn cudgel against his palm. A second later, they rushed forward as one, hunching their shoulders and tucking their heads like bulls charging an opponent.

The first strike of the cudgel came with a sickening crack that sent Richard sprawling to the ground, just near the water's edge. Three toughs were on him like rabid dogs, snarling and kicking. Another held Jasper from behind. He clawed at the man's arm, stomped his feet to get free, and screamed his brother's name.

"Get up, Richard! Don't let them kick you!"

His brother *would* get up. He would jump to his feet and thrash the bullies as they deserved. Richard was tall and strong and had bested most of the other boys in the county. In endless rounds of fisticuffs, he'd proved no one could defeat Richard Douglas Grey, Viscount Winship, the Stanhope heir.

"Gentleman pugilist," Papa boasted of his favorite son. "Golden Hector," Mama called her firstborn, referring to some ancient fighter who'd won all his battles.

Just like Richard.

The bastard at his back lashed an arm around Jasper's neck, squeezing at his throat like a bony noose, but Jasper kept thrashing. Kept shouting. Kept believing his brother would shake off that first blow and defend them both. As he'd always done.

Water splashed and a drop landed on Jasper's cheek. They'd dragged Rich into the lake, and he was struggling now. Arms flying. Fighting back. But there were too many. Blood dripped down his brother's face. He'd stain that damned waistcoat he loved so much.

Jasper scraped his feet on the grass, trying to get away from the man who had him 'round the neck. His captor squeezed tighter, cinching his throat until he couldn't breathe.

"Rich—" Blackness swelled around Jasper like spilled ink, spreading to the corners of his sight, blotting all his strength. "Help me."

But unlike every other moment of his fourteen years, when Richard was there to lift him to his feet, dust off his skinned knees, and beat away his attackers, no help came. Only blackness. Only blows.

A fist slammed the side of his head, and the world tilted. Soggy grass rushed up. He tasted mud as he hit the ground. Boots pummeled his ribs. Jasper found the strength to lift his arms, covering his head with his hands. But another hand came. The man wrenched open Jasper's clenched fingers, scraping and scratching until he'd removed every crumpled bank note, every coin.

"Shouldn't have filched from us, toff."

A final blow. Ringing in his ears. True darkness. Black ink spreading out to cover every sight and sound.

Scattered thoughts came.

Richard needed help. *Get to him.* Papa would be angry. Richard was the heir. He was the one who never failed. Richard mattered. He had to live.

CHAPTER ONE

June 22, 1895

Laughter tickled his ears. Weight bore down on his chest, draped over his hips. A soft weight, pliant under his hands. Heated too. Pleasure in his groin twined with pain in his head as the soft, warm weight moved against him.

He blinked, then again. Colors shimmered and blurred. The light was too dim. The room too smoky. Perfume burned his nose, too spicy and pungent.

What was that sound? A moan. A cry.

A rumbling groan reverberated in his own chest.

"Don't leave me now," a woman whispered near his ear. "I need release."

He flexed his fingers, digging into the warm flesh of smooth feminine legs. Slid his hand up, finding the thicket of curls between the woman's spread thighs.

"Yes, Grey."

She moved against him, her breath quickening as little moans emerged. She clutched at his shoulder, her other hand on his, showing him how to touch her.

He didn't require much direction. The role of lover was one he knew by heart. Some said he was skilled on stage, but he never doubted his expertise in the bedroom.

His own body had numbed. Whether from drink or the drugging effect of the smoke rising in whorls above his head, he wasn't certain. But this, how to touch a woman, how to give pleasure. This he knew intuitively. This was where he excelled.

Heaven knew he'd failed at everything else.

Except acting.

But performing on stage was all a matter of illusion, of lying artfully. Sex and falsehood were his twin aptitudes.

If only he could see the woman clearly and scatter the fog in his mind. He twisted his head on the pillow and noticed a half-empty glass of blue-green liquid glowing in the low gaslight.

"What did I drink?"

A trill of laughter. Red lips. The curve of a grin in a pale face. A waterfall of red hair.

He swirled his fingers in the woman's curls. She stilled and held her breath. He knew he'd found the key. Gently, masterfully, he touched her with all the art he'd learned from countless lovers.

"Oh, Grey." She twitched against his fingers, dug her nails into his shoulder. "Don't stop."

He didn't. Not until she gusted out a long moan, dipped her head, and sank against him as if her bones had melted.

"Absinthe," she murmured against his chest. "A bit of laudanum."

Grey pressed a fist to the throbbing crown of his head and tried to sit up. The lady on his chest stretched like a cat woken from a nap before rising off him and stepping away from the bed.

No, he realized when his vision cleared and he took in the books lining the walls, not a bed. Not his bedroom. He was on a settee in his London townhouse's library, and he and his lady companion were not alone. Half-clothed bodies reclined around the musky, haze-clouded room. Some sleeping. Others smoking from an enormous bubbling hookah. At least one couple was busy, writhing and moaning in the far corner.

A man stumbled past the open library door, nude from the waist up, his shirt and coat rolled in a crumpled ball in his arms. Returning to the threshold, he let out a burp before offering, "Many happy returns, Grey. Smashing birthday party."

Grey waved in the man's direction, though he couldn't have recalled the gent's identity to save his life. Now that his eyesight had cleared, he could make out the bell pull near the fireplace. He kicked a man's leg as he stumbled forward. In his stupor, the partygoer only managed a weak grumble.

Finally reaching the length of fabric to signal the downstairs staff, Grey yanked hard. A seemingly endless ribbon of velvet fabric settled at his feet. Not the bell pull, apparently, but a woman's dismantled gown.

"I need some bloody coffee!" he shouted, instantly regretting the painful echo in his head. No one seemed sober enough to listen anyway.

"Ask the maid to get some," a man called from a deep wingback chair with a giggling woman sprawled across its arms. "As soon as I'm finished with her," the heartless cad added before taking her mouth in a kiss.

"Unless someone gets me coffee, you are all uninvited from my next celebration." He glanced at the scattered bodies. "And if you work for me, you're fired."

"I'll find you some, sweetheart." The woman he'd woken to find on his lap approached and ran a hand down his chest. She'd donned a sheer wrapper that covered her body but hid nothing from his gaze. Lifting her other hand, she offered what he guessed were his trousers hooked on the tip of one finger.

"Thank you, darling." He leaned down to kiss her cheek, still at a complete loss for the woman's name. Of course, it didn't stop him from watching her maneuver out of the room, plump backside swaying with every step, as he pulled on his trousers.

Sinking onto the settee, he ran a hand through his hair and surveyed the wreckage. More than bodies littered the room. Books had been pulled from their shelves. The desk had been swiped clear of its lamp, writing implements, and blotter. A Nippon vase a wealthy widow had gifted him lay in pieces on the windowsill.

"My lord, may I have a word?"

Grey gazed around the room, waiting for an aristocratic guest to pop up and answer the man's request. It had been years since he'd responded to titles or honorifics. Throughout his time in London, he'd done his best to ensure no acquaintances learned of the life he'd left behind.

He had the means to provide lavish entertainment. That was all anyone truly cared to know.

"May I have a word, my lord?" the voice came again. Emotionless. Calm. Hauntingly familiar. A ghost from the past.

Grey turned his head and blinked, pressed two fingers to his blurry eyes. The ghost was corporeal and stood in the doorway as stiff and straight as ever.

"Blessing?" Grey croaked.

"Lord Winship." The man nodded in the curt, almost insulting way of William Blessing, his father's long-suffering butler. But the man couldn't be here in Grey's sinful corner of fashionable London. Derbyshire was where Blessing belonged. The care and keeping of the Stanhope staff and estate was the old man's domain. He was far too loyal a servant to stray from the Earl of Stanhope's side while his master was dying. Unless...

"My father?"

"He perseveres, my lord."

Grey swallowed hard and stood, crossing his arms over his chest. Suddenly, after two days of unfettered revelry, he felt underdressed. "Then why are you here, Blessing?"

"Because I need to speak to you, and he wouldn't let me come alone." Another voice from the past. Rebecca, Lady Fennston, stepped around Blessing, her black hair streaked with gray now and partially covered by a hooded cloak. Her eyes ballooned as she took in the wreckage of Grey's library. Then her cheeks reddened when she noticed Grey's half-naked state.

"My lady, you should have waited in the carriage." Blessing stepped forward to block her view as best he could.

"Go to your carriage, Becca. I'll join you there momentarily." It was the only place he could be sure she wouldn't encounter any further debauchery. Blessing seemed to agree. He offered another of his curt nods and escorted her toward the front door.

"I could only find tea, lover." His scantily clad paramour sashayed into the room and held out a steaming cup. Maeve, that was her name.

"Thank you, sweet." Grey retrieved the cup and took a quick sip, burning his fingers on the scorching porcelain and his tongue on the searing hot liquid. "Could you find me a shirt too?"

She grinned indulgently and bent at the waist, giving him a delicious view as she retrieved his hopelessly wrinkled white dress shirt from a spot near the settee. Handing him the garment, she lifted onto her toes for a kiss. Grey slipped his arms into the shirt and placed a quick peck on the tip of her nose. "I must speak to a lady and will return shortly."

"A lady?" she teased.

"An old family friend." Grey didn't mind the snide pitch of Maeve's tone as much as the thread of jealousy. His strict rules for any liaison were brevity and freedom. He could promise his lovers passion, sensual satisfaction, and nothing more. Ever.

Without another word, he made his way out the front door and into the Fennston carriage. Blessing stood guard outside the vehicle, as if expecting a horde of Grey's drugged, oversexed friends to mount an assault.

Lady Fennston looked relieved to find him dressed, if thoroughly disheveled.

"What is it, Becca? What's brought you to London?"

"Shh." She lifted a gloved finger to her lips. "Blessing knows of the situation, but the coachman does not. We need to keep this as quiet as we can."

Grey noted the fine lines around her chastising eyes, the stubborn set of her mouth. She was still every inch the woman who'd become a kind of older sister to him after his brother's death, offering consolation and censure in equal measure. As Richard would have done.

Despite her frown, she looked well. Apparently, marriage suited the woman his brother had hoped to wed. Strange. Especially since her union had been a hastily arranged match with his boring cousin Alistair Fennston only a year after Richard's death.

"What situation?" Grey whispered, bracing his elbows on his knees.

She gnawed at her lower lip, as if the words were difficult to speak, or she harbored uncertainty about telling him. Her silence ratcheted the tension in his body.

"It's Phyllida."

"Liddy?" Grey's heart sank into his belly and a chill chased down his spine. "Tell me she's all right."

Becca swallowed hard. "I'm afraid I don't know where she is, Jasper. That's the trouble. Liddy has gone missing."

"What the hell are you talking about?" The pounding in his head built to an orchestral crescendo. "How can a sixteen-year-old girl vanish?"

"She's seventeen, as of three months past."

"Yes." Grey clenched his teeth and tried to focus on anything beyond the throbbing rush of blood in his ears. "I sent her a gift, didn't I?"

"The necklace is one of her prized possessions." Becca's voice broke, and she pressed a hand to her chest. "She never took it off."

"Have you gone to the authorities? What does my father say? And Alistair?" Why had she bypassed all the responsible men in the family and come to him?

"Only a trusted few know of her disappearance. And now you." She sat up straight against the cushions but kept her voice low. "I truly believe this involves a passing infatuation with a young man. Informing my husband or the authorities would tarnish her reputation. Alistair can be rather unforgiving about such matters, and telling your father would only cause him to worry. The earl needs all the strength he can muster right now. If we can find Liddy quickly, we might avert lasting consequences. Your sister is too trusting, a bit naïve, but she's not a wanton."

Liddy had always been a silly girl, willing to risk her heart and plunge wholeheartedly into a bit of adventure. A rake wouldn't have to work very hard to gain her trust and lead her astray.

"Who?" Grey cracked his knuckles, already imagining which rotter's face he'd get to pummel.

"I have my suspicions, but they are only that as of yet."

"Tell me."

"She's quite infatuated with the Earl of Westby."

Grey frowned. "Westby? What was he doing in Derbyshire?" And why had anyone allowed the infamous scoundrel anywhere near his impressionable sister?

"Phyllida has been in London for the last few weeks." His cousin's wife bit the inside of her cheek and cast a gaze out the carriage window. "We wished to give her a reprieve from the gloom at Longcross. My aunt Violet agreed to host her for a fortnight, but Liddy asked to extend her visit."

"Your aunt Violet is so old she rarely remembers which day of the week it is. No one bothered to inform me Liddy was in town?"

"Why would we?" Becca faced him now, anger flashing in her hazel eyes. She no longer made any attempt to quiet her voice. "You abandoned your family, your home, your title. Alistair is more of a son to your father than you are. Would you wish—"

She continued speaking, but Grey clambered out of the carriage and slammed the door behind him, stomping back into his iniquitous den.

So much truth so early in the morning was doing his head in. He needed to wash and dress and confront Westby immediately. The thought of his sister anywhere near the man made him nauseated.

"Jasper, I'm sorry. My words were cruel."

He turned to find Rebecca on his doorstep, hesitating as if she did not wish to reenter his nest of sinners.

"You're forgiven, Becca. Nothing you said was untrue." He might be a bloody good actor, but he did his best not to deceive himself. He knew what he was and all the ways he'd failed his family. "Alistair has taken on responsibilities I'm content to ignore. It's a relief to know you both reside at Longcross with Father and…" His sister's name caught in his throat.

"Let's go now and speak to Lord Westby."

"No!" He shouted the word and then worked to tame his temper. "*We* are not going anywhere. I shall go."

"What if he won't speak to you?" Becca took one wary step over the threshold. "I recall how much you dislike the man."

Grey narrowed his gaze. "You remember my complaining about a schoolmate?" His connection with the earl was years past. Now he only knew the wretch via his reputation for seducing innocent young women.

"I recall your coming home at Michaelmas and not wishing to return to Eton." That unwavering amber-green gaze of hers reminded him of a time he preferred to forget.

The first visit home after his brother's death, he'd been awkward and miserable in his own grief. He'd encountered an inconsolable Becca and been completely unable to offer comfort. In fact, he'd railed at her. A childish tantrum. He'd blamed her for his brother's death. Only later did he realize every vitriolic word had been directed at himself. Neither of them had spoken of the incident since.

"I understand men like Westby, Becca. Many would say we're cut from the same cloth." Though Grey took care never to beguile innocents. He favored women who shared his desire for discreet, short-lived affairs.

Becca frowned, assessing him in an apparently unimpressed perusal. He hadn't looked in a mirror in days, but he imagined his unshaven state of dissipation failed to inspire much confidence.

"Go back to Derbyshire. Alistair will wonder where you've gone." For once in his life, Grey needed to do something right.

Taking two more steps inside the townhouse, Becca insisted, "You must find her quickly. She's due back at Longcross next week. Your father and Alistair will begin asking questions if she's gone any longer."

"I understand." He wouldn't need a week. Energy fizzed in his veins. He'd tear London to shreds to find her, if that's what it took.

"Here." She slid a folded bit of paper from the wrist of one of her gloves.

"What's this?"

"A list of Liddy's acquaintances in London, including the gentlemen she mentioned in her letters home."

"She kept extremely busy, I see." There were four gentlemen's names listed, all of whom Grey was sufficiently familiar with to know none was a suitable match for his sister.

"Wouldn't you, if you were seventeen?" Becca glanced toward his shambles of a library. "Perhaps you still do." After pulling up her hood, she started toward the door, then stopped and glanced back at him. "Good luck."

Grey offered a reassuring grin. Yet as he watched Blessing assist her into the Fennston carriage for the long journey back to Derbyshire, one thought dominated.

Luck wouldn't help him now.

He needed what he did not possess. After years of indulging his urges and investing as little of himself as possible, he'd given up on being the kind of man his brother would have been—courageous and honorable.

He squinted at the list of names Becca had given him. All were men he'd known in youth or met through his family's social engagements. None was a friend. He had few of those left from his old life. His gut twisted at the notion of any rogue harming Phyllida, deceiving her, breaking her too-vulnerable heart.

"Bloody rotting hell." He was the wrong man to save anyone. What a sodding irony. The Earl of Stanhope's most debauched offspring was now tasked with preserving his sister's honor.

His twin talents in playacting and seduction would be of no use.

Liddy deserved more than a reprobate actor searching for her. Yet she also deserved more than a lifetime of judgmental glances for what was likely a bit of youthful recklessness. He didn't wish her to begin adulthood burdened with regrets.

He'd chalked up enough of those for both of them.

CHAPTER TWO

"Chance is the detective's greatest ally. An investigator must be prepared to seize upon every opportune moment that comes her way."

—CASEBOOK OF EUPHEMIA
BREEDLOVE, LADY DETECTIVE

Sophia Ruthven never intended to plaster her palm against the man's shapely backside.

In fact, she hadn't intended to encounter the Earl of Westby at all. True, she had stolen into the man's private study. But his sister, Lady Vivian, who'd invited Sophia to speak at her weekly ladies' book club tea, insisted her infamous rake of a brother was not at home.

How could Sophia have known that a simple request to use the ladies' washroom would lead her past the half open door of the earl's study? Who could blame her for succumbing to the mingled aromas of smoke and book leather wafting out of the room?

The chance to inspect a notorious scoundrel's lair was simply too tempting a prospect to ignore.

Purely for research purposes, of course.

For months, Sophia had been working on a story about her fictional lady detective, Euphemia "Effie" Breedlove, but the details weren't right. Her rakish villain lacked verisimilitude. A sheltered upbringing in the countryside had provided few opportunities to observe scoundrels firsthand.

Now her hand was pinned between the room's dark wood paneling, a firm muscled posterior, and the green velvet curtain she'd hidden herself behind. The man and his companion had burst into the room as Sophia stood inspecting the items on the earl's desk. Thankfully, the long drape-covered bay window had been near enough to offer concealment.

"Now. Right here on my desk. You've kept me waiting long enough, sweetling." The man's husky tone drew a moan from the young lady, interspersed with the squelching sound of wet kisses. Who gave with such fervor and who eagerly received, Sophia couldn't be sure.

But she was sure of one thing. The feminine voice beyond the curtain belonged to Miss Emmeline Honeycutt, a fellow guest at the ladies' tea. Sophia had been introduced to the girl not half an hour ago. She guessed her to be quite young, not many years older than her own seventeen-year-old sister, Clarissa. She couldn't stand by and allow the girl to ruin herself.

Shifting her hand, she pushed at the heated swell of the man's derriere.

"What's that?" He stilled, pressing his weight against Sophia's palm. "We don't wish to be caught out, little minx. Seems we must wait a bit longer. You should get back to my sister's gathering."

After a few moments of whining protest and what sounded like the thud of dainty feet stomping thick carpet, Miss Honeycutt retreated with the swish and click of beaded fabric. When the study door slid shut, Sophia reached up to stifle a sneeze. She couldn't get the taste of the earl's pungent cologne off her tongue. Spicy and overly sweet, the scent was laid on so thick it tickled her nose.

"You can come out now, whoever you are." His voice had taken on a hard edge, as firm as the contours of his backside. Not at all the warm murmur he'd offered Miss Honeycutt.

Thankfully, he'd moved enough to free Sophia's hand, but she still hesitated a moment before pulling back the curtain and facing the man she'd read the worst sort of stories about in the gossip columns.

With one push at the drapery, she managed a step forward, keeping her chin up and back straight, lest he think her as brazen as the young woman who'd just left his arms.

"My lord, I can explain…"

But she was apparently going to have to plead her case to an empty room. He'd gone, leaving her with nothing but flame-filled cheeks and the knowledge that, in future, she needed to stem her raging curiosity and keep out of scoundrels' private spaces.

A clock chimed over the mantel and panic set in. She'd been gone too long. Even longer than the silly girl who'd nearly given herself to the earl on his desk.

Starting toward the door, she tripped on the velvet drapery clinging to her ankle.

A vice grip enclosed her wrist to keep her upright. No, not a vice. A hand, large and long fingered, and exceedingly strong, judging by how her own fingers had begun to numb.

"Lord Westby."

With his dark clothing, the man blended into the room's shadows. He'd been watching without her sensing him at all. Cursing her flawed powers of observation, Sophia snatched her arm from his grip. He released her and she quickly righted herself, yanking her boot from the drapery and moving toward the center of the room.

"You're a foolish woman," he whispered, "but I suppose men forgive that once they get a look at your face." He stalked toward her until he was close enough for her to see the glint on his obsidian eyes. Moving slowly, he began circling her like a predator, deciding how he wanted to begin consuming his prey. "And those breasts."

"I must return to your sister's tea, my lord."

"You should have considered as much before hiding away in my study." He drew closer, looming at her back. As his damp breath rushed against her neck, the cloying sweetness of his cologne caught in her throat and burned her eyes.

"I allowed my curiosity to get the better of me, my lord." Sophia started toward the door. "A mistake I shan't repeat."

Westby came around to stand before her, blocking her progress.

Sophia studied the scoundrel for the first time. Dark hair, coal-black eyes, and an arrogant smirk above a strong, squared jaw. Symmetry and sensuality conspired to give the impression of male beauty, as long as one ignored the coldness of his gaze and the cruelty in the set of his mouth.

He seemed to enjoy her perusal. Lifting his arms out at his sides, he urged, "Do your worst. How may I satisfy your curiosity? With a body like that"—he fixed his gaze on the overly ample bosom she'd spent most of her life trying to bind and conceal—"satisfying you would be no burden."

Sophia took his fixation on her breasts as an opportunity to escape. She started past him, gathering a handful of her skirt to keep from tripping on her hem. By the time she reached the study door, he'd sprung into action, rushing up to slam a palm on the panel above her head and pin her against the wood.

"Don't you want a taste before you go? One kiss to remember me by?" He drew his fingers across her cheek and chills raced down Sophia's spine. "I certainly want to taste you," he whispered, his lips hovering near her ear. "Are you the flavor of honey, like the shade of your hair? Or strawberries, like the flush in those perfect lips?"

Blood raced in her veins, flooding her cheeks, heating her chest and neck and the tips of her ears. Her skin pulled taut, muscles cramped.

She'd never been kissed, but she'd been this close to a dangerous man once before.

Flirtation and seduction meant nothing to Westby's sort. But to Sophia, her first kiss was more than an item to tick off the list of all that she'd yet to experience in life.

She still hoped for marriage and even had a prospect in mind. Research for her book was not worth forfeiting favors to a blackguard who reeked of oversweet cologne.

"I've been gone too long," Sophia insisted. The rush of blood in her ears wasn't enough to block the ticking of the clock. Why had no one come to look for her after all this time?

Lord Westby tucked a hand around her waist, twisting her to face him. With one brusque slip of his hand, he palmed her breast, pushed until he'd pressed her back against the door.

"I'll have a kiss before you go." Westby hooked a hand around her neck, sliding his fingers into her pinned hair.

She was on the verge of stomping her foot as Miss Honeycutt had done, but forcefully and on his toes, when Westby dipped his head. A current of shock rioted through her when he swept his tongue across the seam of her lips.

She recoiled, pressing at his chest with one hand and lifting the other to swipe across her mouth. Something had to eclipse the soppy wetness of his tongue, like a warm slug slithering across her lips.

"You do taste like honey," he enthused.

He tasted like cigar smoke and the rose water he'd apparently licked off the lady he'd been kissing moments before.

"Enough of this nonsense, my lord. Let me go." She twisted her body, pushing at him with her hip to create distance between then.

When she finally had the man at her back and the study door latch in her hand, he gripped her arm and whispered, "Did you hear that?"

Somewhere in the house a woman raised her voice. A man shouted in reply, though Sophia couldn't make out his words. Heavy footsteps shook the floorboards, louder as they continued, growing closer to the earl's study.

"Get behind the drape." The earl shoved her toward the window. "Don't look at me like that. You were quite content there a moment ago."

Sophia loathed his dictatorial tone and rough handling. She rubbed at the spot where he'd left a bruising sting around her arm.

"Look, you little fool," he growled, "a forced marriage will never be my fate. And I trust you don't wish to ruin your reputation entirely. Get behind the damned curtain."

Sophia scowled at him as she sheltered behind the velvet drapery. The moment she drew the fabric across her body, the study door swung open.

"Winship?" the earl called out. "Good God, man, it's been an age. I wasn't sure you were still among the living."

"That must be why your housekeeper was so reluctant to admit me." The visitor's voice was as rich and smooth as warm honey. But there was more underneath, a note of barely leashed ire.

"Well, you're here now. Care for a scotch?" Westby seemed oblivious to the thread of fury in the man's tone.

The clink of crystal indicated the earl had turned his attention to the liquor trolley. Sophia sensed the other man moving, the rustle of clothing and thud of his footsteps as he circled the room.

"Did you rip this ribbon off a lady, or did she offer it as a token?" The visitor's voice was humming with anger.

Westby let out an ugly bark of laughter. "Let the fripperies fall where they may, I always say."

Sophia held her breath. She needed to hear the stranger speak again. Something about his voice was oddly familiar.

"You bloody knave, where is she?" He no longer attempted to hide his anger, and Sophia no longer doubted his identity. Westby might call him Winship, but the man's appealing voice gave him away as Jasper Grey, her brother's theater friend.

"What the blasted hell. I don't—" The earl began to sputter before his words cut off, followed by a sickening wallop of flesh colliding with bone.

"Phyllida is besotted with you, as you well know. Tell me where she is, and I'll consider letting you live." Mr. Grey's tone had tempered to a deadly calm.

"Liddy? What business would I have with your sister? Check the bloody nursery."

A struggle ensued, grunts and movement, then the thud of a body hitting a solid piece of furniture. The desk?

"Where is she, Westby?"

"I have…no"—the earl's voice emerged on a breathless choke, as if something, or someone, was cutting off his air—"idea."

"In that case, letting you live seems far too generous."

Sophia fumbled with the drapery, trying to disentangle herself. Westby deserved a walloping, but Mr. Grey would suffer far more if he assaulted a powerful aristocrat.

"Mr. Grey!" she shouted and finally found an opening in the thick fall of velvet fabric.

Both men froze when she emerged. Westby lay atop his desk, face pink with exertion, as Jasper Grey leaned over him, a muscled forearm braced across the earl's throat.

Mr. Grey was just as she recalled him, tall and lean, with tumbling chestnut hair and striking gray eyes, as cool as a January breeze.

"Miss Ruthven?" The infamous actor squinted at her. "What the hell are *you* doing in this bastard's study?" He scowled down at the earl, then straightened and faced her. "I had no idea you possessed such wretched judgement, Sophia."

"And I had no idea murder came so easily to you, Mr. Grey."

They both cast a glance at the Earl of Westby, who'd sat up and begun clawing at his necktie to loosen its folds.

"There, you see. He's alive. I'm not quite a murderer yet."

"What in heaven's name is going on?" The earl's sister skidded to a halt in the study doorway. "The housemaid nearly fainted."

Sophia scooted into the recess of the bay window, hoping to escape notice.

After an assessing glance at her brother, Lady Vivian turned her gaze on Mr. Grey, a grin curving her lips. "Winship," she purred as she approached, "why are you in such a state? Come and have tea with us to soothe your nerves. We've missed your company at Westby House."

This Sophia remembered about Jasper Grey too. The man had a way with women. Not only did they buzz about him, but he seemed to exude a calming affect too. On the day she'd met him, he'd turned an angry woman into a fawning, cooing fool with a few sweet words. The second time she'd seen him, as lead actor in one of her brother's plays, his effect had been even more potent. Ladies in the audience swooned and the clamor to visit him backstage ended with one young woman crying over her trampled hat.

Now Lady Vivian wore the same look other ladies did around him—a sort of blissful, awestruck hunger.

"Leave us, Viv," the earl commanded in a rusty bark. "Close the door behind you."

She shot her brother a look of concern and offered their visitor another simpering grin before doing as Westby instructed.

When Sophia emerged from the window nook, Mr. Grey lifted his arm, and Westby shrunk back as if to avoid a blow.

"Let me take you out of here." Mr. Grey crooked his fingers, bidding her to come toward him.

"You," the earl began, scooting a safe distance away before shoving a finger in the air toward Mr. Grey, "get out of my house. Immediately." He turned his attention toward Sophia, skimming her face before gaping at her breasts. "Do return another time for your kiss."

"I—" Offense and protest perched on the tip of her tongue, but Grey spoke over her.

"Don't speak to her, Westby." He extended his hand as if he expected her to take it. As if he expected her to allow him to make her decisions.

"I will choose when to depart, Mr. Grey." She'd had enough of high-handed men for one day. Never mind that she shouldn't have been snooping in the earl's study in the first place.

"The man is a wretch." He flicked his gaze toward Westby. "An utter scoundrel. A certifiable scalawag."

"I"—the aristocrat cleared his throat—"am standing right here."

"And you cannot deny a single claim."

The earl frowned but offered no rebuttal. "What's become of you, man? A few years on the stage, and you lose all sense?

If you were anyone else, you'd be clapped in irons for assaulting me." He rubbed a hand across his jaw where an abrasion bloomed in shades of red and blue. "We were friends once."

"We were never friends, Westby. You're an arrogant sod and have no respect for the fairer sex."

The earl chortled. "Says the man who's bedded half of London's fairer sex."

Sophia thought she spied a patch of pink on the high cut of Mr. Grey's cheek, but the look he cast her was tinted with more pride than humility. Lifting his hand again, he petitioned her. "Come with me, Sophia. Please."

"I can't simply leave." Sophia owed Westby nothing, but she couldn't say the same for his sister. "Lady Vivian invited me. What shall I tell her?"

"Nothing," Grey said quietly. "Returning to the drawing room will raise questions you won't wish to answer." He tipped his head toward the earl. "Westby will direct the housekeeper to say you fell ill and called a cab to take you home."

"Will I?" Westby asked with arch haughtiness.

Mr. Grey cast him a hard stare, and the earl stomped across the rug. With a dramatic sigh, he yanked his study door open. "Anything to get you out of my house, Winship."

Sophia didn't take Mr. Grey's offered hand, but she moved past him toward the door. For however long she remained in London before returning to the countryside, she suspected her days of receiving invitations from the aristocracy had just come to a crashing end.

"This isn't the time for worrying about etiquette," Grey said, close behind her, a hand heavy at her lower back as he guided her through the door. Once she was across the threshold, he turned back. "Not a word about Liddy to anyone, Westby. If you hear word of her whereabouts, wire me immediately."

"You truly have no idea where your sister is?"

Sophia couldn't detect any concern in the earl's tone for the sister of a man he claimed had once been a friend.

"No." Grey's jaw tensed, his hands tightened to fists against his thighs. "But I will find her." He spun away from Westby and started past Sophia.

For a moment she thought he'd storm out of Westby House without her. Then she felt his fingers, warm and insistent, tangling with hers as he reached for her. He paused in the hallway, waiting for her to respond.

She felt a tremor across his skin. His hands were shaking.

Sophia clasped her fingers around his and let him lead her quickly toward the front door.

CHAPTER THREE

God preserve him from fellow reprobates and gullible women.

Grey wasn't sure which was worse—Westby's cluelessness about his sister's whereabouts or Sophia Ruthven's susceptibility to the man's dubious charms.

A faint blush stained her cheeks, and he suspected the color had more to do with embarrassment than how quickly he'd hustled her from the aristocrat's townhouse.

That was the trouble with principled women. No matter how much they craved passion, peeling back their layers of starch inevitably led to guilt and regret. He preferred women who indulged their desires openly, freely. They were much less trouble and left him blissfully unfettered.

"I shouldn't have departed without a proper leave-taking." Sophia twisted a pair of kid leather gloves between her fingers. "Without even thanking Lady Vivian for the invitation."

"Worry less about propriety and think of facing Viv's circle of lady friends. What would they make of your interlude with Westby in his study?"

"You assume the worst, Mr. Grey." When she turned to face him, the flush in her cheeks deepened to scarlet. "There's no scandal here, I assure you."

He wanted to believe her. In fact, he preferred to think he'd arrived too soon for Westby to do his worst. After all, Sophia Ruthven wasn't the earl's usual sort.

She was too prim, too proper, too watchful with her striking blue-green eyes. He couldn't imagine her falling for Westby's brutish style of seduction.

But Grey *had* imagined the lady. And in ways that would spread that fetching blush on her cheeks to the tips of her toes and the tips of her—*No, best not to contemplate those.* Needless to say, he'd thought of Sophia far too often since their first and only encounter months before. The same day her brother, playwright and now publishing magnate Kit Ruthven, warned Grey not to look at his sister, speak to her, or consider any sort of pursuit.

Unfortunately, the lady's unique brand of beauty wasn't easy to forget.

"Where may I deliver you?" Finding Phyllida had to be his priority. He wasn't sure of his next steps, but a pretty distraction like Sophia Ruthven was one he couldn't afford.

"You're not delivering me anywhere, Mr. Grey. I can see to my own transport." She scanned the far end of the street and offered him a curt "good day" when a hansom cab came into view.

As she began striding away, he fixed his gaze on her slim waist and shapely hips a moment before a faint inner voice scolded him for being a blighter. He'd insisted she leave Westby's home out of a rogue sense of chivalry. The least he could do was see his friend's sister off safely.

"My carriage is here," he called to her. "At least let me take you wherever you wish to go."

"Your carriage?" She turned and took in his family's rarely used London conveyance, arching a brow as if urging him to confess that he'd stolen the polished brougham.

"My father's carriage."

A battle raged across her features. She glanced regretfully at the Westby townhouse and then, with a longing moue, toward the end of the street where the hansom cab had moved along. Finally, she relented and started toward Grey.

"Why did the earl and his sister call you Winship?"

"Because it's one of my names." A title he never wanted. A life he'd left behind.

She stopped in front of him and narrowed her gaze. "A role you've played?"

"A role I'd prefer not to play." He waved off the groom, eager to assist Sophia into the carriage himself.

She rebuffed him, of course, climbing in on her own and wafting fetching scents in her wake. She smelled of innocence. Citrus and lavender and starch, everything clean and fresh. Scents that reminded him of Longcross.

"Shall I take you to the train station? I assume you're returning to the countryside." The notion of sending her away from cads like Westby and himself held enormous appeal. He already suspected Liddy had fallen under some seducer's sway. Sophia Ruthven's ruination was not a prospect he wished to ponder.

Well, he did. But certainly not with a bounder like Westby.

"Wrong again, Mr. Grey. Number six Bloomsbury Square, please. My brother and Ophelia decided they should have a London residence to be nearer the office and theater," she explained as Grey settled himself across from her.

The recently wedded couple were a busy pair, juggling both the publishing enterprise Kit and his sisters had inherited from their father and Kit's success as a playwright. Grey had been honored to be invited to their nuptials, even if it signaled the end of Kit's accompanying him on rambles to pursue the city's less savory entertainments.

"And have you come to reside in London too?"

Apparently, he revealed too much interest in his tone. One of her pale brows winged up.

"For the time being. My sister has departed for a ladies' college in Leicestershire, Kit and Phee will soon embark on a honeymoon journey to France, and Mr. Adamson runs our family's publishing office with remarkable efficiency. I hoped to make myself useful by arranging the new house while they're away." While she spoke of duty and usefulness, there wasn't much enthusiasm in her tone. Grey allowed himself to imagine all the London distractions he could show her. If he had the time. If she was a different sort of woman, and he a better kind of man.

Grey liked the sound of her voice—strong and resonant. He liked her transparency best of all. Despite Sophia's flawless façade, he could detect emotion in her voice, flushed cheeks, and striking eyes. The lady might think herself a paragon of propriety, but she was no good at hiding her feelings as others did.

As he'd been doing for years.

"Here." She pulled a folded handkerchief from her coat.

"What's that for?"

"You're bleeding." She nodded toward his scraped knuckles. He'd caught the sharp edge of the earl's jaw, and one of the abrasions had begun to bleed.

"Nothing more than a scratch." He stretched his fingers, then clenched them into a fist, trying not to wince at the sting. "But I do appreciate your concern, Sophia." After offering her a genuine grin, he dropped his gaze to her lips, willing them to curve in reply.

"Not concern for you, Mr. Grey." Her mouth did twitch up at the edge, but only for a fleeting moment. "I just didn't wish to see you stain this fine upholstery."

"My father's coachman will be most grateful to you."

He'd never met a woman like her. She worked so damn hard at being proper, though not as an affectation. Nothing about her indicated she was playing a role. The lady behaved as if flawless deportment mattered to her.

She sat as straight as he suspected anyone ever had atop the squabs of his father's carriage. Not even the sway of the vehicle as the horses took a clattering turn across cobblestones dislodged her. With her slim gloved hands folded neatly in her lap, she pointed her perfectly squared chin out the window and avoided his gaze.

After being cloistered in the countryside all her life and raised on her father's oppressive etiquette books, he suspected the lady was almost entirely composed of rules and propriety. And lush curves, berry-stained lips, and the prettiest eyes he'd ever seen.

Helen of Troy's face might have launched a thousand ships, but Sophia possessed the poise of a woman who could lead the fleet herself and rout every enemy. Upon first meeting her less than a year before in her brother's home, he'd dubbed her a "goddess," and the appellation still suited.

Pert nose, pink Cupid's-bow lips, thick sable lashes, honey-blonde hair that made him itch to run his fingers through every silken strand. He told himself he could find dozens of ladies in London sporting those charms. But none would have Sophia's eyes. Clear blue, like a cloudless winter sky, but with green fire simmering beneath.

Beyond her face, there was only more to make a man's mouth water—a long, slim figure softened by the flare of full hips and a gloriously plump bosom.

She flicked her gaze toward him, bristling at his scrutiny.

He didn't understand why, but her extreme self-possession sparked an oddly protective urge.

"You needn't worry, Sophia. No one will ever know I found you in Westby's study."

"I did nothing for which I am ashamed, Mr. Grey." Tiny lines furrowed her brow.

"May I expect the same discretion regarding my sister?"

"Of course." She let out a long breath. "Now that you know she isn't at Westby House, what will you do?"

Grey scrubbed a hand across his face but resisted closing his eyes, even for a moment. He feared sleep, losing hours that could be spent searching for Phyllida. Exhaustion bore down, all the gnawing worry of the last few hours piling like bricks on his shoulders. "I will find her." It was his only certainty.

"Where was she last seen?" Sophia leaned toward him, lush lips parted in curiosity, eyes wide. He couldn't help but wonder if it was how she'd looked when offering herself to the earl.

Of all the men to pursue, why on earth had she chosen Westby?

"None of your concern." His words emerged on a gruff volley, reverberating in the carriage's confines. "It's a family matter."

"Of course."

"Why the hell were you in Westby's study?" He watched her porcelain skin for a telltale blush.

"I've done nothing shameful." She met his gaze squarely, without a hint of guile, as if daring him to doubt her.

"So you've said. Twice." Grey couldn't hold back a grin. He liked dares from beautiful women. Unfortunately, long experience taught him exactly what it meant when a person protested too much.

"I was merely curious." She captured the edge of her lower lip between her teeth, causing Grey to ache in places to which he had no time to attend.

"Curious?" he managed on a low rasp, desperate to know the nature of Sophia Ruthven's curiosity. Wishing he had the time to satisfy the lady's every inquisitive urge.

"The earl's townhouse is beautifully appointed," she insisted. "I wished to see some of the other rooms."

Grey's grin deepened until his cheeks ached. She was a terrible actress. Her eyelashes batted too much and her mouth trembled around the edges.

She narrowed her eyes into catlike slits. "If you must know, I passed the study door and was drawn by the scent of books."

"Books?" Westby would be devastated to know his library was more of an enticement than his renowned carnal talents. "I didn't know you liked reading anything other than your father's endless volumes of etiquette."

"How could you know anything about me, Mr. Grey? We're barely acquainted." Finally, a bit of that green fire. The color sparked in her eyes like emerald chips catching the light.

"And yet you jumped out from behind Westby's curtain to keep me from throttling the man." He frowned. "Wait. Was that for my benefit or his?"

"Excellent question. I like that you're not sure of the answer." She finally offered him a smile. An actual, genuine curve of her lips that matched a saucy glint in her sea-mist eyes. "Uncertainty will do you good."

Unless he was very much mistaken, the lady had just flirted with him. He ought to know. Women flirted with him every day. Lots of women—each beautiful, talented, and wanton.

Oddly, none of them intrigued him like Sophia Ruthven.

A surge of victory shot through his veins, but it was short-lived. Just as his time with Sophia must be. The carriage began to slow as it turned into a grass-edged lane near Bloomsbury Square.

"I'm becoming increasingly familiar with uncertainty." He stared at the even lines of black and white in the skirt of Sophia's gown, avoiding her gaze.

"Forgive me." Reaching across the carriage, she gently laid her gloved fingers at the edge of his wounded hand. "I was thoughtless to jest when you're worried about your sister." Straightening on her bench, she retreated so quickly he might have imagined the gesture. Except that his skin was tingling where she'd touched him.

"I'd jest with you, Sophia, any day of the week." He could happily lose himself in her guileless gaze. "But you're right. Phyllida is out there somewhere, and I must find her."

The carriage drew to a stop, and Sophia lurched forward. Grey gripped her arm to steady her and fought the urge to haul her into his lap, to kiss those tempting lips, to forget everything but giving and taking pleasure, if only for a moment.

"Thank you for escorting me home, Mr. Grey." She righted herself and stared at him a moment before glancing down to where he held her arm. "I pray you find your sister soon."

Grey released his hold and hopped out of the carriage when the groom opened the door, reaching inside to help Sophia down. She took his hand, and he held on too tightly, enjoying her touch far too much.

"There are private detectives who could assist you."

"No police or investigators." Grey shook his head. "There's too much risk for rumors to start. I won't allow Liddy's reputation to be ruined over what's likely nothing more than a youthful indiscretion." As the hours ticked past, he tried to convince himself his sister had slipped away for a bit of freedom. She'd always expressed a fancy for Brighton or a visit to some seaside resort, and he could imagine her being hardheaded enough to set out on her own.

"Good day to you then, Mr. Grey." She tipped her head back, and sunshine lightened the blue of her eyes.

As she began striding away, he fought the urge to follow. To spend more time basking in her clean scent and unaffected manner. Perhaps, beyond her blinding beauty and by-the-book propriety, there was more to Sophia Ruthven.

If nothing else, she was a woman who, unlike every other, seemed completely immune to his charms.

Chapter Four

"A detective will meet all sorts during an investigation. Liars, rogues, seducers, and scoundrels. No matter the provocation, never let them rattle you."

—Casebook of euphemia
breedlove, lady detective

Sophia slammed the front door behind her and melted against the wood, struggling to catch her breath.

She loathed the unsettling power of Jasper Grey. The man was too…everything. Charming and handsome and distractingly well built. Flirtatious and brazen. She thought back, trying to recall each word he'd said. Now, out of his presence, nothing struck her as particularly outrageous. Yet everything about the man provoked her. Even his easy smiles and the constant sparkle in his eyes.

Especially those.

How could anyone be so at ease in his own skin?

She pushed the man from her thoughts and fretted as she tugged off her gloves, worrying over her abrupt departure from the Westby townhouse. Wouldn't facing the consequences of her encounter with the earl and maintaining whatever favor she'd found with Lady Vivian have been the better course? She'd accepted the invitation to the noblewoman's tea as a representative of Ruthven Publishing. What would the noblewoman and her friends think of *The New Ruthven Rules for Young Ladies* now that one of its authors had scurried away like a thief escaping in the night?

"Miss Ruthven, I trust you had a good visit." Catherine Cole, the petite, dark-eyed, and impressively efficient housekeeper she'd hired for Kit and Ophelia approached with a list between her fingers. Just a year older than Sophia, Mrs. Cole had made herself indispensable quickly, and the two had built an instant rapport. "Cook would like to discuss the going-away menu for this evening, the mason came to repair the chimney and says he'll return tomorrow to finish, and Mr. and Mrs. Ruthven and their luggage will be picked up for delivery to the station at ten thirty tomorrow morning."

"Very good, Mrs. Cole. I'll speak to Cook after I've changed."

As Sophia started up the stairs toward her room, high-pitched giggles and mischievous whispers filtered through the half-open parlor door.

Mrs. Cole rushed inside and issued one of her no-nonsense commands. "Cease this tomfoolery at once. Back to your duties, girls."

Sophia couldn't resist poking her head into the room. "What's so amusing?"

Two maids stood with their backs to the front parlor window, cheeks flaming. One clapped a hand over her mouth to stifle a round of giggles that emerged as strangled gurgles.

"There's a gentleman out front, miss," the boldest of the two explained before ducking her head.

"Which is no concern of yours," Mrs. Cole insisted. "Now get back to your duties this minute."

When the two scurried from the room, Sophia approached to glance through the sheer lace curtain. Her pulse jumped in her throat, and suddenly she couldn't blame the maids at all.

Jasper Grey hadn't moved from the spot where she'd left him.

The man possessed that elusive characteristic all actors dreamed of—a magnetic allure that made it hard to take one's eyes off him. Not that he was performing *Hamlet* at the moment. In fact, he wasn't doing anything, other than standing next to the impressive closed carriage he claimed belonged to his father and gazing up at Kit and Ophelia's townhouse.

With his disheveled hair and lost expression, he looked a bit like a waif or stray. Though he was an unusually handsome stray, Sophia suspected he had no real interest in being tamed or taken in by one of his many fawning admirers and settling into domestic bliss. Not only did he have a wretched reputation, but he'd stared at her as hungrily as had the Earl of Westby.

Were all men bound to be cads?

Perhaps. Though Mr. Grey seemed a different sort than Lord Westby. He'd touched her to offer assistance and protection, while the earl had left a bruise on her arm and a sickening flavor on her lips. She swept the back of her hand across her mouth, wishing to rid herself of the memory.

Now that she possessed a matrimonial prospect for the first time in her life, Sophia hoped there was at least one honorable gentleman left in England. The mystery to solve was whether Mr. T. Ogilvy, Esquire, would prove to be that man.

Just when she decided Mr. Grey must have forgotten something, he turned and climbed into his carriage, offering one single gaze back at their house before departing. With his sister missing, the man must be mad with worry, but she thought it folly for him to refuse assistance or the name of a reliable detective.

There were endless ways to find trouble in London's sprawl. What if his sister had ventured beyond the city? Most worrying of all was that Mr. Grey seemed to have no notion how to proceed with his hunt for the girl. If Sophia were conducting such a search, she'd start with the girl's friends and confidants, or discover if she kept a journal. Young ladies either confided their secrets to close friends or locked diaries.

"I suppose he is an appealing sight." Mrs. Cole spoke softly from over Sophia's shoulder. "Not that it's my place to say."

When Sophia glanced back to offer the housekeeper a grin, Mrs. Cole pursed her lips in consternation.

"A woman would be blind not to notice his appeal," Sophia admitted. "But one must never forget he's an utter scoundrel. He told me so himself the first time I met the man."

"Are you well acquainted with the gentleman?" Mrs. Cole cocked a dark brow.

"Not well, no." Only well enough to know that his voice was the most appealing she'd ever heard. "He's an actor. A theater friend of my brother's."

"I see." Mrs. Cole raised a hand to her lips to stifle what sounded suspiciously like laughter. "We'll have to blinker the maids if he ever comes for a visit."

"Nonsense. We'll just have to warn them about what kind of man he is." Ironically, he was precisely the sort he must fear his sister had absconded with.

"Do you think so? I suspect that will only make them more determined to fancy him. You know how young ladies carry on. They rush toward adventure without a thought for the consequences." Mrs. Cole crossed to a table near the parlor door and retrieved the morning's post. "Some letters for you, miss."

"Quite a few, I see." Sophia retrieved the stack, hoping for one from her younger sister. Instead, the pile contained business correspondence related to Ruthven Publishing and, on the bottom, an envelope addressed to her in neat italic script from Mr. T. Ogilvy.

The gentleman had been quick about replying, though haste wasn't difficult when the postman delivered several times a day in the city.

A sickly combination of anticipation and dread welled up as she headed to her sitting room to read his letter.

Very like the roil of emotions she'd felt when posting her first reply to his matrimonial advertisement in the *London Inquirer*.

His ad had read:

> *T. Ogilvy, Esq., a professional gentleman of reliable means and moderate age, desires the acquaintance of an accomplished lady of unquestionable character, matrimony being the object. She must be between eighteen and twenty-eight years of age, of genteel education, and accustomed to good society. Preference given to ladies with an interest in books, walks in the park, and the quiet pleasures of home.*

Initially, she hadn't been searching for a husband at all. Just ideas. The personal ads provided an endless crop of story inspiration. Where better to find drama than in the pages of a newspaper?

Despite her willingness to approach matrimony through such modern means, marriage wasn't a prospect Sophia had ever taken lightly. Unlike her sister, she harbored many of her father's traditional notions. She'd never minded the thought that wedlock would be her fate. She'd looked forward to it. Expected it. And with such a goal in mind, she'd applied herself to scrupulously following the rules of etiquette and her father's prescriptions for polite behavior. She believed they'd bring her a husband, a family, and a long, contented dotage.

Of course, her parents hadn't achieved contentment together. But she wasn't like her mother, fitful and moody.

Nor did she intend to be like her father, ignoring his family to pursue business goals and wealth.

There was only one problem—and it was a significant impediment to happily ever after. At six and twenty, not a single proposal had ever come her way. Worse, Sophia wasn't precisely sure why. Men praised her beauty, and she'd passed enough mirrors to consider herself passably pretty. She'd begun to fear that she lacked something inside, a nature and disposition that made others wish to know her beyond her looks.

At her first country ball, gentlemen had vied for her attention the moment she stepped into the room. Her father selected the petitioners he approved of, and at least five respectable young men had whirled her around Lady Pembry's ballroom that evening. During each dance, she'd concentrated on performing the steps gracefully and politely answering every question put to her.

Imagine her surprise when she stepped into her host's maze garden and overheard three gentlemen discussing her merits with all the delicacy they'd afford a mare for purchase at Tattersall's.

Pretty face but cold as ice. Too frigid to desire. Ice queen.

She'd stormed back into the ballroom, eyes stinging with tears she refused to shed, and had chosen the handsomest young man in the room.

Stephen Derringham was tall and dashing, a young rogue ladies whispered about behind their fans.

After catching his eye, Sophia lured him closer with what she hoped was a coquettish grin. He'd drawn scandalously near, whispering to her in a voice so deep it made her shiver.

He invited her into the garden, and when her father was distracted, she'd slipped away.

But Derringham hadn't been interested in romance, only in groping and pulling and attempting to get her onto her back. He'd torn her stocking as he struggled to hike up her dress and steal what she did not wish to give. She'd fought him, pushing and kicking, until he released her with a curse, and she scrambled through the darkened garden to escape.

She still woke in the night sometimes, a cry caught in her throat, arms flailing to keep Derringham's hands away.

The incident had cured her naïveté. Afterward, she'd taken more care with her behavior, found a kind of comfort in her father's rules of etiquette.

Her sister Clary insisted Sophia needed to be more forthright with her feelings. That if she favored a gentleman and revealed her interest, he would respond in kind.

Sophia wasn't convinced. It was a risk no man had ever inspired her to take.

After slicing the letter opener along the envelope's edge, Sophia slipped Mr. Ogilvy's note out carefully, warily. Her first reply had contained mostly banal niceties, assuring him that she met all of the requirements—age, status, and good character—mentioned in his advert. A photographic postcard emerged with the folded foolscap, and Sophia glimpsed only dark hair and a mustache before flipping the card and focusing on the man's letter. She wished to judge Mr. Ogilvy not by his visage but first and foremost by the content of his heart.

Miss Ruthven,

Your reply stood out among all others, and I confess myself most eager to continue our acquaintance.

To that end, I have enclosed a photograph, so that you may judge whether my countenance induces anything like your approbation. If your beauty is half as fulsome as the character you've described yourself as possessing, I shall be beyond pleased to make you my bride. Please enclose a recent photograph with your next reply, which I eagerly await.

Yours respectfully,
T. Ogilvy

"Well, bother." Sophia closed her eyes and sighed. She fiddled with the edge of the postcard but refused to turn the photo over.

Ogilvy had sounded so principled in the newspaper, seeking a match based on character and the harmony of two minds. He'd sparked her notice because his ad mentioned nothing regarding looks or physical measurements. Now it seemed to be the man's only real concern. What of similar interests? What of shared beliefs? What of preferences and inclinations that may or may not be compatible? After waiting so long for a suitor, she refused to jump straight to assessing each other shallowly.

Did she require any greater evidence than the Earl of Westby to prove that a man's beauty could steal one's breath while he offered nothing else in the way of reliability or honor?

She would not send Ogilvy a photograph. Not yet. She knew too little of the man. He hadn't even seen fit to share his given name before asking for a glimpse of her face.

After pulling a clean sheet of foolscap from her desk, she began crafting a response to his letter.

> *Mr. Ogilvy,*
>
> *Your quick reply is greatly appreciated, sir. However, your enclosed photograph was most unexpected. I must inform you that I have set your image aside and shall not look upon your face until we are further acquainted.*
>
> *What are your interests, Mr. Ogilvy? I do not know your occupation, nor by what name your friends address you. For myself, I prefer the county to the city, tea to coffee, and mystery stories like those of Mr. Conan Doyle to any other sort of fiction. I've never been gifted with a nickname. Everyone calls me Sophia.*
>
> *Mayn't we correspond for a while to deepen our understanding of each other?*
>
> > *Sincerely,*
> > *Sophia Ruthven*

When a knock sounded at her door, she blew across the paper to dry the ink from her fountain pen. "Come in."

"Rather than making you go down to the kitchen, Miss Ruthven, I brought up the menu for this evening." Mrs. Cole hustled into the room, holding out a sheet of paper in front of her.

Sophia had taken care to plan a special bon voyage meal for her brother and sister-in-law's last night at home before their departure for France. She wanted to give the newlyweds a pleasant send-off and assure them that all would be taken care of at home during their absence.

"Thank you, Mrs. Cole. Tell Cook this looks perfect." Another thought struck Sophia as the housekeeper started out of the room. "May I speak to you on a delicate matter?"

"Of course, Miss Ruthven." The housekeeper clasped her hands in front of her as she reentered Sophia's room, her shoulders back, body tense, as if she expected a reprimand or interrogation.

"Let's sit for a moment." Sophia gestured to a pair of chairs near the long window looking out onto the townhouse's back garden.

Rather than put Mrs. Cole at ease, the suggestion seemed to make her anxious. She reached up to fiddle with a small brooch at the neck of her blouse. "Is anything amiss with my performance, Miss Ruthven?"

"Not at all." Sophia had already taken a chair and motioned toward the other, offering Mrs. Cole an encouraging grin.

Quickly, as if she didn't wish to waste Sophia's time, the housekeeper seated herself and assumed the same stiff posture she employed when standing. "Yes, miss?"

"You must tell me if this question seems untoward or impolite." Sophia bit her lip and inhaled sharply. "But I wonder, Mrs. Cole, if you'd tell me a bit about Mr. Cole."

The woman's brow crinkled, and one eye narrowed before she said, "My father?"

"No, I mean your husband." Sophia softened her tone. Perhaps this topic was difficult. She began to feel a fool for mentioning it at all.

"My husband?" Now it was Mrs. Cole's turn to bite her lip. She twisted her hands too, over and over each other as if she were kneading a ball of imaginary dough.

"Never mind," Sophia said firmly. "I do not wish to distress you, and the question is too personal. I see that now." She stood and approached the bell pull. "Will you join me for a cup of tea instead?"

"You've found me out, haven't you?" An anguished tone broke Mrs. Cole's usually calm voice. "There is no Mr. Cole." The housekeeper dipped her head and swallowed hard. "I've never been married, Miss Ruthven. I lied."

"Oh." Sophia tugged at the bell pull. "I think this definitely calls for tea." After taking her chair again, she waited. She'd read enough mystery novels to know that most people wished to tell their truth, and waiting patiently was often all the encouragement they needed to confess their tales.

"Many have no wish to hire an unmarried lady, so it was a simple fiction to call myself a widow." Swallowing again, as if she'd taken a huge bite of bread and needed a bit of tea to wash it down, she added, "Not that lying comes easily. I'm generally an honest woman." She let out a gusty sigh. "Doesn't make much difference to tell you as much when confessing a fib, does it? The truth is that I have been working since I was fourteen and never had time for suitors. Those who did show an interest weren't worth my while." She sighed again, but this time it sounded a good deal like relief. "Now you know I'm both a spinster and a liar."

"Please don't fret. Your secret is safe with me, Mrs. Cole. I know what it is to be a spinster, and I understand why a woman would say she's not."

"Oh, I never meant to imply *you're* a spinster, Miss Ruthven."

"But I am." The moment Sophia spoke the words, far louder than she intended, a maid entered the room with a tea tray.

All of them fell into an awkward silence while the girl, one of the gigglers who'd been so affected by the sight of Jasper Grey, unloaded her tray on the table between them, bobbed a curtsy, and departed.

"That's part of why I asked about your husband," Sophia confessed. "I was hoping for your thoughts on matrimony. I'm considering it, you see."

"Are you, indeed?" For the first time since sitting down, Mrs. Cole relaxed a bit, letting her shoulders round, easing the ramrod straightness of her back. "Well, what did you tell all of the other gentlemen who've asked you?"

Sophia swallowed her first sip of tea and frowned. "What other gentlemen?"

"The other men you refused. Must have been dozens who've asked for your hand."

"None." Sophia took a second swig of strong black China tea and gulped too quickly, burning her tongue. "I've never been asked, nor have I truly had any suitors."

"Truly?" Miss Cole pressed her lips together and tipped her head. "I would have expected a bevy of men like the one out front to be nipping at your heels."

"Mr. Grey isn't pursuing me," Sophia quickly corrected. Heaven forbid anyone imagine she'd allow such a disreputable man to court her. Despite the forward-thinking changes she, Ophelia, and Clary had made to *The New Ruthven Rules for Young Ladies*, she couldn't shake the long influence of her father. He'd insisted that she, of all her siblings, must maintain the upstanding reputation he expected of his children. Since Kit and Clary had grown into irrepressible rebels, Father declared her his only hope for carrying on the respectability of the Ruthven name.

She'd often wished she was less reliable, less prone to propriety, with as much liberty as her siblings. Now that Father was gone, she had her freedom. Marriage to an honorable man, she hoped, wouldn't put an end to her newfound independence entirely.

"But you said you're considering matrimony, so I take it you're not sure of the gentleman who *is* pursuing you." Mrs. Cole was as perceptive as she was efficient at managing the staff.

Sophia stood and approached her desk. She retrieved the small rectangle of paper she'd clipped from the newspaper and handed Ogilvy's ad to Mrs. Cole.

"Oh, miss. You found a man in the newspaper? Is that not dangerous?" Judging by the look on the housekeeper's face, she certainly thought so.

"Is it?" Sophia retrieved the clipping and wondered for the hundredth time if she'd been a fool to answer. "I haven't met him yet. I've decided we should correspond for a while first."

"But will he be patient?" Mrs. Cole sipped her tea and shot Sophia a dubious look over the cup's rim. "Seems to me that a man who seeks a wife in the newspaper isn't one who's prepared to let courtship take a leisurely course."

Glancing at her desk and the overturned photograph of Mr. Ogilvy, she couldn't disagree about the man's impatience. And that wouldn't do at all. Patience, which she often lacked herself, was a characteristic Sophia craved in a spouse. Somehow, she'd always imagined an ideal marriage would be one in which a husband and wife improved each other, filling in the qualities the other lacked.

"Perhaps you should meet the gentleman," Mrs. Cole said softly, as if still uncertain whether to offer her opinion. "Might be the quickest way to determine whether you fancy him, Miss Ruthven. Or ever could."

The truth was, Sophia craved another woman's perspective, even more so now that she knew Catherine Cole shared her lot as a spinster. "If you're going to advise me on such delicate matters, I think you should call me Sophia. May I call you Catherine? At least when we're speaking privately?"

"Of course you may. But you might as well call me Cate. Only my father called me Catherine, and he shouted the name more often than not."

"Cate," Sophia started, liking the simple strength of the name. "Must it always boil down to looking upon someone and deciding on that basis alone whether he will suit?" After Derringham, she didn't trust her judgement on that score. "Shouldn't I choose a husband based on more than whether I like his face enough to wake up to it every morning of my life?"

"No, of course, it's right to want a good man. One who's clever and honorable and kind." Cate let out a low chuckle. "Though they say a pretty face can cover a multitude of sins."

"Then I might as well choose Mr. Grey," Sophia teased.

Cate spluttered a mouthful of tea and retrieved a handkerchief from her pocket. As she dabbed at her bodice, her mouth curved in a mischievous grin. "Now isn't that a thought?"

Chapter Five

"Hunch. Hint. Premonition. An echo in one's bones. Call it what you will, an investigator's instincts are her greatest asset when pursuing a clue."

—CASEBOOK OF EUPHEMIA
BREEDLOVE, LADY DETECTIVE

The worst part of playing investigator was revisiting memories and acquaintances he'd been happy to leave behind years ago. Grey dreaded every clash with the four men named on Becca's list, and so far, the first three confrontations had proven to be pointless ventures down rabbit trails that led no closer to finding Liddy.

Now there was one more name to cross off: Clive Holden.

The last time he'd seen Sir Clive, they'd been classmates at university and the man hadn't yet inherited his father's baronetcy. They'd been arrogant bucks, full of far too much bravado and very little good sense. Their adventures usually included an excess of drink, which inevitably lead to a round of fisticuffs, ending in bruises, blood, and a draw. He would have been content to avoid Clive for the rest of his days.

Now, looking back, his chief memory of Clive was how amusing the rogue had found Liddy's childish infatuation with him.

"Right this way, sir." A maid finally retrieved Grey from the parlor, where he'd been waiting for what felt like an hour, and led him into a brightly lit drawing room. The morning light burned his chalk-dry eyes. He'd managed only a few hours of restless sleep before rising early, bathing, and stumbling his way through dressing and shaving.

Somehow, in the madness of his multiday birthday celebration, the remnants of which still littered his townhouse, he'd misplaced his valet.

"Lord Winship!"

Grey spun at the sound of a youthful female voice. "Cecily?"

Clive's sister was still as plump and pretty as she'd been as a young girl, and it immediately struck him that Liddy might have come to the Holden's Cavendish Square townhouse to visit a childhood friend, rather than the young man she'd fancied as a girl.

"What a surprise to see you after all these years." Cecily rushed forward and offered her hand in a familiar way. "My goodness, you're just as I remember. I'm sorry, but Clive isn't at home. The maid should have told you."

"Is he returning soon?" Grey had initially planned to speak to his old schoolmate alone, but now he saw the advantage of a moment with Cecily to inquire about Liddy's recent visits.

"I'm afraid not. He's visiting our uncle in Hampstead before departing on a seaside holiday." She studied him as she spoke, taking in his disheveled clothes and haphazard shave, no doubt drawing semi-scandalous conclusions about what he'd been up to. "Won't you at least stay for a cup of tea? We must catch up after so many years."

"How can I resist?" He only hoped he could keep the liquid down. The alcohol and laudanum had worn off, but he hadn't eaten more than dry toast since Becca's visit.

"Wonderful!" She bounced on her toes and clapped her hands, letting out a giggle that made his chest pinch at how much it reminded him of his sister. "Too bad you didn't bring Liddy with you. We've had such amusing times while she's been in London. I hope she's not indisposed today."

"She is, I'm afraid," he said, to stem more questions, "but I'll be sure to tell her you asked after her." He took a spot on the settee across from where she'd seated herself and swallowed down the bile that rushed up his throat. Lying to acquaintances, he was learning, came far less easily than a performance on stage.

"And I'll be sure to tell Clive of your visit too."

"You were practically in leading strings the last time I saw you, Miss Holden."

"Nonsense. I was at least twelve." The tea arrived just as her cheeks began to bloom in a fearsome blush.

The girl had professed a crush on him years before, just about the time Liddy, who was a couple of years older than Cecily, had developed a soft spot for Clive Holden. Girlish fancies had once seemed as plentiful and easy to ignore as dandelion fluff blowing across one of Longcross's fields.

"Back then, Liddy took quite a liking to Clive, didn't she?" Now he wondered if her affections had turned to something more during the handful of days she'd spent in London.

"Did she?" Cecily poured tea for both of them, averting her eyes. Whatever the girl's fate, she had no future on the stage.

The tea tasted minty and eased into his belly with a soothing warmth. He waited until she'd taken her first sip and looked a bit less anxious. He wasn't quite sure how to begin. He'd confronted every other gentleman on Becca's list directly. Now he needed to find a way to discover the truth from Cecily obliquely.

"What sorts of amusements have you and Liddy got up to in the last couple of weeks?"

Her eyes ballooned and she waved at him in a dismissive gesture. "Oh, the usual sort. A bit of shopping and a few rides in the park."

"Liddy is afraid of horses." After one bolted during a childhood lesson, she'd refused to give the beasts a second chance.

"Is she? Clive gave her a few lessons, and she's become quite a horsewoman."

"In ten days?" Holden must have been awfully persuasive. "Did he take her out alone?"

"Never." Cecily shook her head so emphatically that a blonde curl came loose from her coiffure and bobbed across her forehead. "The three of us went riding together," she insisted as she swiped at the strand. "Ask Liddy. She'll tell you so herself."

Grey smiled to reassure her. "I will." If only he could. He had a dozen questions he wanted to ask his little sister.

"Biscuit?" Her lip trembled as she offered him a digestive from a piled plate. There was more—perhaps much more— the young lady wasn't telling him.

Grey reached for a biscuit and swept his fingers across the edge of Cecily's hand. When she gasped, he offered her a practiced smile. "Thank you, Cecily."

Rather than take a treat herself, she gnawed at her index finger awhile and finally blurted, "They went riding together without me. But only a handful of times."

"When?" Grey cast the plate aside and edged forward on the settee. "Where is Clive now?"

"I told you, Lord Winship. He's gone to Hampstead." She flicked a stray hair from her cheek and crossed an arm across her belly, hugging herself, as if she preferred to keep her secrets. "Liddy hasn't done anything wrong. I promise you that." A look of real fear came into her dark eyes. "Has she said something to the contrary?"

A buzz of anticipation set off a humming in his ears. He sensed that whatever Cecily Holden knew might lead him to Liddy.

"Cecily, please. I promise you won't cause Liddy any trouble." Moving to kneel in front of her chair, Grey made sure he held her gaze. He let his walls down for a moment, tried to let her see the worry in his heart. "But I need you to tell me everything."

"I have a list of sights to see, and we'll send you a postcard from each one," Ophelia promised as she clasped Sophia in a warm embrace for the second time. "But you must enjoy

London while we're gone. Take in a play or visit a museum. Don't spend too much time indoors, and don't work yourself to the bone decorating this house."

Sophia chuckled and gave her sister-in-law's hands a squeeze. "You needn't fret about me, Phee. You and Kit have only to worry about enjoying yourselves. Come back with wonderful stories to tell."

"You know we will," Kit assured, leaning forward to place a kiss on Sophia's cheek while wrapping an arm around his wife's shoulders to maneuver her out the front door.

The carriage had arrived to deliver them to the train station fifteen minutes earlier, but Ophelia was finding it difficult to depart. She was an inveterate worrier. At moments like these, Sophia remembered that her sister-in-law had helped raise her younger sister, Juliet, and, when the day arrived, that she'd make a wonderful mother.

Finally, they stepped onto the pavement, and Sophia followed behind, carrying a hat and gloves Ophelia had forgotten and a satchel they'd packed with reading material for the journey.

After watching their carriage roll away and waving until the vehicle was out of sight, Sophia drew her letter to Mr. Ogilvy out of her pocket.

"I can have a maid deliver it for you, miss," Catherine Cole called from the front step.

"Don't trouble yourself." The morning air was crisp and fresh, and now that Kit and Ophelia had departed, Sophia craved a bit of the outdoors before returning to the house that would feel so much emptier without them. "It's a short walk."

There were only a few ladies and gentleman in Blooms-bury Square this morning, so no one noticed Sophia's hesitation. A few strides forward and she slowed as doubts filled her mind. Despite his request, she'd included no photograph for Mr. Ogilvy. Would he tolerate a slow courtship or wish to rush matrimony, as Cate suggested? Perhaps it *was* dangerous to meet a man from the newspaper. He could represent himself as anyone, designing his character and personality to suit her preferences. As someone who wrote fiction, she understood how easy it was to create a character out of whole cloth.

"Miss Ruthven?" A lady's voice emerged from a carriage slowing near the pavement. A moment later, a gloved hand waved through the open window, and the coachman pulled the horses to a stop. Lady Vivian emerged in a smart turquoise blue traveling suit, a warm smile curving her lips. "I'm glad to see you looking so well. Our housekeeper said you took a bad turn yesterday. We all missed the treat of hearing you read from your book."

"I'm much better now, thank you, Lady Vivian." Sophia prayed her cheeks weren't flaming and giving her away, but she was grateful for a chance to make amends. Ruthven Publishing sales were still struggling, and new titles, like the revamped *New Ruthven Rules for Young Ladies*, needed all the support they could muster. "I hope you'll forgive my hasty departure. Perhaps we can schedule another reading."

"Of course. In fact, I was planning on being imperti-nent and calling on you this morning, Miss Ruthven." She strode forward and reached out to pat Sophia's arm. "I wish to apologize."

"There's no need, my lady. I am the one who left without an explanation."

"You were ill. Goodness knows the megrims strike me at the most inconvenient times." Lady Vivian pressed two fingers to her forehead as if reliving the pain of her last headache. "As it turned out, you were lucky to depart early. My brother returned home unexpectedly, and we had an eventful visit from Lord Winship."

"Lord Winship?" The name Lord Westby had called Mr. Grey. The role, he said, that he did not wish to play.

"An old friend of my brother's." Lady Vivian leaned forward and looked over each shoulder before whispering, "He's an actor now and an utter rogue. Quite scandalous. There was a time when my mother wouldn't even let my brother and me speak his name."

Rogue? Scandalous? Mr. Grey? Imagine that. Sophia had no difficulty ascribing every sort of sin to the man. Yet sins had been ascribed to Lady Vivian's brother too. The noblewoman had to know of his reputation. He was a scandal-rag darling, and based on his behavior while alone with Sophia in his study, she believed every scurrilous word she'd ever read about the man.

"You should meet Winship's sister, Miss Ruthven. Phyllida is a great proponent of women's independence, and I know she'd love your book." The lady stuck a finger in the air and then tapped her bottom lip. "I know what I shall do. Would you fancy a dinner party? They're much more fun than afternoon teas, and we'll make sure to keep my brother and his friends away. Ladies only. I'll expand the invitation list to include Winship's sister and her friend, Miss Holden."

Apparently Lord Westby had kept his word and mentioned nothing of Lady Phyllida's disappearance. But how would Mr. Grey—or Lord Winship, if that was his name—ever keep his sister's disappearance a secret when her friends would keenly feel her absence from social engagements? Sophia still suspected one of them might know precisely what had caused her to slip from her family's oversight in the first place.

"I'll look forward to meeting them both."

"Why not now?" The young lady turned back and waved her hand in the air toward the coachman. "The Holdens are just off Berkeley Square. I was planning to pay a visit this afternoon, but we can have the carriage take us now."

Sophia glanced toward Southampton Row, where she planned to drop her letter to Mr. Ogilvy in the post, and back into Lady Vivian's eager violet eyes. How could she refuse the young woman after ducking out of her home so rudely the day before? "I'll happily accompany you, my lady."

After they were seated and the carriage began rolling the very short distance to Berkeley Square, Lady Vivian ticked off her plans for the dinner party she intended to host. The moment she started on ideas for the menu, the carriage juddered to a stop.

"Was it really such a short distance?" She peered out the carriage window before taking the single step down onto the pavement. "If we're in luck, Phyllida will still be stopping over with the Holdens, and we can invite them both at the same time."

Sophia's heart kicked into a gallop. "She's been staying with Miss Holden?"

"Yes, and it's such a treat for Phyllida, who's spent all her life locked away in the countryside."

They were admitted to the Holden townhouse by a youthful maid who took Lady Vivian's calling card and asked them to wait in a front parlor. Sophia assessed the decor for ideas she might apply to Kit and Ophelia's London home. The Holdens seemed to favor dark polished wood and rich colors. The cherry furniture and deep hunter-green wallpaper gave the sense of cool relief on what would become another hot summer's day.

"Right this way, my lady." The maid reappeared and led them down the hall into a room filled with light. The glare through the long picture windows was so bright that Sophia shaded her eyes and ducked behind Lady Vivian's feathered hat to allow her eyes time to adjust.

"Viv, this isn't at all what you're thinking," a young lady declared from within the room. "He came to call on Clive."

"Well, well, Lord Winship. If you keep turning up everywhere I go, I'll begin to think you're besotted with me."

Sophia's throat went dry, and her heart began an erratic thud against her ribs.

"But I was here before you, Lady Vivian, so perhaps the infatuation is all yours." Mr. Grey, who was apparently Lord Winship, stepped forward to greet Lady Vivian, blotting out the glare of the sun so that Sophia could finally see into the room. What she noticed first was how the warm morning light burnished his hair in shades of copper and bronze. Then the look of shock on his face, causing his dimples to go into hiding when he spotted Sophia.

"Oh, Winship, see how you make me forget my manners," Lady Vivian chastised. "This is Miss Ruthven. She's an author and co-owner of her family's publishing enterprise."

When Lady Vivian rushed forward to greet Miss Holden, he stepped toward Sophia.

"What are you doing here?" he demanded on an irritated whisper, the rudest welcome she'd ever received in her life.

"I was invited." And he was far too close. Rudely close. She could smell his scent, bay and juniper, and see the bluish circles under his bloodshot eyes. She wasn't sure if the man was an actor turned aristocrat or an aristocrat who played at being an actor, but she was certain he had a wretched valet. His servant had missed a patch of stubble near his chin and left a tiny blood-edged nick on his left cheek. She fought the irrational urge to pull out her handkerchief and blot at the cut.

Despite the beautiful symmetry of his features, the gray eyes that had sparked flirtatiously the day before looked desperate now. And exhausted. She wondered if worry had kept him awake all night. She could only imagine how anxious she'd be if her own sister were in danger.

"Did you know Phyllida stayed here in the last few days?" she asked him.

"She visited." He cast a glance back at Lady Vivian to make sure she and Miss Holden were still busy chatting. "That's why I'm here."

"Lady Vivian told me Phyllida lodged here with Miss Holden."

"Did she?" He leaned in closer and kept his voice low. "Apparently she's infatuated with Clive Holden. I must get to Hampstead and find him."

"Are you two going to join us?" Lady Vivian called. "Beware of Lord Winship, Miss Ruthven. He's quite the infamous scoundrel. Come and meet Miss Holden instead. She says she's reading your book and enjoying every word."

Miss Holden stepped forward, and Sophia sucked in a breath. The young lady's petite stature, honey-blonde hair, and ample figure reminded Sophia so much of her sister, Clarissa, that her throat tightened for a moment.

"What a pleasure to meet you, Miss Ruthven." The girl's smile was warm and genuine. "You must know more decorum than all of us put together. My mother made me read the original *Ruthven Rules for Young Ladies* that your father wrote, but I like this one much better."

"Yes, as do I, to be honest." Her father had seen women as meek and demure. Passive creatures who waited on men to guide them. She'd learned how to be everything he expected of her, but she'd often felt the discomfort of playing a role.

"If you ladies will excuse me—"

"Winship, no. You cannot depart just as we arrive. You've been away so long. Stay and tell us about your life on the stage." Lady Vivian positioned herself on a settee and patted the cushion beside her thigh.

Grey cast a longing glance toward the open drawing room door, eager to make his escape.

"Tea, Miss Ruthven, or a biscuit?" Miss Holden approached and offered Sophia a brimming teacup and a gold-edged plate bearing a sampling of biscuits.

"Actually, I fear my pins are coming out." Sophia reached up to surreptitiously tug on one of the pins holding her chignon in place. "Is there someplace where I might fix it?"

Lady Vivian would think her the most indisposed woman in London, but she had a hunch she couldn't quell. The kind of instinct that often led her lady detective, Effie Breedlove, to the clue that solved a mystery.

"Of course," Miss Holden whispered conspiratorially. Privies were not the sort of thing decorous young ladies discussed in front of handsome gentlemen. "There is a closet with a wash basin and mirror at the top of the stairs."

The handsome gentleman in question shot up both brows and dropped his lips in a grimace as he watched Sophia exit the room from which he couldn't seem to find a way to extricate himself.

At the top of the stairs, Sophia discovered that the house was much larger inside than it appeared from the pavement. A hallway ran along the upper level landing, and she counted five doors to choose between. She dismissed the one ahead as the ladies' privy and tried the knob on the next, finding it locked. As she approached the third door, she heard a young woman's voice emerge and froze in place. Tiptoeing forward, she peered through the opening.

Next to the bed, a maid stood fluffing a pillow and singing quietly to herself.

Sophia pushed the door open gently. "Was this Miss Grey's room?"

The maid dropped the pillow and pressed a hand to her chest. "Goodness, miss, you gave me a fright. Yes, miss, this is Lady Phyllida Grey's room." She answered in an obsequious tone, but scanned Sophia from head to toe, as if trying to determine precisely who she was. "Did Miss Holden send you up, miss?"

"She did." And she'd be horrified to know the young woman she thought the most decorous in London was skulking around her home, looking for clues to her friend's disappearance. "She sent me up to fetch a book of Lady Phyllida's." She'd always suspected fibbing got easier the more one practiced, but she was still a much worse actor than her brother or Lord Winship.

The maid squinted one eye, rightfully dubious. "Haven't seen any books in this room, miss."

"Very well, then." Sophia couldn't think of a single fib to get the maid out of the room and allow her to search the space on her own. "Forgive me for interrupting your work."

"No bother, miss." The maid seemed gratified, even shocked, by Sophia's apology and offered her a grin.

Sophia started out of the room, but the maid called her back softly. "Miss?"

When she turned to face the girl, the maid leaned down and lifted the edge of the mattress. She pulled out a slim book covered in a cream fabric. "Is this the book, miss?"

Sophia stepped forward and retrieved the volume. Three pink ribbons along the edge kept the pages tied shut. "I think it very well might be. Thank you."

She struggled to steady her breathing as she made her way downstairs. Perspiration trickled down her neck. Excitement and anticipation zinged through her body. There was no doubt in her mind that she held Lady Phyllida's journal, and its pages might contain information to help Grey in his search.

Unfortunately, she'd brought no reticule and the pockets of her skirt were too narrow to conceal the book. At the bottom of the stairs, she sidestepped behind a potted palm in the hallway and shoved the volume inside her shirtwaist. Her buttons bulged and her corset protested, but the book was mercifully thin.

"Oh, my dear," Lady Vivian said the minute Sophia reentered the drawing room. "Is it another megrim?"

"Where is Lord Winship?" The one time she actually had a reason to see the man, he was nowhere in sight. And asking about him clearly wasn't what Lady Vivian or Miss Holden expected. They exchanged a questioning glance.

"He departed just before you came down," Miss Holden explained.

"I should be going too." Especially since she noticed Miss Holden tipping her head to examine the bulk stretching the front of Sophia's shirtwaist.

"My carriage can deliver you home, if you like," Lady Vivian offered. "As long as you'll promise to come to my dinner party."

"I'd be honored, my lady, but I can see myself home." She listened for the sound of a carriage departing from in front of the house but heard nothing. Perhaps he'd come on foot. "Good day to you both."

Both ladies opened their mouths as if to offer some parting words, but Sophia didn't wait to hear them. She spun on her heel and started toward the door.

She had to move fast if she was going to catch Jasper Grey, or Lord Winship, or whatever his name was.

CHAPTER SIX

The longer Liddy was gone, the more Grey began to wonder if he should relent and hire a discreet detective to assist him with his search. He could try other avenues of inquiry while an investigator wasted time questioning a sixteen-year-old girl for scraps of information.

Wouldn't Sophia Ruthven love to know he was considering her advice? The lady seemed the sort who enjoyed being right. And proper. Good lord, had any woman ever held herself with such perfect poise? He doubted the queen herself managed Sophia's ramrod posture.

"Grey."

He turned as someone called his name. A cluster of ladies and gentlemen on a morning stroll were passing on the other side of the street, but none seemed interested in catching his attention. Perhaps one of the group shared his family's surname.

Quickening his pace, he scanned the main thoroughfare ahead for a hansom cab. A brisk morning walk had seemed a good idea an hour ago. Now he wished he'd taken his father's carriage.

"Lord Winship!"

He stopped and glanced behind him, and his mouth fell open.

Sophia Ruthven rushed toward him, a few long golden curls bouncing at her shoulder, her hem hiked up above her ankle boots. She drew up in front of him and bent at the waist, gripping her chest to catch her breath.

When she finally stood and faced him. Mercy. What a glorious sight. She didn't look proper at all. Cheeks splotchy pink, eyes bright and wide, she opened her mouth just enough to let a few rushing breaths escape.

"I've been chased by women before, but never quite so fetchingly."

"I am *not* chasing you." She lifted a hand to block the sun's glare as she frowned up at him. "Not in the sense you mean, anyway."

Grey stepped closer. "Pursue me in any manner you please, Sophia. I won't complain." His chest tightened as he caught her floral scent. Other parts of his body were tightening too.

She tapped her foot in annoyance. "I need to speak to you."

"You have my full attention." Every inch. Good grief, he'd never found a woman appealing enough to hang on her every breath. He looked away, forcing himself to stop staring at her flushed lips. Glancing back toward the Holden townhouse, he quipped, "Lady Vivian will think you despise her. That's two days in a row you've escaped her company."

Sophia ignored the tease. "We need to speak privately. We're only a mile or so from Kit and Ophelia's townhouse. Shall we walk?"

"Do you think you can manage?" She was still working to steady her breath, her chest rising and falling in the most distracting way. Except...He tipped his head and examined her heaving bosom, which looked oddly square.

"Yes." She pressed a palm to her chest. "I have something here you'll want to see."

"Oh, I'm certain you do."

She huffed out an irritated sigh. "Do you think you could stop being a lecher for an hour?"

"I'll do my best." Though the chances were slim. Nonexistent, really. Especially since the clearest thought he had while she stood before him, breathless and perspiring, was how much he longed to kiss her senseless.

Sophia began striding away in the direction of her brother's townhouse, not bothering to wait on him to follow. She looked quite as appealing departing as she did while stomping toward him. Another tress of hair slipped loose, bouncing down her back, almost to her waist. He couldn't take his eyes off the dangling strand. Then she stopped, turned back, and glared. "Are you coming with me or not?"

Grey swallowed hard and nodded. The woman truly had no notion that half the sentences she'd uttered carried potent double entendres.

He caught up with her and examined the odd shape of her bosom again. "So what is it you have to show me?"

"A book." She spoke the two words out of the corner of her mouth, as if practicing her ventriloquist skills. "I think it may be your sister's journal."

Grey caught Sophia's arm and yanked her to a stop. "Let me see."

"You truly want to examine it here?" She turned and braced a hand against his chest. The gesture was meant to push him away, but he liked the feel of her palm against his body. Though her cheeks were flooded with color, her hand was blessedly cool, and he realized he was the one whose body was overheating. "On the street? In front of anyone who might pass?"

"No." The woman was so bloody practical. And irritatingly correct. "Let's hurry."

His strides were longer than hers, but she kept up admirably. Or tried to. He offered his arm at one point, but she brushed his touch away and fixed her chin even higher. He'd never found a woman's presence at his elbow quite so distracting. It was that hair, like honey silk ribbons bouncing at her back. When they reached the pavement outside Kit and Ophelia's house, he stopped her with a hand on her arm.

"Your hair." He gestured vaguely toward her head. "It's come undone. You might want to…" Words failed him, and he found himself touching her instead, reaching out to tuck a loose tress behind her ear.

Once again, she brushed off his touch and sidestepped away from him. "Yours is disheveled too, Mr. Grey. Or should I call you Lord Winship?"

"Grey will do." As she lifted her arms, shoving that square bosom toward him to draw her rebel tresses into a knot at the back of her head, Grey ran a hand through his hair. He knew he'd made a haphazard mess of his morning ablutions. Count on Sophia Ruthven to point out any sign of untidiness.

Yet as they stood on her brother's front step, righting themselves like two wantons sneaking back into a party after a tryst in a moonlit garden—an experience he knew a thing or two about—it wasn't disdain he saw in Sophia's blue-green eyes. Heat lay beyond the cool ocean hues. And desire. He'd seen that fire in women's eyes too many times to mistake the look.

"Will I have to explain to your brother why your hair is mussed?"

Ignoring him, she twisted the doorknob and pushed open the door, turning back as she stepped across the threshold. "I'm a spinster, Mr. Grey. No one worries about why my hair is out of place."

Then they were fools. And she was too, for thinking of herself as a spinster. She was a ripe, luscious woman who—

"Kit and Ophelia departed for France this morning, so we won't be disturbed."

Grey followed her into a parlor just off the main hall. Before Sophia could secure the door behind him, a woman's voice called, "I heard the door, Miss Ruthven. Shall I have refreshment sent to the parlor?"

A short, dark-haired woman with alert almond-shaped eyes peered at him from the doorway.

"No, Mrs. Cole. We won't be long."

The lady didn't look in a mind to leave him alone with Sophia, so he offered her his most reassuring grin. Which only caused the Cole woman to narrow her eyes, as if she suspected him guilty of the twelve most recent crimes committed in London.

"Letter came for you this morning, Miss Ruthven. I left it on the mantel."

"Very good, Mrs. Cole." Sophia pushed the parlor door toward the woman, inch by inch. "We won't be long."

The moment she turned to face him, Sophia began unbuttoning her shirtwaist. In other circumstances, she would have made a fine seductress. She looked into his eyes boldly as her nimble fingers played over the top two pearlescent buttons of her blouse. Grey licked his lips in anticipation, as much for a glimpse of her soft flesh as for the journal she thought belonged to his sister.

"If you need any help, Sophia." His voice emerged hoarse. "Please don't hesitate to ask."

"Blackguard." She spun away from him and reached inside her blouse. A moment later, she lifted a ribbon-tied book out toward him.

He snatched at the volume, at the hope of finding some clue to his sister's whereabouts. "Where did you get this?"

"I went upstairs at the Holden's. A maid pulled the book out from under the mattress of the room where Phyllida has been lodging. She was under the impression your sister would be returning." Sophia approached as she buttoned her shirt back up to her neck, watching as he fumbled with the knotted ribbons. "Would you like me to untie them?"

"Maybe we should just find a knife and cut them."

But in the time it took him to look around the room pointlessly for a penknife or sharp object, she'd reached across his arms, taken the journal from his hands, and expertly worked the knots loose with her fingers.

She flipped the book open from the last page, skipping backward until she found the first leaf that contained writing. The words had been scribbled in a loopy feminine hand. Sophia turned the book so Grey could read the entry.

He thought it was Liddy's penmanship, but she hadn't written to him in so long he couldn't be sure. Still, the words chilled his blood.

He's promised so much and bids me trust him. Trust is hard, but I've no wish to begin like Mama and Papa. Betrayal won't be my way. And I don't want a thousand lovers like my brother. I do not, will not, ever want for any other lover. I only pray he vows the same.

We depart in two days, and patience, I'm learning, is as difficult to achieve as trust.

"It's dated two days past," Sophia whispered. She'd read the words upside down, apparently.

"Cecily didn't say when Clive departed for Hampstead, but Liddy must have gone with him." Grey couldn't imagine what had taken the two to Hampstead. Perhaps it was the first leg of their journey toward Gretna Green. Only one certainty blazed in his mind. "I have to stop them."

Sophia flipped the book closed, and Grey turned to face her.

"Thank you for finding the journal." He couldn't resist lifting a hand to her cheek. She was as warm and soft as he imagined. For once, she did not flinch from his touch. Taking her lips would be so easy. But if he kissed her, he would not wish to leave. "I must go."

As he started out of the room, he made himself a promise. He would kiss Sophia Ruthven. When he found Liddy and got her safely back to Derbyshire, he'd return and give

Sophia a proper thanks for assisting him. He would kiss her
until she looked at him again as she had on the front stoop.
Until she touched him as she had on the pavement. Until she
said his name, breathlessly, needfully, between kisses.

Jasper Grey dashed away, and despite the sunlight pouring
in through the lace at the parlor window, the room seemed
dimmer without him. And there was a lurch in Sophia's chest,
as if some part of her wanted to follow. To help him solve
the mystery, to see the moment when brother and sister were
reunited.

Clutching her hand, she realized she still held his sister's
journal. She rushed from the room and yanked open the
front door, but he was already gone.

"I thought tea might be in order." Miss Cole appeared,
gripping a tray before her. "If I'm not mistaken, you missed
breakfast this morning."

"Thank you, Cate." The woman's given name slipped
out easily. Despite all Sophia knew of etiquette, calling the
woman she was beginning to consider a friend anything else
seemed too formal. "You'll join me, won't you?"

They had agreed to discuss the household accounts today.
There were repair bills to pay and vendors to select to complete wallpaper and painting projects in several rooms too.
Sophia thought her efficient housekeeper might remind her
of the duties to attend to. Instead, she offered a sharp nod, a
hint of a grin, and began arranging refreshments on a table
between the room's two facing settees.

After a few moments of sipping tea in companionable silence, Cate said quietly, "I think we can breathe a sigh of relief."

"Can we?"

"I don't think Mr. Grey stayed long enough for any of the maids to fall irrevocably in love with him."

"Thank goodness." Sophia smiled before insisting, "It wasn't a proper visit."

"An improper one, then?" Cate ducked her head for another sip of tea, rather than meet Sophia's gaze.

"Impromptu, not improper. I was assisting him." She glanced at the journal that lay on the settee beside her. "He's lost something, and I wished to help him find it."

"Now you have me intrigued. This is beginning to sound like one of those detective stories you like to read."

"I'm attempting to write one too." Sophia held a breath, waiting for the other woman's reaction. She'd never confessed her writing interests or aspirations to anyone.

"Are you? How exciting." Cate edged forward and set her teacup on the table between them. "You must let me read it. May I?"

"Once I've finished and polished it up a bit, I'll let you have a look." Ridiculously, considering that she hoped to publish her story, the notion of anyone else reading the tale terrified her. "There's so much to do before Kit and Ophelia return. Should we get started on the household accounts?"

After gathering the bills, the household ledger, penny post stamps, and fountain pens and seating themselves around a small table in the parlor, Sophia and Cate had the accounts settled, menus sorted, and repairs planned for the coming week in a little over an hour.

As they tidied the table afterward, Cate pointed to the envelope on the fireplace mantel. "Don't forget the post."

Sophia had forgotten all about the letter. Standing to retrieve it, she saw that it was from Mr. Ogilvy. "He's written again before receiving my reply." She didn't know whether to be flattered by his eagerness or bothered by the breach of etiquette.

Slipping the letter from its envelope, Sophia skimmed the short note.

Forgive me for writing again before the favor of your reply, Miss Ruthven. My business enterprises require me to travel, and I have the good fortune of being in London tomorrow, June 24. My intention is to call on you at home in the early afternoon as I confess myself eager to behold the face of the woman who has so fully ignited my interest with her many admirable qualities. Yours, T. Ogilvy, Esq.

"He says he's coming to London tomorrow." Sophia crumpled the letter in her hand. "To see my face."

"And you don't wish him to?" Cate approached to stand beside Sophia.

"Not yet." She pulled the unsent letter to him from her skirt pocket. "In my reply I requested that we correspond for a while to get to know each other. I haven't yet looked at the photograph he sent."

Maybe she wasn't brave enough to trust as Phyllida Grey had, but she could understand the girl's hopefulness. They both craved a happy ending.

"If you hurry, perhaps there's time to send a telegram," Cate suggested.

"Excellent idea." After gathering a few coins and her reticule, Sophia headed for the front door. And stopped the minute she grasped the handle. "Why am I doing this?"

"Doing which?" Cate asked as she joined her in the front vestibule. "Delaying him or meeting him at all?"

"I want to marry. He is eager to. Why should I avoid the man?"

"Because you've never met, and he may be a madman," Cate said solemnly, which only made her words comical.

Sophia slanted her a grin. "That's not my chief concern."

"Well, perhaps"—Cate sniffed and busied herself straightening the perfectly neat cuffs of her plain dark day dress—"you crave a bit of adventure before binding yourself to anyone in matrimony."

Sophia swallowed and stared at the closed door in front of her. She thought of Effie Breedlove, the lady detective she'd created in her stories. Through her, she wrote of adventures, and, yes, perhaps she did crave more experiences than her small countryside village had ever afforded. But marriage would be a new adventure, wouldn't it? She wouldn't shy away from it as she had so much else in her life.

"If he comes to visit as he says he will, I will meet the man. And finally discover his first name."

But the moment she turned away from the front door to head upstairs and look through her wardrobe for an appropriate dress to wear, her thoughts strayed.

Jasper Grey and his lost sister weighed on her mind. Brushing her fingers across the spot where he'd caressed her cheek, she recalled the look in his eyes. Beyond fatigue and worry, she'd glimpsed more. Attraction? Desire?

Nonsense. The man had probably never met a woman he didn't consider seducing.

She'd assisted him. He was grateful. Nothing more.

More important was whether he'd reach Holden and Phyllida in time. What if the couple were already halfway to Scotland? Sophia suspected worry for both of the Greys would plague her until she got word of the young woman's safe return.

Seeking a distraction, she retrieved story pages from her desk and began reading over the last chapter she'd written. As she skimmed lines, she felt the outline of Ogilvy's overturned photograph under her fingers.

Since they were to meet tomorrow, her vow not to look at his photograph seemed pointless. Moving her pages aside, she flipped the photograph, bending over the image to get a good look.

Dark eyes and hair. A neatly trimmed beard; short, pomaded hair; symmetrical features; and a flawlessly arranged necktie. He was a respectable-looking gentleman, serious and unsmiling. Ogilvy's visage inspired nothing more than an interest in cataloging his features.

That was much better than how being in Mr. Grey's company provoked her.

Wasn't it?

Chapter Seven

As he stepped from the hansom cab, the driver scowled down at Grey as if he wished to memorize his face in case he heard later about some mischief committed in Bloomsbury Square.

Grey couldn't blame the man. At shortly after five in the morning, the sun had just begun to come up in warm pink and peach shades, and few were out walking the streets in this respectable district of London. Delivery men were about their business and street sellers had begun to move carts into place, but no fine ladies or gentlemen were out promenading in the square.

He considered approaching the Ruthven front door, then thought better of raising the entire household at such an ungodly hour. Heading down the pavement along the row of whitewashed townhouses, he found an alley leading to a mews. Picking out Sophia Ruthven's townhouse wasn't difficult, but he couldn't be sure which room might be hers.

Someone had left a second-floor window open to let in a bit of cool evening air. Wasn't that just what a lady used to countryside breezes and unacquainted with London's noxious fog might do?

A full moon poured its glow down to light his path into the house's back garden, and Grey bent to retrieve a handful of pebbles from the gravel path next to a freshly planted row of primroses.

On stage he'd climbed bowers, scrabbled over windowsills, and even jumped off "bridges." He sincerely hoped he could rouse Sophia without having to risk life and limb.

He chucked a few of the tiny stones up toward the open window and waited. Just when he ducked his head to choose another from his palm, the window sash shot up.

"Stop it," she whispered. "Are you mad? We just had new window glass installed."

Sophia's hair tumbled over her shoulder and a baggy night dress covered every inch of her arms, chest, and neck, but Grey's body still jolted in response to the sight of her natural and unbound.

"Come down and speak to me." He needed more than a conversation with her, but he'd start there.

"Return at a more reasonable hour, and I'll consider it."

Good God, did the woman think of nothing but propriety?

"Being reasonable is the least of my concerns." It never had been. Not for many years, anyway. And he couldn't worry about the rules of social calls when his sister was in danger of destroying her future. "I need your help, Sophia."

She stared down at him a long moment and then ducked inside. He expected the window to slam shut too, but she poked her head out again a moment later. "Come around to the front door."

As he made his way back onto Bloomsbury Square, Grey went over what he wished to say. He had to convince her, and he practiced his words as if he was about to step on stage.

"Hurry," she said from the Ruthven front step, "before anyone sees you."

If he wasn't so exhausted, he might have found her fussiness amusing.

Once she admitted him to the vestibule inside Kit and Ophelia's front door, he could see by the gaslight that she hadn't gotten much sleep. Puffy circles had begun to form beneath her pretty eyes, and she was frightfully pale.

With the wave of her hand, she bid him follow her into the parlor.

"What help do you need, Mr. Grey?" She was still whispering and crossed her arms over the dark, high-necked day dress she'd donned. Chin high, back straight, she already looked irritated and defiant. He didn't bother mentioning that she'd misaligned the buttons of her gown.

Grey believed in diving in head first, tearing off bandages quickly, and receiving bad news straight on. He sucked in a long breath and blurted what he guessed Sophia Ruthven would take as very bad news. "I need you to come with me to Brighton."

For one fraught moment, she only responded with a crinkled brow. Then she tilted her head, as if she wasn't sure she'd heard him correctly. "You. Want me. To come to Brighton. With you."

"Precisely."

"I'd suspected it from the moment I met you, but now I'm certain." Three graceful strides and she stood slipper to boot with him. She tipped her head to the side, her blonde coil of hair slipping from her shoulder onto her back. "You're not just bad and dangerous to know. You truly are mad."

Byronic compliment aside, he was certain, of all the condemnations that had been hurled at him, that he was not mad. He'd tasted the edge of it once, shortly after his brother's death. But now drink and women and indulgence usually kept the darkness at bay.

"No, Sophia. Just desperate. I've reason to believe my sister is on her way to the seaside with Clive Holden."

"When did they depart?" The furrow in her brow deepened. "How can you be sure she's with him? Did you speak to her?"

Grey tugged his pocket watch from his waistcoat and checked the time. They'd need to head to the train station soon, but he could see from the skepticism in her eyes that she'd require a thorough explanation before agreeing to accompany him.

"After leaving you this afternoon, I went straight to Hampstead. At the home of Holden's uncle, a servant advised me to seek Clive at a local inn." What a wild goose chase that had been. "The innkeeper couldn't recall renting him a room and kept me waiting an hour for his wife's return, so that I might question her. I suspect that delay was a ruse to inform Clive of my presence. A coachman outside the inn told me a young man matching Holden's description tried to hire his rig for a trip to Brighton." Grey scrubbed a hand across his stubble-roughened chin. "He was already promised to another traveler, but Holden did succeed in hiring another coach."

He swayed toward her, not out of desire but exhaustion.

"Perhaps you should sit." Sophia remained standing and pointed to a settee. "When did they depart?"

Grey knew he shouldn't sit. The temptation to rest his head and doze would be too great. But he found himself slumping down with a grateful sigh. "Shortly before I returned to speak to you. Less than an hour ago."

"Why would they take a coach when a train would get them there more quickly?"

"Privacy. Time alone." The same reasons he would choose to travel with a woman via closed carriage rather than a potentially crowded train car. She'd been gone for days. Grey had no illusions about Liddy's chastity, but he couldn't bear to see her promised to a bounder like Holden.

Sophia let out a distressed gasp as realization dawned. "You must go after them. But I cannot accompany you."

Irritation set a muscle ticking in his jaw. "If my suspicions are correct, Clive knows I'm on their trail. They will be expecting me in Brighton." Grey edged forward, braced his elbow on his knees, and gazed into Sophia's eyes. "Neither of them will be expecting you."

"No." She shook her head, slowly at first and then more vehemently as she fiddled with the ribbon at the neck of her gown. "You can't honestly expect *me* to apprehend them." But there was an unexpected flash of interest in her eyes. Unbidden, the image of Sophia as a fearsome lady thief-catcher arose in Grey's mind. She'd be rule-bound and relentless, he suspected.

"If we could separate them, that would be a start." Grey stood, ignoring a wave of dizziness and the aching protest of his sleep-deprived body. "You could approach her, divert her long enough for me to confront Holden."

"I can't accompany you, Mr. Grey." Sophia crossed her arms and began tapping her fingers on the sleeve of her gown. Grey followed the direction of her gaze and noticed an envelope on a corner desk.

Grey should have known his friend's sister would be as stubborn as Kit. And it wasn't as if Grey believed himself short on persuasive powers, particularly when it came to women. But Sophia was a unique challenge.

He stepped away to keep from reaching out and attempting to persuade her in the way he knew best. Crossing toward the desk, he noted the name on the envelope that had snared her interest.

"Is Mr. T. Ogilvy coming to call?" Some scoundrel's sense told him it wasn't a mundane social visit. "A suitor?"

"My callers are none of your concern." Sophia rushed across the room and snatched up the envelope.

Grey looked down into her fierce green-blue eyes. She was close and warm and wafting her virginal lavender scent. When had stubborn spinsters become so bloody tempting? "What would Ogilvy say if he knew you'd been locked away with the Earl of Westby in his study?"

Once the irrational red-hot flash of jealousy waned, Grey was almost as shocked by his words as Sophia. Her eyes had gone wide, and her full lips had fallen open.

He ached to kiss her. Seduction was his way with women, not petition.

She pivoted away and strode toward the unlit fireplace. The tangled tumble of loose honey-gold curls softened the effect of the ramrod straightness of her posture.

"I'm sorry for asking this of you, Sophia, but I've no one else to turn to."

A wry chuckle sounded in the quiet of the room. "Lord Westby said you'd bedded half of London's eligible young ladies. You're a famous actor and, apparently, a notorious aristocrat. You must have dozens of friends in the city."

He didn't. Acquaintances, yes. Connections through his family or the theater. Conquests, lovers, and pursuers. He had hundreds of those. But none were reliable, honorable, or discreet. They were like him, not her. "You're the one I need."

When she turned back to face him, her eyes had softened. "Why?"

"You already know the details of Liddy's poor judgement, and you have a way about you, Sophia. She'll trust you." He dipped his head and cleared his throat. "On very short acquaintance, I trust you."

"I take it you mean to pursue them by train?" She began fussing with the lace at the edge of her dress's bodice.

Grey glanced at his pocket watch again. "If we make the earliest departure, we should arrive in Brighton before they do."

"And then we must find them in a bustling town. How long do you think that will take?"

We. She'd echoed his use of the word. The vice grip of worry that had been choking him since learning of Liddy's disappearance began to ease. Just a bit. "Not long, I expect."

"In a seaside resort teaming with summer visitors?" Sophia offered him what he was coming to recognize as her dubious look, one blonde brow quirked high.

"I'm tempted to simply impress you with my detecting skills once we arrive." Grey reached into his coat pocket and slipped out a small notebook he kept there. "But, honestly, the coachman at the inn told me to which hotel Holden asked to be delivered."

She nibbled her lower lip as she assessed him and then let out a long sigh. He knew that soft wisp of escaping breath spelled victory for him.

"Give me a few moments to prepare." She started toward the door, then changed course and returned to her corner desk. She opened the wide center drawer and drew out Liddy's journal, laying it on the blotter. "You forgot to take this with you."

"Were there any other details about Clive?" A part of him didn't wish to know.

She jerked back in surprise. "It wouldn't have been appropriate for me to read your sister's journal."

"Of course." When she left the room he let out a long exhale of relief. Considering matters from Sophia's very proper perspective, she had conceded a great deal by agreeing to accompany a man alone on a train journey. He glanced at the corner desk, at the spot where he'd seen her envelope from Mr. Ogilvy, and wondered what else she might be risking, beyond her sterling reputation.

Sophia laid her book aside and studied Jasper Grey the moment he began snoring softly.

He'd started their journey by treating her with scrupulous care, making sure not to touch her or even use her given name. Almost as if he realized the impropriety of an unmarried man and woman traveling together. Though they had an entire first-class carriage to themselves, he'd chosen the bench opposite her and kept his gaze fixed out the train car window.

Expecting his usual flirtatious banter to commence the moment they departed the station, she'd pulled out a book and found herself skimming the same paragraphs over and over. But instead of interrupting or attempting to draw her attention, he'd allowed her the quiet to read as his eyes grew steadily heavier. Within an hour, he was sprawled in his seat, chin tucked to his chest, head bobbing from side to side as the train swayed around curves in the track. He'd straightened one leg, so that his boot rested between her feet, pressing against the hem of her gown.

If possible, the man was even more appealing in repose. The same carved Greek sculpture beauty, but none of his cocksure arrogance. No devastating grin. No molten gray gaze to contend with. Just his lean body stretched out before her and a vulnerability in his chiseled jaw and the bow of his mouth that wasn't apparent when he was quipping and flirting and doing his very best to live up to his dreadful reputation.

She forced her gaze away from his body and reached into her small traveling satchel, retrieving her pen and a few pages of manuscript she'd impulsively grabbed before their departure.

Her lady detective was on the verge of a first encounter with the story's killer, a desperate and depraved aristocrat. Sophia tapped the fountain pen on her lower lip and considered how to describe her villain. Lord Westby came to mind, with his cold eyes and dark hair. Then she recalled the slithery feel of his tongue on her lips and winced. Her villain would need to be much better at seduction if she was to convince readers he'd ruined a respectable young lady.

What of Clive Holden? What made him so appealing that Phyllida Grey would risk everything?

Sophia had never met a man who tempted her to risk anything, let alone the reputation her father spent his life urging her to protect. She bent her head, arranged her manuscript page on top of her book, and added a few lines of description about her villain.

Grey shifted, and her glance strayed to his booted foot, then up his long black trouser-clad leg to the buttons of his sapphire waistcoat and finally into two cool gray eyes.

"Enjoying the view?"

"Yes." She turned her head and watched the Surrey countryside rush by. "Beautiful...wildflowers along the line." Daisies and a purple flower dominated. Lupines? She wasn't sure. Clarissa had always been the flower lover in the family.

"I would never have taken you for a wildflower enthusiast." He sat up straight in his seat but didn't fully retract his foot from between hers. "They're untamed. Tenacious. Disorderly." He straightened his waistcoat as he spoke, as if realizing he was as disorderly as the blooms visible through the train car window.

"I don't mind wildflowers when they're in an open field." The openness of the landscape truly was appealing. She'd never been a very good horsewoman, but it put her in mind of dashing across the field on the back of a beautiful stallion.

"And if they pop up in your garden, you simply have someone mow them down?" His teasing tone did nothing to temper her irritation.

"You have a very low opinion of me, Mr. Grey."

"I don't." His mouth tightened, and all the humor drained from his eyes. "I'll always be grateful to you for assisting me today, Sophia. I'll refrain from teasing you." He glanced out the window and crossed his arms, falling silent. Not so much sulking as forcing an end to his usual exuberance.

"So what is your plan?"

"My plan?" His brow crinkled under messy waves of copper hair. "Get my sister back to Derbyshire. I'll carry her over my shoulder the entire way if I must. After thrashing Holden within an inch of his life."

Sophia's brows shot high.

"What?" he queried irritably. "The man deserves as much, and duels, unfortunately, have been outlawed."

"Brute force," Sophia said with a sigh. Somehow, she'd expected more from him. "That's the whole of your strategy."

"What did you expect me to do? Unleash my wit and charm?" The lofty cut of his cheekbones began to simmer with color, and the usual sparkle in his pale eyes sharpened to daggers.

"I thought you might consider unleashing your intellect."

He dipped his head, appearing chastened, even sullen. Then he lashed his arms tighter across his chest and retorted, "I'm not challenging Holden to a quiz. I'm confronting the man about absconding with my sister." He drew in a deep breath and caught her gaze before offering a nod. "But you may be right. A bit of strategy and persuasion might be in order, especially with Liddy."

Sophia's father had allowed her to assist him with his business correspondence, and her brother often listened to her advice, even if he didn't choose to take it. Somehow, none of that compared to the satisfaction of Jasper Grey acknowledging she "may" be right.

"What if we don't find your sister in Brighton?" She asked the question softly, tentatively, knowing the same worry must be weighing on his mind.

"We will," Grey assured in the most serious tone she'd yet heard him employ. "We must."

"And what if it's too late?"

For a moment Grey squinted at her as if she'd begun speaking in a foreign tongue. "You mean if she and Holden have become lovers?"

Now it was Sophia's turn to blush. She willed the heat to cool, even as she sensed it infusing her cheeks.

"You speak of your sister's chastity too flippantly." And too recklessly. To call them *lovers* sounded romantic. Even appealing. But if Mr. Holden had no intention of marrying Phyllida Grey, or if a child resulted from their dalliance, the young woman's life would never be the same. Any prospects for a fortuitous match would be forever ruined.

"Ah, yes, a woman must remain virginal while a man can do as he pleases." He seemed offended on behalf of women and the dual standards applied to each sex. Which she found completely unexpected and the opposite of every man she'd ever known. Certainly the opposite of her father's views.

"That's generally how society sees the matter."

"I disagree." He tipped his head as he assessed her. "Isn't *ruination* a prospect you were considering when I found you alone with Westby in his study?"

"Not at all." Sophia's blood heated a few more degrees when his bow-shaped mouth tipped up in a grin. "Though the earl was intent on kissing me."

Grey's whole demeanor changed, his jaw hardening into sharp angles as thunderclouds banked in his gray eyes. He leaned toward her across the train car, his elbows braced on his knees. "And did he?"

"None of your business." The memory of Westby's tongue on her mouth turned her stomach, and none of what she'd done was any of his concern. She'd already admitted too much.

"I'd wager he did." His gaze fixed on her mouth. He looked into her eyes as if trying to find the truth there.

"You'd lose your wager, Mr. Grey." Sophia lifted the watch fob pinned to her blouse to check the time, and to avoid getting pulled into his magnetic gaze.

"I can't tell you how much that pleases me."

When she looked up, Sophia expected to find a mocking grin curving his mouth.

Instead, he watched her with a solemn gaze. "Did he hurt you?"

"No," Sophia said a bit too vehemently.

Westby had been rude, but the incident served as a reminder that she was no longer the naïve girl who'd once followed a dishonorable man into a moonlit garden.

She understood how tempting scoundrels could be and also how perilous.

Yet as Grey watched her, she glimpsed—just for a moment—something beyond his bravado and charm. Not the dangers of a rakish man but the raw need of one who craved her kiss.

He leaned closer, his gaze flickering to her mouth. All the heat that had bloomed in her cheeks a moment before seemed to gather in her chest. And it spread, simmering beneath her skin, making her pulse race.

A thought came, one she couldn't chase away. Jasper Grey would know how to give a woman a first kiss that she wouldn't soon forget.

Just when she thought he might reach across the space between them and draw her near, the train began to slow. Grey turned to scan the ladies and gentlemen lining the platform.

"Quite a crush." Sophia expected the station to be busy on a midsummer weekend, but the platform was teeming with travelers and carts bearing their luggage.

He lurched toward the window, pressing a hand to the glass. "That's Liddy."

"Where?" Sophia leaned to get a better look, but realized she had no idea of Miss Grey's appearance. "Are you sure?"

"Yes." He stood and reached for her hand, pulling her to her feet. "Come. Let's see if we can catch her."

The moment his foot hit pavement, Grey started off at a sprint.

Sophia rushed after him, skirt and petticoat fighting her every step. Stopping as the crowd rushed past her, she lifted onto her toes.

She couldn't find him. Only a sea of strangers lay ahead.

"You're blocking the pavement," a man snapped as he brushed past.

One more push onto her toes, and Sophia spotted Grey. Lifting the edge of her skirt, she hurried after him, boot heels pounding the pavement as her corset crushed the breath from her lungs.

"Watch yourself, miss." A gentleman jabbed her with his elbow as she attempted to pass. He stalled her, planting himself in her path and slowing his pace.

"Excuse me!" Shooting an arm out, she maneuvered past him and scanned the men ahead for Grey.

Her heart clenched. Across the crowd, his metal-gray gaze held hers. He trudged toward her, face pale, expression stark.

"Your sister?" Sophia held her breath.

"Not Liddy after all," he said when he reached her side. "Let's try that hotel the coachman mentioned. We won't need a carriage," he assured as he assessed the long line of travelers waiting for a hired conveyance. "It's just a few blocks from the station."

As they started through the throng of travelers, Grey took her arm and linked it with his. Sophia allowed him the familiarity, mostly because she had no wish to be trampled by the more aggressive in the crowd.

"Winship?"

Sophia heard the call first and turned to see a blond man striding their way. "I believe he's calling you," she said over the din of chatter in the station, tightening her grip on Grey's arm.

He twisted to glance back and stopped in his tracks, his muscles tensing under her touch. The gentleman was no stranger.

"Who is it?" Sophia asked.

Emotion swirled in Grey's eyes, churning like the waters of the English Channel that lapped the Brighton shore. "Clive Holden."

CHAPTER EIGHT

"As a tenacious lady investigator, I have no shame in admitting I've broken a few rules of propriety in order to solve a case."

—CASEBOOK OF EUPHEMIA
BREEDLOVE, LADY DETECTIVE

The moment Holden approached, looking smug and feigning innocence, Grey longed to wrap his hands around the baronet's scrawny neck. Of course, a fist to the nose would be the wiser choice. If he throttled the blackguard, Holden wouldn't be able to tell him anything about Liddy's whereabouts.

Then Sophia cut in with sense and logic. With the intellect he sorely needed.

"We should get him to a place where we can question him privately," Sophia whispered as she unlatched her arm from his.

Yes. He wasn't used to hearing a voice of reason ringing in his head, cautioning him not to rush into foolishness or pointing him toward the right path. He'd always bucked being managed by anyone, but Sophia had the voice of a siren. A very practical, sensible siren.

Making a scene on the pavement in front of a dozen holiday goers wouldn't do. It would also give Holden a chance to disappear into the crowd if he didn't like their questions. And there was every reason to believe he wouldn't.

"Fancy finding you at the seaside, Winship," Holden called as he planted himself in front of Grey and offered a gloved hand in greeting.

"It's been too long, Clive." Grey gritted his teeth and shook the man's hand as a sour queasiness stewed in his gut.

"Well, yes. Never see you at the usual rounds of parties and balls. Too busy on the West End stage, I suspect." Clive turned his gaze on Sophia. "Enjoying a holiday? You must introduce me to the vision at your side."

Sophia ignored his question and posed her own. "Did you come to Brighton alone, Mr. Holden?"

"I did not," he admitted in a clipped tone.

"Who accompanied you?" Grey clenched his fist at his side. The prospect of throttling the man was more and more appealing.

"My cousin." Holden's mask of friendly joviality slipped as he subjected Sophia to an impudent perusal from her mouth to her breasts to her hips. "A much less enthralling companion than yours, Winship."

"Where is she?" Grey stepped forward and felt a hand on his arm. Sophia seemed to sense his barely leashed ire and was determined to keep him from beating the truth out of Holden.

"I never said my cousin was a lady," Holden sneered. "Isn't one female enough for you? *He* was fatigued from our journey and has already settled in at the hotel." He gazed off in the distance as if he was eager to reach the hotel too. Or simply ready to escape their questioning.

"I had the pleasure of meeting your sister today, Mr. Holden." Sophia spoke the words with a pleasant lilt, but the moment they were out, all the color began to leech from Holden's skin. "She told us Mr. Gr—Lord Winship's sister has been visiting for the last few days."

"Has she?" Holden darted his gaze, doing his best imitation of a nervous squirrel. "I pay no mind to my sister's social calendar." He huffed out what might have been intended as a dismissive chuckle but emerged as if the man was choking on his own tongue.

"She said you took Liddy out riding," Grey added, watching Holden's panic rising. A vein began pulsing in the baronet's neck. "Alone."

"What exactly are you implying, Winship?" Holden sniffed in offense as color rushed up his cheeks. "If you'll excuse me, I will not stand for being cross-questioned." With a finger to the brim of his hat, he ducked in Sophia's direction, then turned and began striding away.

"We have to go after him," Grey insisted, glancing at Sophia.

"I agree. He knows where she is, or at least more than he's admitting."

As they started after him, Sophia pointed to a narrow side lane between two buildings. Grey stretched his legs to catch up with Holden and lashed an arm around the man's shoulders.

"Not so quickly, Clive."

The man attempted to shrug him off, but Grey wrapped his fingers around the back of the scoundrel's neck. When he gave a satisfyingly hard squeeze, Holden attempted to wriggle away, only stopping when Sophia wrapped her arm around his as if he'd offered to escort her along the promenade.

"Keep calm, Mr. Holden," she whispered. "We simply have a few more questions."

Her words had the desired effect. The man settled into a normal stride and allowed Grey to guide him into the narrow stretch of cobblestones between two tall white-washed buildings.

"Where is she?" Grey demanded, struggling to keep his voice under a shout.

"I have no idea what you're talking about." Holden shook his head firmly. "You're mad, Winship. Some said as much when you threw your life away to join a theater troupe. I'm beginning to think they were right."

"You'll forgive me if I don't take your opinion to heart," Grey said, casting a wary glance at Sophia. "All I want from you is an answer." He planted a fist on Holden's chest and pushed the bounder against the brick wall at his back. "Where's my sister?"

"Tell us, Mr. Holden." Sophia placed her hand over Grey's fist, her bare skin a warm and strangely comforting counterpoint to the anger coloring his every thought.

Holden's eyes had gone wild, ballooned so wide the whites were visible all around the discs of blue. He glanced from Sophia to Grey, as if assessing their resolve. "She's not here, if that's what you're thinking. Phyllida is not in Brighton."

"The coachman said he saw you together in Hampstead." Grey didn't think it possible for Holden's eyes to bulge wider, but they did.

"Then he was mistaken. I last saw Lady Phyllida in London." He swiped at Grey's fist to dislodge it from his chest and reached up to straighten his waistcoat. "She planned to embark on a train journey."

"To where?" Sophia asked in a low encouraging tone.

Grey shared her resolve but felt none of her unflappable calm.

"I can't recall," Holden tried.

Grey unbuttoned one cuff, then the other, and began rolling up his sleeves. "Try again, Clive, because I'm struggling for a reason I shouldn't thrash a man with so little concern for my sister's reputation."

Holden looked momentarily abashed, recovered quickly, and had the temerity to sneer. "When have you ever worried about a woman's reputation, Winship?"

Balling his hand, Grey drew his arm back, and whipped forward to strike.

"No!" Sophia called out, latching herself onto his wrist. "Violence will gain you nothing."

Satisfaction, he screamed in his head. Trouncing Holden would give him a good deal of that. Clearly, Sophia didn't agree.

She turned to Holden. "Stop this nonsense, and tell Lord Winship where he can find his sister. How would you feel if Cecily were in danger?"

Her words achieved precisely what Grey intended with his fists. Holden slumped back against the wall, as if the will to resist had seeped out of him.

"She's not in danger. Phyllida is on her way to Cambridge," he blurted on a long exhale. "She took a train not an hour ago."

"Why the hell would she go there?" Grey knew of no one she might know in the university town. She'd never come to visit when he'd spent years there attending college. That period was the only connection he had to the area and men like Westby and Clive Holden. "Why did you send her there?"

"Me? If you know anything about your sister, Winship, you must be aware the lady has a mind of her own." Holden glared at Grey with such seething anger his body began to shake. He thrust out his arms to push Sophia and Grey away. "If you'll excuse me." He started off at a quick stride before breaking into a sprint.

When Grey started after him, Sophia rushed forward and positioned herself in his path. "Chasing after him will get you nothing else."

"He knows more, Sophia. Believe me, the rotter is in this up to his teeth."

"Of course he is, but you won't get a confession by knocking out his teeth."

"I could try, and I'd at least enjoy the effort."

A shadow of a grin ghosted across Sophia's lips, and then she was all business. "What if he's telling the truth? Do you have any idea why she'd go to Cambridge?"

"None at all." Grey planted his hands on his hips and shook his head. "If she's gone to Cambridge, it's at Clive's behest."

Sophia furrowed her brow. "Perhaps Cecily could tell you more. If she knew Clive told you about Cambridge, perhaps she'd confide whatever else she knows."

"Or she might remain as mum as her brother. I'd prefer to locate Liddy and hear the details of this scheme later." A trip back to London held no appeal, especially since it guaranteed him nothing but more frustration as he tried to wheedle information out of a Holden.

"Clive mentioned Cambridge reluctantly, which leads me to believe the claim."

Grey frowned as he considered Sophia's words. He agreed with her logic, but his gut churned with fear. Liddy traveling alone to a city she didn't know? His mind reeled with wretched possibilities. "Perhaps you're right." He preferred Sophia's calm, considered judgement. "Liddy may not know anyone in the city, but Clive does."

"But why would he send her there alone?" She tapped a finger on her lips as she pondered, her gaze distant.

"Perhaps he plans to meet her and travel on to Scotland to elope."

"Then why dally at the seaside with his cousin?"

"I don't know!" Grey slapped his hand against the brick wall as he shouted, his voice ricocheting like a shot off the buildings lining the narrow lane.

Sophia took one backward step, and Grey cursed under his breath. He didn't wish to frighten her or reveal what an impulsive, untamed fool he could be when provoked. The more his frustration built, the more he needed Sophia's good sense to help unravel the mystery of Liddy's disappearance.

"I'm sorry, Sophia. You ask excellent questions. I only wish we had more answers." He buttoned his cuffs, tugged the sleeves of his jacket down, and tried to make himself look like a rational gentleman again. "Cambridge seems the path that might lead us to Liddy. We should return to the train station and begin our journey."

He started past her and made the arrogant assumption she'd follow. When he didn't hear the click of her boot heels echoing his, he turned back.

"I can't accompany you to Cambridge, Mr. Grey." Shoulders back, chin high, hands crossed in front of her, Sophia left no doubt about the firmness of her declaration.

Of course you can. Panic fought its way up Grey's throat, words scrabbling for freedom like caged birds. *You must. I need your help.* He sucked in a gulp of sea air, willed his mind to quiet as he did before a performance. Digging up a sliver of self-respect, he nodded like a gentleman and forced a semblance of a grin to his lips. "Of course you can't. You must return to London and keep your appointment with…Ogilvy. Wasn't that his name?"

"Not because of Mr. Ogilvy." She stared at the ground a moment before meeting his gaze, busying herself with putting on pristine white gloves. "Accompanying you would be improp—"

Before she could finish, Grey took two long strides to stand before her inside the alleyway and catch the edge of her jaw in the cup of his palm. "You needn't explain."

"But…." She hung on the single syllable, lips open, eyes soft as she stared up at him. Her breath quickened.

His entire body quickened in reply. He was acutely aware that she wasn't resisting his touch. Lovely, curious, clever Sophia Ruthven was gazing up at him as if she craved his touch. His. Not Ogilvy's or any other man's. Though he rarely needed encouragement to be bold, the undeniable want in her eyes fired his blood.

Slowly, tentatively, Grey slid an arm around her waist, flattened his hand against the small of her back. Electricity sizzled through his veins, and all he could see and smell and feel was Sophia—the hitch of her breath, the heat of her body, the clean scent of her skin, and the flares of green malachite in her eyes.

It was the wrong time. And definitely the wrong place. But he couldn't resist.

Resisting wasn't his way.

"Sophia," he hissed softly before dipping his head and feathering his lips across hers. "Do you have any idea how much I want to kiss you?" He cupped her head, slid his fingers under the knot of silken hair at her nape, felt her little nod of encouragement. Of *yes*.

One taste and he was lost. Hell with any attempt at civility or gentlemanly behavior. She was so bloody sweet, and she opened to him like a glorious, unexpected gift. He kissed her gently at first, sensing in her gasps and clutching fingers that this was new. She tasted of orange marmalade and innocence. When she emitted a little gasp of shock as he deepened the kiss, he was the one who shivered like a novice who'd never had a woman in his arms. Her hand came up, and Grey expected her to push him away. Instead, she gripped his lapel and pulled him closer.

He wrapped her in his arms and kissed her again. Teased her lips open and tasted as he'd ached to do from the moment they met. She stiffened at first, then melted against him, pressing her bosom to his chest, her hips flush with his. She danced her tongue along his as if testing, exploring, teasing. She lifted a hand to his cheek, stroked his skin with her gloved fingertips.

That undid him, the slide of those very properly covered fingers against his scalp. The stroke went straight to his groin. He wanted her here, now, in a dusty little alleyway in Brighton. When he gripped her backside and began positioning her against the brick wall, she broke their kiss. Gasping for breath, she turned her head away from his.

"I must go," she managed, still breathless.

He came back to the moment as if waking from a dream, shaking his head and releasing her from his arms. She stepped away instantly. Every impulse told him to reach for her, to pull her back, to wrap her in his arms again. Where she'd felt so right and he'd felt a shred of peace, for the first time in days. Who was he kidding? Years.

"I hope you find your sister in Cambridge," she said, a little tremor of emotion shaking her voice, before striding away.

He wanted her back. Craved the strange sense of calm she induced with her gentle touch and firm, unwavering tone. Stepping forward, he opened his mouth to call to her before she walked too far out of reach. But another impulse kept him silent. Fear that the craving he felt for Sophia wouldn't end when they found Liddy.

CHAPTER NINE

"Nothing fires the blood like the discovery of a clue, that bit of Theseus's string that shows an investigator the way."

—CASEBOOK OF EUPHEMIA
BREEDLOVE, LADY DETECTIVE

"Mrs. Cole?" Sophia called out as she closed the front door behind her and began peeling off her gloves. She'd checked the watch pinned to her blouse and tried to stem the panic tightening her chest. The train from Brighton had been delayed twice, and she feared Mr. Ogilvy had come and gone from Bloomsbury Square.

"Thank goodness you're back." Cate strode into the entryway and reached out to take Sophia's gloves. "Your note had me worried."

"It was rather spare on details."

"Bare on details, I think you meant to say." Cate softened her pronouncement with a grin, but stared with a direct gaze that urged Sophia to explain her mysterious journey.

In a hurry to depart with Grey to the train station, she'd scrawled a note, mentioning that she was taking an early train to Brighton and would return soon after the noon hour to meet Mr. Ogilvy. Only Cate knew the purpose of the gentleman's visit and how the success of this first meeting with him could alter Sophia's future.

"Did I miss his visit?"

Cate nodded. "You did, but I take it you had an enjoyable sojourn at the seaside." Her gaze took Sophia in from head to toe. "The sun's lent a bit of color to your cheeks." She stepped near for a closer look. "And you have the lightest sprinkle of freckles across your nose."

Sophia frowned and rubbed a finger down her nose. She'd been in such a rush, she'd forgotten her hat.

"They don't come off," Cate said with a seriousness that belied the twinkle in her maple brown eyes, "though my mother swore by lemon juice to make them fade."

"I shall try some." Sophia clasped her hands behind her back to stop herself from fussing over her freckles. "What did Mr. Ogilvy say? What sort of man did he seem to be? Tell me everything."

Cate craned her neck to glance over one shoulder and then the other, as if she feared one of the young maids might be about and didn't wish anyone to overhear. She pointed toward the newly renovated formal drawing room. "You should see the new wallpaper, Miss Ruthven. The workmen came to hang the last of it this morning."

Sophia followed Cate into the room, sliding the pocket doors shut behind them. "It did turn out lovely," she said as she took in the calming cream and lavender striped pattern before turning to face Cate. "Was he angry?" She crossed her arms and began worrying her lower lip between her teeth.

"No, not angry." Cate cast her an inscrutable glance. "Disappointed, perhaps. Though he didn't say as much, of course."

"He must think me unbearably rude." Sophia slumped down on the new settee, still covered in muslin to keep any wallpaper paste from marring the lovely violet damask Ophelia had chosen. Rudeness was the height of offense in Sophia's estimation. Lapses in etiquette could be overlooked, but rudeness was intentional and therefore unforgivable. "I never dreamed I'd return this late. There was an obstruction on the train line, and then a delay at one of the stations."

"I wouldn't fret much. Mr. Ogilvy struck me as a man who takes disappointments in his stride." Cate took a seat in a straight-backed chair across from Sophia, tipping her head to assess the new wallpaper and the cornice that had been painted to match. "But how is Mr. Grey?"

"So you *do* know a few details of my trip." Sophia wasn't surprised as much as curious how Cate found out.

"Part of a housekeeper's job is knowing who comes and goes." Cate picked an invisible bit of lint from her sleeve. "And one of the kitchen maids heard a man's voice and came to wake me. By the time I dressed and came downstairs, you were both on your way to Brighton." There was a thread of amusement in Cate's tone that Sophia needed to set right.

"We weren't stepping out together." Sophia considered what secrets about Grey and his sister she needed to guard. "He required my assistance."

"At the seaside?" Cate sounded dubious. Her gaze focused with the precision of a microscope lens on Sophia's face.

Sophia stood to look out the window toward the well-manicured patch of grass between the houses in the square. She'd been grateful for Kit and Ophelia's invitation to stay with them in London, rather than remain in the countryside alone. Yet at moments like these she missed the soothing openness of fields and meadows. City spaces cramped one in, and London problems seemed much more tangled than anything she'd ever faced in Hertfordshire.

"I can't tell anyone the details." Sophia turned back to face her only confidant. "But my behavior wasn't as scandalous as it may seem."

Cate ducked her head. "You needn't explain yourself to me."

"In aiding him, I thought I was doing what was right." By which she meant proper, the one quality she'd always striven to embody.

"I'm sure you did, and I trust he was most grateful."

Grateful, indeed. Sophia lifted a hand to her lips, covered her mouth as if she could blot the memory of Grey's kiss. But she never would. His kiss—the first any man had ever pressed to her lips—was indelible. The heat of his breath, the insistent softness of his lips, the delicious taste of him on her tongue. No, she'd never forget the way Grey had touched her, tempted her, branded her with his kiss.

"You're blushing," Cate said in a matter-of-fact tone, as if pointing out that Sophia's gown was unbuttoned or a tress of her hair had come free.

Sophia slid the hand she'd cupped over her mouth to her cheek. Definitely hot. Feverish, in fact. Her whole body had begun to warm the moment her thoughts turned to Grey's kiss.

"I wished to help him with a matter concerning his sister," Sophia confessed, because she trusted Cate and yearned to explain herself, if only a little. "Clarissa is about the same age. Of course I sympathize with him."

"Then that solves one mystery." Cate stood and reached into the wide front pocket of the smock she often wore. "I caught one of the maids reading this in the parlor when she was supposed to be dusting. Looks to be the journal of a Lady Phyllida Grey."

"Did she read anything interesting?" Sophia reached for the small folio. How could Grey have left it behind again? Now, after Clive's refusal to confess much of anything, she found herself more curious than ever to learn what secrets the volume might hold.

"She didn't say. I suspect I frightened the life out of her so thoroughly she wouldn't recall if she did. Curious that the young lady's journal would find its way here."

Sophia couldn't explain its presence without revealing too much about Lady Phyllida's disappearance. "I meant to return it to Mr. Grey—er, Lord Winship."

"A lord?" Cate didn't sound nearly as surprised by the fact as Sophia had been. "Is she heartsick, then, this Lady Phyllida?"

"I'm not sure." For all Sophia knew, the girl thought absconding with Clive Holden to be the grandest adventure of her life. Then again, Phyllida *had* expressed doubt in that single passage from her journal. She narrowed an eye at Cate. "Did you read any of the journal?"

"Me?" Cate belied her offended tone by nodding her head affirmatively. A crimson blush stole across her cheeks. "I may have read a few pages." She cleared her throat. "I'm sorry, Miss Ruthven."

Sophia approached and laid a hand on the housekeeper's arm. "You agreed to call me Sophia. Nothing's changed. But I am curious." She lifted the volume and slipped her fingers through the ribbons loosely tied at the edge. "What did you learn from Lady Phyllida's journal?"

Cate shrugged. "That she's young and in love. That she has fears and hopes, as would any young lady."

Sophia hesitated to flip open the journal. Desire to respect the girl's privacy vied with the potential of what she might learn about her whereabouts. "Did she mention anything about Cambridge?"

"Yes, several times." Cate reached for the journal. "May I?" As she took the little folio, she began flipping pages to one near the end. Near the page where Sophia and Grey had read Phyllida's last entry. "She mentions the River Cam and how she'd always wished to go punting."

"Anything about visiting the city or university?"

"You mean her stay with Mrs. Greenlow?"

"Who?" Sophia moved to stand next to Cate as she pointed to an entry dated two weeks past.

All is arranged with Mrs. Greenlow in Grantchester. Hope
I needn't burden her for long. The waiting will be hellish.

"Grantchester is a small town near the university," Cate explained. "Seems a friend of Lady Phyllida's resides there."

Sophia wasn't so certain. "If this Greenlow woman is a friend, why would the girl feel she was a burden?"

"Even friends can overstay their welcome," Cate very astutely opined.

But what would Lady Phyllida be waiting for in a small town near Cambridge? Perhaps Clive Holden intended to rendezvous with her there. But why would he send her ahead? And why would they travel to Cambridge at all?

"He left you a gift." Cate's words cut into Sophia's woolgathering.

She blinked at her in confusion. "Lord Winship?"

Cate crossed the room, parted the sliding wooden doors, and crossed the hall. A moment later, she returned with a small rectangular box, held out in both hands like an offering. "From Mr. Ogilvy."

"He shouldn't have brought me a present." Gifting someone who was not a friend or close acquaintance was a breech in etiquette, especially when presented to a young lady. The indelicacy arose from the appearance of placing her under obligation or attempting to buy her goodwill. However, Ogilvy's gift was the wrong size for a ring. She suspected she was safe in opening the box. Inside she found a lovely fountain pen with a pearlized barrel and silver accents. "It's lovely."

"Seems a bit too practical for my taste, but it's a pretty writing implement."

"I like practical gifts." Or perhaps she was simply used to them. Her parents had never given her any gifts that weren't useful.

Cate grinned indulgently. "You can use it to send him a thank-you note."

"I should." Sophia nodded, but she was struggling to spare a single thought for Mr. Ogilvy or his pen.

"Or you could thank him in person." Cate slid a calling card from her Pandora's box of an apron pocket. "He plans on remaining in London to see to his business affairs for a few days. He made a note of the hotel where he's staying."

Sophia took the card from Cate and flicked her thumbnail against the edge. "Seeing Mr. Ogilvy will have to wait until I return."

Cate's brows knitted in confusion. "Are you leaving again?"

"I must go to Cambridge." Grey needed to know about Mrs. Greenlow, though Sophia had no idea how she'd contact him once she arrived.

Cate strode from the room and soon returned with a small Bradshaw's Guide of train timetables that Sophia wasn't even aware they kept in the house. "You won't make the last train this afternoon," Cate informed her.

"First departure in the morning, then." She'd make an early start. Despite not knowing her way around Cambridge or how to contact Grey, she did know one thing. The most important fact of all.

She knew where to find Lady Phyllida Grey.

After two days in Cambridge, the Eagle and Stag pub proved to be a haven. Cozily small, its dark-paneled walls offered a welcome retreat from the summer sun.

Grey ordered a pint of ale and a plate of bread and cheese, then retreated to a corner booth and hunkered down. Gulping at the sour beer, he glanced around the sparsely populated public house for any sign of Holden. After taking a bit of food, he'd begin questioning the proprietor. Search every damned room if he had to.

He'd visited his old haunts, the pubs and gathering places he and his classmates had frequented when he'd been at university. On his second day in the city, what had begun to seem an aimless ramble turned fruitful when he encountered a mutual friend of his and Clive's, who now served as professor of mathematics at the university. From him, Grey learned that Clive visited a few weeks past and had lodged at the Eagle and Stag, a coaching inn turned pub.

Grey examined the worn table under his elbows and slid his foot against the sticky floor as the first bite of bread turned to dust in his mouth. Such a grimy interior might suit his debauched tastes, but he loathed the idea of Liddy lodging in such a place.

She'd been brought up gently, sheltered, even from much of their parents' ugliness toward each other.

Damn Clive Holden.

After another swig of ale, Grey straightened his neck cloth and buttoned up his suit. Now was the time to play the role of gentleman. He waited until the publican served another guest before approaching the bar.

"Fine establishment you have here."

"Thank you kindly, sir." In one long scrutinizing glance, the man took in the cut of Grey's garment and the glint on the ebony buttons of his waistcoat. Apparently satisfied, he offered a tentative grin and nod of acknowledgment. "What can I do for you?"

"Sir Clive Holden recommended your accommodations. Says he lodged with you recently."

"We've no rooms available." A buxom older woman approached to stand beside the publican. Grey guessed her to be the innkeeper's wife.

"I'm sorry to hear it," Grey said, catching the lady's wary gaze. "But you do recall Sir Clive's visit?"

Her husband nodded, but the lady shook her head vehemently. "Can't say as I do," she added to emphasize her denial. Her husband immediately ducked his head and began moving away down the bar.

Grey smiled at the older woman. "Memory is such a bugger, but I find this helps." He lifted a folded five-pound banknote from his pocket and unfurled the thin paper on the counter.

She sniffed as if the lucre held no interest. "The Holden gent came and went. That's all I recall, sir." She rushed the words and grabbed the five pounds, folding the note quickly, and shoved it between the top two buttons of her bodice. "Anything else we can do for you, you'll have to ask my husband."

Gladly. Grey waited patiently while the woman returned to wiping off tables, eyeing him with suspicion as she went. After she'd moved out of eavesdropping distance, her husband approached again.

"Refill your glass, sir?"

Grey shook his head. He needed to keep a clear head, though moderation had a terrible way of allowing bad memories to come screeching back to life. "Information is what I'm thirsty for, and I'm willing to pay."

"You'll have to forgive the missus," the man said quietly, keeping one eye trained on the lady in question as she began loading discarded glasses onto a tray. "She's protecting her sister."

"Come again?" Grey pinched the skin between his brow and eyed the bottles of hard liquor behind the bar. His mouth watered for a nip, if only to ease the thunder in his head.

"She provides bed and board, doesn't she? My wife suggested her the moment Sir Clive inquired about private lodgings for a lady acquaintance of his." The man sniffed and wiped his cuff across his nose. "Thought at the time it all sounded rather suspicious. The last thing we want is trouble, sir."

Grey reached across the bar and gripped the man's shirt front. "What's your sister-in-law's name? Her address?"

The man's eyes bloated like overfilled balloons, and he shifted his gaze across the room, as if signaling for his wife's assistance. Grey twisted his head as the woman stomped toward him, knotting a towel in her hands. She lifted her palm when she reached his side. "Another five pounds and we'll tell you."

So much for family loyalty. Grey had never been more grateful for a fellow mercenary spirit in his life. He drew out two five-pound notes. "One for your sister's address," he said, holding the offering out to the pub owner's wife, "and another not to send warning that I'm coming."

CHAPTER TEN

Mrs. Greenlow's lodging house appeared to be a quaint cottage from the exterior but proved to be a spacious hive of activity on the inside.

"We're at sixes and sevens today, miss," a young maid informed Sophia as she swiped a wrist across her flushed brow. "New lodgers coming and two departing. Wait here, if you would, and I'll let Mrs. Greenlow know you wish for a room."

"Thank you." Sophia hadn't asked for a room, but the fib worked as well as any for securing a meeting with the proprietress. After entering the small sitting room the servant indicated, Sophia waited until the young lady shut the door before rushing forward and peeking through the crack in the frame. With so much busy comings and goings in the outer hall, could she sneak up the stairs and search for Grey's sister without drawing notice?

Yes, she decided, if not for the lady and gentleman blocking the sitting room door as they donned hats and gloves. A young man helped them gather luggage at the front door.

When a maid approached the sitting room door, Sophia ducked back and quickly took a seat, trying to appear as if she'd been waiting patiently.

In the end, no one entered, and Sophia sprang up from her chair, too anxious to sit. Her legs still ached from being stuck on the train all afternoon.

The journey from King's Cross Station to Cambridge had taken so long she'd managed to read an entire book of mystery tales and work on her own story, writing out two new chapters as the train drew to shuddering stops at various stations along the way. Unfortunately, when reviewing her new words, she'd found a disturbing description of an aristocratic rogue who would turn out to be an ally for her detective, helping Effie solve the crime.

Hair of cinnamon brown and clear gray eyes, like frosted panes of glass, she'd written, before slashing through the words and struggling to envision any man other than Jasper Grey.

Mr. Ogilvy's bearded visage came to mind, but her character wasn't meant to be a proper gentleman. He was the sort Mr. Ogilvy would likely consider less than respectable. The kind her father would decry as a wastrel. Just the type Jasper Grey—she had to begin thinking of the man as Lord Winship—would no doubt be proud to call a friend.

Now, as she pondered the next complications in her plot, she lifted a notebook and pen from her traveling satchel and tapped her fountain pen against her lower lip. Not the implement Mr. Ogilvy had gifted her. That one felt as if it didn't quite belong to her, especially when the man himself remained a mystery.

Unfortunately, Mr. Ogilvy was an enigma that would have to wait.

"Thank you for your patience, miss." A middle-aged woman bustled through the sitting room door, tucking a few strands of dark hair into pins with one hand and pushing a pair of wire-rimmed spectacles up her nose with the other. "We're not usually in such a scramble, I assure you. Most days, I keep the house quiet and calm. And no unmarried gentlemen are allowed here, if that's of concern to you." Turning to a shelf near the door, she took a tall ledger into her hands, pulled a pencil from behind her ear, and opened the book to a middle page. "How about a room with a view of the fields toward town?"

"A friend recommended your establishment, Mrs. Greenlow. In fact, she may still be lodging with you. Lady Phyllida Grey?"

The lodging house proprietress tipped her head down and stared at Sophia over the rim of her glasses. "Name doesn't ring a bell. When did she make this recommendation?"

Sophia swallowed a lump in her throat and continued doing what she'd never done before in her life. She lied. "Quite recently, ma'am. As I said, I hoped she might still be stopping with you."

Mrs. Greenlow stepped back near the door she'd just entered and gestured toward the front of the house. "Only one unaccompanied young woman has been staying with me, and she's departing today."

Through an oblong front window, Sophia spotted a petite lady in a pretty pink day dress. A wide-brimmed straw hat with matching pink ribbons covered her hair. She stood near the carriage circle with several traveling bags at her feet, as if waiting for a conveyance.

"What's her name?" Sophia strode forward to get a better look. Perhaps she'd recognize Lady Phyllida if she looked like her brother.

"Miss Longcross," Mrs. Greenlow said. "Not your Lady Grey, I take it. You're welcome to her room now that she's off."

Longcross sounded like a fanciful surname, but if Grey's sister arrived in Cambridge under improper circumstances, she'd be a fool to use her own name.

"I can have the room ready within the next quarter hour," Mrs. Greenlow continued, laying her ledger on a low side table and bending to make a notation. "If you'd just add your name and details here."

Sophia wasn't certain when to end the pretense, though securing a room seemed the easiest way to be admitted to the house's upstairs. Bending at the waist, she picked up Mrs. Greenlow's discarded pencil and began writing her name, then stopped herself. A moment's thought and another name came to mind. She wrote *Euphemia Breedlove* in a slow, careful script, scanning the list of names printed above hers. *Miss L. Longcross* was listed near the top of the page, her entry dated over a week prior.

Grey referred to his sister as *Liddy*.

Sophia snapped her gaze toward the girl waiting out front, just as a carriage rumbled into view. A footman disembarked to load luggage, and then a man's arm shot out from the carriage's interior. The young lady stepped up just as a breeze caught her bonnet, loosening a coil of burnished copper hair.

"Excuse me," Sophia muttered as she dropped Mrs. Greenlow's pencil, rushed into the hall, and pulled open the front door. "Wait!"

The carriage door slammed shut, but the young lady tipped her head to gaze out the window. Behind her, a man's face loomed into view. He was blond, but Sophia could make out little else among the interior's shadows.

"Lady Phyllida?" Sophia dashed toward the carriage, but the coachman urged the horses on and the vehicle began rolling away.

The girl lifted one gloved hand to press against the glass. Sophia waved frantically, but the carriage didn't stop. In fact, the horses picked up speed as they left the carriageway and entered the main Grantchester road.

"Was it her?" Mrs. Greenlow called from the front step.

"I don't know." Sophia pressed a hand to her belly where a roil of queasiness had begun. Her gut told her she'd just looked into the face of Grey's sister. Looked at her and lost the girl again.

"Do you still want a room, Miss Breedlove?"

"May I have a look first?" She didn't expect to find anything useful in the room, but she had to discover if the girl had left something behind.

"Suit yourself. I've another new lodger to see to." Mrs. Greenlow pointed to the stairwell once Sophia entered the house again. "First room on your right. Rosebud wallpaper. Very ladylike."

Sophia retrieved her travel satchel from the parlor and made her way up to the room. The air inside still held a hint of violet water, and she moved around slowly from corner to corner, scanning each surface for the merest scrap Phyllida may have unknowingly discarded. She found nothing on the bedside table. The desk drawer held only fresh sheaves of paper, a nib pen, and a pot of ink. Lifting the mattress edge, she slid her hand down the length of the bed but discovered nothing there either.

Dropping into the wooden rocking chair in front of the room's fireplace, Sophia racked her mind for why Phyllida would have lodged at the house for a week. Assuming the young woman she'd seen out front had, in fact, been Grey's sister.

A glint of metal under the bed caught her eye, and she kneeled to find a lady's hair pin. A simple, unadorned hairpin, similar to those worn by every woman in England. The tiny bit of bent metal might have been Phyllida's. Or one of dozens of women who'd lodged in the room.

Sophia shoved the pin into her pocket with a sigh.

From her position near the floor, she heard several voices downstairs. More guests, no doubt. Who knew a lodging house in a sleepy little Cambridge village would be so popular. It was only fair to depart and allow Mrs. Greenlow to rent the room to a paying lodger.

As she gained her feet, Sophia took one long last look around the room, scanning nooks and every cranny that might hold a clue to finding Phyllida Grey. A shape on top of the wardrobe caught her eye, an elevation just a bit higher than the furniture's edge. A book, perhaps? Another journal?

Even on tiptoes, she wasn't tall enough to grasp the object. But she tried, stretching up, straining, her bosom smashed against the wardrobe's door and her cheek pressed to the polished wood.

Body stretched out like a bowstring pulled taut, perspiration pooled on her forehead. Sophia bounced, trying to find another inch in her body to stretch. A sound froze her in place. Her skin prickled and she held her breath. The bedroom door creaked on its hinges as someone slid it open slowly and started inside.

"Sophia?" Grey whispered harshly. "What the hell are you doing here?"

She let out an exhale and drew away from the wardrobe she'd been attempting to climb. "I would imagine that's obvious," she snapped.

Grey lifted a finger to his lips and shut the door behind him. "I snuck by Mrs. Greenlow, but she'll come for me soon enough. Is this the room Liddy rented?"

"I believe so." Sophia retrieved a handkerchief from her skirt pocket and wiped the dust from her fingers.

Despite the shock of finding her in an empty lodging house room, the warmth in Grey's chest was very like relief. From the moment he'd sent Sophia back to London, she'd plagued his thoughts. Not knowing if she'd returned home safely irked him. And more so when she wasn't there across from him when he awoke from a nap on the train ride to Cambridge.

Catching him staring, Sophia turned away. When she looked back again, her gaze didn't fix on his eyes but on his mouth.

That kiss between them had irked him too. Not that they'd shared a kiss, but that he hadn't taken the time to do so properly. He'd pressed her against a grimy brick wall when she was a woman who deserved to be pleasured on velvet cushions.

Good Lord, what drivel. Perhaps it was best to keep his distance from Sophia Ruthven if she inspired such nonsense.

He was here for one reason. Liddy. Recalling that Sophia had found his sister's journal under a mattress, he crossed to the bed and lifted the sheets to gaze underneath.

"I've already searched under there," Sophia informed him in a quieter voice, "but I believe there's something atop this wardrobe."

Grey stepped over to the tall furniture piece and spotted what looked like a book. The volume was far back, almost against the wall. He reached up, grazing his fingertips along the edge of the spine. "Is there something to nudge it forward?" He scanned the room, but there wasn't even a poker near the grate.

"A hanger?" Sophia approached and opened the wardrobe door, pushing him out of the way. "There are only hooks and shelves."

"Then you'll have to do." Considering the distance from her waist to her toes, the lady had deliciously long legs. One small heave and she'd be more than able to grasp the book. He bent his knees, threaded his fingers together, and offered her his joined palms.

"What exactly do you have in mind?" She hitched her hands up her hips.

Plenty. But now was no time to regale Sophia with the sorts of thoughts she inspired.

"Have you never been given a leg up onto a horse?"

"I don't like horses," she insisted, crossing her arms. "Or, rather, they don't like me."

"Then you have that in common with Liddy. Now, if you would, put your foot in my hands."

She eyed him skeptically, as if she didn't trust that he'd merely heave her up and not try to chuck her out the window.

"I'm too heavy."

"Let me be the judge of that." Grey liked all women, every shape and shade and disposition. Sophia was long and curvaceous in every place a man could desire, a woman of substance, but he had no doubt she'd fit perfectly in his hands.

Tentatively, she placed the flat of her boot onto his palms, braced her hands on the wardrobe and gazed into his eyes. When she offered him a tiny nod, he crouched deeper and lifted her.

"I've got it." The moment she uttered the words of victory, she tipped left, one hand braced on his shoulder, her hip plastered against the side of his face.

Grey gripped her lower legs to keep her from dropping too quickly, and she slid down, her lavender-scented curves soft and warm against the hard edges of his body. When her backside rested against his forearm and her feet touched the ground, she braced her hands on his shoulders.

"You should let go of me now."

"Yes." But letting her go was the last thing on his mind. The press of her body felt good. Right. In all his heated, hungry encounters with women, he'd lost this. The tantalizing thrill of simply holding a woman near. Especially one he wanted, yet who was so far out of his reach.

Reluctantly, he released her, but he kept one hand at her waist. She allowed the contact awhile, let the heat of her body seep into his palm, then she pressed a hand to his chest and pushed.

"I'll make you untidy." She lifted the dusty book between them, and Grey's nose began to tickle. "This volume has been up there awhile."

"Not Liddy's, then." He'd suspected it wouldn't be. Why leave clues behind if her objective was to elope with Holden to Scotland? That, he'd decided on the long train ride to Cambridge, was the likeliest explanation for their journey north. "What is it?" he asked Sophia, who'd opened the book to the title page and frowned as she skimmed her finger across the words printed there.

"An autobiography of some sort. The title says it's about a flea. A child's book, perhaps." The moment she began turning pages to read the book's content, Grey lunged for the volume and plucked it from her hands.

"Not a child's book." Grey drew back and tossed the book on top of the wardrobe, returning it to its dusty hiding place. "And not a book you'd find appropriate."

Sophia balled her hands into fists and let out a little growl of frustration. "For a man who revels in doing precisely as he pleases, you seem very determined to manage *me*, Lord Winship." She stomped toward the wardrobe and reached for the book. Apparently, the woman was too stubborn to realize she hadn't sprouted any inches in the last few minutes.

In fact, all she managed to do was arouse him as she stretched and grunted and wiggled her backside, trying to get higher on the toes of her boots.

He planted himself behind her and drew on his meager supply of self-restraint to keep his hands to himself. Softly, he told her, "You can't reach the book, and it is not the sort a proper lady would read." At least, not when anyone was looking.

She guffawed derisively and glanced at him over her shoulder. "What would you know about proper ladies?"

"Fair point." Grey grinned. "But knowing you as I do—"

"You don't know me at all, my lord."

"I allowed you that claim a few days ago. Not anymore." He dropped his gaze to her mouth. Sinfully soft, achingly sweet. He knew those lips now, just as surely as he'd sensed all of Sophia's hidden passion in their kiss. "You wouldn't approve of the book's content."

Whirling on him, she pushed at his chest to create distance between them. "I assure you my prudery does not extend to shying from a flea's biography." She swiped a finger across her cheek to tuck a loose strand of hair behind her ear and unwittingly deposited a smudge of dust.

Seeing her mussed made him imagine her completely unbound, unfettered by laces and stays. What a glorious sight she'd be—Sophia Ruthven, free of all her starch and propriety. Glowing, as she was now, setting free all the fire he'd tasted in her kiss.

He'd never wanted to provoke a woman more, never wanted to devote his days and nights to mining one woman's passion.

"It's pornography, Sophia." When her mouth opened in shock, he reached for her. Just the lightest touch of his fingertips at the edge of her jaw. "A very naughty series of stories, seen through the eyes of an extremely hard-to-shock flea." Lifting his thumb, he swiped at the smudge of dirt on her cheek. But having done his bit of chivalry for the day, he wanted more.

And none of what he wanted was chivalrous.

"You've read it?" she queried in a breathy whisper.

"No," he whispered back. "I don't require erotic stories to fuel my imagination. It's quite vivid enough on its own." He lowered his hand as he spoke the words, more instinct than intent, straying from her jaw. He drew his hand down her body, dipping in at her narrow waist to find the generous camber of her backside. Despite the flint in her gaze, Sophia's body possessed no hard edges, and he craved the time to explore every curve.

Her breath hitched as her hands came up to rest on his chest. Warm, soft, they eased the weight of worry that had been pressing down on him for days. When her body swayed toward his, Grey's blood heated, rioting through his veins.

A bed stood inches away, and the woman in his arms was clever and luscious. A lady who upended every expectation he had of her. But he held back. He didn't want to rush with Sophia.

The bedroom door creaked open, and they sprang away from each other.

"I knew there was something amiss about you, Miss Breedlove. And you, sir. Be off with the both of you." She pointed toward the stairwell. "Now, if you please. Whatever sin you wish to get up to, it won't be under my roof."

Grey bit back a chuckle, dipped his head in agreement, and headed downstairs. Midway down, he turned back. Sophia stopped on the top and cast a gaze back at Mrs. Greenlow.

"The young lady who stayed in this room. Do you know where she was going?"

The older lady crossed her arms and glared at Sophia, then spared a glower for Grey. "Said she was engaged to marry. That and nothing more while she stopped here. The young miss claimed to be waiting on her wedding day."

"Thank you," Sophia said earnestly.

Mrs. Greenlow was having none of it. "Be gone with you. I never wish to lay eyes on the pair of you again."

Sophia followed Grey outside. A moment later, the front door slammed shut behind them. Dusk had fallen over the fields adjacent to Mrs. Greenlow's cottage, and a few lights twinkled from the direction of the university.

"I'm sorry," Sophia said from the edge of the carriageway, head tipped down in defeat.

"We've nothing to be sorry for, despite what Mrs. Greenlow thinks." Grey tried for a smile, but his face felt as tense as the rest of his body. "We both came to Cambridge and have nothing to show for it but a scolding from a lodging house owner."

"Not nothing." Sophia approached, her lower lip caught between her teeth. She wrapped her arms around her body and scuffed the toe of her boot against the ground. "I believe I saw your sister."

"When? Where?" He reached for her, gripped her upper arms too hard and instantly loosened his hold.

"There was a young lady departing when I arrived, standing out here. A carriage appeared with a man inside, but I'm not certain it was Holden." Her mouth trembled, and she lowered her head as if she didn't wish him to see the tremor. "And then she was gone. I couldn't stop her. I'm sorry."

He wrapped an arm around her, then the other, drawing her into an embrace.

"You have nothing to apologize for," he reassured, speaking softly near her ear. "I was too late to catch a glimpse of her. How did she look?" He told himself that if he could just see Liddy, know she was all right, he'd wish her and Holden well. In fact, he'd convince the rotter to marry his sister properly, to ask for her hand and marry her in a church. All the trappings of wedlock Grey could never imagine for himself. His father fostered elevated notions of Phyllida's marital prospects, hoping to see her become a duchess or countess. The Holdens, upper-class gentry at best, would not go over well with Lord Stanhope, but Grey would convince him.

"Well." Tipping back her head, Sophia gazed up at him. "She looked well. Not unhappy or even fretful, but I can't be sure it was Lady Phyllida. If it was, where do you think she's gone now?"

"I don't know. Headed to Scotland, I expect. My father would never give his consent for Holden to marry her. They're a family with no titles and little wealth." Grey stroked his hand up and down Sophia's back. The motion, meant to soothe her, settled his nerves too. Holding her, attempting to give comfort, held his own demons at bay. "She told Mrs. Greenlow she planned to marry. I should wire Longcross and let my cousin know that much at least."

"Longcross?" Sophia wriggled out of his embrace but clutched excitedly at the lapel of his coat. "That's the name the young lady used in the lodging house register."

"Then it was Liddy." A tickle started in the middle of his belly and worked its way up until laughter bubbled in his throat. "And she looked well? She's all right."

Sophia grinned too. Her eyes danced with the shared giddiness of relief, but there were signs of the same exhaustion he felt too.

"Come with me." Grey reached for her hand and gently pulled her along as he started up the village's main road.

"Where?"

"I owe you a pint, Sophia Ruthven."

CHAPTER ELEVEN

---

*"Our conversation skimmed the surface—civility
and niceties. Thus, I dove deeper. Below the surface, where one most often finds the truth."*

—CASEBOOK OF EUPHEMIA
BREEDLOVE, LADY DETECTIVE

Accompanying a scoundrel to a public house was highly
improper.

The worst part of knowing etiquette was that Sophia
couldn't claim ignorance when she broke the rules. Between
her father's books and her mama's lessons, she knew the
guidelines of propriety so well they might as well have been
tattooed on her skin.

Though, of course, tattoos were improper too.

With Grey, she'd gone beyond breaking a few rules, and
he seemed to enjoy every minute.

Sophia knew as much the moment Grey escorted her into the Eagle and Stag, strutting into the Grantchester establishment as if he owned every square inch. The proprietor even seemed to know him, waving eagerly. Then an older woman sweetened the publican's grin by urging them to take a table near the freshly stoked fire to stave off the evening's chill.

Never having been to a public house, including the modest one in her Hertfordshire village, Sophia took in the room with a wide-eyed gape, memorizing details so that she could use them in her stories. Effie Breedlove did much of her best musing over clues while sitting in her local pub.

"Ale?" a barmaid asked, and Sophia nodded. She wasn't sure what else might be on offer at the Eagle and Stag.

"They promised a beef stew if I returned. Shall we have some?" Grey stood too near as he bent to see Sophia into her chair. His breath warmed the back of her neck, the shell of her ear. He had a habit of nearness, of touching her too freely and longer than she should have allowed.

She had a terrible habit of letting him get away with such liberties.

"Sounds excellent." Her stomach concurred, judging by the low growl rumbling up from her belly.

The ale came first, a pale hazy brew served more generously than any beverage Sophia had ever considered sipping in her life. Grey lifted his pint glass immediately for a chug, clearly savoring the flavor and sating a hearty thirst. The tall vessel was half empty by the time he sat it on the scarred wood again.

Sophia took a deep breath and lifted her glass to her lips, tentatively sipping the first dram. And winced. The liquid was warm and unbearably bitter. She covered her mouth to keep from choking, setting the beer away from her with such haste an amber wave sloshed over the edge.

"I'm sorry," she said hoarsely, reaching down to search her reticule for a handkerchief. The bitterness coated her tongue, soured in her throat.

"Not a fan of ale, I see." He removed a pristine square of cloth from his waistcoat pocket and began sopping up the ale. "And stop apologizing." Lifting his gaze, he pinned her with a steel-gray stare. "You've been nothing but helpful to me, and I've yet to repay you."

"I was taught to apologize when I made a mess." Sophia swallowed, wishing she could taste anything but beer.

"You only call this a mess because you've never visited my townhouse on a Friday evening." Grey chuckled. "So apologizing has become a habit, has it? Drilled in by a tyrannical governess or your parents?"

"By my father." Sophia couldn't recall a moment of her childhood that hadn't been intended to please the great Leopold Ruthven.

"I'll bet I could break you of the habit," Grey teased. He settled back until he tipped his chair. Crossing his arms, he revealed the bulky curve of muscle in his upper bicep. So bulky that the seams of his dark coat looked as though they might give up. He tipped his head as he assessed her, studying her so intently she could feel his gaze like a wisp of stray hair she itched to swipe from her skin. Slamming his front two chair legs onto the floor, he dropped forward, elbows braced on the table. "Perhaps I should kiss you every time you apologize."

"You think kissing would cure me?" She hadn't meant the words as tease, or to infuse her tone with a husky timbre. But now that the question was out, she wanted his answer.

He held her gaze, his mouth tipping into a heart-stopping grin. "Kissing you, Sophia, might just cure me."

The eagerness in his eyes warmed the gray to molten silver. Sophia's breath caught in her throat.

"Ale not to your liking, miss?" The barmaid placed two heaping bowls of stew on the table, then a cutting board with still-warm bread. "How about a cider? The missus makes it herself."

"Yes, thank you." Anything to wash away the taste of the beer and distract her from the steady pull of his gaze. A moment later the girl returned with a tall mug containing a beverage that smelled of apples and tasted just as sweet.

"Better?" Grey queried as he tore off a piece of bread and placed it near her bowl.

"Delicious." She took another gulp, and another.

"Slow down," Grey warned. "The cider's sweetness covers its potency. A bit like you."

Sophia quirked a brow, unsure whether he meant to compliment or tease.

He was right about the cider. The brew was already having an effect—a pleasant fizz in her chest, warmth in her bones, as if the liquor was heating her from the inside out.

Grey took his own pint in hand and lifted the glass to his lips. His eyes had shuttered. He'd returned to being a cocksure rogue, winking at her across the table when he caught her staring.

She longed for the bravado to fall away again, to get a glimpse of the man behind the actor's practiced mien.

"How about a question per sip?" Sophia asked before he could take a swig. She had nothing but questions, and the cider, the setting, the look in Grey's eyes all made them feel urgent.

"Go on." He narrowed his gaze before tipping a grin at her over the rim. "Ask your question. I'm thirsty."

"Why don't you want to be Lord Winship?"

He set his glass down with a *thunk*. "Because the title was never meant for me. My older brother was the heir." Swiping up his glass again, he swallowed a long dram. "He would have been better at fulfilling the duties of the title." He grinned before drawing a finger across his lips. "I will fail, as I often do. As I failed him."

Sophia's breath whooshed out on a sharp exhale. "I'm sorry, Grey."

"You're apologizing again," he said in a playful tone that belied his confessions about his brother's death and his own fears. Leaning back in his chair, he stretched out his legs until his boots slid next to hers. "Shall we attempt the kissing cure?"

"No." Sophia ran her finger along the edge of her mug. "But you should ask your question. I want a drink."

He crossed his arms and asked in a low, resonant tone, "Why are you unmarried?"

Irritation made her skin prickle. "Why aren't you, Mr. Grey? Are you a proponent of wedlock?"

"You're cheating." He tipped his chair forward and smiled. "That's two more questions, and you've yet to give an answer."

Sophia lifted her mug to her lips. "No one's ever asked for my hand in marriage." She quaffed the cider, savoring the sweetness on her tongue, focusing on the pleasure of the liquor's warmth rather than Grey's wide-eyed expression.

She knew she was an oddity because she hadn't followed the path of other young women her age.

"They're idiots." Grey signaled to the barmaid to refill their glasses.

"Who?" Sophia forced her gaze to meet his.

"The men who passed up the chance to make you their own," he said gruffly before swigging back the last of his ale.

"You assume I would accept anyone who asked?" The tease in her tone did wonders to cover the lump in her throat.

"No, Sophia." He clutched his spoon and scooped up a heaping mouthful of stew from his bowl. "I believe you're the most discerning woman I've ever met. You're clever enough to choose a man who deserves you."

Sophia dipped her head and focused on her food. For several minutes they ate in companionable silence, each tearing into the meal with the eagerness of famished travelers. She soon gave up on taking dainty bites and ladylike sips.

When she finally laid her spoon down, belly full and head fuzzy with drink, passing thoughts came and went. She should check the time, dig in her satchel and find the train schedule back to London, compose a thank-you note to Mr. Ogilvy.

Ogilvy. She heard his name as if her guilty conscience was reminding her how rude she'd been to the poor man before they'd even had a chance to meet.

"Who is Ogilvy?" Grey's voice. Not her conscience.

"None of your concern." Marriage was the last topic she wished to broach with him again. "He certainly can't help us find your sister." That was what mattered. That was her excuse for sharing supper with a scoundrel in a Cambridge public house.

Grey took a swig of ale, set down his glass, and grinned. "I'm being impertinent." Despite his easy smile and the charming dimples on each side of his mouth, his gaze was steady. Intense.

"Yes, you are." She didn't wish to reveal herself to be a fool when he thought her discerning. Exchanging a few letters with Ogilvy offered no promises. The man might dismiss her or fail to spark her interest, as every other had. "I don't know Mr. Ogilvy well."

"My sister doesn't know Clive Holden well either. Certainly not well enough to trust her future to the bastard."

"What if she loves him?" Sophia toyed with the handle of her mug.

Shock rippled through her when he began laughing. Not a gentle chuckle, but a deep, hearty ripple of sound that echoed in her ears and reverberated in her chest. It was an enticing sound. Naughty and raucous. Loud enough to draw the notice of a table of gentlemen nearby.

"Whatever Liddy feels for Holden, it's not love," he insisted, his voice light and ringing with amusement. "The girl's affections are as flimsy as candy floss." He tossed back another swig of ale, emptying his second pint glass. "Love is a fantasy."

"Is it?" Her parents rowed at times, and no man had ever captured her heart, but Sophia never doubted love's existence.

"Not to mention dangerous." Grey waved a hand at her in an up and down motion, as if to cite her as evidence of his claim.

"Why?"

"Love is a risk. A gamble." He tapped the tabletop to emphasize his point.

"How do you know?" Sophia bit her lip the moment the words were out. Now *she* was being impertinent, but curiosity kept her from taking back her question. Had he merely witnessed his parents' unhappiness or experienced his own broken heart?

"My parents taught me well." His appealing voice turned bitter. "They betrayed each other. Destroyed each other, truth be told." After sipping from a fresh glass deposited by the barmaid, he waved his hand toward her again. "And you? Did you find love during your London Season or back in your country village?"

"I never had a Season." At the time—not long after the incident in Lady Pembry's garden—she'd been relieved to forego the ritual. "A countess in our village offered to sponsor me, but Father refused. He insisted my place was at home caring for my sister." A sip of cider did nothing to loosen the tightness in her throat. "My mother was often ill when Clary was young."

Grey leaned in, flattening his palm on the table near her glass. "So you played housekeeper then as you do now? Nursemaid to your sister. Defender of your brother."

Sophia arched a brow.

"Kit told me you were the one who kept to all the rules he happily broke." He stroked his finger around the handle of her mug. "Did you never have any happiness? Any pleasure?"

"Some say there's more to life than the pursuit of pleasure."

"Fools, every one of them." He smiled wide, dimples on full display. "What else is there?"

"To be useful." Sophia tipped forward until the table edge pressed against the buttons of her shirtwaist. "To have a purpose."

"And when you find your use and purpose, will it bring you happiness?"

Sophia pushed her chair back and stood. Dizziness darkened the edges of her vision. The question was like a pin prick, sharp and pointed, deflating every answer she'd offer if she were conversing with anyone but Jasper Grey. His query made her sense the depths of her foolishness, perfectly underlining a truth she found hard to admit.

After years of striving to be useful, she was miserable. Lonely. Frustrated. Aimless.

She couldn't chastise him for being a pleasure-seeker when, deep in her heart, it was what she longed for too. Pleasure and, yes, happiness.

Looking across the table at him, with his one arm hitched over the back of his chair, one long leg slung over the other, she shook her head. Perhaps they were both foolish for seeking happiness when life never promised any such thing.

"I should return to London, my lord." In the city, she had a purpose. She'd done her bit and devoted all the time she could to helping Grey find his sister.

"You won't be returning this evening." He tugged a chain across his waistcoat and lifted the face of his pocket watch for her inspection. The hour was much later than she realized.

"Surely there's a coach." Though she wasn't sure of any such thing. She cast a glance at the barmaid nearby for confirmation.

"Not as such, miss. Might be able to hire a private coach, though it will cost you a pretty penny." The girl started away and then turned back. "'Course, you could just take a bed here."

"I thought there were none to be had." Grey stood and moved to stand behind Sophia. Too close, as was his way.

"A lodger departed." The pub keeper's wife approached with a brimming bucket of coals to place near the pub's fireplace. "Though unless you've a license and parson to marry the young lady tonight, there's only one bed. Might have a camp bed we could rustle up too."

"We're not sharing a room." The cider might have thickened her tongue to cotton wool, but Sophia's mind was clear about the impropriety of sharing a rented room with a notorious rogue.

The pub owner's wife let out a chuckle. "I meant we could set up a cot down here near the fire once we close our doors."

"Take the room." Grey brushed his hand gently against Sophia's arm. "I'll be fine on the cot." He still looked like a scoundrel, but his voice had taken on a tender note. Gentlemanly.

The drink heightened her exhaustion and made her bones feel as solid as jelly. Grey's eyes were as shadowed as hers. They both needed rest, but he had a long journey to the Scottish border ahead.

"Perhaps you should take the room." She turned to face him and swayed unsteadily. She reached for him, and he gripped her upper arm, his gaze locked on hers.

"I prefer thinking of you tucked up in bed." The hint of grin at the corner of his mouth indicated his suggestive tone was not in the least unintentional.

"Perhaps you two *should* marry," the publican declared as he ambled up to stand beside his wife. "You're already quite good at bickering." When his wife elbowed him in the ribs, he added, "We've one other room, my lord. It's quite small, just under the eaves, but dry and warm and next door to the young lady's."

"Perfect," Grey declared. His hand, a heated steady weight, moved from Sophia's arm to the curve of her waist as he guided her toward the stairs.

She enjoyed his touch too much, could get used to his nearness too easily. She sidestepped away from him. "How will we know which room is which?"

"We'll use our intellect," he teased. "There can't be many rooms, unless the upstairs is larger than the pub below."

"There are only four," the barmaid said from the foot of the stairs. "Yours are that way." She pointed to the left side of the building. "I'll bring a pitcher of hot water up for each of you soon enough."

Sophia nodded to the girl and started up the stairs. The mesmerizing tilt of her hips kept Grey moving forward. His eyes had gone dry, drink had tempered his worries, and now he craved nothing so much as taking Sophia to bed.

He couldn't, of course. No matter how much three pints of ale had blunted his senses, he hadn't forgotten that she was his best friend's sister and the most rule-bound woman he'd ever known.

Those arguments were easy to forget when she was near and her lavender scent sweetened the air.

The moment she retreated from his touch, he wanted her back. He was used to women seeking his hands—pressing themselves into his palms, showing him where to touch and how. Never had he longed for a woman's skin sliding against his own as he did Sophia's. Each time she reached for him felt like a victory.

She stopped on the threshold of a room with an open door, swaying enough to cause her to grip the frame.

"You're tipsy." Instinct told him to reach for her, to carry her to the bed. But she'd never allow him to get through the door.

"I'm not used to drink. My father believed in leading an abstemious life."

"And one absent of any kind of pleasure." No wonder her brother had come to London starving for every enjoyment the city offered.

"I'm not my father." She whirled on him. Reaching out to steady herself, her palm landed flat against his chest, just above his waistcoat. Only the thin starched fabric of his shirt separated her flesh from his. "I am quite capable of enjoying myself, I assure you."

He wanted to see Sophia enjoying herself. Craved her soft feminine laughter, her rare smiles. How satisfying would it be to hear her moan with pleasure and squeal with delight? If only she'd allow him to be the cause of her enjoyment, he could think of a hundred ways to begin.

A flash of fantasy colored his thoughts. Sophia's palm pressed to his body but with no fabric between them. Those loose blonde curls of hers draped across his body, tangled between his fingers, fisted in his hand. Desire pooled in his groin, sharpening his hunger for her, and he fought the urge to dance her three steps back to the edge of the lumpy bed he glimpsed through the doorway.

"When was the last time you enjoyed yourself?" His voice emerged hoarse and low. His fingers itched to follow the lead of the single unfastened button at the high collar of her gown and unhook another. And another. Until he could uncover all those curves hidden behind her pristine white shirtwaist.

"I find pleasure in many endeavors," she insisted in a distinctly dubious tone.

"And the last time?" He couldn't resist running his fingertip along the back of her hand, stroking her velvety skin.

When she gazed up at him, her eyes fixed on his mouth.

"Yes, goddess." He grinned. "That was the last time I enjoyed myself too."

"Don't call me that." She curled her fingers around the placket of his shirt front and gave him a minuscule push.

"It suits you."

"Because I'm cold?"

Grey frowned and gripped her hand, pressing it more firmly against his chest. "There's nothing cold about you, Sophia." He could still remember the warmth of her mouth when he'd kissed her, the delicious heat of her body flush with his. "I call you *goddess* because you're splendid, formidable"—he grinned again—"and perhaps a bit daunting."

She slipped her hand from his, spun away, and started into her room. "I have no wish to be daunting."

Grey followed, taking one step into the low-ceilinged space. "And I've no wish to offend you. Ever. Forgive me." The urge to embrace her nearly overwhelmed him. She was no longer standing with that punishing posture of hers. Her narrow shoulders were hunched, her fingers just visible at the edges of her waist as she hugged her arms around herself.

"Kiss me."

For a moment, Grey thought the command emerged from his lips. Perhaps he was more inebriated than he realized. But there was no telltale rumble in his chest, no vibration in his throat.

She turned to face him, arms loose at her sides, fingers clenched. "Kiss me again, Grey."

Two steps and she was in his arms.

He wrapped a hand around her waist, splayed his fingers against her back, but she pulled him closer. Gripping his necktie, she urged him down. Stretching onto her toes, just as she had to reach the book at Mrs. Greenlow's, Sophia didn't wait for his kiss. She touched her mouth to his. At first their lips brushed and collided softly. Grey wanted her so fiercely, he tensed, knowing how close he was to the edge. Kissing Sophia reminded him of the power of kisses. How they could stoke needs otherwise held at bay, get inside every vulnerable place. The taste of her was dangerous. Made him want impossibilities.

She slid her tongue along the seam of his mouth. Grey opened to her, canted his head to the side to taste her more deeply. He was rewarded with one of those moans of pleasure he'd imagined. The sound was far more arousing than his fantasy.

"I need to see," Sophia said on a breathless shudder as she took his face into her palms, leaving a trail of heat on his skin as she stroked her left thumb across his cheek. She searched his eyes, her bee-stung lips slightly parted.

"What do you see?" Despite his curiosity, he feared her answer. Something about Sophia tore through his defenses, shattered the actor's facade he'd erected.

"Desire."

Yes, from the moment he'd met her.

"And something more?" she asked.

"Yes." Grey swallowed hard. He didn't know what she saw, didn't wish to examine what he felt. Acknowledging the need was too terrifying.

"You like kissing me?"

"Like isn't the word I'd use."

"What word, then?"

He didn't want words. He wanted to show her in the only way he knew how. The way he knew best. But the moment he slid his hand from her narrow waist to the flare of her hip, footsteps sounded on the staircase, and Sophia slipped out of his hands.

"Hot water for you, miss." The barmaid who'd served them downstairs stopped in the doorway of Sophia's room. "And for you too, my lord."

"I'll bid you good night, Sophia." Though nothing in him wanted to part from her. That was the most dangerous aspect of the woman. Whether he'd spent time bantering or kissing her, parting from Sophia never felt right. Never left him with the usual satisfaction of reclaiming his independence.

He sketched a half bow and began backing out of the room. Sophia pressed her lips together, offered him a tiny nod, and then a softly spoken "good night."

The barmaid followed him to the tiny chamber next door. The room was so diminutive, Grey knocked his head on a beam as he approached the bed.

"Watch your head," the young woman warned several seconds too late. "No fire in this room, my lord, but I'll stoke the lady's before I go back down. You'll feel some of her heat in here."

He would much rather be the one stoking Sophia's fire, but he worked to tamp his sensual frustration and smiled appreciatively. "Thank you."

The girl set a pitcher of water in a ceramic bowl on a table near the door and started out, then she suddenly ducked back inside. After shutting the door, she flattened herself against the rough wood. "You're looking for a young lady."

Oh Lord. Grey was used to being propositioned, so the girl's eager gaze wasn't a complete surprise. His body ached for release, but there was only one woman he wanted.

"I'm flattered, miss. Truly, but—"

"I met her once." The serving girl twisted her apron in her hands. "There was something about her. No doubt she was a lady."

Liddy? Grey pressed his palms together, pointed his fingers toward the barmaid. "What did she say to you? Anything at all will be helpful."

"We mostly exchanged niceties. She thought Grantchester a very pretty little village. Everyone does who comes to visit."

With effort, Grey kept his tone calm. "Anything else?"

The girl blinked at him, furrowing her brow. "I sensed sadness," she said hesitantly. "The young lady seemed lonely underneath all of her politeness and smiles."

Chapter Twelve

"Hurts and slights of the past haunt the living like ghosts. Very often, they provide a motive for mischief too."

—CASEBOOK OF EUPHEMIA
BREEDLOVE, LADY DETECTIVE

Sophia woke with a start.

Clenching her fingers, she found a rough blanket wrapped around her body. Sleepy confusion began to clear. She wasn't in her bed at Ruthven House or in her guest room in Kit and Ophelia's London townhouse.

Cambridge. Grantchester. The creaky bed below her was situated above the Eagle and Stag public house. But what had woken her?

She listened in the darkness and heard movement downstairs. Then another sound, much closer. A distinctly masculine rumble and moan.

"No!" Grey cried. Another word came too, but she couldn't make it out. He was in distress. Of that, she had no doubt.

Pushing the blanket aside, Sophia slipped from the low bed. She'd stripped down to her chemise and reached for her skirt, sliding it quickly over her hips and securing the hook. She donned her bodice, and worked one hand along the buttons as she opened her chamber door and crept toward Grey's room. Pressing her ear to the door, she heard his bed groaning as if he was turning and tossing. Rather than call to him, she pushed inside.

Her brother had been prone to night terrors as a child, and she experienced the same sense of urgency to comfort and calm as she had then.

But the moment she ducked into Grey's room, the sight before her swept away any notion she'd come to soothe a child's nightmare.

His lean body sprawled across the tiny bed. One muscled bare leg dangled off the edge. When she followed the line of his leg, she could see that he'd stripped off every scrap of clothing before getting under the covers. The blanket wasn't, in fact, covering him at the moment. Not fully anyway. One side of his body peeked out, exposed from the thick brawn of his thigh to the lean cut of his hips and broad plain of his chest.

Unbidden, and very unhelpfully, Sophia's mouth watered as she studied him. He was no longer calling out or moving, but he slept fitfully, twisting his head on the pillow, his brow drawn in pinched lines.

When he began mumbling again, Sophia crept closer, carefully resting her backside on the edge of his bed. "It's all right," she whispered. "Just sleep."

His brow knitted into deeper grooves, and he gripped the blanket edge so tightly his knuckles paled. Perspiration dotted his forehead, and Sophia reached for the damp cloth discarded near the pitcher and washing bowl. She dabbed gently at his skin. "You're all right," she repeated, as she pressed the back of her hand against his head to determine if he was feverish.

In a flash of movement, he reached for her, sitting up in bed. As he gripped her shoulder, his fingers dug into her flesh.

"Sophia?" Voice feathering out in a raspy whisper, he loosened his hold on her body. But he didn't stop touching her. He slid his hand up her shoulder, pressed his warm palm against her neck, slipped his fingertips along the edge of her hairline.

Her body had never before responded to any man as it did to Grey's touch. Heaven help her, she arched forward to get closer to him. He threaded her hair through his fingers, stroking a strand down her chest.

She hissed when his hand grazed her breast.

Grey immediately retreated. "I'm sorry."

"Don't be," she told him as she reached for the hand he'd planted on the patch of blanket between them. "Touch me again."

His eyes were shadowed when he gazed at her, his movements hesitant as he touched her shoulder. For a moment he simply stared at her, stroking his fingers through her unbound hair. Then lower, to the swell of her breast. Delicious shivers shot down her spine.

"What if I can't stop touching you once I start?" he murmured.

A good question. A rational and proper question. More important, what if she didn't stop him when she should? By any measure, she'd already allowed too much.

When reason wended its way into her desire-hazed mind, it was startling to find that Grey was thinking more sensibly than she was.

"You're right," she admitted. "I came into your room because you called out. Did you have a troubling dream?" She edged away from him on the tiny bed.

"Probably." He let out a ragged sigh and settled back against the bed's headboard. When he crossed his arms over his chest, the blanket rode further down his waist.

"Do you remember what it was about?" She often recalled her own dreams so clearly she noted them in her journal, if only to get them out of her head.

He studied her, watching her face so intently her skin began to heat. "My brother," he finally rasped.

"The one whose title you inherited."

"The one who would still hold the title, if fate were fair." He scrubbed a hand over the dusting of auburn hair on his jaw. "But life doesn't give us what we want."

"What does it give us?" She'd spent her whole life waiting for…something. What she craved was plain enough—marriage, family, contentment. But what would life give her in the end? Strangely, she thought Grey, who'd certainly lived more fully than she had, might have a clue.

"Torment," he said when he looked at her again, his pale eyes brighter and lit with their usual spark. "Temptation," he added, sliding his hand across the blanket until his fingertips grazed hers. But even as he teased her, tempted her, the lines between his brows failed to ease.

"What can I do to ease your torment?" That, after all, was why she'd come to his room.

He glanced through the room's single window, small and rounded like a porthole. Beyond the thick glass, the glow of sunrise had begun to streak the sky in shades of amber and gold. "I can think of a dozen ways." When he gazed back at her, his eyes had heated to molten silver. "But every one of them involves you in this bed beside me, bare and breathless and very sated."

"You're wicked," she said too shakily for him to take the declaration as anything but a compliment. His words worked a strange magic on her body, pebbling gooseflesh along her skin, tautening her nipples, causing heat to pool between her thighs. She looked away, but the crumpled pile of his discarded clothing only brought a rush of heat to her cheeks.

"And you are pure temptation." He smiled as he reached out an inch further, hooking two of her fingers with his. "I wish I had the time to show you all the benefits of tempting a wicked man, but I should rise and prepare for the early train."

He was right and behaving like a proper gentleman. He had a long journey ahead, and she needed to return to London. But in this tiny room with just the two of them as witness, a part of her wondered why he did not wish to play the thorough scoundrel with her as he apparently did with ever other woman of his acquaintance.

"How long do you think the journey will take you?"

"Most of the day. I should arrive on the border by nightfall."

"And then?"

"I search every inn and anvil in Gretna Green until I find them or someone who has encountered them."

Sophia couldn't shake the sense of wishing she could help him finish his search. Not because she desired more time in his company. Being near the man brought out the worst of her impulses, but hunting for his sister was a worthy endeavor. Much more important that overseeing the selection of wallpaper in Kit and Ophelia's guest rooms. More significant than attempting a courtship with a man she didn't know any better than a stranger at the Eagle and Stag.

"I should dress." He began pulling aside the blanket at his hips. "I have no problem with you watching, but you'll have to at least stand up so I can get out of bed."

Sophia scrambled to her feet. *This* was the man she harbored regrets about abandoning. An utter, irredeemable rogue. A saucy smirk perched on his sensual mouth, if she had any doubts.

"I'll leave you to your ablutions." When she took the two steps toward the door, she tipped her chin up in indignation and the top of her head grazed the ceiling beam.

"Have a care, Sophia." He was behind her in an instant, one hand braced over her head, the other lightly clasping her arm. "Are you all right?"

She carved an inch of space between them and spun to face him. "Perfectly. You needn't…" Her retort fizzled on her tongue because Grey was pressed against her in the small space, and he wasn't wearing a stitch. She'd known as much as soon as she'd entered his chamber, but seeing his naked thigh and chest was wholly different from glimpsing his bare…everything.

Keep your eyes up. But they were rebellious eyes, and her body had committed an all-out coup d'etat. She glanced. No, it was more of a long gaze, but they were pressed so close together in the tight space that she couldn't see much beyond the flat, muscled expanse of his belly, marked by a coppery line of hair right down the center.

His hand obscured her view as he hooked a finger under her chin and lifted until her gaze met his. "One of these days, when we have nothing but time, I hope you'll let me strip you bare and gaze at your nakedness with as much eagerness."

"I'm not eager." She swiped at his—very bare, very warm—arm to free her chin. "Just...curious."

"Yes." He tipped his head, assessing her, smiling as if he liked whatever he found when he looked at her. "I do love that about you." His brows drew together in a frown the moment the word *love* was out and echoing in the air between them.

"I should go. The first train to London departs just after yours heads north." She peeked at him over her shoulder as she eased the door open, but he said nothing more. She didn't speak either. But she looked. A single glance, but one she would not soon forget.

Grey sensed something was amiss. Some trouble beyond the fact that he was tired, hungry, and had worn the same necktie three days in a row. Some bother beyond the tragedy that he hadn't consumed a decent cup of coffee in days. Greater than all of the irritations of travel and the grind of anxiety over Liddy was that he'd lost his usual sense of *joie de vivre*.

Most disturbingly of all, he wasn't particularly interested in finding it.

He suddenly cared more about bantering with Sophia than all the parties carrying on in London without him. Even more than the adulation of audiences at Fleet Theater, no doubt being flung at the feet of the young man who'd stepped into his role as lead in one of the most anticipated plays of the Season.

He'd always found bidding others good-bye uncomfortable. Yet now the prospect of parting from her was a physical weight constricting his chest as he watched her exit the station-master's booth.

"Apparently my train departs twelve minutes before yours," she said blithely, approaching with a ticket clasped between her fingers.

Wonderful. So he would get to stand on the platform like a besotted fool, watching until her train churned out of view.

Gazing along the railroad tracks, as if she could envision the entire path from Cambridge to King's Cross Station in London, Sophia bit her lip. It was one of her many nervous habits he'd begun to note, much like the way her nose took to rabbit-like twitching when she was irritated, or her habit of ducking her head when embarrassed, not to mention her very irritating tendency to apologize for events that were in no way her fault.

Wouldn't it be a relief to free himself of a woman burdened with so many quirks? As he watched her check the watch pinned to her shirtwaist, a strand of hair slipped from behind her ear, and he couldn't convince himself of anything other than how much he would miss not having her near.

"Do you have everything?" He offered the inane question for the sheer pleasure of having her eyes on him.

Sophia frowned. "I only have a small satchel." She pointed to her lumpy, embroidered bag.

"Yes." He was so pathetic he thought he might even miss her hideous travel satchel. "What do you carry in that thing, anyway?" Upon toting it upstairs for her the night before, he'd found it surprisingly heavy and unwieldy.

She shrugged. "A few books and notes." Her eyes widened as she looked at him, then she ducked down to dig in her ever-present bag. "I almost forgot to give this back to you. You left your sister's journal the last time you were at Bloomsbury Square."

Grey took the slim book, and a shiver of anxiety crept along his shoulders. It felt odd to hold something of Liddy's. Something she should rightfully have in her own keeping. "Thank you."

"I'm afraid Cate and I may have peeked at a few passages." Sophia did her embarrassed head-ducking thing before tilting her gaze up at him. "Her entries are what led me to Cambridge."

"Then I'm glad you read them." Grey stuffed the book inside his waistcoat for safe keeping. "What books?"

"Pardon?" She squinted in confusion.

"You said you carry books in your bag. Which ones?" Far easier to discuss her choice of reading material than stare at the station clock over their heads as the minutes counted down to her departure.

"Detective stories, mostly. I'm fond of them."

"Are you?" After spending most of the previous two days with her, even the few feet of distance between them seemed a troublesome expanse. Grey approached, and his body responded instantly to her citrus and lavender scent and the way her gazed veered between wary and intrigued as she watched him. "What draws you to such stories, I wonder?"

She hadn't yet pushed the stray strand of hair off her cheek, and he seized the opportunity to touch her. "The danger?" The silky tress tickled his skin as he tucked it behind the delicate curve of her ear. He couldn't resist bending to whisper. "Intrigue—is that what you desire? An adventure all your own?"

He felt like an ass the moment the taunt was out. The words reminded him too much of his sister.

Sophia confirmed his foolishness with a firm shake of her head. "The stories I read are fiction. Scandal is all very well between the pages of a book, but I wish for marriage and a quiet life." Her nose quivered, and Grey wasn't certain if she was speaking truthfully or merely saying what she knew she should.

How could he divine the honest cravings of their heart?

He shook himself as if shaking rain from his coat. Why worry about Sophia's heart, or any woman's, for that matter? If she was telling the truth, the lady claimed to want marriage. A quiet life. Both of which struck him as precisely as appealing as the pox.

Her train approached the station platform, brakes squealing as metal slid against metal, and steam puffed up in billowing clouds.

His disquietude ratcheted to panic. As if an hourglass had been tipped, and he was running out of time. But for what?

Sophia would loathe his world of late-night celebrations and constant frivolity. And he had no right to her time or her kisses when he could offer her nothing in return.

"I know you'll find your sister, and I wish you a safe journey." Halfway to the train carriage, she turned back. "I've amended my opinion."

"Which one?" He strode forward, eager to close distance between them.

"I no longer think you're irredeemably wicked." Her expression bloomed into a dazzling smile. "But you are exceedingly good at being a scoundrel."

Grey wasn't used to denying his urges. But he battled the impulse to follow her, stop her, call her back to his side. Instead, he watched until she'd boarded the train. She didn't bid him good-bye, and he was grateful. He couldn't have managed the word.

A moment later, his own locomotive drew into the station on the opposite side of the platform, but he ignored the stationmaster's call to board.

Stubbornly, he waited. He needed her to go, needed to see that she was safely on her way before he could begin his journey.

"Lord Winship!"

Grey snapped his gaze toward the path that led into Grantchester. A young woman rushed toward him, one hand clamped over her straw bonnet.

"Feared I'd missed you," she said, her face as flushed and tired as when he'd first met the young servant girl from Mrs.

Greenlow's boarding house. "I couldn't let you go without telling you what the young lady said to me."

Sophia's train began to move, piston rods pumping as the driving wheels began to roll. Grey spotted her at a window, her eyes shadowed, mouth drawn tight. She watched him, turning her head and twisting her shoulders to keep him in view until her train took a turn and sped out of sight.

"She said she was going home, my lord." The girl moved closer to snag his attention and looked relieved to get the words out. "Said she was happy to be returning home."

"Home?" It didn't make any sense. Why would Holden send her to a Cambridge lodging house only to take her back to Derbyshire? He dug into his waistcoat pocket and handed the girl a few coins. "Thank you for finding me."

"When you see her again, hope she's as well as when she left us, my lord." She bobbed a curtsy before striding toward the village.

Grey spun on his heel and started for the ticket window. He needed a westbound train. Rushing forward to claim a spot on the next departing train, he caught a fresh green scent on the air.

He searched the platform for Sophia, scanning every blonde female traveler's face. Past the station, he spotted a field of purple-topped lavender blooms dancing in the breeze.

Changing course, he headed for the stationmaster's office. He wasn't sure why he had to let her know of his new destination, didn't take the time to consider. He simply strode toward the window where there was a telegraph and a man who could exchange his northbound ticket for one headed to Derbyshire.

CHAPTER THIRTEEN

With no difficulties along the line, the return train from Cambridge deposited Sophia in London midmorning, leaving much of the day stretched before her. And yet, for the first time since coming to stay with Kit and Ophelia in London, she didn't look forward to entering their tidy townhouse on Bloomsbury Square.

She was eager to see Cate and hear how all of the house improvements had proceeded in her absence. But unease plagued her, as if she'd misplaced something essential or left a valuable behind in Cambridge. She hadn't, of course. Her traveling case hung over her arm.

It was Grey's search that remained unfinished, not hers. Would he let her know when he'd found his sister?

As if on cue, her satchel strap broke the moment she stepped inside the front door. Books thudded to the floor, manuscript pages scattered, and she dropped down on one knee to catch her fountain pen before it rolled away.

"Would you care for a cup of tea while you wait?" Cate's voice filtered through the half-open door of the formal drawing room. A moment later, she stepped into the hallway. "Oh thank goodness." She rushed forward, crouched to help Sophia gather her belongings, and then tugged her into the front parlor across the hall. "He arrived first thing this morning," Cate said breathlessly. "I tried to turn him away, but he insisted on waiting."

"Who?" In her gut, she knew the answer. Before she could confirm her suspicion, heavy footsteps clip-clopped across the marble hallway floor, tracing Cate's path.

"Mrs. Cole, I wonder if I might trouble you for—" The bearded, bespectacled gentleman stopped in his tracks. "Oh, forgive me. I did not mean to interrupt."

Ogilvy. Crow-black close-cropped hair, neatly trimmed mustache, hooded eyes that gave nothing away. He was precisely the man of his photograph, except in living color. Though, as coloring went, the man favored stark. His pitch-black suit contrasted with the snowiest shirt Sophia had ever seen. For a moment he stood as still as the man captured in his picture postcard, then the hair over his lip began to twitch as he grinned. "Miss Ruthven, I presume."

"Mr. Ogilvy." Sophia straightened, prayed travel hadn't left her terribly mussed, and took one step forward. "I'm sorry I was not at home to greet you earlier."

Despite an attempt at smiling, her mouth remained stubbornly stiff, her voice threaded with a note of irritation she hoped he didn't catch. Though, honestly, the man's tenacity verged on worrisome. He'd visited twice, and she had yet to extend a single formal invitation.

"I cannot express what pleasure it gives me to meet you, Miss Ruthven." He sketched a stiff little bow, which warmed Sophia's old-fashioned sense of social graces sufficiently to remind her that Jasper Grey, Lord Winship, had never received an invitation to visit either.

"Must have been a particularly long walk this morning," Cate said after clearing her throat. "All the way to Regent's Park, Miss Ruthven?" She shot Sophia a quick wink to ensure she understood the subterfuge employed to explain her early morning absence to Mr. Ogilvy.

"Perhaps you consider me rude for calling uninvited, Miss Ruthven, but I hoped to see you before I depart from the city." He glanced back at the drawing room from which he'd emerged. "May I beg the favor of speaking privately with you for a moment?"

Sophia glanced at Cate, who, as usual, read her thoughts.

"I'll have refreshments sent to the drawing room," she assured before heading toward the kitchen.

Ogilvy possessed a heavy tread, his footsteps echoing in the hallway as he followed Sophia into the recently decorated room. A gentleman who knew his manners well, he waited politely until she lowered herself to the settee and gestured for him to join her.

"The house is impressive," he declared, glancing apprais- ingly around the room. "How do you manage all of this space on your own?"

"Oh, this is my brother's home. He and his wife invited me to visit, and I offered to assist with updating the decor." There was so much she'd not yet found the opportunity to share with him via letter.

"Then you own no London property of your own?" The intersection of his dark brows indicated displeasure at the revelation.

"No, I usually stay at my father's home, now my brother's property, in Hertfordshire. We grew up in a small village called Briar Heath."

"When I saw your address, I assumed you resided in London." He was quite displeased to learn otherwise, if his frown was any indication. Had the man truly chosen to reply to her letter because he hoped to acquire her equity in a London townhouse?

"You reside in Bristol?"

Before he could answer, a maid entered the room and deposited a tray with tea and biscuits on the table between them.

"I would much prefer to find a place in London," he said as Sophia poured him a cup of tea. "Are you fond of the city, Miss Ruthven?"

"Exceedingly so." More than she ever dreamed possible. Beyond those moments when the countryside called to her and she yearend for its open spaces, she couldn't deny how much the light and noise and energy of London intrigued her.

"Perfect." His grin returned, and he nodded approvingly after his first sip of tea. "We can live here rather than Bristol. Business opportunities abound in London." With an abrupt porcelain clatter, he set his teacup down and edged forward on the settee, his hands clasped before him. "When would you wish to marry?"

Sophia choked on her tea. Scorching liquid seared a path across her tongue. Mr. Ogilvy snapped a long white kerchief from his pocket and dangled it in the space between them.

"Forgive me, Miss Ruthven. I've taken you by surprise. Perhaps you think my boldness indelicate. I am a man of business, not fancy words." He reached into his pocket again and extracted a small square box.

Oh no. Please no. She wasn't ready to disappoint him nor to accept him, if an offer was what he had in mind.

When he moved off the settee and lowered himself to one knee, Sophia shot up, nearly overturning the table between them. "Mr. Ogilvy—"

"Miss Ruthven, you cannot be unaware of my intentions."

"No, or rather, yes, I am aware of your intentions." Hadn't that been much of the appeal of replying to his ad? No pretense. No uncertainty. "I hoped there might be more time for us to know each other better."

"As you can see, I am not a patient man."

Clearly. Just as Cate had intuited.

"Wait," she said as he flipped the hook holding the tiny box shut. He stared up at her expectantly, but her tongue had twisted into a tangled knot. The longer she was silent, the fiercer the scowl on his face.

"Have I come too late? Do you have another suitor?"

A little trill of panicky laughter burst out before she could stop herself. "No." There had never been suitors. Certainly none with the determination and tenacity of the man kneeling before her.

"Then, may I have your hand in marriage, Miss Ruthven?" He flipped the box's latch with his thumbnail to display a dainty silver band with an oval sapphire at its center.

Sophia stared at the ring until her eyes watered. She'd known the question was coming, but a proposal, especially one from a man wearing Ogilvy's earnest expression, caught her off guard.

"Ah," he said as he got to his feet. "You need time to consider."

"I insist on time, Mr. Ogilvy. I won't be rushed into a decision." A refusal to be coerced wasn't at all what weighed on her mind.

Grey. His voice echoed in her head, flashes of his bare skin flitted through her mind. Even his bay scent wafted up from her clothes. Everything about the man conspired to cloud her thoughts.

And yet to what end? Kisses were not commitment. Nor contentment. Wasn't that what she'd sought when replying to Ogilvy's newspaper ad? A few days in the company of a scoundrel—no matter how appealing—couldn't alter what she wanted for her future.

"I understand, Miss Ruthven," Ogilvy said, though his bowed shoulders and clenched fists said otherwise. He glanced at the standing clock in the corner. "I must depart. My train leaves for Bristol within the hour, and London traffic is unpredictable."

She'd offended him. Displeased him, at the very least. A panicky flutter welled up in her chest. A foolish sense that her single chance at marriage was walking out the door. "Will you return to London soon, Mr. Ogilvy?"

"Undoubtedly, and I vow to give you fair warning next time." His tone was almost playful.

A smile tickled around the edges of Sophia's mouth. Ogilvy exhaled, his chest deflating like a balloon. For the first moment since their meeting, Sophia wished for him to stay, wished to know more of this man whose ad had sparked her interest.

He started toward the door, stopping on the threshold to turn back. "May I kiss you before I depart?"

The tentative ease she'd begun to feel with him dissolved like morning dew.

She didn't answer; he stepped forward. Scandalously near, considering they'd only met twenty minutes ago. Hovering at her side, he leaned in eagerly, his ragged breath against her cheek.

"A kiss would hardly be appropriate, Mr. Ogilvy." Funny how those words had not passed her lips when Grey lowered his mouth to hers.

She was behaving like a fool. She'd allowed liberties with a libertine. Yet with a respectable gentleman, she clung to the same outdated notions that had brought her nothing but spinsterhood.

Ogilvy brushed his fingers against hers with the lightest of strokes. "Your hand, at least?"

Sophia pointed to her cheek, the one closest to where Ogilvy loomed. Out of the corner of her eye, she saw a flash of a smile, and then he lowered his head, brushing his whiskered lips against her skin. His beard scraped her cheek like the bristles of a brush, and his lips were shockingly cool.

An unbidden shiver made her flinch away from his touch, but he edged forward. His gaze fixed on her mouth, as if he intended to take the kiss she'd denied him.

"You forget yourself, Mr. Ogilvy." Planting a hand on the snow white of his shirt, Sophia gave the overeager man a shove. "I've agreed to nothing, and I don't even know your given name."

"'Timothy," he said, his voice husky, eyes blazing. "May I call you Sophia?"

"Perhaps when we know each other better." Delay was what she needed, a chance to sort her muddled feelings into the clearer thoughts. "I look forward to our future correspondence."

The prospect of a husband seemed so much more appealing when he was a name in a newspaper or ink strokes on a piece of foolscap. A man she could just imagine—and foolishly idealize.

Ogilvy bowed as he had upon their introduction, though when he stood his expression turned hard, his voice firm and unyielding. "I am pleased to continue our correspondence for a while, Miss Ruthven, but the goal of my ad was wedlock. I trust that is yours too."

"Yes. Marriage to a man I know and trust." After spending years of enduring her father's high-handed manner, Ogilvy's imperious tone was as irksome as an overtight corset. She refused to commit herself to any man who expected her to be cowed by a gruff voice and fearsome glower.

"Will you see me to the door?"

"Of course," she said, relieved their sparring had ended. He waited just beyond the drawing room threshold and shamelessly assessed her from forehead to toe as she approached.

As Sophia passed, he followed her down the hall in his heavy-footed gait. There was an awkward moment as he proceeded onto the front step. He drifted toward her so that his body brushed hers from hip to shoulder. Settling his hat over his pomaded hair, he cast her another a terse look. No smile, nothing to indicate he'd enjoyed their visit any more than she had.

"I shall send you a letter when I return home, disclosing all a woman could wish to know before considering a gentleman's suit." He gripped her hand and bent his head to place a breathy kiss on her knuckles. When he straightened, a heated, hungry look lit his gaze. "You're a beauty, Miss Ruthven. That I cannot deny. But I wish to be settled, to move into the coming year with a wife by my side. I won't wait forever." He touched the brim of his hat, spun on his heel, and started off down the pavement.

Sophia shut the front door, pressed her forehead against the wood, and released a long exhale of relief.

"Is that enormous sigh because you've just met the man you plan to marry, or because you're glad he's gone?" Cate's perceptive question would have made Sophia laugh if not for the guilt she felt at acknowledging the answer.

"More the latter, I'm afraid," she said, turning to face Cate. "The good news is that you were right. I'm beginning to agree with you about the folly of choosing a husband from a newspaper ad." Sophia crossed her arms. "Tell me what you think of him."

"He seems no-nonsense, impatient, perhaps a bit bullish." Cate answered as if she'd anticipated Sophia's question and given a good deal of thought to the matter. "He knows his manners and has learned the social niceties, but I suspect he'd rather dispense with formalities."

"Not an appealing assessment."

Cate shook her head. "I find his all-business attitude admirable, but I can't detect any sign of the romantic in him."

With a shrug, she added, "All depends what you seek in a marriage, I suppose."

Trust, above all. Then mutual respect and admiration. She might never find the passionate variety of love Kit and Ophelia shared, years ago. But could she truly live her whole life without a scrap of romance?

Every encounter with Grey left her flushed and frustrated, yearning for something just out of reach, even as she told herself it was a mirage. Her first encounter with Ogilvy had simply left her uncertain.

"I should go up and write a note to thank him for his visit." Sophia retrieved her travel case from the front hall table and started for the stairs, eager to change out of the day dress she'd worn two days in a row.

"Was your trip to Cambridge a success?"

Sophia stopped on a middle step, fingers tense on the handrail. She knew Cate's curiosity couldn't be avoided for long. At least Kit and Ophelia weren't at home to add their questions to the chorus.

Before she could offer Cate any details of her adventure with Grey, two quick raps at the front door saved her from answering. Cate started down the hall, and Sophia continued up the stairs. After washing and changing, she'd be better equipped to answer Cate's questions. And hopefully a bit more clearheaded.

"Telegram for you," Cate called at the precise moment Sophia reached the top step.

"What does it say?" Her tired, overwrought mind spun a hundred dire scenarios fit for her detective story, and Sophia sent up a quick prayer the telegram contained no bad news regarding Kit or Clarissa.

Cate unfolded the thin cream slip of paper and read.

Change of plans. Headed to Derbyshire now. Hope to find L there. Ever grateful for your aid. G.

Cate tipped her gaze up at Sophia. "What will you do now?"

"Do?" Sophia frowned. "Change my gown, take some tea, eat my first decent meal in days. Lord Winship has made no request of me in that telegram."

Cate bowed her head as she folded the telegram and placed it into her apron pocket, but Sophia didn't miss her plumped cheeks and her mouth stretched in a grin.

"What?" Sophia propped a hand on her hip. "Clearly you disagree. Tell me why."

"The man took the time to send you a telegram for the express purpose of telling you the very place in England where you might find him." Cate sniffed and quirked an eyebrow. "An invitation if not an outright request, don't you think?"

Thinking had once been Sophia's strength. She'd always learned quickly and had often been the sole Ruthven family member to remain levelheaded when everyone else was in an emotional tumult. While Papa was shouting, Mama crying, and her brother sulking angrily in his room, Sophia never forgot to tuck Clary into bed with a kiss.

My sensible child, Father called her, and she'd cherished that bit of approval from him.

Apparently age didn't always bring greater wisdom. She felt anything but sensible now. Because as she stood looking down at Cate, she fought a completely impulsive urge. To follow Grey to Derbyshire, to offer whatever assistance she could in this leg of his journey to find his sister. Yet she knew to her bones that nothing could be more improper.

Returning Cate's expectant gaze, Sophia said, "At the very least I need a bath before deciding anything. Can you have hot water sent up?"

"So you are considering a trip to Derbyshire?"

"No." She was beginning to wonder if Cate was her advisor or the devil on her shoulder, encouraging her to chase every capricious whim.

"Derbyshire is quite close to Leicestershire, is it not? You could visit your sister at her ladies' college."

"A rational argument won't persuade me to do something completely ridiculous."

"Of course not," Cate agreed with a slow nod. "But you have been missing your sister, haven't you?"

She did miss Clary. More than she'd imagined she would, especially considering how her sister's rebellious nature clashed with Sophia's traditional—Clary would say rule-bound—attitudes. "If I go anywhere, it will be to Leicestershire. Not Derbyshire, mind you. I will have traveled more in the week than I have in my entire life."

"Should that not be counted a good thing? New experiences are excellent fodder for a writer's stories, are they not?"

"You're very convincing." Sophia couldn't help but grin. "If you ever tire of household management, you should consider a career as a barrister, Cate."

Chapter Fourteen

"I do love an investigation that takes me far afield. What is familiar becomes stale. New endeavors sharpen a detective's wits and powers of observation."

—Casebook of euphemia
breedlove, lady detective

Richard was there, just at the corner of his periphery. If he could only get to him. If he could only reach his side, he'd fight off the thugs. They couldn't truly mean to kill his brother. Impossible. Richard was indestructible. He was the heir, the one everyone prayed would make the Scandalous Stanhopes respectable again. Everyone needed Richard.

Now Richard needed him, and he couldn't fail this test.

"Ouch!" A girl's voice rang out like the sharp clang of church bells, waking Grey from the dream he'd dreamed a thousand times. "Watch yourself, sir."

Around him, the world tilted, and he clutched the edge of his seat to keep from falling. But he wasn't falling. He was waking on a moving train, dragging his mind up from dark memories hidden in the murky deep of the past.

Blinking hard to clear his gaze, he found himself staring into huge caramel brown eyes. The dark-haired young woman across from him snapped her mouth shut, as if she'd intended to continue with her chastisement but suddenly thought better of it. Between them, his legs were sprawled nearly to the edge of her knees, and he'd stuck out a booted foot, which was tangled in the pleated hem of her gown.

"You crushed my foot under yours," she said in a voice that was decidedly warmer than her initial shout, more coyness than offense. "What shall you do to make it up to me?"

Yes, definitely coy. Flirtatious even. Considering he hadn't had a woman in his bed in days, he should have been tempted. But he wasn't. The girl couldn't have been much older than Liddy.

She grimaced, as if shocked at her own brazen question.

For Grey's part, he was tired, achy, and eager to see the end of another train journey. Damnably, this one would end in Derbyshire, the place he'd been avoiding for a decade.

"I offer you my heartiest apologies, miss," he said, firing off a practiced grin and sitting up straight in his seat so that their legs were no longer in danger of tangling.

The young lady glanced at the train car door before leaning toward him. "Can't you offer anything more scandalous?"

Grey pinched the bridge of his nose and studied the girl's pale skin, silt brown hair, and eager eyes. With her pristine gloves and fashionably modest gown, she was the picture of feminine innocence. Yet above her buttoned-to-the-chin neckline, she gazed at him in breathless anticipation of mischief.

"I'm afraid I cannot." Grey shook his head. Honestly, he claimed no understanding of young women. He'd never bedded a virgin in his life. Indeed, he steered clear of women of propriety.

Like Sophia Ruthven.

At the thought of her, he shifted in his seat. Why couldn't he have awoken to find Sophia seated across from him? He wondered if he'd ever be able to embark on a train journey again without missing the sight of her perched on the opposite bench.

"Trust me, scandal is not as appealing as it seems." After growing up in a family endlessly sullied by the infidelities of his parents, he'd spun his own brand of outrage by abandoning his title to seek fame on the stage.

Despite the debaucheries he'd enjoyed, he couldn't recommend the stain of scandal to a young woman with her whole life ahead. For Liddy, he hoped for a better future. Their father insisted his sister's marriage to a powerful aristocrat would keep whispers of Stanhope scandals from following her into adulthood. Marrying well worked for his eldest sister, Olivia, who remained blissfully ensconced with her Scottish duke in a Dunkirk castle.

"Is it because I'm plain?" His train companion slumped against her cushioned bench, crossed her arms, and glared at him. "My sister's the pretty one. Gentlemen trip over themselves to compete for her attention, but nothing remotely exciting ever happens to me."

Had that been Liddy's motive too? The prospect of excitement, even if it led to social ruin? Derbyshire could be dreadfully quiet.

Before he could reassure the young lady, the train's whistle drew his attention. They couldn't be at the Derby station yet. Grey glanced out the window. Far down the line, he spotted a gathering of enormous ruddy brown cows. Though one perked an ear and turned its head at the whistle's screech, none of the beasts seemed inclined to abandon their spot on the tracks.

"Brace yourself," Grey urged as a series of high-pitched air whistles sounded again.

"For what?"

After the piercing screech of crushing metal, the train car jerked to a stop. The girl lurched toward his bench, and Grey positioned himself to blunt her fall. She cried out in pain as they crashed together. They held each other a moment, and then he released her gently, helping her back onto her bench.

Tears spilled over her cheeks.

"Are you all right?" Grey scanned the girl for any outward sign of injury.

"My arm and shoulder smart a bit, but I'm in one piece."

"You can move your arm all right?" Grey stood and handed the girl a handkerchief to wipe her eyes. She moved her arm gingerly as she gripped the square of cloth.

"Yes," she said, swiping at the dampness on her cheeks. When he started out of their train carriage, the young woman called out, "Where are you going?" Her crystal sharp voice took on a panicked note.

"To find out what's happened. I'll return shortly."

Grey proceeded down the train car hall. Cries, shouts, and grumbles were overrun by a terrible grinding squeal emerging from below the train car itself. Outside the windows, a billow of black smoke clouded his view.

A man in a conductor's uniform approached. "Are you injured, sir?"

"No, but it sounds as though others might be."

"We've already sent to the local village for a doctor. If you're able-bodied, we need assistance to disembark passengers."

"Here?" Grey hunched his shoulders and peeked out beyond the rising smoke. "In the middle of a field?"

" 'Fraid the train's not moving for a while. Seems we have a bad cylinder, and it will take time to check the cranks and line."

Grey could read Ovid in the original Latin, Sappho in Greek, and memorize lines for a play within a few hours' time, but the mechanics of locomotion were beyond his knowledge and interest. He did, however, know how to calm overwrought young women. Dozens thronged around the stage doors to see him after every performance.

"I'll help. Tell me what to do."

Nothing about Rothley Ladies College was as Sophia expected.

Kit and Ophelia had traveled with Clary to get her settled in, and their only descriptions on returning had been about the institution's admirable curriculum and fearsome headmistress. Having been educated at home, first by a governess and later by various tutors in art, music, and decorum, Sophia imagined a ladies' boarding school to be a place of strictures as forbidding as her father's. Dull uniforms and general drudgery. Now, she thought perhaps she was relying too much on visions of *Jane Eyre*'s Lowood School for expectations.

Filled with trees, Rothley's campus brimmed with carefully snipped box hedges and clusters of flowers around stone benches. On carved balustrades, dozens of female students sat or reclined in the sun with books in hand. The severity of the three-story main building was tempered by riots of ivy festooning every brick. From one of the windows, a beautiful harmony of voices lifted in song.

"You're here!" Clary shouted, her arms encircling Sophia from behind.

She patted her sister's clasped hands and smiled. "You'll have to let go so I can get a look at you."

One glance and Sophia could see that Clary had changed. Not in the measure of her exuberance or blinding smiles, but something in her face and eyes. A leanness she hadn't recalled, a maturity she hadn't expected.

Yet examining Clary from head to toe, much remained the same. Paint-splotched fingers, a flower tucked behind her ear, and ribbon rosettes decorating her school uniform. The bodice and skirt were a decidedly odd color. All the other young ladies dotting the campus wore a simple cream shirtwaist over a straight black skirt. Clary's blouse was a strange shade of pink on purple.

"It's mauve," she proudly announced. "I dyed it myself in chemistry class."

"You definitely stand out among your classmates." Clearly a few months at college hadn't hampered Clary's unique sense of style or her rebellious nature. Sophia had to admit there was a soothing appeal in the shade. If nothing else, the color set off Clary's violet eyes. "What does your teacher say?"

"What could she say? She's the one who taught us the formula." Clary clasped Sophia around the arm. "Come up to my dormitory where we can chat privately. The rest of my dorm sisters are at choir practice or the monthly tennis tournament."

Clutter was a gentle description of the chaos reigning in Clary's shared dormitory. Amid four spartan beds, lady residents had scattered books, sporting equipment, and clothing. An apparatus that had the air of a medieval torture device dominated an oval rug in the center of the room.

"Impressive, isn't it? One of my dorm mates has been working on that engineering project for weeks." Clary tidied as she spoke. After clearing books and empty teacups off a wingback chair, she wiped the seat clean with the edge of her sleeve. She gestured toward the chair proudly afterward. Sophia restrained a wince and took the chair.

"I would fully explain the mathematics of it all to you, but you know how despairingly I feel about mathematics."

None of the Ruthvens had ever been numerically inclined. Words were their domain. Even as a child, Sophia had kept a hidden box full of unfinished story starts under her bed, and Clary endlessly scribbled tales of fright and tragic romance, which she allowed no one to read. The few scraps Sophia had been able to get a glimpse of included mention of ghouls and misery. Despite her sunny disposition, Clary's artistic and reading tastes possessed a darker bent.

When she finally plopped down into a chair opposite Sophia, Clary let out an unladylike whoosh. "When Juliet gets old enough, we must convince her to come to Rothley too."

"I agree. She's not fond of London, but I suspect she'd feel at home here in the countryside." Their sister-in-law, Juliet, was a few years younger than Clary. Only her love for mathematics matched her disdain for social graces. Preferring the country, she resided with her aunt in Briar Heath. Juliet staunchly refused to relocate to London, but Rothley, nestled in the Leicestershire countryside, seemed a place she might flourish.

"Should I attempt to scare up some tea and biscuits? Later, I can speak to our headmistress about securing you a seat in the dining hall this evening."

"No need, my dear. I only came to see how you are. I've purchased a return to London on the afternoon train." Perhaps if she didn't stay long, saying good-bye wouldn't prove as gut-wrenching as the day Clary had first set off for college.

"Then we must be quick." Clary took up a pencil and paper, centering them on her lap. "Do you mind if I sketch you while listening to your stories of London and how ridiculously happy our newlywed brother is?"

"If you must." Sophia patted at the chignon at the back of her head, which had been infinitely tidier when she'd pinned it up early in the morning. "Should I move near the window to catch the light?"

"Not at all," Clary said as she began laying long vigorous strokes on the paper. "We've just the shadows needed for a true chiaroscuro sketch." When Sophia said nothing, Clary glanced up. "Go on. Tell me all I've missed."

Sophia cleared her throat and stared at the carpet under her feet, considering what to tell her sister and what to leave for another time. Ogilvy was best left out. No use giving Clary hope of another forthcoming family wedding. She didn't wish to give her little sister fodder with which to tease her mercilessly in the meanwhile. Mention of Grey seemed inappropriate too. He wanted his sister's disappearance to remain a private matter, just as Sophia preferred to conceal every example of her lack of restraint in the man's presence.

"My goodness," Clary said quietly. "What's happened? It must be awful. You've gone positively crimson." She set aside her art supplies and dropped off her chair to kneel in front of Sophia, gripping her hand as if she could save them both from blowing away.

A breeze would do quite nicely, Sophia thought, if only to cool the heat in her cheeks. None was to be had on this sunny summer day, though the tall dormitory windows had been left open wide.

"Nothing awful, I assure you. Don't fret." After patting her sister's hand reassuringly, she urged Clary back into her chair. "Kit and Phee are as you say. Happy. Incandescent most days. They departed for France on Friday and promise to send postcards as soon as they're able." Sophia scanned her memory for any other pleasant facts to share. "The new lady housekeeper I've hired has proven to be extraordinarily adept at her duties. I believe you'll like Mrs. Cole immensely."

After a moment of silence, Clary tipped her head, her eyes narrowed. "You're still very good at hiding, aren't you?"

"I don't know what you mean." But even as she denied the claim Sophia fought the urge to bolt and conceal herself from Clary's searching gaze.

"No matter the crisis or family squabble," Clary said as she began sketching again, intermittently glancing up. "I could always count on you to be calm. To be the sensible one. The strong one. But I always knew you were more volcano than mountain."

Sophia made a little harrumphing sound and flicked an invisible speck of lint from her skirt.

"So which is it, sister dear?" Hunched over her drawing, Clary's pencil stilled as she stared at Sophia. "That color in your face indicates you've done something you don't wish to confess. Since I can't imagine you doing anything truly horrible, it must be something slightly scandalous."

"Nonsense." Sophia longed for a bit of tea to clear the sudden dryness in her throat.

She'd spent so many years of her life striving to live up to their father's expectations. Even if it meant her life was quiet and cloistered. Or that she never ventured far from Briar Heath. Bad behavior was to be avoided. No exceptions.

Now she'd skirted scandal every day of the past week between her run-in with Lord Westby and her interactions with Lord Winship everywhere else.

"Is it a gentleman?" Clary set her drawing aside and leaned forward, one elbow braced on her knee as she perched her chin on her fist. "Or more than one gentleman? Now that truly would make for intrigue!" She edged forward, eyes dancing with amusement and the prospect of gossip.

Sophia swallowed against the lump that stuck in her throat like a bite of over dry scone. Aside from reassurances when their parents were at odds, Sophia had never lied to her sister. She loathed falsehood in others. Now she yearned for some easy prevarication to avoid telling Clary about Grey.

Wasn't it sufficient that the man hadn't left her thoughts since the day she'd met him?

"When I was a child, Kit used to tickle me until I confessed where I'd hidden all the boiled sweets." Clary slumped back and sighed. "I don't suppose that would work with you, so go ahead and tell me. Perhaps you'll feel better if you do. Right now you look like a balloon in need of bursting."

A volcano and now a balloon. If Clary was to have any success in society, she'd need to attempt more delicacy in her assessment of others. Never mind that she was unerringly correct. No one liked having someone hold a lamp to her distress.

"I'm considering marriage." Sophia rushed the words so that they nearly melded together into one. A bit like air bursting from an overstuffed balloon.

Eyes wide, mouth agape, Clary sat motionless for a moment, then rose from her chair and began pacing. "When? Who? Why have you shared none of this with me before now?" She stopped behind her chair, gripping the wooden frame. "I know you prefer to conceal emotion, but I'm your only sister. Should sisters not share such details with each other?"

The hurt in Clary's voice surprised Sophia.

"I'm sorry. Please come and sit, and I'll explain." When Clary resumed her seat, Sophia edged forward and took one of her sister's hands. "You're rushing ahead. I merely said I'm considering marriage, not that one is in the planning stages or even that a groom has been selected." She managed a wan smile. "Much is undecided. I only know that I wish to be settled. Kit and Phee have their home in London. Kit will wish to sell Ruthven House, as is his right. It's far too large for me to manage on my own. Why not begin planning for my own home?"

Clary knitted her brow. "So you wish for a home more than a husband? Shouldn't falling rapturously in love with a dashing gentleman come first?"

Clearly, despite her ladies' college curriculum, romance and high drama still formed a large part of Clary's reading material.

Sophia pressed her lips together. What was worst was that she'd once harbored romantic expectations like Clary's. When there were men like Jasper Grey in the world, how could a woman's thoughts not turn to passion? Yet he'd been the one to insist he was not a gentleman for whom any proper young lady should set her cap. Not that Sophia had. Or ever would. Temptation. That's what he'd called her. That's all he was. A tempting man.

"There is someone," Clary said past one of her beaming smiles. "You speak of practical choices, but being sensible wouldn't make you color as if you'd sat near the fire too long."

"It's a warm day."

"What's his name? Tell me that much at least."

"Timothy Ogilvy. Esquire," Sophia added. The honorarium seemed important to him and thus an affront to leave off.

One of Clary's brow arched up. "Impressive, I suppose. But there's more you're not saying. Your nose is twitching."

Clary peered closer, giving Sophia's face a disturbingly intense perusal. "And you have freckles," she whispered in a shocked tone. "I've known you for eighteen years, and I've never seen a single spot to mar that perfect skin of yours."

Sophia rolled her eyes and wished she'd taken Cate's lemon juice advice. "I went out in the sun without a hat. Hardly evidence of a crime."

Clary began circling her chair, assessing as she chewed her nail. Sophia stifled the urge to reprimand her younger sister as she'd spent so many years doing as her caretaker. Not that it had done much good. Clary, she feared, would always do precisely as she pleased.

Her sister's burning gaze made Sophia's skin itch. "Mr. Grey," she finally blurted out, just to make Clary's roving stop. "Kit's actor friend. I encountered him in London last week. Not purposely, of course. Quite unintentionally. But none of that matters. He's likely in Derbyshire now."

"How do you know?"

"He said so in a telegram."

Clary stopped in front of Sophia. "Why would he inform you where he's going?"

That was the question, wasn't it? One she'd been wrestling with since Cate read his telegraphed message aloud. "I'm not sure," she admitted, unable to come up with any reasonable guess.

"Perhaps it's an invitation." Clary sounded suspiciously like Cate. If she hadn't known better, she'd suspect the two were conspiring. "And what a coincidence. Here you are, less than fifty miles from Derbyshire."

"To see you."

"I'm thrilled you came to visit, but I don't believe in happenstance." Eyes fierce and wide, Clary said in a low tone, "I believe in fate."

A shiver chased down Sophia's spine, followed by a rush of heat that made her hot and itchy. One foot began drumming the floor. She couldn't imagine anything worse than fate. Some unseen power scheming to move people about like chess pieces. Father controlled them all with his rules and anger. To cope, she'd learned to comply, but she'd never enjoy being unable to make her own choices.

She was mistress of her own destiny now, right or wrong.

"I've never been to Derbyshire," she heard herself state pointlessly.

Clary's face lit with one of her infectious grins, dimples punctuating her mirth. "But now you're considering it?"

"I am." Relief accompanied the confession. Because after setting aside Father's rules and society's expectations, what Sophia truly wished was to finish what she'd started. From the moment she'd agreed to accompany Grey to Brighton, she'd come to care about his sister's fate. His quest to find her was Sophia's now too.

"You should go," Clary insisted brightly. "When will you travel so far north again?"

"Probably sooner than you think, since I do miss you."

"Me too." Clary sniffed as her eyes grew glassy. "Go to Derbyshire, Sophia. I can't leave Rothley until Michaelmas. You must go and have an adventure for us both."

Would it be an adventure or pure folly? Sophia's only certainty was the bubble of anticipation in her belly, the impulse to go. She stood and pulled her bodice down straight, swiping to arrange the pleats of her gown. "I'll need to exchange my ticket at the station."

"Yes!" Clary sprang from her chair and pulled Sophia into an embrace.

"I'm going to Derbyshire," she said, sealing her determination. The decision was more than impulse. She was taking Cate's advice and Clary's encouragement. She was following her instincts, like Effie Breedlove would.

CHAPTER FIFTEEN

Grey woke in a sweat and lifted his arm to block the blinding glare of light riding dust motes across his room above the coaching inn. He'd overslept, judging by the oven-like heat of the room and the unrelenting glare of the midday sun. Scents assailed him—sour beer, damp wool, roasting meat. Hunger stoked his belly into a series of rumbles, but they were nothing to the drumbeat in his head.

The swelling in his left temple had eased, but the spot was still tender to the touch.

Worse than the train's sudden halt was the fact that it hadn't moved again, and they'd forced passengers to disembark in a small village near the county border with Derbyshire. A few determined travelers hired coaches to the nearby city of Derby. A handful took to the fields and baked in the late afternoon sun while the train and rail were checked for damage. The rest fanned out on foot into the village of Beeston, seeking shelter for the night.

Grey chose to join the last group and was lucky to secure a room at the Seven Winds. Their ale was dark and stout, their victuals hot, and the rooms were spacious and comfortable, despite the scratchy woolen blanket covering his body.

When he plopped his head on the lumpy pillow, a familiar scent wafted up, and he clenched his fingers on the blanket. Lavender. All the bedding smelled of the flower's essence. He'd fallen asleep plagued by Sophia's scent, and now the aroma was a reminder of her absence.

No, not her absence. That implied she belonged here with him or had left some emptiness behind. Ridiculous. She'd gone back to her life, and he would return to his.

He simply wasn't used to waking in a bed alone. When he did, he was used to regretting the absence of soft, warm feminine curves pressed against his body. But this morning he missed Sophia Ruthven, and that was unsettling. Frightening. Far too specific, especially considering the tenacity of his longing for the woman. In a few short days, she'd cast a spell, snared a man she considered the worst sort of scoundrel. And so he was, but still he wanted her. Perhaps the more so because he shouldn't.

"Mr. Grey?" a young woman's voice, soft and sweet, carried past the booming in his head. "Coffee, sir?"

"God, yes," he called, but his voice emerged on a hoarse squawk.

He surged from the low bedstead, pulling the blanket along to cover the essential parts of his anatomy. Gripping the wooden latch, he swung the door open and the innkeeper's daughter's jaw dropped to her chin.

"Coffee?" she squeaked as her gaze wandered to his waist.

"You're a true heroine," Grey told her, retrieving a steaming mug from her laden tray. "Thank you."

She nodded as he swung the door shut. He settled on the bed's edge and let the dark bitter coffee shock his brain into wakefulness. Beyond the inn's window he glimpsed a copse of trees and a flat field beyond. That way lay Longcross, and nothing in him wanted to face either the estate or the memories it housed. A decade had passed since he'd spoken to his father, longer since he'd seen his mother. As far as he knew, she was still living in France. After Richard's death, his parents had gradually given up on maintaining the pretense of a contented marriage and parted ways. Grey hadn't kept in close enough touch to know if his mother had ever returned from the continent.

The estate lay north of Derby. As a youth, he might have crossed the distance in a day of countryside rambles. Now he decided the best strategy was to head to the train station, where he could both check to see if Becca had responded to the telegram he'd sent the previous night and hire a carriage to take him to Longcross.

He dressed quickly and started for the station without bothering to draw a razor across his jaw. Hours had already been lost.

The Derby station was surprisingly busy, and he queued impatiently before reaching a telegraph operator. The man searched a series of wooden cubby holes in an enormous cupboard running the length of his office. When his finger paused at the edge of a stuffed box, Grey held his breath. "We do have one here for you, sir."

Hands shaking, Grey unfolded the crepe-thin paper. His heart began thrashing behind his ribs as he read.

Liddy has returned but not to Longcross. Still reason for concern. Come at once. Becca.

He needed more coffee or a finger of stiff scotch. His knees felt as solid as jelly but relief made him consider embracing the dour man standing behind the telegraph counter. Instead, he offered him a crown and set off in search of a carriage.

A train had just pulled up to the platform, its smoke stack puffing white plumes that obscured his view. He glanced down at Becca's telegram again. How could Liddy have returned but not to Longcross? Another mystery to solve, apparently. Becca had him intrigued, but whatever "concerns" remained regarding his sister could be conquered. She was safe and at home in Derbyshire. That was the essential fact.

More important, it meant he could soon return to his life. To the den of iniquity he called his London townhouse, to the stage, where he rarely failed.

Casting a gaze toward the front of the station, he spotted a few carriages where passengers were loading their luggage before the conveyances rolled away. One coachman lounged against the side of his rig smoking a pipe. Grey beelined for the man.

"Already promised," he growled as Grey approached.

"Ah, but are you persuadable, sir?" Luckily, he'd brought along all the cash he usually kept stashed in his London townhouse.

"Did you not hear me? Promised my coach to a lady." The man sniffed, and his eyes widened when Grey removed a shiny crown coin from his pocket. "Might've agreed if it were another gentleman, but I can't leave the lady stuck at the station on a blazing day." The man stepped forward, dangling a wrinkled hand over Grey's coin. "Tell you what. I'll deliver the lady and return for you sharpish. Will that do, sir?"

With a sweeping look around the other packed carriages, Grey had to agree. "Suppose it will have to do." But his usual inclination toward impatience sparked another possibility. "Where is the lady who's hired you? Perhaps we could share your coach." Unless the woman was traveling with a brood of children, he suspected she and he could abide comfortably in the confines of the rig without brushing shoulders.

"Said she needed to send a message to London." The coachman pointed a crooked finger toward the station office. "Here the lassie comes now."

A weight pressed on Grey's chest, and he struggled to breathe.

Sophia.

What am I doing?

Sophia couldn't locate Grey's ancestral home on a map of Derbyshire. Not that she'd had sufficient foresight to consult such a document before setting off on her journey. She'd have to rely on her coachman for directions. He seemed an able man. Though her judgement may have been based on hope over reason. She wasn't sure her discernment counted for much at all anymore.

Hours ago, in Clary's dormitory, coming to Derbyshire seemed an exceedingly logical end to an endeavor she'd committed to days before. The sort of adventure she'd long denied herself. Now, as she stood at a train station in the midlands of England, her plan seemed fragile and flimsy at best.

Calling in at an aristocrat's home without an invitation? How had that ever seemed like a good idea?

Her impulsivity was beginning to verge on frightening. From Clary, she expected such recklessness. But Sophia had always valued checking off lists, a carefully set table, clothes that fit to perfection, gardens planted in neat rows. *A place for everything, and everything in its place.* She'd stitched it once during needlepoint lessons with her governess.

Now it seemed the sensible nature she'd always relied on had derailed, and she was careening into chaos.

Cate urged her to send word when she arrived safely, and she'd at least accomplished that sensible task by sending a telegram at the station office. As she studied the dusty path beneath her feet and approached the coachman she'd hired to take her to Longcross, she weighed her choices. This was the last chance to decide whether to go or turn back.

"Sophia."

Lifting her head, she spotted him instantly. He stood out like a beacon; a tall, cool spectacle of male beauty in a cluster of dusty travelers fanning themselves with folded train timetables. His buff linen trousers and waistcoat hugged his thighs and chest, both wrinkled but fashionably cut. His hair glinted like polished bronze in the scorching sun, but it was his grin that left her speechless.

He started toward her, slowly at first and then so quickly his hair riffled in the breeze. His mouth ebbed up as he approached, bursting into a brilliant smile. A few steps away from her, he lifted his arms, the start of an embrace.

"I received your telegram." Her words stopped him short, pinning him in place.

"And you came." He thrust his hands in his pockets as if he wasn't quite sure what to do with them.

"Is my arrival very awkward?"

Grey dipped his head and examined the ground between his feet. "Not the word I'd choose." He took one step forward as he caught her gaze again.

"What then?" She edged forward, closing the single footstep of distance between them. She had to know if she'd made an utter fool of herself. Squinting up at him, she offered suggestions. "Rude? Brazen? Impertinent?"

"Serendipitous." His hand shot out, and he cupped her elbow, drawing her an inch closer. For an endless moment he simply took her in, brushing his gaze over her hair, her hat, each feature of her face, and then settling on her mouth. His perusal stoked a humming in her veins.

Sophie was grateful for her long sleeves to hide the goosebumps dotting her arms, but, for once, she had no wish to turn away. To hide from the giddiness he might read in her eyes, the eagerness in her expression. Seeing him reminded her why she'd come. Glimpsing the relief in his eyes swept away all doubt that coming had been the right course.

"Thank you," he said, bending to brush his lips against her cheek.

Her knees locked, and a primal pulse began low in her belly. "Why serendipitous?" she whispered in his ear.

A soft rumbling chuckle emerged from the firm chest a hairsbreadth from her own. "Must there always be a reason?" He slid a hand to her back and raised his head to stare down at her. Amusement teased at the corners of his mouth.

"Of course. There is always a reason."

"And you will always be determined to investigate the facts, ever-curious Sophia?" He was holding her now, both arms wrapped lightly around her waist. Despite the warm day, the heat of his touch felt good. Reassuring. If not proper, then impossibly...right.

"Probably."

"Will you be wanting the carriage or not?" The coachman had finished with his pipe. He stood watching them with his thumbs hooked in the pockets of his trousers.

"I hired him to take me to Longcross," Sophia admitted.

"I tried to do the same, but he insisted on loyalty to you. Shall we set off?" Grey took her hand, wrapping it gently in the crook of his arm. He bent to retrieve her traveling satchel, and the coachman picked up his larger case. As they headed toward the carriage, Sophia sensed tension rippling off him—a tightness in the way he held her arm and the firm line of his jaw.

"You're not looking forward to returning home?"

"Dreading the prospect." The closer they got to the carriage, the tighter his grip. "That's why your presence is serendipitous," he said as he helped her up. "Before I looked across the station and saw your face, I was considering any excuse to delay my arrival." He took the bench across from her. The carriage's narrow interior pinned their legs side by side. "Your arrival has given me a reason to go."

She wondered if he could hear the clamor of her thumping heartbeat. "And Lady Phyllida?" Discovering the young lady's fate was the rational, logical reason she'd come.

"She's safe, but apparently not at Longcross. Another conundrum to solve." He rapped on the side of the carriage to signal the driver to proceed. "Luckily, I'll have your sleuthing skills to assist me."

The moment the carriage rolled into motion, Sophia's belly began to cartwheel. Grey's discomfort at the prospect of visiting his family's estate didn't bode well. From every point of propriety, she had no business accompanying an unmarried man. "What will you tell them?"

She caught him staring at her mouth, and he glanced up guiltily.

"Tell who?"

"Your family, the servants, anyone at Longcross who wishes to know why I am arriving with you."

He lifted his broad shoulders in a languid shrug. "Whatever you wish me to tell them. As much or as little as you like."

"You intend to lie."

"Actor. Remember? I have a talent for deception." He drew in a deep breath. "My cousin's wife, Becca, will be glad of your company, I assure you. Country life can be lonely and limiting." He frowned as realization dawned and leaned forward. "I'm sorry, Sophia. I didn't mean—"

"What you say is true." No one had to remind her how cloistering life in a small village could be. "I prefer when you tell me the truth."

He burst into a wicked laugh that resonated through her chest and settled at the pinnacle of her thighs. "If I told you the truth of what I'm thinking when you're near, you'd never travel alone in a carriage with me again."

She recognized his tease for the temptation he offered. Though she longed to know precisely what he thought of her, there was something else she wished to know first. "Why do you dread returning home?"

He turned to watch the passing countryside though the carriage window. When he gazed back, his eyes had hardened to metal gray under his thick ebony lashes. "If only we had a pint of ale between us and could play questions again."

"I never told you about the rest of the game." She'd learned the rules from her brother as a child. "If you refuse to answer a question, the other player may issue a command."

Grey leaned toward her, edging forward until her knees were caught between his. He placed his palms on the bench on either side of her thighs, where her hands rested on the upholstery. "How would you command me, Sophia?" As her blood thrashed in her ears, he lifted a thumb to stroke the edge of her hand. "What would you demand of me here, where no one else can see us?"

"A kiss?" She wanted more than a kiss. Wanted that moment in the Eagle and Stag back, when he was gloriously bare and pressed against her. Wished she'd been braver at that moment and given in to the temptation burning her up from the inside.

Why cling to propriety when she might spend the rest of her days a spinster?

"You need only ask, sweetheart." He covered her hands with his, edged closer until his mouth was inches from hers. "I'm yours to command."

"Kiss m—"

He took her mouth. Reached up to stroke her cheek, her neck, sliding his fingertips into her hairline.

Sophia reached for him too, clutching at his shoulder, tangling her hand in his hair. The short soft waves sifted through her fingers. When she pulled him nearer, teased at his tongue with her own, he emitted a low growl that fired her blood. She reached down for the open neck of his shirt and slipped the top button free, then the next, snaking her hand inside to feel the heated muscle beneath. He flexed under her touch, but she wanted more. All of him, to see every part of the man behind the masks he wore.

"Sophia," he said when she retreated to catch her breath, his voice hoarse and reverent. "Do you know how much I want you?"

Shaking her head, she busied herself freeing another button on his shirt, then lowered her head to taste his skin. Salt and heat and bay-scented male flavored her tongue, and Grey hissed as his fingers tightened in her hair. She kissed another inch of his skin, then another, finding a scar that stretched from his upper chest to the muscled bulge of his shoulder. She traced the line with her finger, then with her mouth.

"Stop." He cupped her face between his palms to hold her still. A moment later he released her, and Sophia scooted away, flattening herself against her carriage bench. Breathless and aching, she felt the heat of mortification scorching her cheeks.

"I'm sor—"

Grey pressed a finger to her bee-stung lips. "Don't you dare apologize. You did everything right, and I'm a greedy man. I want your passion, sweetheart." He swallowed hard and lowered his finger. Dropping a hand to her knee, he said, "I want *you*." His face lit in a sensual grin. "We were moments away from you finding out how much."

"You presume I would let you do more than kiss me." The snipe was born of frazzled nerves and wounded pride. They both knew she was no longer the proper woman she'd long attempted to be.

"Who's refusing to tell the truth now?" He rubbed gently at her leg, causing her skirt to ride above the edge of her boot. Grey took advantage, slipping his hand down to stroke at her stockinged leg before dragging his fingers up the back of her calf. "When I make love to you, I intend to do so properly." Slipping his hand under her skirt, he stroked higher. "To take my time. To pleasure you until you scream my name."

"You mistake me for one of the ladies clamoring for you outside the stage door." In complete contradiction to her words, she parted her knees to ease his way.

"Never." He stilled at the top edge of her stocking before dragging his fingers across the skin of her bare thigh, just at the lacy edge of her drawers. "I see you, Sophia. I know who you are behind that unforgiving corset and all those damned buttons."

"Grey." Sophia hissed his name because she sensed they were on an edge from which there was no turning back.

He withdrew his hand slowly, then resettled the folds of her gown over her legs. "You can't hide from me behind your father's rules. I don't want you to."

When she could think again, when the throbbing need in her body eased, she looked over, where he sat hunched and tense across from her. "But you'll continue to hide?"

Lightning fast, he reached for her hand, pressed her palm flat against his chest. "I can't hide this." Under her palm, his heart thrashed wildly. "Nor this." He moved her hand down to hover near his groin. Her fingers grazed the stiff ridge of his arousal.

When he released her, she snatched her hand back and pressed it to the upholstery. "Many women spark that reaction in you, I'm sure."

"Not like you do." He crossed his arms, turned his face toward the carriage window. She thought perhaps he'd told her the absolute truth. She yearned for his claim to be true. To believe that somehow she, a cold country spinster, could tempt a scoundrel as no other woman ever had.

At the moment her heartbeat began to settle back into its natural rhythm, and the carriage made a sharp turn. The crunch of pebbles indicated they'd turned off the road into a private drive.

"There it is," Grey said in an ominous murmur as he dipped his body toward the window to peer beyond. "Longcross."

CHAPTER SIXTEEN

"*I take especial care not to judge a case or a suspect too quickly. When a solution seems simple, I dig deeper.*"

—CASEBOOK OF EUPHEMIA
BREEDLOVE, LADY DETECTIVE

Sophia's gasp was what he'd come to expect when visitors got their first glimpse of the Stanhope estate.

Grey peered out the window and stifled his own nervous inhale. Not because he felt any sense of awe in response to the house's sumptuous grandeur. Nor because the building housed only miserable memories. Until Richard's death, he'd found his share of happiness as a child, despite his parent's marital scandals. He'd been luckier than his siblings. No one ever expected much of the Stanhope spare.

His reaction to Longcross centered on the moment when everything changed. When the estate became not a luxurious stomping grounds but a mausoleum to the tragedy he'd caused. A moment he'd given anything to reverse. A nightmare he'd gladly strike from his memory if he could.

"It's extraordinary." Sophia pressed to the carriage glass with childlike eagerness. Watching her, remembering the silken texture of her cheek, studying the elegant bones of her beautiful face, gave him ease. Her nearness tempered the queasiness in his gut, stayed his urge to bolt. To get out. To flee this bloody moving box and go back to the life he'd made.

In a matter of hours, he could catch a train to London, buy a bottle, and find a willing woman. Lose himself in sex and indulgence.

"All those windows," she said on an awestruck breath. "Twenty-six windows on the front facade alone."

"Twenty-four panes in every window," he conveyed with no enthusiasm, reciting details drilled in as a child.

"You must have an army of servants."

"The Stanhopes have always measured their worth by the size of their houses and the multitude of their staff." He couldn't bring himself to claim the pile, no matter how appealing. He stared vacantly at the endless swath of emerald lawn hugging every edge of the house, blinked as waning sunlight glinted off gilded pediments above each window. Not even the majestic bronze horses charging up from the enormous fountain sparked a hint of interest, despite how they'd fascinated him as a child.

More than the house, or his father ailing inside its walls, what he truly couldn't bear to face was the responsibility for Longcross. Soon, it would be his alone.

"I'm not dressed well enough to enter those doors."

"You're perfect." The sight of her made his mouth water. Not only because he wanted her desperately but for the pure pleasure of having her close. Her sweet scent and good sense seemed essential if he was going to step from the carriage and through Longcross's elaborately carved front door.

Sophia turned from the window, eyes brightened by the sun. "Is that how you seduce all women? Compliments and exaggeration?"

"In fairness, I haven't seduced *all* women." He hated to admit to her how little he worked at seduction. His style was short on words. More a matter of heated glances, the entice-ment of a touch, a stolen kiss filled with promise.

"But you wish to seduce me?" She swiped a hand across her sleeve, straightening the seam, as if that action was much more vital than meeting his eyes.

He caught her nervous hand and sensed a little tremor along her skin. Bringing her fingers to his mouth, he kissed the back of each, touching the tip of his tongue to the last. "I'd prefer we seduced each other."

She drew in a ragged breath that lifted her bosom, and he wished, as he'd hadn't wished for anything in years, that they were alone in that shabby room above the Eagle and Stag. That he had time to undress her slowly and dispose of every doubt and pretense and strip of clothing between them.

"One more kiss, Sophia?"

She pressed a hand to his chest to keep him at bay and glanced nervously out the window. Longcross loomed nearer. "I don't think we should."

"Please." He released her hand, stared at the floor of the carriage, and clenched a fist against the upholstered bench below him. He'd never pleaded for a woman's affection in his life.

She cupped a palm against his cheek. Bending forward, she pressed her lush strawberry mouth to his. A gentle kiss, full of tenderness, sweetened by the stroke of her fingers along his jaw. When she pulled away, the heat of her gaze quelled his unease.

A moment later the carriage jerked to a stop in front of Longcross. Sophia sat back and waited patiently for the coachman to unload their luggage.

As Grey handed her down, she said, "Perhaps we should tell your cousin and his wife that I am an acquaintance of Liddy's." Explaining her presence still worried her, but he was simply grateful to have her by his side.

"We should tell Becca the truth, at least."

"What is the truth?" she asked as he approached the house's tall oak door.

Grey turned back. "That you're the sister of a friend and have assisted in my search for Liddy." *That I need you here.*

After a moment, she nodded and joined him on the threshold, glancing at him expectantly. Tension rode his shoulders, tightened his neck. He looked down into Sophia's sea foam gaze and drew in a sharp breath, catching her clean lavender scent on the breeze. "Prepare yourself," he warned. "The entry hall can be a bit overwhelming."

He almost grinned when lines of confusion knitted the silken arch of her brows. Before he could explain, the door swung open with a heavy groan, and Blessing strode forward.

"Lord Winship," the hoary older man pronounced, as if he was not a bit surprised to find the heir of Stanhope on the doorstep after ten years' absence. "My lady." He offered Sophia a curt bow. The man was much like Grey's father. Always a soft spot for the ladies. Shuffling back, he urged them inside and then squinted at their two bags. "Is this all you've brought, my lord?"

"The large one's mine," Grey said defensively, immediately back in the role of child at Blessing's judgmental commentary.

"Welcome to you both." Becca's voice echoed off the high-ceilinged entry hall. "Blessing, have one of the maids take the young lady's bag up and prepare a guest room." She'd never been intimidated by the tall, domineering man in the least. The butler immediately snapped into action, casting Sophia one more appreciative glance before directing a footman to retrieve their bags.

"Come in so we can shut out that heat." Becca waved them into the foyer, gave Grey a brief hug, and then offered her hand to Sophia.

"Becca, may I introduce Sophia Ruthven. Sophia, Lady Rebecca Fennston, my cousin's very capable wife. She has the run of Longcross, and I suspect the entire estate is better for her guidance."

"Pleased to meet you, Miss Ruthven."

As the two exchanged niceties, Grey strode through the carved wooden arch that led to the house's multistory main hall and stopped to take in the familiar display. A renowned Italian artist had been employed to paint a spectacular bacchanalian fresco full of fleshy bodies on the ceiling and upper walls. Gilt had been plentifully applied to stairwells, railings, and cornices around the room, and the bold black-and-white checkerboard tile floor had always made him dizzy.

"Oh my," Sophia said on a breath as she came up next to him, tipping her head this way and that to take in the frescos, art, and tapestries. Which was exactly what the wealth had been spent for in the first place. To catch the eye, to mesmerize. To blind visitors with beauty, so they'd forget all the petty hurts and unforgivable infidelities committed within the house's walls.

He longed to reach for Sophia's hand, to offer her reassurance as much as to steel his own resolve.

Heavy footsteps sounded on the polished tile. Grey's body tensed, ready for a fight, expecting his father to come barreling around the corner. But it couldn't be Father. Somewhere up above, in his parent's palatial suite, the man was dying.

"Liddy?" A young man's hopeful voice called out.

Grey pivoted toward the sound, and the world went red. He lunged past Sophia, heard her cry out. Then nothing more. Just the gush of blood in his ears as he wrapped his hands around Clive Holden's neck.

"Jasper, no!" Becca's shriek filtered past his rage.

Holden's pale skin began to mottle in shades of crimson and purple as the man clawed at Grey's hands.

"Grey." A firmer voice, resonant and warm. "Please," Sophia pleaded as she laid her hand on his arm, gentleness against the violent contraction of his muscles as he choked the life out of his former school friend.

He loosened his hold before shoving Clive away. The man pinwheeled toward the wall, clutching at his throat, gasping for air. A maid and two footmen gathered nearby, whispering nervously.

"Have a tea service sent to the yellow drawing room," Becca instructed as she took Sophia's arm and led her away.

"Shall we send for a doctor, my lady?" one of the maids squeaked.

"No," Clive rasped. "Not necessary." He stared wild-eyed at Grey. "Winship, you must allow me to explain."

Grey nudged his chin toward the drawing room, indicating Holden should precede him. He didn't trust the bastard at his back.

The ladies had taken seats on adjacent settees. Grey couldn't sit. Couldn't stop pacing. Furious energy rattled through his body, and he gripped the cool marble of the fireplace mantel to steady himself.

Glancing up, he sought Sophia's gaze. She watched him worriedly as a maid wheeled a tea trolley into the room. Becca began pouring tea and distributing plates of biscuits and finger sandwiches. So civilized. So perfectly proper. So oblivious to the murderous impulse still bubbling in his blood.

Once they were all served and the room fell silent but for the clink of teaspoons on porcelain, Grey clenched the marble until his knuckles paled and demanded, "Explain yourself. Use as few words as possible. My patience has run thin."

"Mr. Holden only meant—" Becca began.

"No!" *Breathe, man. Control yourself.* "Forgive me, Becca, but I must hear from Clive. He is the rotter who led Miss Ruthven and me on a merry chase from Brighton to Cambridge."

Becca harrumphed and fussed with the cuff of her gown, muttering, "If you wished to hear from him, perhaps you shouldn't have strangled him."

Clive cleared his throat. "Liddy swore me to secrecy."

"You're blaming my sister?" Grey couldn't stop the seething. The urge to silence the man overwhelmed him, despite how much he needed to know why Liddy fled to London in the first place.

"I think we should allow him to finish," Sophia said quietly.

Grey nodded at her and then managed to force his tense body into motion, joining her on the settee.

"When she came to London," Clive continued, "I hadn't seen your sister in years. She'd grown so much, become a vibrant, intelligent young woman. And I became completely besotted. An utter love-struck fool." Clive dropped his head in his hands before looking up again. "I thought she cared for me too. I planned to ask for her hand in marriage. I didn't know he'd already seduced her."

"Who?" Grey barked, edging forward. He needed a target for the storm raging inside.

"Lord Westby," Sophia murmured under her breath.

Becca's eyes widened, and Clive gave a sharp nod.

"You knew?" Grey managed past his clenched jaw. Everyone else could keep secrets from him, but he couldn't stomach falsehood from Sophia.

"No," she insisted. "Just intuition based on my own…encounter with the earl. Logically speaking, Mr. Holden seemed a much more obvious suspect."

Clive grimaced and lifted his hands. "I only lied to protect Liddy."

At that moment, Grey would have happily throttled Holden and Westby both, at the same time, one neck squeezed in each fist.

"Why Cambridge?" Sophia asked. "And where is Lady Phyllida now?"

"With my aunt," Becca said as she stood to refill her teacup.

"The same aunt," Grey cut in, "who was supposed to serve as chaperone in London but allowed her to slip away?"

"Lady Fennston's aunt isn't to blame." Holden's voice had returned to its usual mellow pitch. "Liddy is clever. And determined to do precisely as she pleases." His face pinched in a sad grin, as if he admired her tenacity, no matter how much heartache she'd caused him. "She went to Cambridge in the hope Westby would join her there. Elope with her to Scotland. He said as much, apparently, but I suspect it was merely a ruse to get her away from London. She'd begun to become a nuisance, you see. Expecting more than he ever intended to give."

"And you retrieved her from Cambridge and brought her home?" Sophia, as Grey had come to expect, was doing an excellent job of sorting out the facts. Her steady voice was also working wonders at calming his wrath. A bit.

"Yes, but she refused to return to Longcross. She insisted on going to Lady Fennston's aunt's cottage on the Hartley estate."

Grey worked to moderate his breathing as he studied Sophia sipping daintily at her tea. He memorized the striking curves and angles of her profile, gilded in the waning afternoon light. Her hair, her skin, even her gown had taken on a golden cast.

"Why wouldn't she wish to come home?" she asked softly.

Grey could name a dozen reasons. Perhaps Becca understood too because she remained quiet.

Holden glanced at each of them in turn. "She feared that perhaps she is…" He paused and caught Becca's gaze, only continuing when she offered him a minute nod. "She fears she is with child." Holden stood and took a single step toward Grey. "No matter her circumstances, Winship, I wish to marry Liddy." He bowed his head and let out a weary sigh. "But I've yet to convince her."

"You've also yet to receive the blessing of this family." A begrudging kernel of respect for Holden and his commitment to Liddy was lingering somewhere inside of Grey, but a ruddy haze of anger still dominated. The man led him on a wild goose chase when he might have confessed all of this in Brighton.

"Jasper." Rebecca's voice held that tone. The motherly, chastising tone he'd always loathed. "I'll go and speak to Phyllida again," she said more gently. "Perhaps you could accompany me, Miss Ruthven. We are both fond of your *New Ruthven Rules for Young Ladies*."

Grey snorted. For all the good those rules had done Liddy. Standing, he immediately felt heavier, more burdened, for stepping away from Sophia. She provided a sense of calm more quickly than any liquor he'd ever consumed. And he was quite sure he'd tried them all.

"We must convince Liddy to come home," he announced. "Whatever dilemma she's facing, let her be at Longcross. I won't have her exiled from her family."

Becca's gaze shot to his, and Grey stared back. He, better than anyone, understood the hypocrisy of his words. He couldn't blame his sister for following the example provided by their parents. Not to mention his own debauched lifestyle. None of them had protected her as they should have.

"Once I know she's safe," he added, "I'll go to London and confront Westby."

"You needn't go to London." Clive ran a shaky hand through his guinea-gold hair. "He is due to arrive in Derbyshire for the opening of the hunting season."

"She's determined to challenge him at the Westby masquerade ball," Becca added. "If we can't dissuade her, Alistair must be told." She pinched the bridge of her nose. Grey didn't look forward to informing his cousin of the debacle either. The man was always more eager to condemn than sympathize. "If Liddy plans to make a scene, he must be forewarned."

"She says Lord Fennston will send her away to a nunnery," Clive protested. "I won't allow that."

"And will your father allow you to marry a young lady who's carrying another man's child?" Becca shot back. "Being an earl's daughter won't atone for that sort of scandal."

"If we marry soon, no one need ever know."

A drumbeat began pounding behind Grey's eyes. The quest to find Liddy had derailed his own life, but the pursuit had been a simple and singular one. A narrow tunnel, with his sister safe and well and home at Longcross at the end of his efforts. Now it seemed that finding her unraveled a single knot only to reveal a dozen more.

He glanced at Sophia.

She tugged at the edge of her lip with her teeth. Light flickered behind her eyes, as if that cunning mind of hers was churning.

"What do you think we should do?" His question drew everyone's gaze to Sophia.

"I favor honesty in all undertakings." She set her teacup aside and stood, facing Grey. "But surely your family should decide these matters."

"I want your opinion."

"Very well." She nodded at Becca, who returned a tight grin. "Persuading Lady Phyllida to return home seems a fine idea. But most of all, I hope she'll be convinced to cease her pursuit of Lord Westby. Despite his title, he's no gentleman. The man is"—she gazed guiltily into Grey's eyes—"a scoundrel."

She spoke of Westby, but the sentiments struck with the precision of a prize fighter's blows. A fist to the gut, all accomplished with five softly spoken words.

He knew what he was. He'd spent years celebrating his dissipation. But he'd been different with Sophia. Held back when he wanted to take her, refrained when she looked at him with fire in her eyes.

Her words were a reminder of who he was. Of how she'd always see him. Dishonorable. Not a gentleman. Just a scoundrel.

The room had fallen silent as the others watched him, waiting for him to scoff or crumble.

His father's voice played in his head. *"Love is a snare, boy. A tempting trap. Take my advice, and never allow yourself to be caught in its web."*

But this wasn't love. This was lust. Sophia's compelling beauty and repressed sensuality presented an enticing challenge. Nothing more. The woman had an odd calming effect on his overwrought nature, but so did liquor, if he drank enough of it.

He did not love Sophia Ruthven. She represented everything he wished to avoid. Prudery. Propriety. Virginal innocence.

Half the times he'd touched her, she'd retreated. Perhaps whatever glimpses he'd seen of her passion would always be constrained by her father's rules.

She looked at him and saw a bounder. No better than Westby. Perhaps she was right. His and Westby's piles of sins would stack up to the sky. But on one certainty he would never waver. He was not and never would be an honorable man. Honorable men lost their lives for fools like him.

Twisting on his heel, he turned his back on all of them. Strode from the drawing room as they shouted his name. Kept going until he'd passed through the front door, crossed the carriage drive, and felt his boot heels sink into the cushion of lawn on the west side of the house.

He needed to think. To escape the scents of lavender and Longcross and that disappointed shadow in Sophia's eyes.

Chapter Seventeen

Sophia sat up in bed and rubbed her eyes, uncertain if a sound had woken her or the racing thoughts she'd sifted for hours before falling asleep.

A few embers still burned in the fireplace across the room, giving off an intermittent glow, but the spacious suite had grown cold. She waited, listening for any repetition of whatever noise might have broken through her fitful sleep. Only the normal creaks and groans of the enormous house replied.

Edging back against the headboard, she pulled the counterpane up to her chin and surveyed the bedroom suite a Stanhope maid had led her to once it became clear Grey wouldn't return after storming from the drawing room.

The jade silk wallpaper shimmered in the faint firelight, not to be undone by the excessive application of gilt on furniture edges, drawer knobs, and the mermaids carved into the fireplace mantle. Everything about Longcross announced the family's wealth and love of comfort. She'd encountered no unpolished or cushionless surfaces.

For all the apprehension Grey expressed about coming to this place, the house reminded Sophia of him. There was a sultry sort of unapologetic beauty about every inch of the estate. Not that she'd explored very far. After being installed in her room and hanging her single change of clothes in the suite's connecting dressing room, she'd taken up the pages of her novel. Effie had discovered another clue, the one that would eventually lead her to solve the mystery. Sophia had reviewed old words, made a few changes, but had been unable to write anything new.

Concentrating on writing proved impossible when Grey's wounded expression haunted her.

She hadn't meant to injure him. Only to speak the truth about Westby. Too late, she realized the words cut both ways.

Hours ago they'd been kissing in a carriage. Now she suspected he wanted nothing so much as to find her gone from his home whenever he decided to return. She planned to leave on the first morning train if she could find a coachman willing to transport her to the station.

A voice sounded in the silence, and Sophia snapped her gaze toward the door.

"Please." The single word rang clear. A man's voice, deep but faint, as if echoing from many rooms away. Then louder. "Someone, please."

Slipping from bed, Sophia grabbed the heavy brocade dressing gown a maid had provided after fetching buckets of warm water for her bath. She eased the bedroom door latch gently, trying not to make a sound.

Gaslight sconces lined the dark wood-paneled hall. They'd been turned low but seemed bright after the darkness of her room.

"Please," the man repeated. A mournful, needy cry.

Sophia moved toward the sound, tiptoeing past room after room until she reached a set of double doors at the end of the hall. She pressed her ear to the wood and heard movement, the creak of bedsprings and heavy breathing interspersed with the distinct sound of a man moaning, quietly, miserably, muttering to himself.

If there were a bell pull nearby, she would have given it a tug. As it was, she detected no other movement in the rooms nearby.

"May I help?" she asked quietly as she slid the door open and stepped into the room.

The sharp tang of antiseptic stung her nose. *Mama.* Her mother's room had smelled of carbolic and roses, and she'd tiptoed tentatively toward her bed as a child much as she now approached the enormous canopied bedstead of Grey's father. The cut of the man's face, the shape of his jaw, left no doubt he was the Earl of Stanhope. The man Grey had been avoiding for years. He lay twisting his head back and forth on his pillows, continuing to groan. Beside him, an overturned glass lay on its side, and a bell had fallen to the floor below.

"Lord Stanhope?"

He opened his eyes and stared at her. "Jocelyn? Is that you?"

"No, my lord. My name is Sophia."

"Another? Haven't I sufficient nursemaids already?" He waved a gnarled hand toward the table near his bed. "Well, make yourself useful. Fetch me a drink, girl."

She was beginning to get a subtle inkling about why coming home hadn't appealed to Grey. But she complied with the earl's command, tipping his glass aright and pouring water from a pitcher nearby.

When she lifted the glass to his lips, he clasped her wrist in a painful squeeze. "Jocelyn? It is you, isn't it?"

Sophia shook her head, but he gripped her more tightly.

"Oh, Jossie." Despite the frailty writ in every line of the earl's aged face, the man still possessed surprising strength. He yanked Sophia closer. "I've missed you almost enough to forget how much I hate you."

"Sophia, my lord." She pushed at him with her elbow, sloshing water on him from the glass in her hand.

He wailed as if he'd been doused with acid, releasing her wrist and flailing his arms. Fists striking out blindly, he landed a blow on her cheek, and Sophia reeled back. After stumbling to catch her balance, she dropped the water glass, reaching out uselessly as it slammed onto an uncarpeted patch of marble tile and shattered in a watery mess.

Behind her, the room's doors burst open, cracking against the walls like gunshots.

"What the hell do you think you're doing?" Grey loomed between the open doors, wearing a half-buttoned shirt, black trousers, and a ferocious scowl.

"There he is, son of mine." Oddly, Grey's shout settled his father, who immediately stopped striking the air and reclined quietly against his pillows.

"Yes, Father," Grey said, tempering his tone. "I'll see you again tomorrow. Rest now."

"I…" Sophia tried to speak and found her throat burning, her voice raspy and raw. The burning spread to the corners of her eyes, but she fought the tears. She never allowed herself to cry. "I heard a noise and thought I could help him."

"You're not here to help him."

A maid appeared in the doorway behind Grey, an oil lamp in her hand.

"I'll get his nurse and a brush to clear away the glass, my lord," the girl said before bolting down the hall.

"I'm sorry." The words tumbled out unbidden. Grey said nothing in reply, and she couldn't blame him. Her apology was insufficient.

Sophia cast a final glance at the earl, who gazed at her as if he'd never seen her before that moment. Two heavy footsteps sounded from the doorway, and she turned as Grey approached, his boot heels crunching over shattered glass. He kept toward her, eyes grim, mouth a slashed line, until his chest brushed hers.

Without a word, he reached down and lifted her in his arms.

Squirming against him, Sophia insisted, "I can walk on my own, thank you very much."

"In bare feet? Over glass? You're not nearly as sensible as you think you are, Sophia." He wouldn't look at her, not into her eyes. But he skimmed his gaze down her body, where the dressing gown gaped, exposing her bare legs. "Save your outrage and propriety until I've gotten you out of this room."

With a little tsk of frustration, she hooked an arm around his neck and allowed him the chivalrous gesture.

But, like a true scoundrel, Grey didn't put her down when they reached the hallway. He continued on, forcing her attention to the friction between their bodies, the clean pine scent of his skin, the warm, insistent gust of his breath against her cheek. His hair was wet where it curled at his shirt collar. He'd recently bathed and that thought—water sluicing down his naked body—quickened her pulse.

"Where are you taking me?" Her voice was smaller, breathier than she intended.

"Where would you like me to *take* you, goddess?" His husky tone infused the words with another meaning. More scandalous offer than innocent query.

"Back to the train station so that I can return to London." Licking her lips, she stared at the patch of skin above his gaping shirt. Which did nothing to assist her with any logical thought.

He smirked, a flash of white in the darkened hall. "So you intend to leave me?" All the while he kept on, striding toward a room past hers on the opposite side of the long hall. When he reached the threshold, he kicked the unlatched door open with his boot, stepped inside, kicked the door shut, and deposited her on a plush armless chair in front of a stoked fire.

"This isn't my room," she protested. It was the single fact she could muster. All else was feeling—the humming in her veins, the pulse and throb in her body, ratcheting each moment she'd moved and shifted against Grey's. She'd never anticipated this need that built to a fierce hunger. For one man's nearness. For one man's touch. For the taste of him on her tongue.

"No," he said, as he crossed the room to a low table. After filling a tumbler with amber liquid, he tipped back the whole in a single swallow. "This is my room." He lifted a finger in the air. "That's a lie. This is a guest room. I haven't set foot in my old room in years." Refilling his glass and another, he caught both vessels between his fingers and approached, offering her one. "Shall we start, from this moment, vowing to tell each other the truth?"

"I always tell the truth." Sophia took the glass, hoping a swig of whatever was inside might steady her nerves. Just one sip. Not enough to melt her bones and turn her into a wanton fool, as she'd been at the Eagle and Stag. The first sip seared her tongue but curled with a comforting warmth into her belly.

"Yes, of course you do." He smirked before tipping back his liquor. "Why are you here?" Hooking a wingback with his boot, he slid the chair near hers and settled against the velvet.

"You carried me." And the entire side of her body that had been pressed to his was still warm.

"At Longcross, Sophia. Tell me why you came to Derbyshire." He leaned forward in his chair, elbows balanced on his knees. There was no mockery in his expression. If anything, he cast her the most earnest gaze she'd ever seen in his stormy gray eyes.

"I received your telegram." A simple truth to stall while she sorted and sifted. There had to be a series of rational decisions that led her from her from meeting with Ogilvy to Leicestershire to visit Clary, and now here, to this fraught moment, sitting across from a man who had the irritating power to make her blood sizzle in her veins. Whose scent and smile made her struggle to think at all.

"So you've said." His voice had lowered to a gentle purr. Not a hint of his usual teasing tone. None of his flirtatious arrogance. He sounded raw. "But why come all the way from London?"

Swallowing, she opened her mouth to explain that she'd come north to see Clary.

"Truth, Sophia. Only truth between us tonight."

"I wanted to see you again." The admission caused her heart to lurch in her chest as if the organ was breaking free of its moorings. Casting a gaze toward his bed, she considered lunging for a blanket to cover herself. She felt bare, stripped naked before him.

When his beautiful lips tipped in a soft grin, she realized her moment of blurted frankness was precisely what he wanted.

"Yes," he said on an exhale. "I missed you too, sweetheart."

Sophia bristled. "We were apart for a day. I never said I missed you." Scooting to the edge of her chair, she prepared to bolt from the room if he demanded more. She'd already admitted too much. Pulling the edges of her dressing gown together, she wrapped the brocade around her like a shield.

"But you did miss me." Grey reached between the slit in the fabric and laid his palm on her knee. "Maybe it's not an honorable man you need at all."

Ridiculous. All she'd ever wanted in life was honor and honesty and a simple happily ever after. Sophia twisted her head to deny his brazen claim, and the single ribbon tying her hair back came loose. She reached up to gather the mess of haphazard waves, and Grey touched her arm.

"Please don't." He stroked his fingers along her skin, sifting through the pile of fallen tresses. "Let me see you."

What if she gave him what he asked? Not simply let down her hair, but pulled down her walls, allowing him to see every inch of her, inside and out. Every worry and wayward thought. Every fear.

The prospect terrified her. She'd never considered exposing herself to any man.

For a fleeting moment, Derringham had tempted her, and that had ended in bruises and shame.

Grey would offer her nothing. She'd be a conquest to add to his pile.

Why didn't that knowledge stop her from wanting him? Why didn't reason stem the longing to know all his secrets, the yearning to see every inch of his body? Perhaps she wasn't the proper faultless woman she'd always believed herself to be. Maybe she no longer wished to abide by every rule.

"You first," she said softly.

He didn't react, and a part of her hoped he hadn't heard. That they could part from each other without risking anything more.

But then his mouth curved. He'd heard, and he reached up with both hands to grip the collar of his open shirt. He pulled the whole over his head, leaving his unruly waves of cinnamon hair even more disheveled.

Firelight lit his bare chest, highlighting every hard and smooth place she wished to touch.

"Your turn, sweetheart." He reached for the edge of her dressing gown and tugged lightly. Eager glints sparked in his slate gaze.

Underneath, she wore only a sheer chemise. But she'd been the one to start this shedding of clothing and guises. Standing to untangle herself from the heavy fabric, she unbuttoned two fastenings over her breasts and peeled the edges back, letting the gown pool at her feet.

"*Bloody hell, Sophia.*" Grey murmured the curse, and she immediately dipped to retrieve the garment and cover herself. He stopped her, kicking the pile away. Reaching out, he curled his hand around her hip, stroking across her belly with his other hand. "It wasn't a complaint, sweet. You took me by surprise." His fingertips brushed the underside of her breasts. "You're exquisite."

Despite their agreement to speak only truth, she didn't trust his effusive praise. But she sensed the eagerness in his touch and leaned forward to urge his hand higher.

"You take my breath away." He did sound breathless as he husked out each word.

His long, elegant fingers closed over her breast, and she moaned from the sudden pleasure of his heat against her body. Her response emboldened him. He wrapped an arm around her hips and drew her close. Gazing up at her, he allowed his hands to roam, stroking the backs of her calves, dipping into the dent at the back of her knees, skimming up her thighs, dragging her chemise higher and higher.

"Stay with me tonight." As he spoke, he lowered his head, pressing a kiss to her stomach, then lower, to the taught stretch of skin above her curls.

As her body shuddered beneath his touch, she weighed his proposition. He offered this night alone. The chance to sate her desire, let him pleasure her in the all the wicked ways he knew how. But no more. No promises for a future. Nothing to hold onto tomorrow.

"I want to stay." Sinking her hands into his hair, she slid her fingers through the thick waves. "But we both know I should not."

Tipping his head to press into her touch, he flashed a grin. "I'm dishonorable, darling. I never concern myself with what I should do. Only what I want to do. You, Sophia. I want you." Resting his chin on her stomach, he clasped his arms around her body and gazed up at her. "Tell me what you want."

Love. Marriage. A happy home in the countryside. Those truths she could not confess, because nothing was clearer than his disdain for each.

But neither could she deny her desire for the scoundrel in her arms. Jasper Grey, Viscount Winship, the man who never wished to be heir to an earldom. Here, in the glorious estate most men could only dream of and which he wished to avoid, he seemed vulnerable. As if he might truly need her this night as much as she desired him. He let her glimpse the man behind the many roles he bragged of playing, and she wanted that man most of all.

No other had ever made her heart thrash in her chest, her body throb and heat the moment he looked her way. Perhaps none ever would.

Why deny herself one night of passion?

"We'll have tonight." She spoke the words quietly, solemnly, as she would a vow. Now that she'd decided, she wouldn't turn back.

Grey froze. Hands stilled on her body, his mouth fell slack.

"Unless…" Sophia dropped her hands from his hair and clasped an arm across her breasts. "You've changed your mind."

He stood and wrapped an arm around her, gripping her backside to pull her flush against his body. The hard pulsing thrust of him answered her doubt. Sinking a hand into the tumbled tresses at her neck, he tipped her head back and took her mouth. Urged her to open to him with the press of his tongue. He kissed her hungrily, deeply, stroking her back with one hand as he reached between them with the other to find the damp, hot center of her arousal.

Breaking their kiss long enough to reach down, he caught her knees in the crook of his arm and carried her swiftly to the high bed in the corner of the room.

Sophia lay back, one arm still clinging to his neck, expecting his hard, warm body to come down on top of hers. Instead, he unhooked her arm gently, kissing from her elbow to her hand before standing before her at the foot of the bed. He licked his lips as he took her in, from her unkempt hair to the spot where her chemise had slid high to reveal the tops of her thighs to the tips of her bare toes.

He reached for his waistband and began flicking buttons free. Sliding her legs together, Sophia watched hungrily as he peeled back his fly and shucked his trousers, letting the dark fabric slide over his chiseled hips. *Mercy.* Statues in museums and etchings in history books had misled her entirely.

"I want to make this perfect for you," he said as the bed dipped under the weight of his knee. He reached for the hem of her chemise, sliding the fabric up to expose more of her body to his gaze. "We should dispense with this," he said, gripping her hand and pulling her to a sitting position. He helped her removed the garment and then stared, as if awestruck.

Sophia wrapped an arm across her breasts. "Surely you've seen breasts before."

"Not yours." He leaned forward. "Everything about you is a wonder to be explored."

"Including my shyness?"

"Are you shy, sweet?" He bent to kiss the arm she still had braced across her chest, then the swell above. "You needn't ever be shy with me, Sophia. Share your thoughts. Tell me what you want. Be your true self. Just let go."

Drawing in a long breath, Sophia lowered her arm. Grey sucked in a breath and reached out to stroke her cheek, avoiding the spot where his father's hand had landed. "Does it hurt?"

She shook her head as his continued touching her. Down her neck, over her chest to the tip of her breast. He bent and kissed her nipple, sucking the tender point into his mouth until she bucked off the bed. Shifting, he took her other nipple in his mouth, teasing at the taut berry with his tongue, his hand sliding lower, all the way to the shallow of her belly button. Then lower, into the warm tangle of curls between her thighs.

Yes. That spot, the center of aching need was precisely where she craved him. And he knew exactly how to touch her. Gently, tenderly. He smiled down at her, watched her, their gazes locked.

When his fingers delved deeper, Sophia tensed, one hand clutching the bedclothes.

Grey froze before dipping his head to kiss her. "Tell me what you want, sweet," he whispered against her lips.

"You," she said, dragging her fingers through the hair dipping over his forehead. "More of you."

He began moving again, his fingers exploring, while he bent his head and took the tip of her breast into his mouth again. His tongue moved like hot velvet against her bud while his fingers worked magic. Each stroke driving her closer, pulling her tighter. "More," she cried out, unsure what she needed, only that a desperate craving grew inside her. A craving for him. To be closer. To risk everything. To give him all the parts of herself she'd never shared with any man.

As soon as her demand was out, he moved on the bed, shifting down her body, nudging her legs apart with one long, muscled thigh. She lifted her hips, eager for the feel of him against her.

Grey swept his gaze up at her, his eyes searing and intense. There was a question in his eyes, a vulnerability. As if he too was risking himself, giving more than just his body to her.

Then he hunched his shoulders, lowered his head, and pressed his mouth to the wet heat between her thighs.

Shock, pleasure, panic struck at once. She pushed at his shoulders. "What are you doing?"

A low chuckle tickled her sensitive flesh before she felt the heat of his tongue against her slit. He continued to taste as her knees dropped open, and she twisted her head on the pillow, trying to get away, trying to get closer. A shudder began building from her center, up her back, inside her chest. She shook as if fever had overtaken her. She couldn't breathe, couldn't speak, couldn't move. Grey was here, with her, and the heat and weight of his body was all she knew. All that mattered. And then she shattered. Heat flooded her veins, a melting warmth. Sensation exploded along every nerve. She dug her fingers into Grey's shoulder, tangling her other hand in his hair.

He kissed a trail up her body.

"What? Why?" Words emerged from her lips, queries swimming up from her boggled mind.

"This may hurt, sweetheart," he said, his voice muffled by the haze of pleasure still clouding her brain. "I never want to hurt you."

His hands were on her thighs, stroking gently, then the thick hard length of him was there, where she was slick and raw and impossibly warm. She spread her legs, no longer wishing to hide any part of herself. He positioned himself with infinite care, then breached her in one confident thrust. The flash of pain went quickly, but nothing could have prepared her for the fullness. She wrapped a leg around his, stroking her heel up his calf, reveling in the feel of him inside her, nudging her hips toward him because she wanted more.

"Easy, goddess." Breathless, his voice emerged on a strained whisper. "Never," he said and then sucked in a breath. "I never want to cause you pain."

"There's no pain." Reaching up to stroke his cheek, she promised, "It's all right, Jasper."

"Grey," he said as he settled his body over hers, began to pump in a delicious rhythm as he buried his face against her neck. "Call me Grey." He kissed and nipped at her skin as he thrust. "So sweet," he groaned as he filled her again.

The tautness built once more, pleasure sparking her every nerve, soaking every muscle. Grey paused, held himself above her, pressed a hand to her face to make sure she met his gaze. "Sophia," he hissed as he began to withdraw. But she wouldn't let him go. She tilted her hips to draw him deeper, reached down and gripped his backside to pull him closer.

"Wait, sweet."

She could build a rhythm too. He'd taught her how. She bucked against him as he stared down at her in amazement.

"Soph—" he started, then tipped his head back and emitted a virile roar as warmth flooded her insides. He collapsed atop her, his body slick and fevered. A moment later, he rolled to his side and pulled her with him, tucking their bodies together as he drew the blanket up. "Stay with me. Don't leave."

Just for tonight. Sleeping in his arms would make facing tomorrow harder. But as he clasped an arm around her body, threw his leg over hers, nuzzled his face in her hair, she couldn't imagine anyplace else she wished to be.

CHAPTER EIGHTEEN

"There are occasions when a mystery's solution brings nothing but fresh dilemmas."

—CASEBOOK OF EUPHEMIA
BREEDLOVE, LADY DETECTIVE

Grey reached for Sophia and clutched a fistful of bedsheets.

The smooth linen retained a bit of warmth from her body and her floral citrus scent. He could still taste her too, remember the texture of every inch of skin he'd kissed, recall the warmth of each spot where he'd lingered, exploring her with his tongue. He'd woken in the night, retreating from a nightmare into her soothing embrace. Her kisses of comfort had soon deepened, and he'd taken her again. More slowly, more expertly, focusing on her pleasure, giving her release before seeking his own. Not spilling as he had the first time, like a novice without a shred of control.

She had been incomparable. Trusting him as he never dreamed she would, giving herself with passionate abandon. He licked his lips and gripped the sheet tighter. He wanted her again. Now. Wanted her beside him. To hear her voice, her moans of pleasure, to look into her fathomless eyes.

"*We'll have tonight.*" When she'd slipped away shortly after dawn, thinking him asleep, she'd whispered a choked *good-bye.* Her departure was expected. Hell, he didn't want to remain at Longcross for another day himself. But she wasn't simply planning to leave Derbyshire. Her farewell was for him.

Liddy had been found. Sophia had done all he'd asked of her and more.

He bloody well planned to go back to his life in London too. Why shouldn't she return to hers? Let her go back to the house she felt a duty to improve for her brother. To a housekeeper who seemed more confidant than servant. To some knave named Ogilvy, who did not deserve her. Whoever he was.

Grey wasn't certain which he hated more—the fact that he might never make love to Sophia again or the prospect of waking every day for the rest of his days without her in his bed.

He sat up and scrubbed his hands through his hair, staring out at the long expanse of wooded meadow where he'd roamed much of the previous evening, attempting to clear his head and forget the disappointed look in Sophia's eyes. Today the weather seemed determined to be as sullen as his mood. The sun-soaked days of early summer were giving way to rain. Storm clouds loomed in the sky as a breeze whipped treetops to and fro.

Damn Sophia and how much he longed for her. He wasn't a man for commitment or longevity. Yet she *had* managed what no other woman ever achieved. She'd gotten under his skin, into his blood. Hell, perhaps he did have a heart, because something in his chest hurt like the devil at the prospect of parting from her for good.

Still, *carpe diem* had long been his motto. He took each day afresh, unfettered and free. Planning for the week ahead seemed daunting, let alone making choices to determine the rest of his days. Duty, responsibility—he understood they would be thrust upon him when his father died. But he planned to shape that future to impact his London life as little as possible. Acting and debauchery were all he'd ever been good at. He wouldn't give them up.

Marriage would be forced upon him one day. Every earl needs an heir, after all. In his youth, his mother selected a duke's third daughter as his future bride, but he'd only met the girl once and couldn't recall her name. Mariah? Madeline? Margaret? It mattered not. Wedlock, when faced, would be a practical arrangement with a lady who understood he could offer nothing but a title and a gilt-crusted estate to reside in. He would live in London. The future Lady Stanhope could have Longcross to herself.

A soft knock sounded at the door, and a maid pushed in a moment later, ducking a brief curtsy before approaching the fireplace and brushing ash and soot into a bucket.

"Has Lady Fennston risen?"

"I believe she is taking breakfast in the morning room with Lord Fennston, my lord."

Alistair. Wonderful. Grey's head began thumping. "And Miss Ruthven?"

"She is at table too, my lord."

"Is Turnbull still at Longcross?" The man had served as his brother's valet and then his own before Grey left home.

The girl turned her gaze his way, blowing a stray hair from her cheek. "Lord Fennston's valet? Yes, my lord, he's been at Longcross forever, so they say. Shall I send him up to you?"

"Yes, thank you." Grey tried for a charming grin. "Could you have the kitchen procure some coffee too?"

The young maid finished blacking the grate, took her pail and brush, and departed.

Grey reached for his discarded trousers and then stood to retrieve his shirt. The faint scent of Sophia's perfume wafted up off the fabric. At least he'd get to take some part of her with him when he embarked on a task that was long overdue.

Striding to his father's suite, he battled the urge to retreat. Despite the man's dotage and the possibility he might not know Grey from one moment to the next, he was still his father. Grey needed to face him.

"No!" the old man's refusal echoed down the long upper-story hall. "I won't have another."

A woman's voice followed, gentle and coaxing. "Come, my lord. We'll build the fire high so the room's warm."

"Let me speak with him," Grey instructed from the threshold. One maid stoked fireplace coals, another poured water into a tub, while a third held his father's hand, urging him to bathe. At least his father had plenty of attentive caretakers.

The servants filed out of the room quickly, each casting him a nervous glance before departing.

"No more baths!" the Earl of Stamford shouted before falling silent and closing his eyes, as if he might have drifted off to sleep.

"Father?"

One eye opened, a clouded gray orb surrounded by wrinkled flesh. "Richard?"

"No, Pater." What he wouldn't have given Richard to be here, ready, as he'd always been, to take on the earldom. "Jasper."

Both brows winged high, and the earl lifted off his pillow for a closer look. "Thought you'd be in London plowing into some whore."

Grey clenched his fists and waited. After a decade of shirking his duty to the family, he deserved a bit of the man's ire.

"Certainly what I'd be doing if I had the strength," his father added before collapsing against his pillow. "Fetch your mother, boy."

"Mother isn't at Longcross anymore." She'd been gone longer than Grey.

"Bollocks. Saw her in my room last night." After closing his eyes, he began murmuring her name. "Jossie. Jossie."

Only his father had ever called the Countess of Stanhope by the nickname, which she'd deemed coarse and childish. Grey's mother had never been much for nicknames or familial warmth and affection. Though she spared plenty of attention for her many paramours, Grey couldn't recall her hugging Rich or offering either of them a kiss on the rare occasions she visited the nursery.

His father struck out a hand and clasped Grey's wrist. "Bring her to me. Tell her all is forgiven."

"Mother isn't here." Perhaps he'd mistaken Sophia for his countess, since both women were fair-haired. Though in nature, Sophia's honesty and determination to see a commitment to its end were the exact opposite of his mother.

"You must..." The earl began to cough, a terrible, deep rattling sound that made Grey's own chest ache.

"What must I do, Father? Tell me." How in the hell was he supposed to be master of an estate that brought back memories he longed to banish?

Squeezing tighter, his father gripped Grey's forearm. "If you find her, son, never let her go."

Slim, dark-haired Lady Fennston invited Sophia to join her on a visit to her aunt as they shared a civil but awkward breakfast with Lord Fennston in Longcross's elegant dining room.

No mention of Lady Phyllida, of course.

Despite Lady Fennston's insistence the previous day that she'd tell her husband all, the man seemed unaware of anything more troubling than the newspaper's mention of a railroad strike that would postpone a coming business trip north. For most of breakfast, he hid behind his morning paper, assessing Sophia over the rim of his spectacles now and then.

Sophia managed to swallow a few bites of toast and sips of tea, but she failed miserably at thinking of anything but Grey. Luckily, the bruise from his father's inadvertent blow was barely visible on her face.

"Where did you say you'd met my cousins, Miss Ruthven?" Lord Fennston lowered his newspaper as he addressed her.

"She met Jasper and Liddy in London, of course," Lady Fennston said, casting Sophia a warning glance.

"And yet she and Winship are here, while Phyllida is not." He folded his paper with a fearsome rattle, fussing until he got the seams perfectly even.

"Her train has been delayed." Lady Fennston pointed to the newspaper report he'd just been bemoaning. "You know how disappointing the trains can be."

"Mmm." After emptying his teacup and swiping a napkin across his mustache, Alistair Fennston turned the full power of his dark, bespectacled gaze on Sophia. "And you're twice unlucky, Miss Ruthven. Not only has Phyllida been delayed, but you had the distinct misfortune of arriving with the prodigal Stanhope heir. Tell me, how well do you know Lord Winship?"

Sophia swallowed down a mouthful of tea and cast her inquisitor what she hoped was an unaffected grin. "He is a friend of my brother's."

Leaning back in his chair, Fennston crossed his arms and asked, "And how well do you know Lady Phyllida?"

"So many questions, my dear." The tiny thread of chastisement in Lady Fennston's tone was far gentler than the manner in which she'd rebuked Grey.

Her husband was equally undeterred. "Phyllida is young and silly, but you, Miss Ruthven, seem a lady of manners. Perhaps even sense."

"Thank you, my lord." *I think.* His compliments sounded suspiciously like insults. Very like her father's way of never delivering praise without adding a bit of stinging critique at the end.

"Miss Ruthven is eminently sensible, my dear. In fact, she wrote a book of etiquette rules for young ladies."

"Really?" Fennston lifted his teacup toward her in mock salute. "Ah yes, *Ruthven Rules*, wasn't it? But your father wrote those volumes. Not you."

Sophia narrowed one eye at him. "My siblings and I inherited my father's publishing enterprise, and we've updated his etiquette books."

Fennston snorted. "The rules of society do not change, Miss Ruthven. Though I commend any book that seeks to remind ladies of their duties. If only Phyllida had adhered to such a book."

"Actually, the *New Ruthven Rules* encourages young women to think for themselves, to become educated in order to discern which rules are worth applying and which are outdated and must be discarded." Sophia cocked the baron a grin before taking a dainty sip of Earl Grey tea.

Fennston choked on his own gulp and slammed his teacup down, missing the saucer entirely. "That sounds more like anarchy than etiquette."

"My siblings and I like to think of it as progress, my lord." Sophia beamed at him.

He yanked his napkin from his collar and cast his wife a scowl. "Do you think Winship intends to rise before noon? I've business matters to attend to in my study." After tugging a pocket watch from his waistcoat, he glowered at the dining room threshold.

Sophia looked too, swallowing quickly and swiping away crumbs from her mouth. Would Grey finally appear?

After several fraught moments, he did not.

"Go up to your study, my dear. Miss Ruthven and I will make our way to Aunt Violet's. You can speak to Jasper at dinner."

"Mmm," Lord Fennston grumbled. He rose, kissed his wife on the cheek, and left the room as if escaping to his business affairs was what he'd wished for all morning.

"Shall we set off?" Lady Fennston stood and shook out the folds of her elaborate day dress. "I must speak to Cook about this evening's menu. Let's meet in the front hall in ten minutes."

Sophia cast one more agitated glance at the empty doorway and nodded at Lady Fennston. There was an early afternoon train she planned to catch back to London, and she'd brought her travel case down to the front hall earlier, anticipating her departure.

She was ready to go, but now she couldn't imagine leaving without seeing Grey again. She'd whispered a *good-bye* when parting from him in the early morning, but she'd been fighting the impulse to return to the warmth of his embrace ever since.

"*You're not as sensible as you think you are, Sophia.*" After a week's acquaintance and a deeper intimacy than she'd shared with any man, he did know her. Perhaps better than she knew herself.

This morning she did not feel sensible. She felt like a rule-breaker, a creature of passion and wanton possibilities. Bindings had been loosed in those lovemaking hours with Grey, fears conquered, a fire lit inside that she hoped never extinguished. She felt alive. Fully and without restraint. Consequences might come. She sensed them closing in already. Marriage appeared a dimmer prospect than ever before. Perhaps she'd never know a man's touch again. What if she carried Grey's child? She was acutely aware she could find herself living with the same uncertainties as Lady Phyllida.

After making her way to Longcross's front hall, a maid approached with her traveling case, gloves, and hat. "Oh, I'm not departing for good." Not yet. "But after returning with Lady Fennston, I plan to catch the one o'clock train to London. Could you arrange for someone to take me to the station?"

"I'll make sure a cart and driver are ready for you, miss." The young woman took back Sophia's travel bag and pushed it under a table near the door.

Lady Fennston appeared soon after, and they set off in an elegant closed carriage with windows on every side. Even under gloomy skies, the fields around Longcross reminded Sophia why she loved the countryside. Broad meadows, green as far as her eye could see, fresh air rather than London's fog of smoke and soot.

"I should warn you that Liddy can be quite stubborn. Impossible at times." Lady Fennston was different away from Longcross, more relaxed, her voice warm and mellow. "Without a mother to guide her and with a father more interested in his own diversions than running the estate, she often did precisely as she pleased."

An image of Clary rose in Sophia's mind. Stubborn, willful, and yet, for the most part, she'd abided by their father's rules. Perhaps the Stanhopes had never had any rules to curb their impulses.

Seemingly reading her thoughts, Lady Fennston added, "Lord Winship is much the same. Though I suspect, for Jasper, guilt drives him more than willfulness." Her voice had grown quiet, her gaze distant.

"What guilt?" Sophia suspected she knew the answer.

"Richard." Lady Fennston dipped her head and picked at a loose thread on her gloves. "His brother. Once upon a time, he was my betrothed. Jasper has always blamed himself for Richard's death."

"Why?" Sophia leaned forward. In the answer, perhaps there was a key to his need for masks.

"Oh, look, there's the cottage." The baroness's voice had taken on a bright pitch. She reached out and touched Sophia's arm. "If you have any persuasive skills, Miss Ruthven, please employ them as you see fit. I don't plan to leave Aunt Violet's without Liddy in tow."

Pungent, wilting summer roses clung to a trellis on either side of the cottage door. A maid took their hats and gloves and led them down a narrow hall to a plump silver-haired woman. Lady Fennston's aunt smiled warmly, but her overall expression was one of long-suffering exasperation.

"Darling, Becca, I've been looking forward to your visit for days. And you must be Miss Ruthven." Clasping Sophia's hand, she offered a welcoming grin. "Becca sent a note last evening about your arrival. We rarely have guests at Rose Cottage, so this is a rare pleasure. Come in, please."

Inside the diminutive sitting room, a fluffy orange-and-white cat stretched along a windowsill near a seated young lady. There was no mistaking Grey's sister. She lounged on the dainty dove-gray settee with the same boneless ease her brother seemed to employ when confronted with a piece of furniture.

She did know some manners, though, because she immediately rose to greet them, offering Lady Fennston a warm hug and kiss on the cheek before looking curiously at Sophia. "Hello to you. I am Lady Phyllida Grey." She stuck out her hand in a guileless way that reminded Sophia of Clary. "And you are?"

"Sophia Ruthven. Pleased to meet you, Lady Phyllida." Again. Not that they'd actually met before, but there was no doubt in Sophia's mind she was looking at the same young woman who'd left Mrs. Greenlow's rooming house in Cambridge a few days earlier.

Dipping her head of auburn curls forward, she whispered to Sophia, "Call me Liddy. Everyone does." Then she squealed and covered her mouth. "Wait! Are you *the* Sophia Ruthven? The one who wrote *Guidelines for Young Ladies?*"

Sophia smiled. "That was my sister-in-law. Ophelia Ruthven."

"She's very clever."

"I cannot disagree." There were times when she wondered if her brother deserved such a wife after being fool enough to break her heart years before.

"Miss Ruthven *did* co-write the *Ruthven Rules for Young Ladies,*" Lady Fennston added, as if coming to her defense.

Liddy nodded approvingly. "I like that one too, but I do loathe the word *rules*." She cast a pointed gaze at Lady Fennston, who stood in the corner speaking quietly with her aunt. "When they make some rule to curb me, it's as if they've issued a challenge."

"I doubt that's the intent." Yes, very like Clary indeed. And someone else. "Your brother seems to have a similar philosophy."

"Do you know Grey?" She sounded eager and wistful at the same time. "How is my brother? Is he at Longcross?"

"He is, and I know he'd be pleased to see you." Surely the anger he'd unleashed on Clive Holden wasn't a harbinger of how he'd react to seeing his little sister after years apart.

"I can't go back," Liddy insisted. "Not yet. I must speak to Dominic first."

Dominic, the Earl of Westby. The girl's eyes glazed over when she said his name, as if the man held her in his thrall. Sophia understood, now more than ever, how a lady could be tempted by such a man. "I met Lord Westby in London."

"Did you?" Liddy's whole demeanor altered. Eyes narrow and body tense, she whispered, "Please don't tell me he flirted with you and such a man cannot be trusted. I've heard all the smears against him a hundred times." She sniffed haughtily but then began nervously chewing her nail. "He didn't flirt with you, did he?"

"Let's just say he didn't treat me with the respect a lady deserves." Sophia tried to smooth her expression and measure her tone. She knew Liddy wouldn't wish to be lectured about Westby's faults, but the girl needed to know the truth about him.

"Ladies, join us for tea," Lady Fennston called from a chair near her aunt, gesturing toward an empty settee.

"If you come back to Longcross," Sophia whispered to Liddy, "I'll tell you all about the time I met Lord Westby. And you'll get to see your brother."

Liddy bit her lip before answering. "How long will you be staying? Believe me, I do wish to see Grey. He's the one person in our family who'll take my side in this whole affair."

The girl didn't seem aware of the double meaning in her choice of words and flounced onto the settee she'd been occupying before their arrival.

"Clive Holden has been to visit us at Longcross," Lady Fennston said as she offered Liddy a cup of tea.

"Really? I'm surprised he has the time to visit when he's been here at the cottage so often." Grey's sister sounded supremely unimpressed with the man's tenacity. She cast a gaze at Sophia. "Have you met him, Miss Ruthven?"

"I have." She was itching to admit she'd saved the man from being strangled by Grey. Twice. "He seems very fond of you, Lady Phyllida."

"Yes." Liddy screwed her face into an irritated moue. "Unfortunately, I do not love him."

"Liddy." Lady Fennston had a way of drawing out a person's name, infusing the syllables with a tincture of reprimand.

"What? Is it impolite to speak of love? Why not discuss what is essential? The very reason we were born at all." After her impassioned outburst, Liddy let out a huff of frustration.

"You're a writer, Miss Ruthven. Surely you believe that true love is necessary for any real happiness in life."

"No, she doesn't." Grey stepped into the room, ducking his head to clear the low door frame. "She's far too sensible for such nonsense."

His voice vibrated down Sophia's back as if they were in his darkened room again, and he was whispering oaths against her skin. Heat flared in her cheeks, her breasts, her thighs, everywhere she remembered the sear of his mouth on her.

Sophia's gaze snagged on his a moment before Liddy cried out.

"Jasper!" She leapt from the settee straight into her brother's arms.

Grey held his sister tight, closing his eyes and tucking his head against her shoulder. "Come home, Liddy."

She pushed away from him. "I can't. Please understand."

"No." He shook his head vehemently. "I don't understand. Longcross is your home and where you should be. Forget your foolish pursuit of Westby."

Liddy gasped and turned a wounded gaze toward Lady Fennston before facing Grey again. "So you know my secrets too?" Lashing her arms across her chest, Liddy insisted, "I will never marry for anything but love."

Grey clenched his fists and cast Sophia a gaze of frustration. Of desperation.

Liddy threw up her hands. "Why would I expect you to understand? You don't believe in love, and you'll marry Miss Cathright anyway."

"Who?" Grey and Sophia asked in chorus.

Liddy rolled her eyes. "The poor woman who's been waiting to marry you since she was a child. You've don't even remember her."

Grey pinched the skin between his brows. "I remember her name starts with an *M*."

Sophia set her teacup down, got to her feet, and stepped toward a sash window. She longed to be out in the field beyond, for a bracing walk and the chance to fill her lungs with fresh country air. The warmth in her cheeks flared, and she had no wish for everyone to see. Grey approached to stand behind her. His scent and heat only made her more eager to escape, to leave him to Longcross's gilded halls and Miss Cathright, whoever she was.

"You'll be miserable," Liddy continued. "Marriage without love is a hollow pit."

"Stop being so bloody melodramatic." Grey's shout rattled against the window in front of Sophia. "I'm not marrying anyone, but you are coming home. Go and gather your belongings. Now."

After emitting a little growl of frustration, Liddy swiveled away from him and stomped from the room.

"Well," was all Lady Fennston's aunt managed before rising from her chair and following Liddy.

"You needn't have been quite so heavy-handed." Lady Fennston cast Grey a grateful grin. "But well done. I'll go and help her along so that we can all get back home."

When they were alone, Grey stepped closer. Sophia felt the warmth of his breath against her neck. He laid a hand lightly on her upper back, teased his finger against a loose strand of hair. "Sophia."

No one said her name as he did, with a lush kind of reverence, stroking intently over each syllable. After parting from him, would anyone ever treat her name with such care?

"I wanted you there with me when I woke." His voice sounded rusty.

"It was hard to leave you."

Grey laid his hands on her shoulders and pressed his lips to her nape. "Then don't."

He was convincing. Tempting. The most appealing man she'd ever met in her life. Except that he wanted nothing she did.

He'd said as much himself. He had no intention of marrying anyone.

Twisting away from his touch, Sophia steeled herself and started toward the door. Her chest pinched with every step. Her body ached, as if lodging its own protest against her decision.

"Sophia, where are you going?" His beautiful actor's voice, an instrument he could pitch a dozen ways, had gone rough and raw.

What if she never heard his voice again?

"I have a train to catch." She didn't turn back. If she looked into his eyes, she'd never be able to walk away. "Goodbye, Grey."

CHAPTER NINETEEN

By the time Liddy and Becca came down with half a dozen hat boxes and bags, Grey had all but worn a hole in Aunt Violet's Aubusson carpet. He'd been violently pacing the floral oval for the half hour since Sophia's departure. More than once, he'd made his way to the cottage's front door, only to turn back.

He needed to get Liddy home. Then he needed to find Sophia.

"If Cousin Alistair sends me to a nunnery, I shall never forgive you," Liddy lamented as Grey took up her bags and followed her out to the Stanhope carriage.

"No one is sending you anywhere you do not wish to go."

She stopped, planted her hands on her hips, and shot him an exasperated stare. "Says the man who is dragging me back to Longcross."

"Longcross *is* your home."

"Yours too, but I haven't seen you there in years."

"I have a life in London, Liddy."

"As will I, once Westby marries me."

"He is not the man you want him to be." Grey longed to take his sister by the arms and shake sense into her, but he knew Stanhope stubbornness well enough to know its futility. Nothing but the pain of experience would convince her. Even then, she'd probably resist.

"He's not like you, Grey. Dominic believes in love, and he adores me."

"Then where is the man?" Grey lifted a hand to his brow and scanned the nearby landscape. "I don't see him lurking behind any hedgerows. I've been at Longcross for two days without a single glimpse of the rotter. Though Holden's been there, moping about, as miserable as a kicked dog."

"Dominic will come, and then you'll see." Liddy pointed, getting close enough to plunk Grey on the nose. "When he arrives and requests my hand, I look forward to watching you eat your hat."

"It will be a long wait." Grey watched his sister's cocky grin droop and felt like an ass. The fiercer her devotion to Westby now, the more devastating her heartache would be later. To make light of his claim, he winked and added, "I never wear hats."

She conceded him a half-hearted grin.

"Stop fighting, children," Becca said sharply as she took Liddy by the arm and helped her up into the carriage. After settling next to her, she looked out expectantly at Grey. "You're coming back with us, aren't you?"

For a moment he debated his answer. All he truly wished to do was catch the first train back to London and intercept Sophia. But Liddy wasn't home yet. "Yes, let's go."

They all stared out the windows, avoiding each other's gazes, as the horses started the short journey home. Halfway to Longcross, Liddy looked around the carriage as if seeing the interior for the first time.

"Where's Miss Ruthven?"

Yes, where the hell was she? At the station? On a train chugging its way back to the city?

"She planned to depart today, I believe." Becca caught Grey's gaze and added, "I wish she could have stayed awhile longer."

Becca suspected. Or perhaps she simply knew him too well. He doubted Sophia had confessed anything to her, but there was a knowing look in his old friend's eyes.

"Well, we must send her a note and ask her to return," Liddy insisted. "I've never met a lady writer before. I was looking forward to getting to know her better."

Me too. A great rumble of thunder rolled across the sky, and Grey watched as storm clouds swirled overhead.

"Perhaps the weather will delay her journey," Becca said as they approached Longcross's lengthy drive. "I'd hate to be locked in a train car in weather like this."

"They don't actually lock you in." Liddy's teasing tone was the first lightness he'd heard from her, the first sign of the girl he used to know.

Grey winked at her and smirked, but then he recalled when she'd last been on a train. Her journey to Cambridge, or perhaps while traveling back to Longcross with Holden.

He hoped she'd marry the man. Holden had been as foolish as the rest of them in their university days, but he was a good sort. Grey didn't think him capable of Westby's brand of deception, or his own history of debauchery.

"She's very pretty," Liddy said absently as she twirled a strand of hair around her finger. "Miss Ruthven, I mean."

Pretty didn't begin to describe Sophia's beauty. Now he knew there was more. That for all the lovely aspects of her face and mouthwatering lushness of her curves, they were nothing to the appeal of the woman underneath. The strength and cleverness. Her curious mind and benevolent impulses.

They were so very different.

Sophia saw a need and dashed straight toward it. He brushed up against duty and bolted the other way.

Once they reached Longcross, disembarking the ladies took much less time than getting them into the carriage had. Liddy actually stopped to gaze up at the house wistfully before brushing past Blessing and bounding up the stairs to her room.

"Alistair wishes to speak to you at dinner," Becca said as she peeled off her gloves. "Thought I'd give you fair warning." She leaned closer and whispered. "I still haven't told him about Liddy's adventure."

"Is that what we're calling the whole debacle now?"

After her gaze around to ensure no servants were nearby, Becca said under her breath, "Aunt Violet says she's out of danger. Liddy isn't carrying Westby's child."

Grey's gut clenched, and he swallowed hard. Liddy could free herself from Westby now. But only time would tell whether Sophia might be carrying *his* child. The thought didn't disturb him nearly as much as it should have.

"What have you told Alistair?" In other words, how pompous and overbearing did the man intend to be? How much would he have to fight to keep his cousin from punishing Liddy if Fennston discovered her recklessness?

"Nothing." Becca lowered her head and peeked up at him through her lashes. "All's well now. We only have to keep Liddy from pursuing Westby at the upcoming ball and convince Alistair to let her marry Holden."

"A marriage she does not desire."

"She will come around. Unlike you, Liddy wishes to be wed. She simply has to discard her notions of romantic love. Few are lucky enough to find that."

There was a catch in her voice that made Grey's throat burn. "And you, Becca? Have you discarded those notions?" Whatever he'd thought of her match with Richard, he'd never doubted the two had been in love.

"I am content with Alistair," she said defensively. "He is a good man. Faithful and trustworthy."

"An honorable man."

"Yes," she said quietly. "I do love him, Jasper."

"How do you know?" The question wasn't intended as mockery or jest, though Becca frowned up at him suspiciously. He simply craved a fair definition of that elusive emotion that others pursued with such reckless abandon.

"I cannot imagine spending a day of my life without him," she said earnestly. "That's how I know." She left him standing alone in the entry hall, the clip of her boot heels echoing on the tile floor moments after she'd departed.

He stood frozen in place so long a maid approached and asked if she could assist him.

"Where's Miss Ruthven? When did she depart?"

The girl frowned and pointed to her hat and gloves on the hall table. "She came for her bag, Lord Winship, but left the rest behind. I've arranged for a cart to take her to the station, but that's not for a good hour or so."

Grey glanced through the open drawing room door and the window behind. Rain had begun to patter lightly against the panes. "She's wandering the estate?"

"Can't rightly say, my lord. Only that she's not in the house."

Grey started for the front door, his eagerness to find her matched by the questions plaguing his mind.

Where had she gone, and why had she taken her travel bag? Surely she hadn't been so desperate to leave him that's she'd walk to the station in the rain.

Sophia wasn't sure where she was going, but the walk felt good. Stretching her legs, pumping her arms, energy firing her muscles. She never walked enough in London. Hansom cabs were too plentiful and omnibuses too cheap. This was what she missed about the countryside. Its open spaces begging to be explored.

Hitching her satchel strap higher on her shoulder, she stopped and surveyed Stanhope land from a small rise next to a soaring maple tree. Not a single other estate was visible in the distance, only swaths of land boxed in by darker green hedgerows. A breeze blew from the west, and she cast her gaze eastward, spotting a tree-ringed body of water. A pond? A lake? She headed off to explore.

By the time she reached the water's edge, the sky had darkened to an indigo gray. A few intermittent raindrops fell softly against her cheek, but Sophia refused to be deterred. Spotting a knoll near the water that beckoned as a suitable stopping place, she approached and lowered herself onto a dry patch of grass under a leafy tree.

After a few minutes, the drizzle of rain let up, and she retrieved a few manuscript pages from her bag. She'd drafted the chapter revealing the crime's resolution, but she found the next pages harder. What would Effie do now that she'd successfully solved her first mystery? Would she part from the handsome aristocrat who'd assisted her? A few ideas about the next story played in her mind, but she struggled with how to bridge her current tale with the next.

An idea came, but it forced her to change earlier chapters too. Digging more pages from her bag, she spread them out and anchored a few with nearby pebbles and obliging stones. Wind kicked up now and then, but the cluster of trees nearby sheltered her from the worst.

What if the spark of interest between Effie and her handsome, aristocratic, crime-solving partner developed into more in future stories? Could a lady detective maintain her work and independence if she married?

As Lord Redmane strode away, a phantom pinch of unease squeezed Effie's chest. As if a piece of her that had always been intact was missing now.

Sophia sat back and rolled her eyes. One night of lovemaking had turned her into a sentimentalist. She poised her pen at the start of the line to strike the words away but found herself writing more. Paragraphs and paragraphs flowed as she hunched over the paper and prayed her fountain pen didn't run out of ink.

She flicked away a raindrop on her cheek, then another. A drop plopped onto her manuscript page, running the ink like watercolor paint. Sophia dug in her bag for a handkerchief and dabbed at the paper, then began collecting the sheaves she'd spread out around her. Raindrops came faster, heavier, pattering against the tree leaves above her head like coins poured from a torn pocket.

Stretching to retrieve one manuscript page the breeze had blown from its pebble holder, she crushed another under her rain-spattered dress and cursed. "Dammit!"

Wind lashed sodden strands of hair against her face. When she reached up to swipe them away, a gust sent several of her manuscript pages sailing for the water. They floated on top like paper boats. Sophia got to her feet, hiked up her hem, and started toward the lake's edge. Hunching on the bank, she caught two of the pages and stuffed them inside her blouse. A few more squares of soaked foolscap floated out of reach.

Lowering a foot into the lake, she winced as water rushed up her leg, drenching her boots and stockings. She stepped forward tentatively, unsure how deep the bottom might be. She'd never learned to swim, but if the water was shallow, she could wade toward the floating pages. They weren't too far out yet.

Each step drew her deeper into the water, to her knees, up her thighs, and then to her waist. The weight of her skirt and petticoats dragged her down like lead ballast. Maddeningly, as she moved forward, a wave of rippling water pushed the rogue pages farther. She stopped, bent, reaching as far as she could and got her fingertips onto the edge of one precious rain-soaked piece of her story. One more inch forward and she clasped the foolscap between her fingers. Another step forward and her foot sank in the soft lake bed, tipping her off balance.

Sophia cried out. Flailing forward, one hand splashed against the surface of the water to break her fall. As she went down, she clasped her manuscript page to her chest.

Grey stopped believing in luck on the day his brother died.

He knew other men considered him a favored sod. If one tallied a man's success by the number of women who'd shared his bed, then perhaps he was fortunate man.

But he'd long ago lost faith in a mythical Lady Luck who looked down and capriciously dispensed her goodwill to those of her choosing. That was complete and utter rot. He rarely gambled anymore. When he did, he never expected to win. Calamity would never take him by surprise again. He expected misfortune, distracting himself with pleasure and indulgence in the meantime.

Half an hour after stepping out of Longcross's front door, wandering through meadows and groves with no sign of Sophia, Grey's well-honed sense of pessimism told him she'd be at the one spot on the estate he'd avoided since his fourteenth birthday.

A skitter of trepidation chased down his spine, but he turned and made his way toward the lake. Each step felt heavier, as if the grass was turning to quicksand under his feet. The muscles of his body tensed too, preparing for a fight.

Danger lay ahead. He could never envision that body of water and think of anything but the battered body of his brother laying lifeless on its banks.

Rain started in a gentle patter, soft drops pelting his skin. But the drizzle turned quickly to a steady stream. The sky bucketed down a deluge, and the ground grew soggy and slippery under his feet. Mud splashed up as he stomped across the rise leading down to the lake.

At the top, he spotted her. Her skirt ballooned as she floated in the water. His heart stopped. His breath stalled. Then his heart began hammering wildly in his chest.

He ran toward her, sliding on the sodden ground. Stumbling to one knee, clawing at the mud to get to his feet again. He had to reach her. Help her.

Flashes came of Richard. Flailing in the lake. Fighting for his life. But there was no monster holding Grey back now. No bony arm cutting off his air.

He wouldn't fail this time.

"Sophia!" He sprinted toward the water's edge and sloshed into the water.

She moved, turning to face him. Eyes huge, hair hanging in sodden strips over her shoulders, gown muddy, she was the most beautiful sight he'd ever seen.

She was breathing. Alive.

A choked exhale burst from his lungs. "Are you hurt?"

He couldn't be sure whether the water streaming down her face in fat rivulets was rain or tears.

Standing waist deep in the water, her whole gown sopping, she shook her head and slapped angrily at the lake's surface as he strode toward her.

"Come here." Grey reached out his hand. "What the devil are you doing in the water, woman?"

"My manuscript," she cried, her voice scratchy and desperate. "Please help me get the pages." She pointed to a few waterlogged cream patches on the water's surface, too far off for him to give a damn about.

She mattered. He needed to get her home and dry.

As soon as he drew close, Grey grabbed her arm, pulled Sophia toward him, and dipped into the water to lift her into his arms. She wriggled against him as she had that night in his father's suite.

"My story. I can't lose those pages."

"Shh, sweetheart. I need you more than you need those pages."

She settled against him as he carried her to the water's edge, tried to keep his footing as he clambered up the muddy rise, and set her safely on her feet. She was shaking and cold. He shucked his jacket and settled it around her shoulders. She cast her gaze toward the water and said on a shaky breath, "They're gone."

"Wait here," he told her as he headed back toward the water.

"No." She started after him.

"Stop, Sophia. It's too slippery down here." He pointed her back toward the spot where he'd left her. "Just wait for me."

The grass had receded into sloppy clumps of mud, and he lifted his boots high as he squelched through the muck.

"Be careful. The water might be deep at that end," she called from the bank.

Very deep. He'd learned to swim in this water. Loved this spot so much that Blessing had to retrieve him from the lake at the end of more than one long summer's day. He wouldn't behave for anyone else. Except Richard. When his brother went away to university, Grey had been left with little guidance and a good deal of childish mischief in his heart.

Which had led to this damned lake, that harrowing day, and the calamity he'd give his very soul to undo.

As he waded deeper, Sophia called out again. "Just leave them. Please come out."

But he had to get her pages. She was safe and alive, and he would have given her the bloody moon to see her smile again.

They were little more than soggy squares of pulp by the time he swam out to collect the tangle of pages floating half under and half atop the lake's surface. The writing was faint, ink smearing as he lifted them from the water. Still, swimming toward her with them clutched in his fist felt like a victory. Seeing her standing on the rise above the lake felled old ghosts.

He'd come back to these murky waters and, for whatever fickle reason, Lady Luck had smiled on him today.

Sophia bounced on her toes as he approached, held out her hands, and Grey laid his tattered offering on her palms.

"Thank you." She shoved the pages inside her mucky shirtwaist and stepped closer, lifting to press a quick kiss to his lips.

Grey lashed an arm around her waist and held her tight, cupping the back of her head and deepening their kiss. He was done with quick. Done with teasing and temptation. He needed to feel her in his arms, give her some of his heat, convince his galloping heart that she was safe and uninjured.

"We should get inside," she murmured against his lips as rain and wind buffeted them.

"Yes." They held on to each other as they made their way back, each trying to keep the other from slipping in the soaking lawn.

For the first time in years, the sight of Longcross brought a sense of relief instead of dread. Grey was so eager to get Sophia inside he was tempted to hitch her into his arms and sprint across the threshold. Instead, they continued on, arm in arm, causing Blessing to shudder in horror as they dragged bits of grass, mud, and pools of water onto his pristine checkered tile floor.

"What in heaven's name happened to you two?" Becca clasped a hand over her mouth as she entered the hall and scanned them from head to toe. "Is either of you hurt?"

"Just wet and dirty," Grey assured her.

"Guess you won't be needing that cart to the station, miss," a maid said as she slipped his sopping jacket from Sophia's shoulders.

"Of course not. Let's get you upstairs and into some dry clothes." Becca reached for Sophia's hand.

"My bag is back at the lake," Sophia said miserably. "I have no other clothes."

"I have plenty." Becca turned to Blessing. "We should send one of the footmen out to retrieve Miss Ruthven's case."

The old butler nodded and set off to do his duty, casting bereft glances back at the water dripping from their clothes onto the entry hall floor.

Grey had removed his arm from Sophia's body as soon as they stepped through the front door, but he didn't want to let her go. She glanced back as she followed Becca up the stairs, casting him a soft grin that soothed him like the stroke of her hands on his skin.

He could let her walk away, knowing he'd see her again after she'd gotten warm and dry. The greater question was whether he would survive letting her walk out of his life for good.

CHAPTER TWENTY

Inspecting herself in the dressing room mirror, Sophia gave the bodice of Lady Fennston's loaned gown a tug. She loved the electric blue shade and intricate beading along the hem and neckline. The velveteen fabric felt heavenly against her skin, not only soft, but heavy enough to chase away her persistent chill. She and the baroness were close in height and shape, so the length and fit of the dress suited her well, but the bodice was far too meager to contain her bosom. Perhaps if she hunched through most of the evening meal, she could keep from exposing every member of the household to her cleavage.

She doubted Grey would complain. In fact, she had half a mind to walk across the hall and let him decide whether she looked too scandalous for the dinner table. Of course, he'd be freshly bathed, clean-shaven, smelling of bay soap and his unique masculine scent.

If she sought him out now, she doubted they'd make it down to dinner at all.

Potent memories flooded her mind—the hunger of his kiss on the bank of that impossibly cold lake. The way he held her, tenderly, protectively, as if he'd never let her go. The warmth of his body thawed her the minute he pulled her from the water, but the relief in his eyes melted any doubt. He was more than the scandalous blackguard he claimed to be.

Grey desired her. He'd never hidden that fact. But stomping into the water to retrieve waterlogged sheaves of her story wasn't an act of lust.

He cared about her. But did he love her?

Pushing *those* distracting thoughts away, she returned to the bedroom portion of her suite. Kneeling before the fire, she examined the manuscript pages laid out on the rug nearby. Still damp but decidedly drier. All had begun to curl 'round the edges, but the ink had proven tenacious, despite a thorough wash in lake water and rain. She could read most of every page. The challenge would be putting them back in order, along with the few Grey had rescued.

Retrieving them was a perfect excuse to visit his room.

Sophia started toward the door and jumped when someone knocked on the other side. She held her breath and twisted the knob, expecting Grey to step through. Instead, the maid who'd helped Sophia remove her wet clothes peeked in.

"Some more clothing for you, miss. From Lady Fennston." The young woman stepped inside, carrying a pile of folded fabric in one arm and several gowns draped over the other.

"Oh, I don't think I'll need all of those." Judging by the multiple colors and styles, Lady Fennston expected her to stay at Longcross for some time. Sophia planned to leave on the next day's train.

"No matter. Better to plan ahead than come up short."

Sophia grinned and nodded as the girl continued sorting the dresses into the tall wardrobe. She was the efficient sort of servant Cate would appreciate.

"Shall I take you down to the dining room, miss?" the girl asked when she'd finished in the dressing room. "They'll be ringing the gong soon, but you can wait in the red drawing room in the meantime."

Since she didn't know where either the dining or red room was, Sophia agreed and followed the young woman down the stairs. "How many drawing rooms are there at Longcross?"

"Three, though one is used as the countess's private parlor."

"And where is the countess?" Grey had never mentioned his mother. Even after the incident in his father's bedroom, no one spoke openly of the earl or his wife. The house seemed full of secrets and mysteries to solve.

"I've never seen her, miss," the maid whispered back. "She hasn't lived at Longcross for all the while I've been in service."

Sophia began to ask more, but the deep reverberating chime of the dinner gong echoed through the house, and the maid picked up her pace.

"Good luck, miss," she said, depositing Sophia outside the door of a room wafting scents of roasted meat and Grey's crisp woodsy cologne.

Sophia drew in a bolstering breath and started across the threshold.

"Mercy." Grey murmured the single word of praise and froze as he stared at her, a small aperitif glass halfway to his lips. His gray eyes sparked with glints of silver as he drew his gaze down her body and back up again.

Sophia fought the urge to yank up her bodice.

Grey looked devastating in a spotless white vest and tie and ebony black suit. His eyes were those of a rogue, but he wore his suit like the most fashionable of aristocratic gentlemen.

At the end of the table, Lord Fennston stood and pointed to a chair across from his wife. "Miss Ruthven, if you please."

Sophia started toward the chair he indicated, but Grey stepped close. His clean pine scent made her mouth water. "Sit next to me," he said quietly as he offered his arm and led her toward the end of the table opposite Lord Fennston.

The two men had each claimed their sides, the baron at the head of the table, Grey at the other end. Liddy sat in the middle catty-corner from Lady Fennston, and Sophia took a chair across from hers, closest to Grey.

Lord Fennston grumbled something inaudible, then happily tucked in to his soup the moment a servant placed a steaming bowl in front of him.

Grey sipped his wine, flicking his gaze across Sophia's face, her neck, her cleavage. She tasted her soup and licked a dribble off her lip. Out of the corner of her eye, she saw Grey lick his lips too. Their gazes clashed and heat swept up her body.

"I never imagined I'd see either of you dry again after that downpour," Becca said over the clink of silver spoons and crystal. "And I'm glad to see my dress suits you so... well, Miss Ruthven."

Lady Phyllida stifled a chuckle, covering her mouth with a gloved hand as she cast a nervous glance toward Lord Fennston.

Sophia willed her cheeks not to flush.

"Your father is pleased to have you at Longcross, Winship." The baron spoke the words without any ire or judgement, but Grey seemed to bristle at the sound of the man's voice.

"Is he?" he said before swigging down more wine. "When I visited him this morning, Father barely recognized me."

"He's very forgetful," Liddy put in quietly.

"Indeed," Lord Fennston said with what sounded like genuine regret in his tone. "When do you plan to return to live at Longcross permanently?"

Grey chuckled and leaned back in his chair, bracing his hands on the table's edge. "You know that's never been my plan, Alistair."

"But surely when Lord Stanhope..." Lady Fennston's voice trailed off, and she cast a regretful glance at Phyllida.

"What, Becca?" Grey drained his wine and gestured for a footman to refill his glass. "You thought I would go from reprobate to responsible earl over night? Dishonorable men don't wake up honorable one day." He caught Sophia's gaze and watched her intently, waiting for her reaction. "Do they, Miss Ruthven?"

Sophia's throat burned. A ringing, like an echo of the dinner gong, began thrumming in her head. She wanted to give him the answer he needed, find the words that would ease the misery in his eyes. Most of all, she wanted to touch him. He was tantalizingly close, yet everything she knew of propriety dictated she keep her hands to herself.

"Perhaps a man can change." Lady Phyllida's voice was soft and hesitant. Hopeful. Sophia suspected she was thinking of Lord Westby.

"Not in my experience," Fennston said decidedly, welcoming the arrival of the second course by tucking his napkin behind his neck cloth. "A man's nature is set from an early age, and his character often worsens with age."

"That's worrying," Lady Fennston teased. "What character flaws shall you begin exhibiting in your dotage, Alistair?"

"Lucky for you, there is no chance of my character worsening." The man tipped his head and cast his wife a mock-stern gaze over his spectacles. "I had the very good fortune of marrying a wife who inspires me to be a better man each day." He lifted his glass and Lady Fennston raised her own for an impromptu toast.

Sophia couldn't help but grin at the display of marital bliss. Not as effusive as her brother and his new wife, but one could live happily on the sort of contentment she glimpsed in the baron's and baroness's gazes as they beamed at each other.

"Well said." Lady Phyllida lifted her glass and broke into a toothy smile.

Beside Sophia, Grey pressed two fingers to his temple as if his head had begun to thud as fiercely as hers.

"Speaking of marriage, Winship." Fennston cast his gaze down the table. "You should consider pursuing that happy state for yourself."

Grey grasped his wine glass at the same moment Sophia reached for her fork. Their hands collided and, for a scandalous moment, he clasped her fingers in his, stroking his thumb across her skin. His touch sent sparks of heat radiating up her arm, tingling in her veins. She wished they were anywhere but at a table in view of his sister and family.

Too quickly, he let her go, and no one else seemed to notice the exchange that left her quivering.

"Perhaps I should consider marriage," Grey said, his voice taut.

Lady Fennston and Phyllida snapped their heads toward him. Sophia held her breath.

"It won't be Miss Cathright; I promise you that, Alistair."

Lord Fennston frowned and pushed his spectacles up his nose. "Who?"

"Lady Stanhope chose her for Jasper, just before—" Midsentence, Lady Fennston fell silent.

"Ah," the baron said, as if understanding had suddenly dawned. "Aunt Jocelyn was keen on arranging marriages for her children, wasn't she? But you needn't worry, Winship. None of them were ever legally binding. You have no contractual obligation to marry Miss Cathright."

"Even if you wished to do so," Lady Fennston added, "you'd have to find the lady first. Last I heard, she'd set off for America."

"What a relief," Grey said, raising his glass in a mock salute. "I wish her well."

"So you should feel free to marry whomever you wish." Lady Fennston cast a knowing glance in Sophia's direction.

"Within reason, of course," her husband added.

"I think everyone should be able to marry whomever they wish," Liddy proclaimed. Leaning forward to meet the gaze of each of them at table one by one, she added earnestly. "And only ever for love."

"There are other considerations, Phyllida." Lady Fennston cast a wary glance at her husband before continuing. "Duty, responsibility, there are often practical reasons for making a match that will bloom into love with time."

"Miss Ruthven, what do you think?" Liddy turned in her chair so that she was no longer facing Lady Fennston. "I should like to hear from a writer on this matter."

The girl seemed to have a very high opinion of writers or at least an abiding belief that they'd always champion romantic love.

Queasiness began to brew in Sophia's belly, and she slid a hand to her stomach. Everyone's gaze was on her, pressing, waiting for a brilliant answer that would settle the impossible dispute. She was most aware of Grey, his nearness, his scent, his steady perusal as he waited for her to speak on the topic they'd once broached with each other over ale and cider.

"I think," she started, gently patting at her stomach, hoping the soup she'd consumed would stay down, "if one is lucky enough to marry for love, one should. My brother did, and I've never seen him so happy."

Grey smiled at that. Sophia caught the flash and looked into his eyes. Before their unexpected encounter in Lord Westby's study, Kit had been the one thing they had in common. She knew their friendship mattered a great deal to both men.

"There. You see," Liddy said triumphantly.

"But…" Sophia wasn't finished yet, and she wanted to finish before she did something unforgivable, like lose her supper at the dinner table. "There are other considerations too." She thought of Ogilvy and her own practical reasons for responding to his ad. Perhaps no one understood the sensible reasons for marriage better than Timothy Ogilvy, with his list of requisite qualities for a bride.

"Such as?" Grey prompted. He waited, body tense, his gaze fixed on her face.

He wanted her list, her logical, practical reasons for choosing a husband. They'd seemed so unwavering when she'd clipped Ogilvy's ad from the newspaper. Then Grey had come bursting into Westby's study and into her life. He'd thrown pebbles at Kit and Ophelia's new windows. Given her the most exquisite first kiss. Made love to her with such tenderness and passion, she couldn't ever imagine another man's hands on her body.

Now nothing was clear, except that her heart was in her throat, her belly was roiling, and she wanted to be in Grey's arms.

He looked bereft, as if he needed her there too.

"Grey," she managed, sliding her hand closer to his on the table.

He clasped her fingers, and his eyes widened. "You're burning up."

"I'm not feeling well."

Lady Fennston dropped her napkin and rose from her chair. "We should get her upstairs. Have Blessing send for Dr. Keene."

"I'll take her up." Grey's voice carried just enough steel that no one questioned the appropriateness of his helping her from her chair.

"Be careful with her," Liddy called, as if she thought Sophia a piece of delicate porcelain.

At the moment she felt more like a wrung-out rag.

Grey held her close as he led her toward the main hall. She swayed as they neared the stairs, and he turned as if he might sweep her into his arms.

"Don't you dare pick me up again. I am quite capable of walking on my own."

He braced his hand on her back as she started up the first step. "Perhaps I pick you up for my benefit as much as your own." Leaning in, he added, "I'll take any excuse to have you in my arms."

"You should keep your distance in case I'm contagious."

He hugged her closer. "I'll take the risk."

By the time they reached her room, Sophia wouldn't have minded being in his arms. Her nausea was waning, but the pounding in her head had built to a dizzying crescendo. As soon as he opened the door, she beelined for the bed, crumpling onto the coverlet. Shivers wracked her body, and she tried to curl up, drawing her knees in close.

Grey pressed a warm broad palm to her back, curling the other around her shoulder. "Come, sweetheart, let me get the cover over you." Turning her onto her back, Grey reached down, slipped off her shoes, and pulled the coverlet up. When he began to step away, Sophia stuck her hand out to stop him.

"Don't go."

"I'm not leaving you. Just going to stoke the fire." He kept his word, returning as soon he'd agitated the coals into blazing heat.

Sophia couldn't stop shivering. She stared into the flames, but her body shook as if the bed was filled with ice.

Grey shucked his jacket and settled the fine dark fabric over her chest and shoulders. He laid a blessedly warm hand on her forehead. "Definitely feverish."

"I-I'll be all right." Sophia swept a finger over the frown burrowing lines between his brows.

He chuckled and captured her arm, lifting her hand to his lips and placing a tender kiss on each knuckle. "I'm no expert at caring for the ailing, but shouldn't I be the one comforting you?" Flattening a palm against her cheek, he added, "Give someone a chance to take care of you for a change."

She studied Grey as he bent to kiss the center of her palm. Firelight limned his bronze waves, outlined all the chiseled edges of his face. When he gazed back at her, his brow was still knitted with worry.

She loved him. No protest, no reasoning. The truth was there in her heart, as if it had slipped in without her noticing.

"Grey," she whispered. Her throat ached as if she'd swallowed a wire brush, but she had to get the words out.

"Shh, sweet." He stroked her hair away from her brow, then leaned up to press a kiss to her forehead.

Her skin was so warm, his lips felt cool.

From the doorway, a man cleared his throat. Sophia was too tired to lift her head, but Grey stood and faced the intruder, keeping her hand clasped in his.

"Dr. Keene, thank God you're here. She's shaking and feverish. What can you do?"

"A good deal more without you hovering like a nervous hen." The man's booming voice made Sophia wince. "Leave the lady in my care, Lord Winship, and ask a maid to send up some ice and cold compresses."

Grey leaned over her, one hand sunk in the pillow next to her head. "I'm coming back. Keene will take care of you in the meantime."

As his footsteps retreated, a bearded old man came into view, frowning down at her with grim concentration. His cold wrinkled hand came up to rest on her forehead. "You've quite captured the boy, haven't you, my dear?"

Sophia frowned, unable to make sense of his words beyond the clatter in her head.

"The Stanhopes have been in my care since the earl was a child," he said in his low baritone as he lifted an instrument from his bag. "Delivered all three of the countess's children myself." The doctor pressed the metal disk of a stethoscope to her chest and listened intently for a moment. "I've only seen that look of terror on the boy's face once before. On the day his brother died." After drawing the gas lamp on the bedside table nearer, Dr. Keene lifted her wrist and pressed two fingers firmly against her pulse. "Fear is good for a man once in a while. Reminds him what matters most."

"I love him," Sophia confessed.

"Of course you do, my dear." Dr. Keene patted her arm in a fatherly manner. "I diagnosed that condition the moment I walked through the door."

CHAPTER TWENTY-ONE

"I've encountered many during my investigations who crave knowledge and will pay anything to discover facts, only to find the truth very hard to face."

—CASEBOOK OF EUPHEMIA
BREEDLOVE, LADY DETECTIVE

Someone kicked Grey's foot, and he sat up with a start, orienting himself quickly. He'd been keeping sentry in Sophia's room for two days, crumpled in a chair, watching over her.

Dr. Keene loomed near, lifting a finger to his lips before casting his gaze toward where Sophia slumbered in bed. "Fever's down," the old man said quietly. "Just a cold to contend with now."

Lurching out of his chair, Grey clasped the doctor's hand. "Thank you, Keene."

"Might want to spruce up a bit, Lord Winship, if you plan to woo the lady properly." The doctor arched a brow as he took in the rumpled clothes Grey had been wearing for two days.

"Good advice." Now that he knew she was out of danger, he could justify leaving her side for an hour to bathe and pull a razor across his scruff.

"Shall I offer more?"

"Go on, then." Grey suspected a lecture was coming. Keene was prone to them, or at least he had been when Grey or Richard had gotten into scrapes as boys.

"Spend more time at Longcross, my lord." He patted Grey's shoulder. "What are a dozen city diversions when you can have one lovely woman by your side?" He glanced again at Sophia, then lifted his bag and strode for the door. "Keep her in bed for a few days, my lord."

Grey arched an eyebrow as the medical man closed the door behind him.

"I'm not staying in bed," Sophia called in a rusty voice. "I feel much better."

"Doctor's orders, I'm afraid." Grey approached her bedside and swallowed hard at the sight of the dark crescents under her eyes. Despite the determination in her blue-green gaze, he was equally determined for her to get the rest she needed.

"He also advised you to retire to Longcross and keep a woman by your side. Do you plan to take that advice?"

Maybe. He doubted he'd ever run the estate with the efficiency that seemed to come naturally to Alistair and Becca, but he didn't dread the place anymore. In a few short days, the estate had become more than a mausoleum to painful memories of the past. With Sophia, he'd made new memories. Vivid and much more pleasant ones.

"I plan to do whatever it takes to keep you in this bed for a few days." He took her hand, because touching her had become a necessity. For the first time in two days, she was warm but not feverish. His chest swelled with relief.

"And what is your strategy?"

He'd failed this quiz before. She'd chided him for rushing in with brute force rather than employing his intellect. He scoured his tired brain for some distraction that would keep her satisfied to remain abed. "I could read to you. Judging by the story you're writing, you favor mysteries."

Sophia rose onto her elbows and stared in horror at the thick rug in front of the fireplace. "You took up my pages? You *read* my story?"

"I…" Grey hesitated, running a hand through his hair. He wanted to get this answer right. She'd written a story, and writers generally wrote so that others might read their tales. Or so he'd assumed. "I assembled them, adding the ones I retrieved from the lake." He pointed to where he'd collected the warped sheaves of foolscap. "Reading the story was necessary to put the whole back in order."

She grimaced and sank down further into the covers.

"I quite like Lord Redmane, and Miss Breedlove is a fearsome sleuth."

"Do you think so?" Sophia edged up, scooting into a sitting position.

"Absolutely."

"I haven't decided how they should continue."

"Well, then you must decide and finish the tale." Grey reached around to add another pillow to support her back, inadvertently brushing her breast. She let out a little a hiss of surprise and clutched his hand before he could pull back.

"Thank you for staying with me." The touch of her fingers was feather light, but warmth radiated through his body. "I sensed you were here through the worst of the fever."

Through every minute. He'd never considered leaving her side. "No place else I wished to be." Sifting his fingers through the honey-blonde waves of hair spilling over her shoulder, he told himself he had to stop touching her. She needed rest, not him hovering over her, yearning to divest her of every stitch of clothing and climb into bed with her.

A soft rap at the door preceded the arrival of a maid carrying a pile of linens. "Lady Fennston says I am to help miss with her bath."

Grey swallowed down the reply on the tip of his tongue. What he wouldn't give to be the one tasked with helping Sophia to bathe. But he'd already broken every rule of etiquette by remaining in her room. He stood and promised, "I'll return soon."

"Can I take you up on your offer?" Sophia called when he was two steps from the door.

Grey lifted a brow. Had he actually made his offer to bathe her out loud?

"Will you come back and read to me?" she clarified.

Grey smiled for the first time in days. His face ached as if his muscles had forgotten how. "Let me guess. Detective stories?"

Sophia grinned back. "Conan Doyle will do quite nicely. I have a copy of *The Memoirs of Sherlock Holmes* in my bag."

Grey walked quickly as he began his search for Sophia's leather traveling case. According to the upstairs maid, a footman had retrieved it from the lakeside but failed to take the bag up to her room. While Grey searched its contents in Longcross's entry hall, Liddy appeared.

"You must plead my case," she demanded in strident tones. "Becca says I can't go to the Westby ball because I'm not formally out until next year."

"Sounds sensible to me." Not to mention a useful means of keeping her away from the Earl of Westby.

She sighed dramatically. "When have you ever been sensible in your life? Please help me, Jasper."

"Helping you is why I'm here."

She scrunched her nose and tipped her head. "Whatever do you mean?"

"Liddy, you disappeared." Grey scooped up a collection of papers and a thin blue clothbound book from a side compartment of Sophia's bag. "You gallivanted to Brighton with Clive Holden, then took yourself off to Cambridge. Sophia and I followed you for days. Why do you think we're at Longcross?"

"I thought she'd come as a friend of Becca's, and that you followed her here because you're besotted with her."

Well, she had half the story right. Grey glanced around to ensure no servants were about. He'd never worried about his own reputation, nor those of the women he'd carried on affairs with. But he cared about Sophia's, despite being the lucky scoundrel who'd taken her to his bed a few nights ago.

"Her brother is my friend." And he had Kit's murderous rage to contend with when the man learned how close Grey and Sophia had become in a week's time. "She agreed to assist me in my search for you."

"Oh." Pressing her lips together, his sister clasped her hands behind her back and almost looked contrite. Almost. "I'm sorry if I caused anyone worry."

"If?" Worry was the least of what she'd caused. Some half-wit actor had taken his part on Fleet Theater's stage. Sophia had jumped into the lake and been abed with fever for two days as a result. Grey hadn't slept in his own bed in far longer. Though, in truth, his unprincipled friends were likely using his Belgrave Square home to come and go, and sleep and revel, just as they did while he was in residence. He usually hated quiet and being alone, but the prospect of returning to the bacchanalian wreck of his townhouse no longer held any appeal.

"I don't know how you can lecture me when everyone knows you engage in the worst sorts of excesses." Despite her defensive tone, she stared at the tile floor, unable to meet his gaze.

"No one should follow my example." He hooked a finger under her chin and nudged her head up. "Especially a clever, lovely young lady who could win the heart of an honorable young man."

"I've found the man I wish to spend the rest of days with, but I am capable of pursuits beyond flirtation and matrimony." She lifted her chin from his finger and stepped away. "Perhaps you should read Miss Ruthven's and her sister-in-law's books."

Grey frowned as his sister stomped away. "Why?"

"You might learn a thing or two about women and what they truly crave in life and love."

After a thorough search of her still-damp bag, Grey found no other book than the volume of Sherlock Holmes tales. He separated the *Memoirs* from a pile of papers it had been stored with and kneeled down to put them back in Sophia's bag. Then a name caught his eye.

Ogilvy.

The ink on the man's letter had run, but Grey could decipher most of the words. Apparently Sophia had written to Ogilvy, and he mentioned enclosing a photograph in reply. Sifting the papers, his fingers struck a harder bond of paper, a photo card of a stern-looking middle-aged man with pale skin and dark everything else. Beside the photograph, a small clipped rectangle of newsprint bore a matrimonial ad such as one might find in the London papers.

Grey considered such ads sad, often comical. At the theater, some of his fellow acting troupe took to amusing each other by reading them aloud backstage. Companionship was plentiful in the city, whether acquired through charm or coin. Why petition for a mate in the newspapers?

But he knew the answer. He sought affection when he liked and with women who cared about their reputations as little as he did. Sophia had spent her life upholding all those constraining principles and ethics her father had been known for. She was the kind of woman who would give herself to spinsterhood rather than engage in an affair with a man who offered her passion and nothing more. Like Westby. Like Grey.

His hands shook as he shoved the sundry papers back in her bag. One stuck up at an odd angle, and he pulled the sheet free. A list written in a flawless italic script, the same hand as Ogilvy had used in his letters. *Qualities Required in a Wife.* The list was ridiculously long, the product of a pompous man who seemed to think women were akin to a carriage or suit that one could order designed to one's specifications.

What made his gut clench were the marks on the page. He could only imagine they'd been made by Sophia. She'd ticked off several of the qualities on Ogilvy's list, as if she'd sought to meet his demands and be the perfect matrimonial prospect he sought. But she'd fallen short. Two items— "meekness" and "no pursuits outside the home"—had no tick mark, and "purity of body and mind" contained a series of question marks in the margin.

Grey crushed the paper in his fist, shoved the volume of Sherlock Holmes stories under his arm, and sprinted up the stairs to Sophia's room. He pushed the door open so hard it bounced off the wall.

She gasped, nearly sloshing tea from the cup in her hands. "My goodness, what's wrong? Are you all right?" Her pretty blonde brows tented on her forehead.

As he strode toward the bed, he straightened Ogilvy's stupid bloody list and held the page out for her to see. "This is utter hogwash."

She narrowed her eyes to read the faded writing, and her brows winged high. "Where did you get that?"

When Sophia reached out, Grey crushed the paper in his hand and flung it toward the fireplace.

Then he leaned down and kissed her. He didn't try for finesse or skill. He wasn't gentle, as he should have been. Fingers twisted in her hair, hand skimming over her cheek, her neck, her breast, he poured all his worry, need, and desire into the kiss.

She clung to him, her hands as eager as his. Her moans and gasps were a symphony to his ears. When he pulled back, breathless, she stared at him with a stunned look in her verdigris eyes.

He told her, "You're perfect, just as you are."

"I'm far from perfect."

"If you argue this point with me, I'll simply kiss you senseless until you agree."

She laughed, a warm delicious sound that made his whole body ache to have her underneath him. Or on top of him. Any way he could have her would do.

"Is that how you win all of your arguments with ladies?"

"No," he said brusquely, sitting back on the bed, one hand still twined with hers. "Only you." He could hardly admit that he rarely argued with any woman. None of his previous entanglements had lasted long enough for a disagreement. And if one arose, it was always a signal for him to bolt.

Funny, then, that he was quite content to spend the rest of his days settling rows with Sophia Ruthven. Especially if each ended with kissing her. But would she be content to spend her days with him? With her beauty, she'd likely been propositioned by more than a few scoundrels, beyond him and Westby, yet she'd responded to the matrimonial ad of a pompous sod like Ogilvy.

In his haste to kiss her, Grey had dropped her book of detective stories on the bed.

Sophia took up the volume and lifted it toward him. "You did say you'd read to me."

"Is there a particular one I should I start with, or have you already read them all?" He couldn't tell if the book was well thumbed. Its page edges were rippled from being doused with rain.

"Surprise me. I enjoy the stories no matter how many times I've read them."

Grey began thumbing the pages and arched a brow. "Even though you know the answer to who committed the crime?"

"I suppose I enjoy Holmes's methods for solving a conundrum as much as the mystery itself."

He recalled her calm demeanor and insightful questions throughout their search for Liddy. Her intrepid Effie Breedlove character seemed more an ideal of Sophia's than simply a character on the page. But if she saw herself as Effie, why had she written a character who became smitten with the roguish aristocrat who'd helped her solve the mystery?

Grey stood and lifted the wingback chair over to her bedside. He opened the volume of tales to *The Yellow Face* and began reading.

Sophia settled back against the pillows with a little grin curving her mouth. "That's a good one," she said quietly. "The very story where I got the name for my detective."

"Shh, I'm reading," Grey teased, and then read on, drawing on his acting skills to give each character a unique voice.

Sure enough, the Conan Doyle mystery centered around a character named Effie Munro and her husband's suspicions about his wife's past. The story proved quite short, but within ten minutes Grey was thoroughly engrossed, sitting forward in his chair, the book balanced on his knees.

Sophia watched him, as enrapt as a theater audience, one hand clasped over her mouth.

He read more quickly, but tried to steady himself. For Sophia's sake, he tried to perform the story with emotion and skill. He looked up at her in amazement as the mystery was revealed, then bowed his head to continue.

" 'I am not a very good man, Effie,' " Grey's voice roughened as he read the husband's reaction to his wife's deceit, " 'but I think I am a better one than you have given me credit for being.' " Just four paragraphs remained in the story, and Grey stumbled through them before snapping the book shut.

Sophia beamed at him and clapped her hands. "Beautifully done. Now I know why ladies line up at the stage doors for you."

"Why do you want to marry Ogilvy?" Grey regretted the question instantly. Not because he wasn't desperate to know the answer, but because his words swept away all the admiration in her eyes and wiped the dazzling smile from her face.

"You shouldn't have rummaged through my belongings."

"I was retrieving your book so that I could read to you." Like a detective claiming his evidence, he lifted the volume to prove his point. "Judging by his photograph and letters, Ogilvy's as dull as dry toast. Why would you want to marry such a man?"

"And you judge everyone by appearance, don't you? The handsome actor with a bevy of beautiful woman on his arm every night." She threw back the covers and swung her legs around as if she intended to get out of bed.

"Don't get out. Dr. Keene said you must stay in bed."

"Dr. Keene isn't my doctor, this isn't my house, and you have no right to instruct me in what I must do." In spite of her determined shout, Sophia remained in bed. She lifted a hand to her head as if she was in pain, and Grey rushed to her side.

"No." Her hand shot out. "I can't think clearly when you touch me."

"Likewise." He couldn't resist smirking.

She caught the flash and scowled up at him. "You shouldn't be in the room when I'm half-dressed anyway. It's not proper."

"We're way past propriety, sweetheart." Grey caught her scent, bergamot and warm woman, and his mouth watered. "I'm not leaving until you answer my question."

"My decisions are my own, and Mr. Ogilvy is none of your business." She got back into bed and tucked the blanket firmly around her, as if attempting to create a barrier to keep him away.

"You write of an adventurous woman." Grey pointed to the stack of pages from her manuscript. "A clever woman who bests all the men around her at solving crimes and every other endeavor." Walking toward the fireplace, he kicked the crinkled ball of Ogilvy's list with the toe of his boot. "And yet you wish to give yourself to some sorry sod who wants a custom-order wife? Who thinks women can be reduced to a neatly written list. I didn't see passion on the fool's list. I saw no mention of stubbornness, tenacity, courage, or intelligence. You possess those qualities in spades, Sophia."

"I suppose I'll never suit any man, then." Clasping her arms across her lush breasts, she insisted, "I'm fully prepared to be a spinster."

Grey chuckled, and she cast him a glare full of emerald fire. "Sophia." Her name always felt so good on his tongue, right and somehow familiar, as if he'd been waiting his whole life for her. "Solve the mystery for me, won't you? Tell me why a woman like you, lush and lovely and full of passion, would even consider marrying a man like T. Ogilvy, Esquire."

She was silent so long he thought she'd refuse to answer. Staring at the fire, she finally murmured, "Because he wants a wife." Slowly, she lifted her head and cast her gaze his way. "Do you?"

Grey's mouth went dry, his chest hollow and tight. He backed out of the room, his view of Sophia retreating. The opposite of his nightmares, when he ran toward Richard and never got closer. At the threshold, he turned away from her, kept going, and never looked back.

CHAPTER TWENTY-TWO

*"Along with a finely tuned ear, sharp eyes, and
sundry detecting tools, I find a sturdy parasol and
study in the defensive arts serve a lady detective
well."*

—CASEBOOK OF EUPHEMIA
BREEDLOVE, LADY DETECTIVE

"I have no business attending an aristocrat's ball." Sophia
instantly realized the futility of her refusal, especially considering that a seamstress kneeled at her feet, finishing off hemming stitches to ensure Lady Fennston's borrowed gown fit
her properly. "I'm not an aristocrat." And she had a terrible
feeling about the ball.

The first and last ball she'd ever attended was still the
stuff of her nightmares.

"There are at least four reasons you should attend," Liddy
insisted from the slipper chair in Sophia's dressing room.

"After days of begging Becca and Alistair, I will be there, and I want you there too. Alistair arranged a special invitation for you since Becca likes you so much. You'll look positively ravishing in that gown, and Grey will have the opportunity to dance with you."

"He won't." Sophia examined the gown's bust. The fabric was plentiful enough to cover her cleavage, yet hugged her in beautiful shimmering peach satin. "That would require him to speak to me." Which he hadn't done for three days. Not since he scurried from her room as if his heels were on fire.

The following day she'd done her best to get out of bed, dress herself in the gown she'd worn to Longcross, and secure a cart to the station. Circumstance and the estate's inhabitants had thwarted her at every turn. A maid claimed she couldn't locate Sophia's boots. Another informed her that the cart and carriages were all in use or need of repair, and when Becca and Liddy heard of her plan to depart, they convened an emergency afternoon tea in her sitting room to convince her to stay.

Becca, as Lady Fennston insisted on being addressed, had urged Sophia to remain at Longcross and rest for a few more days. When cajoling didn't have much effect, Liddy turned to begging. She spoke with heart-wrenching honesty of the loneliness of Longcross. Sophia could easily imagine how the huge estate must seem confining to a young woman of energy and spirit. Liddy also enthused about a Gothic romance story she'd written and how eager she was to speak to Sophia at length about books and publishing.

No one mentioned Grey, yet he was constantly on Sophia's mind. Half a dozen times, she'd started toward his door across the hall, only to think better of confronting him.

Then last night, he'd stunned her by coming to her room.

He'd swung the door open and gazed at her, his eyes full of smoke and fire, fists clenched at his sides. Hunger had glowed in his gaze, a kind of desperation. But neither of them had taken the next step. She'd wanted to reach for him, soothe the struggle tensing his body, answer the question in his eyes.

But she was still waiting for *his* answer.

Minutes after bursting in without a word, he'd silently retreated.

"There, miss." The seamstress who'd come to assist with the fitting of Becca's new ball gown stepped back and surveyed her work. "I think that will do quite nicely."

"Thank you."

The young woman ducked her head. "I should go and assist with Lady Fennston's fitting."

She hadn't meant to embarrass the girl, but Sophia wasn't used to the kind of attentiveness from servants and staff that the Fennstons and Stanhopes took for granted. She wondered how Cate would fare in such a household. Most of all, she missed Cate's good sense and excellent advice. Except for the parts about being adventurous. That encouragement had led her to a gilded estate she found it difficult to escape and a man she was sure she'd never forget.

"Grey may seem like a bit of a riddle, but he's clear as day to me." Liddy was willing to give Sophia advice, apparently. But speaking about him to his sister seemed inappropriate, if not unfair. She shuddered to think how Kit or Clary might explain away her behavior. According to Clary, she was volcanic, and she still wasn't quite sure what the description was supposed to mean.

"Tell me about your story," Sophia tried as a diversion. She'd been encouraging Liddy's literary efforts and was curious how far her tale had progressed.

Liddy pealed with gusty laughter. "So he's avoiding speaking *to* you, and you're avoiding speaking *of* my brother altogether?"

Sophia sat gingerly on the edge of a chaise lounge, trying not to loosen any of the careful stitches the seamstress had worked so hard to sew.

"What you have to know about Grey is that he tends to walk away from anything he cares for deeply."

"That makes no logical sense whatsoever." Which was what Sophia was beginning to conclude about men in general.

"Richard's the cause. Well, his death." Liddy grew uncharacteristically somber, tucking her chin against her chest. "I was born after he died. I only know what Jasper told me. That once he'd gone, nothing was ever the same again."

"What happened to him?" Sophia asked gently, loath to pry but eager to know about any event that had such a devastating effect on Grey.

"Only Grey knows for sure," Liddy said, regaining her light tone. "He witnessed our brother being attacked by a gang of thieves. Jasper was gravely injured himself. The guilt colored all his choices, I suspect. Any time good fortune comes his way, he bolts. He left university on the cusp of a degree, left home when he came of age to inherit, and now..." Liddy bit her lip and shrugged.

"He'll bolt again?"

"I hope not." Liddy lifted a finger to chew on her nail. "He'd be a fool not to see what's right in front of him, wouldn't he?"

Sophia sensed the girl was referring to Westby as much as her brother and tried for a reassuring smile. Westby was a cad, but perhaps she was as foolish as Liddy for imagining a man like Grey might wish to transform from scoundrel to husband.

*M*en *can change.*

Grey repeated the words to himself as he tipped back a glass of whisky and gazed out of the Westby smoking room into the quickly filling ballroom. He'd come to the Westby estate early, planning to pummel Dominic. Of course, the scoundrel knew better than to show his face.

Which left Grey far too much time to brood.

He fixed on Kit Ruthven as his exemplar of change. The man had embraced London's diversions with Grey's brand of abandon. Affairs and dalliances with scads of fervent feminine admirers had been his chief pursuits the moment he stepped off the train from Hertfordshire. Then he'd changed. Returned to his first love and had enough sense never to let her go again.

Marriage. The very word gave Grey the shivers, but not when he thought of Sophia. If he thought of matrimony as a means of having her in his life, the prospect became tempting. Tantalizing. His desire for her, his love for her, was no longer worth questioning.

What Grey doubted was his own nature. He could live with marrying Sophia, knowing that he did not deserve her. But did she deserve his failings, the aspects of his nature he loathed to face?

"I didn't think you ever set foot past London these days, Winship."

Grey turned at the sound of Westby's voice. The man had closed the smoking room door and held a small pistol in his hand, the barrel pointed in Grey's direction.

"Put the gun down, Westby." The chambers Grey could see were empty and the Webley's hammer wasn't cocked. "You have no intention of using the thing."

Westby lowered the pistol hesitantly. "What I don't intend is for you to wrap your hands around my neck again. Ever."

"Then you should keep *your* hands off my sister."

The earl dropped onto a low settee and laid the pistol on the cushion beside him. "I'm sorry, Winship. Honestly. But I have no further interest in your sister. Believe me when I tell you her persistence disturbs me almost as much as your tendency toward violence."

Grey deposited his empty whiskey glass on the liquor trolley and strode to face Westby, flexing his hands, yearning to plant a fist in the man's smug face.

"You almost look the part of a gentleman in white tie and suit. But you and I, we both know what we are. Black hearts through and through." Westby gestured toward the ballroom. "If you've forgotten, I saw one of your old paramours here. I'm sure she'll be keen to remind you."

"Who?" He couldn't imagine any ladies from his past would wish to make their way to Derbyshire. The countryside was too staid for those who relished London entertainments.

Westby shrugged. "A redhead. Asked after you."

Flexing his fingers, he pondered whether to go for Westby's jaw or bloody his nose. Yet he knew trouncing the fool would solve nothing. Grey would appear uncivilized, and Liddy would only take the bastard's side more fiercely.

He hated his sister's preoccupation with the man, but he didn't doubt her feelings. For the first time in his life, Grey understood the tenacity of love. Devotion despite every rational reason to let go.

"You've given Liddy false hope, Westby. That needs to end. Tell her the truth of who you are."

"Have you told your blonde beauty the truth?" He flicked his hand in Grey's direction and chuckled. "Surely, you understand. We black hearts never reveal our hands. A friend and I were at Fleet Theater last week. Ladies in attendance burst into tears when the curtain rose, and they discovered you'd abandoned your role." He smirked as he rose to fix himself a drink. "Does Miss Ruthven know of all the tasty pieces panting for your return to the city?"

Grey stormed toward Westby. To hell with civility. The man needed a trouncing.

"I take it you've found your sister, Winship."

Mention of Liddy stopped him short. She'd never forgive him if he beat Westby as the man deserved.

"She's at the ball tonight." Grey caught Westby from behind, spun him by the shoulders, and gripped his lapels. "Tell her the truth, Dominic. And then keep your distance. If I see you breathe in her direction after this evening, there will be hell to pay."

"I have no wish to speak to her." The earl swiped at Grey's hands and punched a palm flat against Grey's chest. "Keep your brazen sister away from me, Winship. If she persists in her pursuit, I'll do more than ruin her in private. I shall let everyone know she's a little wanton. Like all the rest of the Stanhopes."

After a final sneer, Westby scurried from the room.

Grey waited a moment before exiting. He needed to cool his rage.

He needed to see and speak to Sophia.

As he stalked into the ballroom, fifty masked faces reminded him to slip his own strip of black satin from his pocket. He'd once favored masquerade balls, at least the dissipated sort he'd put on in Belgrave Square. Now they seemed more annoyance than amusement.

Even with a golden mask held up to cover half her face, Sophia stood apart from every other woman in the room. Her gown was the hue of blushes he'd seen color her cheeks, the shade of her mouth after he'd kissed her.

Throat parched, he strode toward her like a man dying of thirst rushes toward an oasis. He did thirst for the taste of her. More than he'd ever yearned for any woman in his life.

She stood in profile, surveying the growing ballroom.

"Dance with me?" he asked as he approached her side and caught her floral scent.

"Are you certain you recognize me, Lord Winship?"

Yes. With breath-stealing awareness. "I could never mistake you."

"So we're speaking to each other again?" Irritation made her mouth twitch, which only made him more eager to kiss her.

A quartet of musicians began tuning their instruments in the corner of the ballroom.

Grey leaned in close. "Meet me in the library. Across the hall from the ballroom." The music would be too loud, and the other guests too close, for them to speak during a dance.

"Someone needs to keep an eye on Liddy. She's already searching for Westby."

Grey glanced around the room and spotted his sister's auburn curls. "I'll have a word with her." He skimmed his ungloved fingers across Sophia's arm, finding a warm bare patch of skin above her evening gloves and below her puffed sleeves. "Then I'll come to the library."

Sophia glanced behind her as she exited the ballroom, hoping to avoid Becca's watchful gaze. She spotted her sweeping around the dance floor with her husband for the first waltz of the evening.

"The library?" she quizzed a passing footman. The young man pointed in the direction of several closed doors on the other side of the Westbys' circular main hall.

She attempted to enter one door and found it locked. Trying the next, the gilded latch gave way, and she stepped into the dark room. The air reeked of smoke, not the pleasant smell of book leather, and she wrinkled her nose. Sliding a hand along the wall near the door, she searched for a knob to turn up the gaslights.

"I prefer the darkness."

Starting at the deep voice, Sophia plastered herself against the closed door. Grey's voice was warmer, much more appealing. But she recognized this man's low baritone too. "Lord Westby."

"The beauty with the breasts."

Though her eyes were still adjusting to the darkness, Sophia saw the outline of him, heard the rustle of his movements. She turned to twist the door latch and make her escape. The moment the door slid open, flooding the room with light from the hall, he struck a fist against the panel over her head. The door slammed shut, and he crushed his body against hers.

Liquor fumes burned her eyes. The earl was soused, and she sensed he intended far worse than the boorish seduction he'd attempted in his study. He was rough and unyielding, his weight painful against her back. One of his hands came up to grip her head. He pushed her toward the door, smashed her cheek against the polished wood.

"I thought of you and pleasured myself. Imagined your sweet mouth on me."

Sophia couldn't breathe. She bucked hard to get an inch of space between them.

Westby laughed and gripped her hips. "Oh yes," he slurred. "I'll take you this way, if you like." With one hand pressed to her back, he reached down and grabbed for the hem of her gown.

Memories rushed in. Of Derringham's hands on her, his bulk crushing her, stealing her air as he clawed at her legs, desperate to get under her dress.

"Get off me!" Sophia braced herself against the door with her arms, using her weight to fight Westby's hold. The man was bulky, but he was also drunk and distracted. In the inch of space she'd created between them, she lifted her heel and stomped his foot with all her might.

"Bloody hell," he squawked, lurching away from her.

Sophia twisted the door latch and sprinted from the room. Guests crowded around the ballroom threshold, watching the dancers and sipping champagne.

She had no wish to dance or enter the fray. She needed to find Grey and headed for the only door she hadn't tried. As she twisted the latch, Westby stumbled from the smoke-scented room, and Sophia quickly closed the door of what she prayed was the library behind her.

Definitely the library. Books lined every wall, and unlike the room she'd just exited, the gaslight sconces were lit but turned low. Unfortunately, the space was empty. No Grey or anyone else, but she spied a set of French doors ajar at the far end of the room and started toward them.

Grey stood in profile near the corner of the gaslit balcony, staring up into the starlit sky. His hair glittered like polished copper in the glow of the gas lamps, especially when he turned and noticed her approach. "Sophia." He said her name tenderly. "I was wishing you were here to see the stars." A warm smile began to curve his mouth.

Until she stepped into the gaslight.

His jaw dropped as he rushed toward her and curved a hand around her shoulder.

"What's happened to you?"

Her coiffure had come loose. Westby pulled her hair at some point. She remembered that now. Reaching up, she tried her best to stuff the loose tresses back into pins.

"What happened?" he demanded as he gently cupped her cheek. "Tell me why your hair is down." Despite the forced calm of his tone, his hands quivered against her skin.

"Westby—" Before she could explain, Grey shot past her. Sophia spun and followed him out of the library.

"Where?" he barked without looking back.

"Don't do this." Sophia laid her hand on the sleeve of his jacket. "I'm fine. I got away from him."

He jerked to a stop, and she moved to stand at his side. A muscle ticked in his jaw, and his arm felt hard as marble under her fingers.

"Grey, you'll only cause a scene."

His mouth softened a fraction, and he cast her a tense gaze. "I'm an actor, sweetheart. Creating scenes is what I do best." He reached for her, hooking two fingers under her chin and caressing her jaw as if she was precious. "He'll never touch you again. I promise."

"If you resort to violence, you'll be no better than he is," she reasoned.

A tight grin tipped the edges of his mouth. "Did you ever think I was better than Westby?"

"Yes." In every way that mattered, he was a better man. On the cusp of telling him, of confessing her love, an ear-piercing boom rang out.

Grey sprang forward to position his body in front of hers.

"What is it?"

"A gunshot." He started toward the sound and called back. "Stay put."

Sophia ignored his command and followed him to the room where Westby had assaulted her. Grey grimaced at the threshold when he noticed her at his back.

"You're not walking into danger with me," he insisted.

Sophia nodded and forced herself not to follow when he pushed the door open. A young woman's desperate cries rebounded off the walls.

"Liddy." Grey retrieved a revolver from the carpet and slipped it into his jacket pocket before kneeling beside his sister. On her knees, she bent over Westby's prone body, weeping uncontrollably.

Sophia stepped inside the room and closed the door on a group of guests attempting to peer inside. Bile rushed up her throat when she drew close to Grey. Blood pooled on the floor near the earl's head.

"I-I didn't mean to," Liddy rasped. "He laughed at me. Called me awful names."

Grey gently pushed his sister aside and leaned over the earl. After a moment, he let out a gusty exhale and glanced back at Sophia. "He's fine. All the blood seems to be coming from a nick on his ear."

"He fainted," Liddy explained. "I only meant to give him a fright. I tried not to aim at him."

"How did you know to cock the hammer?" Grey stared at his sister, a dumbstruck expression slackening his jaw. "Where did you even learn how to shoot?"

"Penny dreadfuls," she said, hitching an eyebrow as if the answer should have been obvious.

All of them turned when the smoking room door swung open and the elderly Countess of Westby planted herself on the threshold, securing the door at her back.

"What in God's name is going on?" Westby's mother lifted a quizzing glass to her right eye and inspected each of them one by one. A gasp escaped when she pointed her lens at her son. "Dominic, whatever are you doing on the floor?"

"He fell," Sophia said when the earl didn't move.

"Cut his ear," Grey added.

"I'm afraid he fainted," Liddy whispered past a tearful hiccup.

"Was he being reckless again? Showing off?" Lady Westby twitched her nose and sniffed the air. "Where's the revolver?"

"My lady?" Grey queried innocently.

"He plays with the weapon like a child with a toy. I've told him he'll shoot himself one day." She cast an imperious gaze around the room. "I can smell the gunpowder."

At the same moment Grey drew the revolver from his pocket, Westby sat up and pressed a hand to his wounded ear.

His eyes bulged wildly as he glared at Liddy. "You bloody bit—"

"Dominic!" Lady Westby slammed her walking cane on the floor. "I bear your debauchery and spendthrift ways, but I will not tolerate profanity in my home."

Grey gathered Liddy to his side with one arm and laid his hand on Sophia's shoulder. "We should depart." He'd deposited the revolver on Westby's desk and tipped his chin toward the gun as they passed the countess.

"Say nothing to the others as you go," Lady Westby demanded. "If anyone understands the need for discretion and hiding a family's shame, you do, Lord Winship."

"Of course, my lady," Grey bit out.

In the vestibule beyond the library, guests milled and whispered. When one couple noticed the library door slide open, several others rushed forward to question Grey. Out of the crush, Becca and Lord Fennston emerged. Liddy went straight into Lady Fennston's arms.

"Take her and return to Longcross," Grey directed.

Fennston offered a grim nod in reply and led his wife and cousin around the gathered guests toward the house's front door.

"Aren't we going with them?" Sophia longed to be away from the Westby estate. And to never attend another blasted ball for as long as she lived.

Grey bent to whisper near her ear. "I want you with me." He plowed ahead, and the crowd parted with only a few grumbled protests.

At the carriage circle, Sophia barely resisted the urge to press herself to Grey, to hold him, breathe in his rich scent, bask in his warmth. He seemed less eager and stood stiff and rigid at her side, his arms braced across his chest.

When he finally helped her into the carriage, the weight of his hand on her back made her wince. Pain radiated out from the spot, and she drew in a sharp breath.

After joining her on the carriage bench, Grey leaned forward, elbows on his knees. "What did he do to you?"

"He pushed me." Sophia shook her head, eager to forget the whole incident. "He said vile things. Nothing more."

"I should have pummeled him when I had the chance." Grey raked his fingers roughly through his hair. His elbow bumped her shoulder, and he flinched away. "I'm sorry."

"You needn't be afraid of touching me. I shan't break." She enfolded Grey's hand and pressed his palm to her lap to prove her point.

He dug his fingers into her gown, his hand closing around her thigh as he gathered fabric, pulling until the dress's hem rested on her knee. Sophia bit her lip when he caressed her stockinged leg, sliding his fingers up and down in delicious ribbons of heat. When he reached higher, pushing the fabric up to the edge of her drawers, she shivered and emitted a breathy moan.

Grey retreated instantly, his hand stilling on her thigh before he pulled down her dress and swung his body onto the opposite carriage bench.

"That was a moan of pleasure." Sophia clenched her fist against the upholstery. Shouldn't a scoundrel know as much? "I didn't want you to stop."

"You deserve better than being tupped in a carriage after you've been…" He scrubbed a hand over his mouth.

"Nothing happened with Lord Westby." She had to make him understand. All she needed was for Grey to hold her again, to love her.

"He touched you, and I wasn't there to stop him." He slouched back against the upholstery and laughed. A horrible hollow sound that made her own chest ache. "I am never where I'm needed. Even when I am, I fail." He glanced out the carriage glass at a moonlit field. "Remember that, goddess, when you tell yourself I'm not like Westby."

"You were there when I would have cut myself on broken glass in your father's room. And when I nearly lost half my manuscript in the lake."

"I'm not a bloody hero." He leaned forward. Even in the dim interior, Sophia sensed the tension rippling off his body. "That room I carried you out of? My father will die in that room. He's been there, wasting away, for years, while I've been in London. Hiding. Indulging." He dipped his head, his chest inflating on a ragged breath before he continued. "And that lake I dragged you out of? My brother—"

"Grey, I know." His hand was warm and broad, his fingers clasping hers eagerly when she reached for him. "You needn't explain."

"I couldn't reach him," he said quietly. "I didn't save him."

Sophia scooted to the edge of her bench, slid her fingers along Grey's jaw to tip his head up, and lowered her mouth to his. She kissed him tenderly, stroking the stubble on his cheek.

Grey groaned and cupped the back of her neck, pulling her closer. He wrapped an arm around her hips to ease her onto his lap.

The heat and hardness of his body drew a moan from her lips. Grey swallowed the sound with a deep kiss, his tongue tangling with hers as he clutched at her waist to get her closer. She needed to be close to him too. Needed to be back in his bed, with nothing between them—not a stitch of clothing and no pretense, no doubts.

This was the man she wanted. Needed with an intensity that didn't frighten her anymore.

He dipped his head to kiss her neck, then lower, laving the slit of her cleavage.

"I love you" emerged from her lips on a gasp.

He nestled his face against her neck, kissing and suckling the tender flesh before he whispered "I love you, Sophia" against her skin.

The words she'd craved. Words she'd been waiting her whole life to hear. Heat blossomed in her chest, but there was a squeeze of pain too. An echo of the misery she heard in his voice.

"I can't lose you." He ceased kissing her but continued to hold her in his arms, stroking his hand down her back.

Heart in her throat, she said, "Are you asking me to marry you?" She had to know.

"I don't deserve you." He swallowed hard and opened his mouth, but no sound emerged. Then, finally, choking on his words, he said, "I want you. That much I know."

All the heat, all the tentative fragile joy, flowed out of her as if she was a pin-stuck balloon, deflating without any air to buoy her up.

As the carriage clattered to a stop at Longcross, she disentangled herself from Grey's arms.

"Sophia, please." He held fast to her hand. "I can't lose you."

She had no answer for him. Only questions flooded her mind. Had he felt the same way about Maeve once? She didn't doubt he'd bedded both of them. Why was she different? Why did he shout at Maeve to get out and beg her to stay? He didn't want marriage. Refused to commit himself that much.

If Liddy was right, the more he cared for her, the greater likelihood he'd bolt.

"I can't stay," she heard herself say. She was prepared to commit her whole heart, her body, her soul, but she needed a man who would do the same.

She commanded her legs to move. Even when he called her name in that reverent way of his, she willed herself to keep walking.

Chapter Twenty-Three

One month later

Grey woke with a start and stared in confusion at the pristine shelves across from him. Each book stood up straight and perfectly aligned. Not a single shelf contained discarded lingerie or empty wine glasses. He gazed around, confirming that he was, in fact, in his Belgrave Square townhouse. That's when he remembered.

He'd turned a new leaf.

After Sophia leapt from the family carriage and strode out of his life, everything turned black. She'd fled Derbyshire the next morning. No note. No parting words. No second thoughts.

He'd stayed on at Longcross and wallowed in self-pity for days.

Becca couldn't get through to him, Liddy did her best to annoy him into animation, and Alistair knew enough to leave a gentleman alone to stew in his own heartache. Only one voice shook him from his misery. His father's. He'd been summoned to the earl's sickroom and given a ferocious lecture about duty and responsibility and finding a suitable countess that was, unfortunately, twenty years overdue.

Still, Grey had mulled the old man's words. Mulled and wallowed, and then finally returned to London. With titanic effort, he'd kept himself from Bloomsbury Square. Of course, he didn't need to haunt Sophia's doorstep to see her face everywhere he looked. She haunted his dreams and his days. He laughed out loud, recalling something amusing she'd said. Chuckled to himself like a madman, remembering some moment of her cleverness. Tossed and turned in his bed because she was not beside him. He ached for her unceasingly.

So he'd done what he could to prove to himself that a man could change, creating outward signs as evidence of his transformation. He'd hired new staff, had the townhouse cleaned and several rooms repainted or wallpapered. While Sophia was no doubt carrying on redecorating Kit and Ophelia's house, Grey was becoming adept at choosing colors and patterns himself for Belgrave Square.

But now the house was deadly quiet. No more raucous parties. No more drunken revels. No scantily clad women and heaving bodies grinding against each other in the library corner. The place was emptier than Longcross, and he didn't even miss the noise.

He only missed her. He only missed Sophia.

After a scratch at the door, the new housekeeper, a wizened, fearsome woman, stuck her head in. "Visitor for you, Lord Winship. Says he knows you from Fleet Theater."

Grey rolled his eyes and waved to indicate the visitor should enter. They'd come in droves at first. Old friends and comrades in sin, begging for admittance back into his Belgrave Square playhouse. He'd had a sort of cathartic satisfaction in telling them of its end. Of watching their eyes bulge or turn down in disappointment when he proclaimed himself an altered man.

Mr. Fleet himself had made a visit too, insisting Grey return to the stage. After negotiating the completion of one final play, the man departed in a door-slamming, profanity-laden huff. It couldn't be the theater impresario calling again. The man had too much stubborn pride.

The visitor who strode into his library was the last man Grey expected.

"Have you come to murder me?" he asked Sophia's brother, standing and reaching out to offer his friend a hand.

"I haven't decided," Kit said, rocking back on his heels, as if to remind Grey of his considerable heft and height. "But I'm not ready for that yet either." He cocked a brow toward Grey's outstretched hand.

"Fair enough." Grey gestured toward one of the new leather furniture pieces he'd ordered for the library.

Kit sat on one side. Grey lowered himself to the opposite sofa.

"I truly believed Sophia too clever to succumb to your charms."

Grey ran a hand across his scruffy jaw. Despite the pristine house around him, he hadn't shaved in days. "I don't believe she ever did." Succumb was too weak a word for Sophia. As if she was a heroine in some Gothic novel who'd crumpled in his arms. Her affection, her love, whatever she felt for him, hadn't come easily. Perhaps that was why he valued it so much. "She only stopped loathing me when I ceased attempting to charm her."

Kit's dark eyes lit with amusement. "Interesting strategy."

"Sophia is honest and true. She wouldn't be wooed any other way."

"So you love her?"

"Yes, I love her," he rasped out the word he'd taken too long to say to her. And why? It came so easily now. He'd shout *love* from the bloody rooftops if she'd hear him.

"But you've no wish to marry her? Commit to her?" Kit's hand tensed into a fist along the sofa back. "My sister deserves more than to warm the bed of a man who won't give her his name."

Grey shot to his feet and lunged for the liquor trolley. Except that the damned thing wasn't there anymore. He'd given up sipping at spirits too.

"Would you have me wed your sister? Me?" He pointed to himself and then at Kit. "You, of all men, know who I am. What I've done. Sins piled so high they'd bury me if I turned around."

"You're no less melodramatic, I see." Kit hooked an ankle on the opposite knee.

"I'm an actor, remember?" Grey stared out the window onto the other whitewashed houses in the square. Weren't all his redecorating attempts just an effort to whitewash his past? "A professional liar. Do you really wish your honest, beautiful sister to marry such a man?"

"Frankly, no, I don't wish her to marry a liar. But the man I knew usually left those skills on stage each night." Kit's eyes were stark, but his mouth twitched in a grin. "I also know your good qualities. Your loyalty—"

"I abandoned my family."

"So did I. We were self-indulgent asses while it lasted, and now we've changed. Ophelia changed me. I admit as much." Kit looked around the spotless library. "Apparently, Sophia has turned you tidy."

"Our last encounter didn't…end well. If I ask your sister to marry me, do you believe she'll say yes?"

Kit sat forward, hunching his shoulders and planting his elbows on his knees. He smiled up at Grey. "Now you're asking the right question."

"Will she?" All he could see in his mind's eye was the moment she'd left him. The moment she'd walked away. The pain of it stabbed at him every single day.

Kit stood and clasped Grey's shoulder. "That is the question. That is risk. When you're willing to take it, you're ready to give her everything she deserves." Kit reached into his waistcoat pocket and extracted a folded note.

"Is this from Sophia?" Grey clutched the folded foolscap, stroking the paper as if he'd found a bar of gold.

"No. From Mrs. Cole, our housekeeper. She said you'd understand."

"**P**lease don't tell me it's another letter from Ogilvy." Sophia lifted her hand, heaved out a sigh, and waited for Cate to drop the envelope into her hand. "My last note to him was firm. He couldn't have mistaken my request to stop writing."

"He did seem a tenacious sort." Cate laid the letter in Sophia's palm. "You're going to read this one, aren't you?"

"Why should I? I've no wish to be hounded by any man." Sniffing, holding back tears as she had for days, she reached for a penknife and sliced the paper open. "I'd rather remain a lonely spinster than fend off men in whom I have no interest whatsoever."

"Oh, to have that sort of problem." Cate grinned, tipping her head, as if urging Sophia to give in to mirth too.

Unfortunately, Sophia still felt hollow inside. No mirth, no eagerness for the future, not even any true ire for Ogilvy. In truth, the man had only sent two letters, and the second had likely been written before he received her first reply. Though this third was worrisome. The last thing she wanted was for him to turn up on Kit and Ophelia's doorstep again. Now that they were back home, there would be myriad questions she had no wish to answer.

"It's typed," Sophia said as she unfolded Ogilvy's note.

"He *is* a businessman. Typewriters are plentiful these days, as you well know." Cat nudged her arm.

Sophia had recently purchased her own typewriter. She'd learned to type while helping her father with his business correspondence, and now she found writing her new story on the machine made the words pour out quickly. Something about the clack and rhythm of hitting the keys made the ideas flow.

In the weeks since parting from Grey, writing had been her one source of solace. Well, one of two sources. Her spirits were incrementally lifted by Effie Breedlove's adventures and Cate's good-natured friendship.

Cate remained the only person in the household aware of Sophia's feelings for Grey. She'd been tempted to confide in Ophelia, but it didn't seem fair to ask her sister-in-law not to tell Kit.

"He's requesting a meeting." Sophia lowered the note and frowned at Cate. "I can't meet him. He'll get ideas, and I've no wish to give him hope."

Cate began tidying the umbrellas in the hall stand and dusting off the table they used to collect hats and gloves. "Where does he wish to meet you?"

"Hyde Park."

"No place better," Cate insisted as she rubbed at a spot on the hallway mirror glass. "Busy, open, very public. If he proves bothersome, you can simply walk away."

"Or run away." Sophia surprised herself with her first attempt at humor in days.

Cate tipped a grin. "Just keep your corset loose. Makes running easier."

"Do you really think I should meet him?" Sophia relied on Cate's advice.

Though she hadn't yet confessed everything about her time with Grey, a few details had slipped out. Then gradually more. Cate was clever enough to deduce the rest, but she'd kept surprisingly mum about how Sophia should handle her heartache. Cate didn't condemn Grey, nor did she urge Sophia to seek him out and go rushing back into his arms. Assuming he wished her to do any such thing. Sophia wasn't certain at all. He'd made no attempt to contact her. No notes, no visits. He hadn't even made an appearance at Bloomsbury

Square to welcome Kit and Ophelia back from their tour of France.

"Might do you good to get out and catch a bit of sun." Cate sorted a pile of magazines into perfect order. "You've been in the house too much these past days."

Hiding was what she meant to say. Sophia thought leaving Derbyshire would help her forget Grey, but London reminded her of him too. More so. Had he returned to his London lodgings? Was he back up on stage each night at Fleet Theater? She dared not read the papers for fear of seeing his name mentioned.

Though Cate had clipped one notice she insisted Sophia read. From a gossip rag, of all sources. A report that the "infamous Earl of W—— had set off for the Continent to flee whispers of madness." A tour of Europe seemed too easy an escape for the man, but Sophia suspected his mother had come to the end of her tether with the man's escapades.

Along with attempting to forget Westby, her time in Derbyshire, and Grey, Sophia strove to find value in spinsterhood. She'd begun attending a lecture series on writing given at the local college, and she'd joined a ladies' auxiliary that sewed clothes for needy children in the East End. Never mind that she'd always been awful with a needle. The struggle to improve her stitches occupied her mind, and that was at least halfway to distracting her heart.

She'd *almost* convinced herself their parting and his disinterest was for the best. They were too different. In character, they were opposites. He didn't want anything for his future that she wished for hers.

"I suppose I should go up and change," Sophia said wearily. Lately, she'd felt achy and listless, fatigued by heartache, and prepared to tear up at the least provocation. Perhaps a bit of sun and air would do her good.

"Oh, are you going to see him now?" Cate had begun scrubbing a cloth along the freshly painted wainscoting.

"In an hour." A thought struck, and Sophia turned back as she stepped up the first rung of the stairs. "Would you come with me?"

"Me?" Cate shook her head until one of her dark pinned curls came loose. "You don't need me tagging along."

"Please, Cate. It's utterly proper for me to have a chaperone, and I nominate you." Sophia managed a grin. Or at least she thought she did. Her cheeks felt odd and stretched.

Cate sighed and returned a tight smile. "Very well. I'll accompany you. Let me go and speak to the housemaids and cook to let them know I'll be out for a bit."

"Excellent." Something rattled around in Sophia's chest. Not quite joy or even happiness, but a lift of eagerness to be out of doors and spend time with Cate. If she could finish her chat with Ogilvy quickly, they could stop in at a teahouse for scones and a warm cup of Earl Grey before Kit and Ophelia returned from the Ruthven publishing offices.

After changing into a modest day dress, brushing her hair, and finding her new pair of boots—that were not stained and waterlogged from diving into Longcross lake—she returned downstairs to find Cate waiting by the door, tapping her foot impatiently.

"You're suddenly eager for this venture." Sophia pulled on gloves but dispensed with a hat.

"We'll need to find a cab or omnibus," Cate said as she started out the door.

"Will we? I thought we might simply walk up Oxford Street." She tipped her head back, closed her eyes, and basked in the afternoon sun.

Cate reached for her hand and tugged. "You know how I loathe being late."

She didn't know that about Cate, though the fact didn't surprise Sophia. Cate had been five minutes early to her interview regarding the housekeeper job at Kit and Ophelia's, and anytime she stepped out, she made a habit of returning before she was due.

"All right," she agreed, "let's find a cab. The omnibus is often overflowing in the afternoons."

A polished two-seater hansom appeared as if by magic, and Cate rushed toward the rig to secure their ride. Sophia followed at a more sedate pace, fighting a wave of queasiness, and took a spot beside Cate. And they waited. Carriage traffic thickened as they approached Oxford Street. More than once, she turned to Cate, on the cusp of suggesting they return to her original notion and walk. But then the clog finally gave way and the horse clopped a few more paces toward Hyde Park.

The cabbie let them off near Marble Arch, and they headed into the park. Cate set a blistering pace.

"How do you know where we're going? Did you read Ogil-vy's letter while I was upstairs?" Sophia asked, if only to slow her companion down and catch her breath.

"Not at all. Just assumed he'd want to meet near the carriage drive. It's in view of the Serpentine and has a line of benches. There aren't benches everywhere in the park, are there?"

Sophia shrugged. She hadn't taken enough time to search the huge green swath in the center of London well enough to know.

"There we are." Cate pointed to an empty stretch of benches near a line of trees that were just beginning to feel the nip of early autumn in the air. The tips of their leaves had begun to change color.

Sophia took a seat, but Cate remained standing. "Think I'll have a peek at the Italian Gardens," she said. "Just down the way. I'll return soon."

"Why don't I come with you?"

Cate lifted the watch pinned to her shirtwaist. "Don't want to miss him, do you?"

Sophia didn't blame Cate for wishing to avoid Ogilvy. She had half a mind to escape before his arrival herself. "Very well. I'll come and find you once he's gone."

As Cate bustled north, Sophia craned her neck to look south, down the long stretch of the Serpentine. Ladies and gentlemen and children were ambling throughout the greenery, but she spotted no gentlemen with Timothy Ogilvy's features. She'd forgotten her own pin watch, so she didn't know the time, but even a few minutes of waiting seemed interminable. She stood and stretched her back, rubbed at the churning in her belly, and cast a gaze toward the east end of the park.

In the distance, behind the thick trunk of a tree, she caught a glimpse of a woman who looked very like Cate. Narrowing her eyes, she shifted to get a better view around two gentlemen who stood nearby smoking pipes and discussing horses.

The woman moved, so that most of her body was obscured by the tree, and then a man stepped back on the opposite side of the trunk. A tall man, long and lean, with bronze hair.

"Excuse me, miss." A nanny pushing a baby in a pram tried to get around Sophia.

She'd inadvertently planted herself in the middle of a walking path and dodged back to make way. When she cast her gaze toward the tree again, both figures she'd seen—one very like Cate and the other very like Grey—were gone.

Rubbing at the center of her chest, at the spot that ached whenever she thought of him, she turned back to her bench, only to find two elegantly dressed young ladies had taken the spot she'd vacated.

Pivoting on her heel, she started toward another area of seating closer to the lake. Grey stepped out of the tree line onto the path in front of her.

Her mouth dropped open as goose bumps pebbled her skin.

She narrowed her gaze. Perhaps the water sparkling off the Serpentine had created a mirage. She'd read about such optical illusions in a magazine.

"I fear I'm not the man you expected to encounter."

"Not expected, no." Her body fizzed from head to toe. Was her voice vibrating too? He wasn't the man she expected to see, but he was the one she'd longed for a glimpse of for days, weeks that had dragged on like years.

"Unfortunately"—he lifted his right hand, where he held a letter between two fingers—"you have a conspirator in your midst."

"Cate."

"She told me where you'd be, if I wished to speak to you alone." He stepped toward her, didn't stop until he was close enough to touch. Until his juniper scent made her mouth water. "I do want to speak to you, Sophia." He reached out as if he'd touch her, then pulled back. "It's the least of what I wish to do."

"Speak quickly." Not because she didn't wish to hear every word or savor the sound of his voice. But because the longer he stood there, his hair glinting in the afternoon sun as the Serpentine reflected daylight back on him like his own bank of limelights, Sophia knew she couldn't hold out much longer.

Every nerve and muscle in her body pulsed with the urge to go into his arms.

"Quickly?" The dimples that had been flickering to life in his cheeks dimmed. Crumpling Cate's letter in his hands, he gazed at Sophia, panic-stricken, like an actor who'd forgotten his lines. "Kit came to visit."

"Did he?" So there was more than one conspirator in her midst. Who else knew about this plot? Ophelia? Clary? The postman?

"He gave me hope that you might wish to see me." Quieter, he added. "He reminded me what you deserve."

A frown tautened the skin between her brows. "Did you need reminding?"

"No." He frowned too, and she remembered the times she'd smoothed her fingers over those lines on his forehead. "Perhaps. I can be a thick-headed man."

Sophia pressed two fingers to her temple, where warning bells had begun to clang. Nothing would be easier than rushing into Grey's arms, getting lost in his clear gray gaze. But she didn't hear enough certainty in his tone. She'd pulled herself back from the agony of walking away from him. She had her writing now, her ladies' auxiliary, her class at the college. That could sustain her.

Enough to keep her from risking her heart ever again.

She sucked in a deep breath, tasting the soot and rust of London air.

"I prefer the countryside." She wrapped her arms around her middle and continued. "London has its appeal but preferably in short doses."

"All right." Grey arched one brow as if flummoxed by the changed of topic.

"I only ever want to make love to one man. My husband. And I want children. Two, so they aren't lonely. Maybe more."

He tilted his head like a confused puppy, licked his lips, and swiped a hand through the impossibly perfect and yet completely untamed waves of his hair. "Understood."

"I prefer tea. You like coffee. Cleanliness is a preoccupation with me, and I've noticed your tendency to be messy."

"A man can change," he said, as a grin began teasing at the corners of his mouth. "Come to Belgrave Square with me, and you'll see. As to the countryside, I'm returning to Derbyshire."

"What of London and the theater?"

"I've left Fleet."

"But you love acting." And he was marvelous on stage. She'd never forget the single performance she'd seen.

"What I love," he said, taking one step closer, "is you. Acting may be a talent, but it served mostly as a means of escape. From the past. From myself." He cocked a rakish grin. "Is it my turn to convince you why we should never part again?"

Sophia shook her head and searched for more. There had to be other reasons they were wrong for each other. They were too different. Opposites in essential ways. He was an aristocrat, and her father had worked for his money. He was an actor—former actor, apparently—and she was a writer, of sorts. She was a spinster, and he was a notorious scoundrel.

"We are too different."

"Perfectly so." He took one long step, one that brought his chest close to hers, tangled his legs in her gown. "I need your cleverness and good sense. Your goodness and refusal to give up." His grin burst into a smile. "I admit you're getting the worst of this deal, Sophia, but I do promise to encourage you to be impure in body and mind, to be bold rather than meek, to seek as many pursuits as you like outside the home. As long as you always come back to me."

Sophia opened her mouth to reply, and he finally touched her. One finger slid with aching tenderness against her cheek.

"I know you say we're different," he said softly. "But I've changed. You, Sophia." He slid an arm around her waist, gently, tentatively. "You inspire me to be a better man."

"Are you?"

"Marry me, and I'll show you how much." He pulled her tighter against his body.

Sophia felt her ramparts of rational arguments falling away. Her heart didn't wish to be wary, even as her mind spun for any vestige of doubt.

"Shouldn't you have altered *before* we marry?"

"I have." He bent his head back, tipping his mouth in contemplation. "Though the process is ongoing, I suspect."

Catching her gaze, he vowed, "I never want to lose you again. I have changed, love."

She saw the truth in his eyes. Heard the certainty in his voice. She couldn't deny the rightness of being in his arms.

"Not too much, I hope." Slipping her hand along the edge of Grey's lapel, Sophia savored the heat of his chest against the backs of her fingers. "I did fall in love with a scoundrel, after all."

Confusion shaded his eyes, and then he smiled. A brilliant, dazzling, dimple-popping display that kicked her heart into a gallop. That was new. For days she'd felt hollow, but now her pulse thudded wildly in her ears.

"Are you rejecting my attempts at reform?" There was a question in his eyes, a tentative hopefulness, a hint of fear.

"Not entirely." Sophia tipped onto her toes and nuzzled the delicious bay soap-scented plane of his cheek. "I love you, Grey. Now. The man you are right this minute."

"So you want me, scoundrel and all?"

"I do." Sophia smiled and pressed closer, wrapping her arms around the man she was going to marry. "As long as you're *my* scoundrel."

Derbyshire, October 1895

Sophia held a curl of hair in place while Cate searched for an additional hairpin.

"Should have brought more from London," Cate grumbled as she scoured her traveling bag.

"Perhaps Liddy has extra."

"Have you seen the girl's coiffure? Between the two of you, I doubt there's any pins left in Derbyshire." A moment later, she drew back her hand and thrust a piece of bent metal in the air, as if she'd just pulled Excalibur from the stone. "I've found one."

Sophia smiled, and then her eyes bulged. "Oh no."

Cate dropped the pin and lunged for a small stone basin in the corner of the vestry, quickly returning to Sophia's side.

"Are you sure that's not for holy water?" Sophia slapped a hand over her mouth.

"I have no idea, but if you don't wish to cast up your accounts all over your wedding gown, I suggest you make use of it."

Sophia lowered her hand, bent over the basin, and shook her head. "It's gone." She shrugged and straightened in her chair. "Probably just nerves."

Cate narrowed her eyes and dragged a chair up next to Sophia's. After settling onto the creaking wood, she clasped Sophia's hand. "You may keep news of the babe from others as long as you like, but I've known you were increasing from the moment you returned from Derbyshire."

Sophia gazed in the mirror she'd used to don her gown and dress her hair. "That obvious, is it?" A persistent ruddiness lit her cheeks, but her belly had only rounded slightly. She stroked her fingers over her stomach, and her breath caught in her throat.

Joy welled up inside, so much happiness after so many years of doubting she would ever find contentment.

"Why have you not told the man?" Cate asked softly.

Sophia swiped away a tear. "Today Grey is vowing himself to me for the rest of his life. A wife seems enough to take on for one day." She turned her head and grinned at Cate. "I plan to tell him tomorrow."

"I wager he'll be over the moon. Never seen a man so smitten as yours is with you." Cate bent to retrieve the pin and stood to place the final touches on Sophia's coiffure.

Sophia didn't interrupt while Cate worked at rearranging a few curls, but as soon as she'd finished and stepped back to survey her work, she asked, "Cate? Who is the gentleman I saw you speaking to in the church this morning?"

Cate's dark eyes widened. "Mr. Lassiter? He's a gentleman from London."

"Yes, that must be where I've seen him. He's come to call at Kit and Phee's, hasn't he? I thought he was a workman or one of the designers who have been working on the townhouse."

"No." Cate shook her head. "He's a brewer by trade."

"How intriguing." Sophia pressed her lips together to suppress a grin. "And how did you meet this gentleman brewer?"

Cate planted a hand on one hip. "Did one of the housemaids tell you?"

"Not at all," Sophia insisted, bending her head so that Cate could clasp the Ruthven family pearls around her neck. "I solved the mystery on my own."

"Go on, then, lady detective," Cate teased. She'd read every word Sophia had written about Effie Breedlove and continually asked for more pages. "Tell me how you solved this one."

"Not terribly challenging. A pair of missing scissors, a newspaper with rectangles cut out of the personal ads, and a tenacious smile on one Catherine Cole's lips."

Cate's cheeks pinked as she patted Sophia's shoulders. "Very well, Miss Sleuth. He's a good man, but there's been no mention of marriage. I'm content to take each day as it comes."

Sophia patted her friend's hand. "I wish you happiness."

Cate smiled back at her in the mirror. "And I'm so glad you've found yours."

A rap at the door and they both turned as ladies filed in. Liddy led the way, lifting the beaded hem of her gown to keep from tripping. Clary followed behind, garbed in her signature mauve hue. Phee and Juliet finished the queue, both bearing bouquets of white freesia and myrtle sprigged with ivy leaves.

Cate took both bouquets and fussed with the ribbons surrounding each, making sure they were perfectly wrapped. Clary positioned herself behind Sophia's chair and wrapped an arm around her shoulder.

"You look perfect," Clary said wistfully. "Like a fairy tale princess. Or a Greek goddess."

"A viscountess," Liddy enthused. "That's what she'll be."

Sophia's tummy gave a lurch again, and she slid a hand over her belly. She only wanted to be Grey's wife. And to manage to say her vows without losing her breakfast.

"I won't have a title," Liddy announced dramatically. The other ladies in the room quieted, waiting for her to say more.

"Why is that?" Clary finally asked.

"Because I'm going to marry Clive Holden."

Clary, Phee, Juliet, and Cate frowned in confusion, but Sophia sprang up from her chair and embraced Liddy. When she pulled back, she took care not to mar the girl's elaborate upswept curls.

"You love him, then?" Sophia asked. Liddy insisted love was the only quality that mattered in marriage. While she didn't wish to see the girl with a monster like Westby, she no longer believed in settling for half measures either.

"I do." Liddy beamed. "He dotes on me as no one ever has. The more time I spend with him, the more I love his kindness and devotion."

Beyond the vestry walls, an organ burst into the notes of Mendelssohn's Wedding March.

"Good grief, it's time." Sophia cast her gaze at Cate.

She thrust one bouquet into Sophia's hands and the other into Clary's. Before Phee, Juliet, and Liddy filed out, they stopped to peck a kiss on Sophia's cheek. Each whispered words of encouragement and smiled with the same giddiness bubbling in her chest.

Outside the vestry door, Kit waited, bouncing on his heels. He smiled the moment she walked through and thrust an elbow out for her to clasp.

"Ready?" he whispered.

"I've been ready for this moment for a few years." More than ready. In a few moments, she would be his spinster sister no more.

He led her around the side of the church so that they could proceed down the nave. At the country church's porch, she tipped her head up and saw Grey.

Her mouth went dry, and then a wave washed over her. Not cold like those waters back at Longcross lake. But warmth, a lightness and joy that made her whole body tingle. This moment was what she'd always wished for. That man was the only one she wanted. Ever.

He seemed to catch her sense of wonder and smiled back.

As Kit led her up the aisle, everything else faded. The organ music, the smiling faces turned her way, even the heady scent of the flowers clutched in her hands.

Only Grey mattered. The world narrowed to him and her. To them, their future, and the child growing inside of her.

His gaze locked on hers as she reached his side. He kept watching her, his mouth tipping in a grin now and then as the clergyman read their vows, and they dutifully repeated solemn promises to each other.

When Grey lifted her veil and bent to kiss her, the parson cleared his throat.

"Long tradition states that the Stanhope earl does not kiss his bride, my lord."

Grey cast a gaze back at Kit, who served as his grooms-man. Her brother shrugged unhelpfully.

From the front pew, Lord Fennston intoned, "It's tradi-tion, Winship. Every Stanhope earl has followed the same etiquette."

Grey looked into Sophia's eyes, caught her cheek against his palm, and smiled. "I'm not the earl yet, and my wife has had her fill of etiquette, I think." He dipped his head and took her lips. A warm, tender, breath-stealing kiss. Then another. And one more for good measure.

"Besides," he murmured for Sophia's ears and anyone close enough to hear, "she knows she's married a scoundrel."

Gasps emerged from the pews. One lady squealed in out-rage. A gentleman coughed contemptuously.

Grey stood up tall and wrapped Sophia's arm around his. She stroked her fingers along the muscles flexing under her touch, too filled with joy for words.

Which was an odd sensation, for a writer.

As he led her back down the nave, Grey tipped his mouth her way and whispered, "How soon can we be done with the nuptial festivities? I want you and you alone for all my fore-seeable days."

"That's very unsociable," Sophia insisted. "And we'll have to make room for at least one other."

"Will we?" Grey's footsteps slowed as he frowned at her. "Who?"

"That's a matter I'll need your help deciding."

"Is this a riddle?" At the porch of the church, he turned to face her. "I'll help you with anything, wife. What do we need to decide?"

As the pews began to empty and well-wishers started a procession past them, Sophia stretched onto her tiptoes, clutched Grey's shoulder, and whispered in his ear. "The name of our child."

His mouth dropped open at the same moment his gray eyes lit like diamonds catching the light. He glanced down at her belly, then gently laid his palm across her waist. "I love you," he said, his voice ragged and low. "I love both of you."

Keep reading for an excerpt to the delightful first book in
Christy Carlyle's Romancing the Rules series,

RULES FOR A ROGUE

Kit Ruthven's Rules (for Rogues)
#1 Love freely but guard your heart, no matter how tempting the invader.
#2 Embrace temptation, indulge your sensual impulses, and never apologize.
#3 Scorn rules and do as you please. You are a rogue, after all.

Rules never brought anything but misery to Christopher "Kit" Ruthven. After rebelling against his controlling father and leaving the family's etiquette empire behind, Kit has been breaking every one imaginable for the past four years. He's enjoyed London's sensual pleasures, but he's failed to achieve the success he craves as London's premier playwright. When his father dies, Kit returns to the countryside and is forced back into the life he never wanted. Worse, he must face Ophelia Marsden, the woman he left behind years before.

After losing her father, Ophelia has learned to rely on herself. To maintain the family home and support her younger sister, she tutors young girls in deportment and decorum. But her pupils would be scandalized if they knew she was also the author of a guidebook encouraging ladies to embrace their independence.

As Kit rediscovers the life, and the woman, he left behind, Ophelia must choose between the practicalities she never truly believed in, or the love she's never been able to extinguish.

Available now from Avon Impulse

CHAPTER ONE

"Duty foremost. A true gentleman puts no appetite, ambition, or enterprise above duty."

—THE RUTHVEN RULES FOR YOUNG MEN

London, September 1894

He always searched for her.

Call it perversity or a reckless brand of tenacity. Heaven knew he'd been accused of both.

Pacing the scuffed wooden floorboards at the edge of the stage, Christopher Ruthven shoved a hand through his black hair and skimmed his dark gaze across each seat in the main theater stalls of Merrick Theater for the woman he needed to forget.

Damn the mad impulse to look for her.

He was a fool to imagine he'd ever find her staring back. The anticipation roiling in his belly should be for the play, not the past.

Finding her would be folly. Considering how they'd parted, the lady would be as likely to lash out as to embrace him with open arms.

But searching for her had become his habit. His ritual.

Other thespians had rituals too. Some refused to eat before a performance. Others feasted like a king. A few repeated incantations, mumbling to themselves when the curtains rose. As the son of a publishing magnate, Kit should have devised his own maxim to repeat, but the time for words was past. He'd written the play, and the first act was about to begin.

Now he only craved a glimpse of Ophelia Marsden.

The four years since he'd last seen her mattered not. Her bright blue eyes, heart-shaped face, and striking red hair had always distinguished her from other women, but Kit knew they were the least of the qualities that set her apart. Clever, stubborn to the core, and overflowing with more spirit than anyone he'd ever known—that's how he remembered Phee.

But looking for her wasn't mere folly; it was futile. She wouldn't come. He, after all, was the man who'd broken her heart.

As stagehands lit the limelights, Kit shaded his eyes from their glare and stepped behind the curtain. The thrumming in his veins was about the play now, the same giddiness he felt before every performance.

Hunching his shoulders, he braced his arms across his chest and listened intently, half his attention on the lines being delivered on stage, half on the pandemonium backstage. He adored the energy of the theater, the frenetic chaos of actors and stagehands rushing about madly behind the curtains to produce rehearsed magic for the audience. Economies at Merrick's meant he might write a play, perform in it, assist with scene changes from the catwalk, and direct other actors—all in one evening.

Tonight though, beyond writing the words spoken on stage, the production was out of his hands, and that heightened his nerves. Idleness made him brood.

Behind him a husky female voice cried out, and Kit turned to intercept the woman as she rushed forward, filling his arms with soft curves.

"There's a mouse!" Tess, the playhouse's leading lady, batted thick lashes and stuck out a vermillion-stained lower lip. "Vile creatures. Every one of them."

"Tell me where." Kit gently dislodged the petite blonde from his embrace.

"Scurried underneath, so it did." She indicated a battered chest of drawers, sometimes used for storage, more often as a set piece.

Kit approached the bulky wooden chest, crouched down, and saw nothing but darkness and dust. Bracing his palms on the floor, he lowered until his chest pressed against wood and he spied the little creature huddling in the farthest corner. The tiny mouse looked far more frightened of him than Tess was of it.

"Can you catch the beast? We can find a cage or give it to the stray cats hanging about the stage doors."

"Too far out of reach." He could move the chest, but the mouse would no doubt scurry away. Seemed kinder to allow the animal to find its own way to freedom. Kit knew what it was to be trapped and frightened. To cower in darkness covered in dust. His father hadn't shut him up in a cage, just a closet now and then, but Kit would be damned if he'd confine any creature.

Tess made an odd sound. Of protest, Kit assumed. But when he cast a glance over his shoulder, her gaze raked hungrily over his legs and backside as he got to his feet.

"The little thing will no doubt find its way out of doors, Tess. Not much food to be had here."

Tess took his attempt at reassurance as an invitation and launched herself into his arms.

She was an appealing woman, with tousled golden curls, catlike green eyes, and an exceedingly ample—*Ah, yes, there they are*—bosom that she shifted enticingly against his chest, as if she knew precisely how good her lush body felt against his. Without a hint of shame or restraint, she moved her hands down his arms, slid them under his unbuttoned sack coat, and stroked her fingers up his back.

"Goodness, you're deliciously tall."

Kit grinned. He found female praise for his awkward height amusing, since he'd been mercilessly teased for his long frame as a child. In a theater world full of handsome, charming actors, his stature and whatever skill he possessed with the written word were all that set him apart.

"You're like a tree I long to climb," she purred. "Feels so right in your arms. Perhaps the gods are telling us that's where I belong."

Tess wasn't merely generously built. From the day she arrived, she'd been generous with her affections too. Half the men at Merrick's were smitten, but Kit kept to his rule about avoiding intrigues with ladies in the troupe. Since coming to London, he'd never sought more than a short-lived entanglement with any woman. He relished his liberty too much to allow himself more.

"Perhaps the gods are unaware you're due on stage for the next act," he teased, making light of her flirtation as he'd done since their introduction.

"Always concerned about your play, aren't you, lovie?" She slid a hand up his body, snaking a finger between the buttons of his waistcoat. "I know my part. Don't worry, Kitten."

The pet name she'd chosen for him grated on his nerves.

"The music's risen, Tess." Kit gripped the actress's hand when she reached toward his waistband. "That's your cue."

"I'll make you proud." She winked and lifted onto her toes, placing a damp kiss on his cheek. "You're a difficult man to seduce," she whispered, "but I do so love a challenge." After sauntering to the curtain's edge, she offered him a final come-hither glance before sashaying on stage.

"Already breaking hearts, *Kitten*? The evening's only just begun." Jasper Grey, Merrick Theater's lead actor and Kit's closest friend, exited stage left and sidled up beside him. With a few swipes across his head, Grey disheveled his coppery brown hair and loosened the faux silk cravat at his throat. The changes were subtle, but sufficient to signal to the audience that his character would begin a descent into madness and debauchery during the second act. Having explored many of London's diversions at the man's side, Kit could attest to Grey's knack for debauchery, on and off the stage.

"I'm sure you'll be more than happy to offer solace. Or have you already?" Choosing a new lover each night of the week was more Grey's style than Kit's, though both had attracted their share of stage-door admirers and earned their reputations as rogues.

Grey's smirk gave everything away. "Whatever the nature of my private moments with our lovely leading lady, the minx is determined to offer you her heart."

"Bollocks to that. I've no interest in claiming anyone's heart." The very thought chased a chill up Kit's spine. Marriage. Commitment. Those were for other men. If his parents were any lesson, marriage was a miserable prison, and he had no wish to be shackled.

Kit turned his attention back to the audience.

"Still looking for your phantom lady?" Grey often tweaked Kit about his habit of searching the crowd. Rather than reveal parts of his past he wished to forget, Kit allowed his friend to assume he sought a feminine ideal, not a very specific woman of flesh and freckles and fetching red hair. "What will you do if she finally appears?"

"She won't." And if he were less of a fool, he'd stop looking for her.

"Come, man. We've packed the house again tonight. This evening we celebrate." Grey swiped at the perspiration on his brow. "You've been downright monkish of late. There must be a woman in London who can turn your head. What about the buxom widow who threw herself at you backstage after last week's performance?"

"The lady stumbled. I simply caught her fall."

"Mmm, and quite artfully too. I particularly admired the way her lush backside landed squarely in your lap."

The curvaceous widow had been all too willing to further their acquaintance, but she'd collided with Kit on opening night. Having written the play and performed in a minor role for an indisposed actor, he'd been too distracted fretting over success to bother with a dalliance.

Of late, something in him had altered. Perhaps he'd had his fill of the city's amusements. Grey's appetite never seemed to wane, but shallow seductions no longer brought Kit satisfaction. He worried less about pleasure and more about success. Four years in London and what had he accomplished? Coming to the city had never been about indulging in vice but about making his mark as a playwright. He'd allowed himself to be distracted. *Far too impulsive* should have been his nickname, for as often as his father had shouted the words at him in his youth.

"How about the angel in the second balcony?" Grey gestured to a gaudily painted box, high in the theater's eastern wall. "I've never been able to resist a woman with titian red hair."

Kit snapped his gaze to the spot Grey indicated, heartbeat ratcheting until it thundered in his ears. Spotting the woman, he expelled a trapped breath. The lady's hair shone in appealing russet waves in the gaslight, but she wasn't Ophelia. Phee's hair was a rich auburn, and her jaw narrower. At least until it sharpened into an adorably squared chin that punctuated her usual air of stubborn defiance.

"No?" Grey continued his perusal of ladies among the sea of faces. "How about the giggling vision in the third row?"

The strawberry blonde laughed with such raucous abandon her bosom bounced as she turned to speak to her companion. Kit admired her profile a moment, letting his gaze dip lower before glancing at the man beside her.

"That's Dominic Fleet." Kit's pulse jumped at the base of his throat. Opportunity sat just a few feet away.

He'd never met the theater impresario, but he knew the man by reputation. Unlike Merrick's shabby playhouse, known for its comedies and melodramas, Fleet Theater featured long-running plays by the best dramatists in London. Lit entirely with electric lights, the modern theater seated up to three thousand.

"What's he doing slumming at Merrick's?" Grey turned to face Kit. "Did you invite him?"

"Months ago." Kit had sent a letter of introduction to Fleet, enclosing a portion of a play he'd written but been unable to sell. "He never replied." Yet here he was, attending the performance of a piece that revealed none of Kit's true skill as a playwright. Merrick had demanded a bawdy farce. In order to pay his rent, Kit had provided it.

"You bloody traitor." Grey smiled, his sarcastic tone belying his words. "You wouldn't dare abandon Merrick and set out for greener fields."

"Why? Because he compensates us so generously?"

Though they shared a love of theater, Grey and Kit had different cares. Grey possessed family money and worried little about meeting the expenses of a lavish London lifestyle. Kit could never take a penny from his father, even if it was on offer. Any aid from Leopold Ruthven would come with demands and expectations—precisely the sort of control he'd left Hertfordshire to escape.

"You belong here, my friend." Grey clapped him on the shoulder. "With our band of misfits and miscreants. Orphans from lives better left behind."

Belonging. The theater had given him that in a way his father's home never had. Flouting rules, tenacity, making decisions intuitively—every characteristic his father loathed were assets in the theater. Kit had no desire to abandon the life he'd made for himself, just improve upon it.

"We came to London to make something of ourselves. Do you truly believe we'll find success at Merrick's?" Kit lifted his elbow and nudged the dingy curtain tucked at the edge of the stage. "Among tattered furnishings?"

"That's only the backside of the curtain. Merrick puts the best side out front. We all have our flaws. The art is in how well we hide them." Grey had such a way with words Kit often thought *he* should be a playwright. "Would you truly jump ship?"

"I bloody well would." Kit slanted a glance at his friend. "And so would you."

Merrick paid them both a dribble, producing plays with minimal expense in a building that leaked when it rained. Cultivating favor with the wealthiest theater manager in London had been Kit's goal for months. With a long-running Fleet-produced play, he could repay his debts and move out of his cramped lodgings. Hunger had turned him into a hack writer for Merrick, but he craved more. Success, wealth, a chance to prove his skill as a writer. To prove that his decision to come to London had been the right one. To prove to his father that he could succeed on his own merits.

"Never!" Tess, performing the role of virginal damsel, shrieked from center stage. "Never shall I marry Lord Mallet. He is the worst sort of scoundrel."

"That's my cue." Grey grinned as he tugged once more at his cravat and dashed back into the glow of the limelights. Just before stepping on stage, he skidded to stop and turned to Kit. "You'd better write me a part in whatever play you sell to Fleet."

With a mock salute, Kit offered his friend a grin. He had every intention of creating a role for Grey. The man's acting skills deserved a grander stage too.

Kit fixed his gaze on Fleet. He seemed to be enjoying the play, a trifling modernized *Hamlet* parody Kit called *The King's Ghost and the Mad Damsel*. He'd changed the heroine's name to Mordelia, unable to endure the sound of Ophelia's name bouncing off theater walls for weeks. Months, if the play did well.

After his eyes adjusted to the stage-light glow, he pointlessly, compulsively scanned the crowd one last time for a woman whose inner beauty glowed as fiercely as her outer charms. He wouldn't find her. As far as he knew, Phee was home in the village where they'd grown up. When he'd come to London to escape his father, she'd insisted on loyalty to hers and remained in Hertfordshire to care for him. All but one of his letters had gone unanswered, including a note the previous year expressing sorrow over her father's passing.

He didn't need to reach into his pocket and unfold the scrap of paper he carried with him everywhere. The five words of Ophelia's only reply remained seared in his mind.

"*Follow your heart and flourish.*" They were her mother's words, stitched in a sampler that hung in the family's drawing room. Kit kept the fragment, but he still wondered whether Ophelia had written the words in sincerity or sarcasm.

A flash of gems caught his eye, and Kit spied Fleet's pretty companion rising from her seat. The theater impresario stood too, following her into the aisle. Both made their way toward the doors at the rear of the house.

He couldn't let the man leave without an introduction. Kit lurched toward a door leading to a back hall and sprinted down the dimly lit corridor. He caught up to Fleet near the ladies' retiring room.

"Mr. Fleet, I am—"

"Christopher Ruthven, the scribe of this evening's entertainment." The man extended a gloved hand. "Forgive me, Ruthven. It's taken far too long for me to take in one of your plays."

Attempting not to crush the slighter man in his grip, Kit offered an enthusiastic handshake.

"I want to have a look at your next play." Fleet withdrew an engraved calling card from his waistcoat pocket. "Bring it in person to my office at the theater. Not the one you sent. Something new. More like this one."

"You'll have it." Kit schooled his features, forcing his furrowed brow to smooth. So what if the man wanted a farce rather than serious drama? He craved an opportunity to succeed, and Fleet could provide it. "Thank you."

"If we can come to terms and you manage to fill my playhouse every night as you have Merrick's, I shall be thanking you."

Kit started backstage, his head spinning with ideas for a bigger, grander play than Merrick's could produce. Never mind that it had taken years to grasp the chance Fleet offered. Good fortune had come, and he intended to make the most of it.

As he reached the inconspicuous door that led to the back corridor, a man called his name.

"Mr. Ruthven? Christopher Leopold Ruthven?"

Two gentlemen approached, both tall, black-suited, and dour. Debt collectors? The instinct to bolt dissipated when the two made it impossible, crowding him on either side of the narrow passageway.

"I'm Ruthven." Taller than both men and broader by half, Kit still braced himself for whatever might come. "What do you want?"

The one who'd yet to say anything took a step closer, and Kit recognized his wrinkled face.

"Mr. Sheridan? What brings you to Merrick's?" Kit never imagined the Ruthven family solicitor would venture to a London theater under any circumstances.

"Ill tidings, I regret to say." Sheridan reached into his coat and withdrew an envelope blacked with ink around the edges. "Your father is dead, Mr. Ruthven. I'm sorry. Our letter to you was returned. My messenger visited your address twice and could not locate you. I thought we might find you here."

"Moved lodgings." Kit took the letter, willing his hand not to tremble. "Weeks ago."

"Your sister has made arrangements for a ceremony in Briar Heath." Sheridan lifted a card from his pocket and handed it to Kit. "Visit my office before you depart, and I can provide you with details of your father's will."

The men watched him a moment, waiting for a reaction. When none came, Sheridan muttered condolences before they departed.

Kit lost track of time. He shoved Sheridan's card into his coat pocket to join Fleet's, crushed the unread solicitor's letter in his hand, and stood rooted to the spot where they'd left him. Father. Dead. The two words refused to congeal in his mind. So many of the choices Kit made in his twenty-eight years had been driven by his father's wrath, attempts to escape his stifling control.

Now Kit could think only of what he should do. Must do. Look after his sisters. Return to Briar Heath.

He'd leave after speaking to Merrick. Any work on a play to impress Fleet would have to be undertaken while he was back home.

Home. The countryside, the village, the oversized house his father built with profits from his publishing enterprise—none of it had been home for such a very long time. It was a place he'd felt shunned and loathed most of his life. He'd never visited in four years. Never dared set foot in his father's house after his flamboyant departure.

As he headed toward Merrick's office to tell the man his news, worry for his sisters tightened Kit's jaw until it ached. Then another thought struck.

After all these years, night after night of futile searching, he would finally see Ophelia Marsden again.

Clary Ruthven's story is next in

HOW TO WOO A WALLFLOWER

Coming Fall 2017!

Dear Reader,

I hope you liked the latest romance from Avon Impulse! If you're looking for another steamy, fun, emotional read, be sure to check out some of our recent and upcoming titles.

For fans of historical romance, we have a fabulous new novella from Lorraine Heath! WHEN THE MARQUESS FALLS is a stunning love story about a very traditional marquess who knows he will never be the same when the beautiful—and totally unsuitable—daughter of the village baker snags his heart. As any true #Heathen (a Lorraine Heath super-fan!) knows, her books are deeply emotional, sometimes gut-wrenching, and always end with a glorious HEA. This novella is no different!

Contemporary romance lovers will be thrilled to hear there's a new novel from T. J. Kline coming soon! RISKING IT ALL is a heartwarming, swoon-worthy tale of second chance love . . . but you'll have to buy it to find out if charming play-boy Andrew can win back Gia, the one who got away! Full of steamy secrets, tons of emotion, and an adorable baby, T. J.'s latest is sure to hit all the points on your romance checklist.

And if you like military romances, you're in luck! Cheryl Etchinson is back with FROM THE START another American Valor novel featuring her signature tough, strong, sexy heroes. Army Ranger Michael trains hard and plays harder, but nothing could have prepared him for falling in love . . . especially with a woman who wants nothing to do with him. Don't miss this slow burn romance that will have you sighing with happiness when the hardened military man finally lands his lady!

You can purchase these titles by clicking the links above or by visiting our website, www.AvonRomance.com. Thank you for loving romance as much as we do . . . enjoy!

Sincerely,

Nicole
Editorial Director
Avon Impulse

Fueled by Pacific Northwest coffee and inspired by multiple viewings of every British costume drama she can get her hands on, *USA Today* bestselling author **CHRISTY CARLYLE** writes sensual historical romance set in the Victorian era. She loves heroes who struggle against all odds and heroines who are ahead of their time. A former teacher with a degree in history, she finds there's nothing better than being able to combine her love of the past with a die-hard belief in happy endings.

Discover great authors, exclusive offers, and more at hc.com.